ANDREW

BOY SLAVE *to* FREE REBEL

BY

D.N. BRYAN

BOOK ONE

CHAPTER I

A FEW MINUTES past noon, a short, portly man in his forties with tied-back salt and pepper hair led a small, slightly built slave boy along a wide dirt path. William Bryan, or Will, as he liked to be called, was innkeeper, constable, and resident slave dealer of the town. Currently, he wore the hat of slave dealer, having accepted the boy to be sold. The boy looked not more than ten. The boy was frightened, and moved with hesitation. In a rare gesture of compassion toward a slave, Will placed a hand on the boy's shoulder as he guided him along the path, trying to reassure him that no harm would befall him.

Will had no moral reservation about selling and buying human souls, nor had he ever thought of it as right or wrong. To him, it was an honest business, and dated back to before man could remember. It delivered a needed service, helped add to the economy, fed thousands of the otherwise unemployed, and put food on his table. Why a few niggers sometime caused so much trouble about it was beyond him. All you had to do was treat them right, just as you would treat any other animal. Take those two slavers putting up at his inn; they were lowlife scum of the worse kind. The last time they had been in town to sell their commodities, he had witnessed one of them split one of his slave's heads in half with an ax because he got sick on bad food and vomited on the slaver's leg. No enforceable law against killing a slave or an animal—but would a man do that to a horse or dog? No. So, why treat a slave in such a manner? You have to take care of your property.

Before opening the oak door to enter the jail, Will looked in through the barred windows in front to be sure the slaves were in their cells. Satisfied, he opened the door and stepped in, guiding the boy in front of him to an area of well-tramped dirt with nothing else except a long table with benches on each side. Down the middle of the table ran a small version of a cattle-feed trough.

On the other side of the earthen floor were six half-a-rod-square jail cells, made of iron straps crisscrossed and riveted in such a manner that they formed squares not quite large enough for the average man to pass his head. Four of the cells were occupied, and the other two empty.

Will opened the empty cell on the end and said to the boy, "Don't want to put you in with all these others, Andrew. They were recently unloaded from a boat. Don't know their nature. I'm given by the slavers they were baptized before being brought here, but that don't mean nothin'. I doubt they even know what it was all about. So, I'm going to put you in this cell by yourself where they won't be a problem to you." Reluctantly, the boy slave entered the cell and stood still as he looked at the other captives.

As Will closed the cell door, he gave Andrew a piece of advice: "Be polite, speak clear, and look a buyer in the face when he speaks to you, and you could be bought by a good master. Why Mister Carter couldn't keep you, I can't understand. Of course, knowing Carter, it's all about money. That's what's important to him. I wish you well. If I needed another boy, I'd buy you myself."

Then he added, "I'll make sure you get good food, Andrew, and see to it you eat alone so these others don't steal it from you."

Andrew took a position almost in the center of the jail cell. Standing there in a daze, he looked around and did not know what was happening. The oak door slammed shut, breaking Andrew's stupor. He backed against the far wall of his cell and slumped to the floor. The straw spread on the floor smelled of excrement—not only in his cell, but in all of them. Some cells had holes in the earthen floor to relieve oneself; in others, no such hole had been dug, and a person would just let it go, perhaps in the furthest corner of the cell. Either way, the straw was used for cleanup. He tried to keep his mind busy by listening to the chatter of the others, crammed four or five to a cell. They spoke a language he didn't understand, even though some of the slaves on Carter's plantation had seemed to speak something similar.

The day had begun like previous days, with a morning chill. Before long, it would turn hot and humid as the day wore on. You could count on a late-afternoon thunderstorm dropping its torrential load of rain and clear just as abruptly, leaving a breath-stifling period of humidity until the cooling breezes blew in the evening.

After the storm, Will, true to his word, had a meal of boiled goat and beans brought to the jail, and Andrew, sitting alone at the table, downed the meal and drank from a fresh bucket of water until he was sated. Back in his cell, his full stomach caused him to become drowsy, and he fell asleep on the straw-covered floor.

Andrew woke at the sound of the big door being opened. He sat up, and saw Will and another man bringing in another slave. The slave's feet were shackled and his hands manacled in back, and he stumbled as he was pushed down the row of cells.

Andrew noticed the man who had come with Will more than he did the slave, as he thought the man looked odd. He was just over five and a half feet tall, but he was stout and wide, made of muscle and fat in a bundle hard as rock. As he walked, he shifted from side to side in a rocking motion. His neck, what little was shown of it, was thick, and it balanced an oversized head.

Black hair grew out of his shirt collar opening, and seemed to be one with his full-bearded face.

They approached Andrew's cell, and Will said, "You be careful of this one, boy. He's a mean one. Should be a prisoner rather than being put up for sale. Sorry to put him next to you, but the other cells are full. Better get back some."

Andrew backed against the far side of his cell. Will opened the cell next to Andrew, and the odd-looking man placed his boot on the slave's rump and pushed. The slave stumbled into the cell and fell face down. The man followed him, kicking the downed slave in the side. As the man backed out of the cell, the slave rolled over enough to look up at the man and smiled. In return, the man spit at him.

With the cell door closed and with the sound of the main door closing, the slave rolled over, sat up, and looked about. He was barefoot and shirtless, his exposed back revealed a history of past beatings and whippings, and there were fresh cuts still open and bleeding. The back of his head had an open wound with caked blood that had run down his neck. A stubble of beard grew over a branded *R* on his left cheek. That, and the evidence of whippings, gave proof this slave was trouble.

He looked around at his surroundings, then at Andrew, and said, "This place don't change much. I've been here a few times after being caught off the plantation. Who're you, boy?"

Andrew did not answer, and pressed himself harder against the far side of his cell.

"Hey, I ain't going to hurt you. Even if I wanted to, I ain't so dumb to do it in here. Don't be afraid, child."

"I'm not scared of you, and I'm no child. I'm twelve, and do a man's work."

"Twelve! You don't look over eight, maybe seven. You're just a runt. Nobody's going to buy you to do fieldwork, that's for sure. Chances are, you're a houseboy of some kind. What kinds of man's work you ever done?"

"I helped Miz Jane raise her kids and take care of the other young'uns. She died having a baby, and Master didn't need me anymore."

"Miz Jane, she the missus of the house?"

"No. She belonged to Master."

"A breeder, huh. Where's your mam and pap?"

"Don't know where they are. Don't know who they are. Miz Jane says the overseer found me in the tobacco field, and Master gave me to her to bring up."

"Well, they both must've been from over the water, 'cause you're as black as you can get, same as me. Be proud of it. You hear me?"

"Yes, sir, I hear you."

"I ain't no sir. I'm Jim, just Jim. My other name don't get used. Mostly I get called 'that damned nigger.' Makes me smile now. What they call you?"

"Andrew. Never had a last name. Master was Master Carter, so maybe my name's Andrew Carter."

"You don't want that name. That's a white man's name. What you want a white man's name for?"

"Don't most of us get named after our master?"

"Guess so, but that don't mean you have to. Why don't you figure a name you want to be called and name yourself?"

"I can do that?"

"Try it, and see what happens."

The man had a disarming way about him, and in spite of himself, Andrew began to feel less concerned that he might be in harm's way. "What kind of name? I mean, how do I know what name isn't a white man's name?"

"Something will come to you. Don't hurry it."

"What's wrong with a white man's name? Your name's Jim. Ain't that a white man's name?"

"It is. The whites call me that. I've got another name, same as my dad's, but nobody's going to call me anything but Jim or *damned nigger*, so I let it go. Name's Samba Mohomet. See, it don't make no difference; nobody going to call me Samba."

Jim looked around. Seeing nobody to be concerned about, he rolled onto his back, arched his butt off the floor, brought his manacled wrists under his butt, and drew them under his legs; his hands were now in front. He scooted closer to one of the cell's sides and felt along the bottom.

Finding what he was looking for—a place close to the floor where the water and moisture had rusted the iron straps—he pulled on one of the straps and the rusted rivet popped out, separating the straps where they crossed. He pulled upward on the bottom of a vertical strap and it bent up such that it was pointed toward him. He looked around and saw a couple of the captives in the far cell looking at him in an interested and curious way.

"What you doing?" asked Andrew.

"You'll see. Just be quiet about this and keep talking. You like talking?"

"Yes, but—"

Jim slid one of the shackle's chain links over the strap. He began sliding the link back and forth on the bar as if he were trying to saw the chain link in half, which was what he was trying to do. "Tell me more about what you did when you were at the Carter place."

"They had me—what's those whip marks on your back? They whip you?"

"Me and Big Bull the overseer, the guy who kicked me in here, didn't always agree. I wasn't what you might call the best slave around the place. I never cared much about being a slave, and I let everybody know; the overseer and the master. The master used to just tell the overseer to take care of the situation, and he did. He'd hit me or give me ninety-nine; that's something you don't ever want to experience. He was meaner than a two-headed rattle-snake. When I could, I'd hit him back; he never knew when I was going to do it, but he knew if he whipped me or hit me, I was gonna get him back sooner or later. Then I used to run away to another place where I had a lady friend, an Indian; they was never going to give me a pass, so off I'd go, figuring the whipping was gonna be worth it. One of them times after they caught me off the plantation, Master said to make it known I was a runaway. They burned that 'R' on my cheek and gave me ninety-nine. They let me lie there on the ground, and told the other slaves not to help me. I stayed there most all night. It rained, and it seemed to revive me some. I pulled myself out of the mud and crawled to the cabin I stayed in. The other slaves wouldn't let me in, I guess because of the warning they had been given about helping me. I fell asleep outside the cabin thinking I was going to die. Come morning, Big Bull came a lookin' for me. He grabbed me by the arm and dragged me toward the fields. He must'uv thought I was still weak, but I wasn't. My strength had returned, and other than aching all over from the branding and the whipping, I felt good. I stood up and charged him; got him in the small of his back, and he must'uv flew twenty feet. He tried to stand up, but I was on him before he could clear his head. I beat him until someone hit me on the head from behind, and I was out. Guess they gave up on me. I 'woke in chains, and here I am. I'm hoping someone will buy me who ain't so damn mean. 'Course, I'd still do the same things."

"You trying to break your chains? You going to escape?"

"Chain ain't made well. Looks like soft iron, like nails are made of. Yeah, I'm trying to get ready to run, cause if I ain't bought, I go back with Littlefield and Big Bull, and I know for sure they gonna kill me. They'd already have killed me if the master didn't think I might be worth something in his pocket. So they try to sell me first, and if that don't work...well. We'll just see what happens. What about what your man's work was?"

"Miz Jane had nine children of her own, and took care of the other children when their mamas were working. Must've been another ten or twenty children, sometimes. My job was making food sometimes, and watching the older children to make sure they didn't get in anybody's way or get into trouble. I couldn't play with them, or Miz Jane would beat my behind with a pan. She said I weren't no child, and I had a job to do and that didn't include playing games."

"Well, now, I'd say for twelve years old, you did do a man's work at that; that's for sure. What else you do around there?"

"Nothing; there weren't anything else I was allowed to do."

"Could you read?"

"Don't know how to read. We weren't told how to do that."

"Did anybody read around there?"

"There was a group who didn't talk to the rest of us. They used to make marks on wood with charcoal or in the dirt. Some of them talked, and I couldn't understand them. Miz Jane said they came from over the water and talk different."

"They were Muslims, boy. Your place had Muslims. My pap was a Muslim. He came from a place over the water he called Africa. Said he was a Mandinka. He tried to get me interested in that stuff when he visited my mam, but I wasn't interested. I was more interested in other things."

"What other things? You mean fishing and hunting?"

"Yes, but let me tell you something, and don't ever forget what I'm about to tell you. I wanted to learn how to read. See, I'm smart. I see the white man reading stuff and writing stuff, and I know the secret to not being a slave is knowing how to read and write. You learn it, and you won't always be a slave."

"What's wrong with being a slave?"

"Boy, if you don't know, you're just plain dumb—no, stupid. That's what you are. You're stupid."

Andrew had never been called stupid. He'd been called a lot of things, but not stupid.

"Why stupid?"

"I hope you find out, Andrew, because you don't seem stupid. It's just you ain't been around to see what else is out there. My pap used to tell me stories about the place he'd come from, the wars he'd been in, and the places he'd been after. He said freedom was the thing he missed more than even his wives and children he left behind in Africa."

"Where's this place, Africa?"

"Africa. That's the place we talk about when we say *over the water.*"

"He had more than one wife?"

"Yes, it's a Muslim way. He had a wife here, my mam, and he was allowed to visit her on Sundays. I remember him visiting us and trying to teach me about being a Muslim. He could quote word for word from their book; its call the Koran. As I said, I didn't want any part of learning that stuff. But I did want to learn to read, and that was what we did together on his visits: he taught me to read the Koran. He'd read it, and then write it on wood with charcoal in English and show me the words. That's one of the things my overseer hated about me—I could read, and he couldn't. He said it should be against the law for a slave to read. I've heard it is against the law in some places."

"Would you teach me to read, Jim?"

"I would if I could, but I doubt if we'll get a chance to be together long enough."

"How am I supposed to learn to read if there's nobody to teach me?"

"You don't know what's in your future or what opportunities you're going to get. Keep your eyes open for the opportunity. If you see something written, ask somebody if they know what it says. If they read it to you, remember the shape of the words and what they mean, and memorize it. Other than that, watch for someone who knows how to read and learn from them."

"Sounds hard."

"It is. Anything worth anything is hard. You'll figure out how if it's important to you."

Jim kept the motion up into the late hours of the night. At last, the link wore thin, and after some twisting, it opened. Jim examined his efforts, and, pleased, he smiled. He didn't notice the others who had been watching him also smiling. He re-closed the link on itself such that a casual observer would not notice it. He focused his attention on the now-worn, sharp strap he had used as a saw. He pushed the strap down and up several times until the strap broke off in his hand, and hid it inside his pants.

CHAPTER II

"I'M GOING TO sleep tonight, Martin, that's for damn sure," Ignatius said. Every bump in the road reminded him of his sixty-six years. His fingers found it painful to relax their grip on the reins. A younger man might complain, but as one grows older, pain becomes a routine part of life, and complaining becomes tiring to you as well as to others. Accepting in silence the bitter ignominy of age becomes a matter of course. He was not a religious man, but thought it made sense that something was responsible for all that was, and calling it God or a god was good enough for him. If anything, he might be called a Deist, which was common among many who thought about and questioned these things. He did not blame his image of a god for his condition or the things that went wrong in his life, but he questioned the purpose of such a flawed plan.

To ease his aches and pains Miss Millie made salves from animal fat and secret plants, and insisted Ignatius rub the concoctions over his sore parts. The remedies spread the odor of old about him, but there was no relief. He thought it best to use it on horses, but Miss Millie was not to be argued with.

"Did I not offer to drive?"

"Yes, I suppose you did. But it's difficult to give up the reins in more ways than one."

"You're still having a problem turning it over to Mary and me, aren't you?"

"The plantation is the only thing I've ever known, Martin. But I know I'm no good for it anymore. I'd just run it down. I get angry at everything anybody does that's just a bit out of line, or even different from how I would do it. I never used to yell and take a swing at the niggers the way I do now."

"No, I know you didn't. You've always prided yourself on treating them well."

"That boy, the one Norton Carter calls Andrew—I hope he's the way Norton spoke of him. He'd help me no end to make living a whole lot easier. I'll try my best not to lay a log along the side of him," Ignatius joked.

"Norton's quite a salesman, you know. He's not about to tell you the bad things about this boy. If he's such a fine young man, why doesn't he keep him?"

"All I know is what he said; he no longer needs him, and is trying to cut his expenses. I've known Norton a long time, and I can trust him on this."

"Will he take him back if he isn't what he said?"

"He didn't say so. I'll take it up with Will when we get there."

Trees on each side of the stage road shaded the journey, giving relief to what was beginning to be another hot day. Ignatius's mind wandered, and blurred images of the past came and went. He thought of some of the many things that had happened in his life; he pictured the day he had married Mary's mother, Elizabeth. He had been born into the Catholic faith, but it had never set well with him. The Father had paid him many an unwelcome visit, trying to convince him to attend Mass and confess the sins that he had accumulated through his churchless adult lifetime. On one such visit, he was annoyed by the Father's stubbornness, and to be rid of him, accepted his invitation to a church picnic.

She was just nineteen when he saw her at the picnic. She wore a plain white dress, and was carrying a platter with a hog's head from the fire pit to a table. She was the prettiest girl he had ever seen. She looked straight ahead, but he thought he saw her take an ever-so-slight glance his way, and with just the hint of a smile. There and then, he told himself that girl was going to warm his bed for the rest of his life.

As she laid the tray down on the community table, Ignatius forgot the reservations and decorum of the day, and made his way to her side. "Mind if I sit with you?" he blurted. Her father, having wandered up behind the two, originally to help his daughter but now taking the role of the protector, asked "And who might you be?"

Some might have been startled, but Ignatius had always been self-assured and ready to take on any situation, be it with Indian, slave, or white.

"I'm Ignatius Attaway, and I would guess you're this girl's father." Holding out his hand to shake, he continued to say, "I was asking her if I could sit with her."

Her father was starting to say something when Elizabeth interrupted. "I would love to have you sit and eat with us. My name's Elizabeth, and yes, this is my father, Mister Curtis."

The meal was a bit one-sided. Ignatius and Elizabeth, not meaning to exclude anyone, talked mostly to each other. The church father gave a speech and several other members did the same, talking about what their committees were up to—but Ignatius and Elizabeth scarcely heard a word. By the end of the picnic, Ignatius had asked Elizabeth if he could drive her home. She said yes before her mother or father could say a word.

Elizabeth and her mother knew it was the right thing by the time the picnic was over. Her father, however, harbored doubts about this man who had come into his little girl's life. As Ignatius drove Elizabeth home, her father and mother followed close behind in their buggy. Her father tried to hear everything the young couple was saying, but with the sounds of the buggies and Elizabeth's mother talking in his ear about what a wonderful man this Ignatius was, he could not hear a thing. He could still see what they were doing, though. *Just keep your hands on the reins, Mister Ignatius,* he kept saying to himself.

Love makes a man do things he would never do otherwise. He attended every service, always sitting next to Elizabeth. After a while, he went to confession, and an audible gasp was heard from the Father when Ignatius confessed his many sins of killings in the war.

In fact, Ignatius disliked the Father as well as religion, and he exaggerated his deeds and sins, knowing the Father would have a difficult time with what he heard. Ignatius could not help himself for the pleasure it gave him to listen to the Father anguish over it.

The courtship lasted long enough to satisfy Elizabeth's father, and no more.

AS IF ELIZABETH had eavesdropped on Ignatius's thoughts, she had her father's slaves make a bed of cherry wood, complete with a golden yellow silk canopy with tassels hanging down. The best seamstress of all her father's slaves made a goose down mattress to her specification: not too hard, not too soft. The first two attempts did not suit her, and she had them made over until the mattress was just right. The night before they were married, her father's driver delivered it to Ignatius as he was finishing a pipe and just getting ready for bed, suffering from a headache from the party his friends had given him an hour or so before. He had his slaves carry it to the big room on the third floor of the mansion, the room reserved for entertaining guests—and, a few hours earlier, the room chosen by his friends for his bachelor party.

The room had served as his mother and father's bedroom, and was built within the roof of the big house. It was the only bedroom on the top floor, but it was complete with a connected study and small room where a chamber pot and basin were discretely hidden from view. The room had allowed his parents to enjoy complete privacy, and now it would serve Ignatius and his bride.

With the order of "Put it up over there and clean this place so it's suitable for a lady," the bed was put in place until Elizabeth, after the wedding night, had other thoughts about how the room should be arranged in a proper manner suitable for husband and wife.

The day following the wedding, Elizabeth had the bed moved to the far wall, between two gable windows looking out over the plantation. This left most of the room, the door side, open for activities, such as trying on and changing Elizabeth's many dresses and gowns with the help of her entourage of slave servants. Another door, seldom used, led to a staircase that wound its way down two floors to the kitchen where Miss Millie slept. The original purpose of the entry had been to allow servants to access the room with food and drinks without having to go through the house proper. Elizabeth thought the idea quaint, and revived its use and purpose.

She warmed the bed, and Ignatius, too; and it was in that bed, in that room, that she died two years later giving birth to Mary, their only child.

Ignatius cremated Elizabeth as she lay in the bed in a clearing next to the family graveyard. It was covered with firewood ten or twelve feet high. Ignatius lighted the pile with a torch. Flames leapt to the dark sky, and Elizabeth took her place among the many who had gone before her. The ashes of the cremation were raked over the graveyard, and a wooden memorial was placed in the middle of the yard. Each year, on the anniversary of her death, all, including the slaves, were given the day off, and the marker was renewed with a new carved one.

Tears ran down Ignatius's cheeks from reddened eyes, and Martin pretended not to notice. *Leave him be*, he thought. *He's remembering again.*

Then there were friends he had known since he was a boy, many becoming farmers, as he had done; most dead or dying now. Damn! How he missed them, all of them. He wished he could go back in time, but knew it was not to be. Maybe this boy he was going to see about buying could help him do the things he found more difficult to do; things like riding down to the swamp and shooting deer or turkey, and lying back against a tree and fishing for whatever happened to bite. He thought of a dozen other things he liked to do, but somehow just never had the time for. It came to him that he hadn't thought at all about having the boy help with his duties as master of the plantation. He might miss it a bit, but not much. Yes, it was time to turn it over. Martin had made Mary a fine husband, and he brought several rich acres of adjoining land with him. If they would give him a few grandchildren, he would be a happy man. Well…give them time, and who knew what might happen?

Martin, seeing Ignatius going deeper and deeper into his depressive slump, put a hand on his shoulder and shook him. Ignatius looked up at Martin and blinked his eyes, trying to clear them as well as his mind. "Huh? What?"

"You hear the news about what happened up in Boston?"

"You mean about soldiers shooting into a crowd of people?"

"I do. What you think 'bout it?"

"Only thing I heard was the soldiers who did the shooting were arrested. They killed one of 'em…a colored boy, I heard. Sounds like the crowd was getting out of hand and the soldiers was trigger happy. I understand the captain in charge was arrested. Guess they had to do something to calm the masses."

"Strange thing I heard is the crowd was organized by that troublemaker Sam Adam, and Sam's cousin, John, is going to defend him. Doesn't that make a pair?" Martin said, shaking his head from side to side in disbelief.

"I guess I don't understand what the problem is, Martin. Seems everything was alright and all of a sudden people got on edge about almost nothing. Can't figure out what the nothing part is."

"The problem is, those people listen to that troublemaker rather than tending to their own business."

"Don't know, Martin. You might be right; it's not any of my business."

"I've got an uneasy feeling about things, Iggy. Something's going to happen sooner or later, and it's not going to be good."

"I suppose you're right," Ignatius said wiping the last of the moisture from his eyes. Then, rubbing the small of his back, he said, "On the way back, you can drive. I'm going to spread a thick layer of straw in the back of the wagon and tell you how to drive all the way back."

"You old…whatever, if you do, I'm going to hit every hole in the road." They laughed and went back to their private thoughts.

"Springs."

"What'd you say, Iggy?"

"I was just thinking, I should've had softer springs put in under this seat."

"It's not but a mile up the road. You'll make it."

"You wouldn't say that if you were inside this body, son-in-law. Your turn will come someday."

They sat in silence, other than the occasional grunt and moan from Ignatius as the wagon seemed to find every bump and rut in the road.

The sun was well on its way down when Martin said, "That's Bryan Town ahead of us."

In a few minutes, they stopped in front of the inn.

"We're here, Martin. Give me a hand; don't think I can move too well. It's not that I'm getting old, it's just this damn wagon's hard springs," he said, with a slight painful smile of self-deprecation.

The inn was of rough-cut wood, weathered almost white. A wooden sign swung above the inn door, with "Bryan's Inn" painted in white paint. Thick plank stairs led up to the porch, and from there, a heavy door allowed entrance by stepping over an old flea-covered hound lying on his side licking his genitals. A sign posted on the door read:

NEWLY ARRIVED BY WAY OF THE INDIES
NEGROS FROM AFRICA
RECENTLY OFFLOADED FROM THE BOAT
INDIGO RUN
AT THE PORT OF ST. MARY'S
TO BE AUCTIONED FRIDAY MORNING
JUNE, 21, 1765
14 ADULT MALES, 1 ADULT FEMALE
POSSIBLY LOCAL OTHERS

THE DOOR LED into the inn's tavern. Inside, the air was filled with smoke, and the smell of burned grease floated throughout; men at tables and the bar smoked pipes and drank pints. Against an end wall was an immense fireplace in which a boar was roasting. An old, wrinkled black woman watched over it as she rocked in a chair and puffed a pipe of her own, turning the spit when she thought fit. An occasional rat sneaked out from a crack in the woodwork and scurried to claim a fallen crumb. Three soldiers in red and white uniforms sat at a table and ate outside cuts from the roasting boar. One of them poured a round of ale from a flagon.

Another table hosted a lone free black who everyone knew as Isaac Attaway. He owned several acres of rich land, which he had been able to purchase along with his freedom from Ignatius Attaway some three years previous. Since then, he had been able to purchase three or four older slaves from other planters. The slaves had been deemed just about worn out after fifteen or twenty years of hard fieldwork, but Isaac thought they would still be able to give a few more years of work before they died, and at the price of "take 'em off my hands" plus a few pounds, he couldn't pass up the offers.

Why Isaac had come to Bryan Town this day was a mystery to all, and speculation filled many a conversation. Seated at the bar were two slave dealers talking among themselves, but also answering questions the locals were asking about the slaves they had brought up from the port of St. Mary's. Around the rest of the tables sat planters, all having come to Bryan Town for the auction. They had not seen each other for long spells, and were eager to talk about the latest news, rumors, and farm talk in general.

Will, the innkeeper, was no stranger to Ignatius and Martin, or, for that matter, most of the other local patrons of the inn. Upon seeing the travelers enter, he was quick to ask them if they would like an ale. "Perhaps later, Will," Martin said. "Right now, we'd like our wagon and horses put up, and to get a good bed for the night."

"One of my boys will take care of your rig. We have a room that has a bed not taken. The rest of the beds in the room are full, or you can put your roll on the floor just about anywhere if you prefer. The other rooms are about the same, but this one smells...well, agreeable enough. Chamber pots are around the room, and dug latrines are in the back of the building next to the jail. If you wish, we have a bath house. The water comes from a well, and it is a bit cold, but there are no bugs in it. For a small charge, we can heat it, but it takes an hour or two."

"Bath?! Why? We have no need for a bath. We'll only be here long enough for the sale tomorrow," said Ignatius. "And have your boy load the back of the wagon with straw, enough to sit on so a man won't feel the wagon when it hits a hole in the road."

"I'll have it taken care of, Ignatius. Perhaps you might wish to view the Negroes. They're in the jail, and can be viewed at any time. We have lighted lanterns inside just for the purpose. The slaves are chained for your protection, though I've been assured by the traders over there," pointing to the two slaver dealers, "the slaves are not violent. However, who knows for sure? One of them might decide to go north at any time."

"I'm interested in a young Negro by the name of Andrew. Norton Carter had him brought here for me to take a look-see. If I want him, I can buy him outright, and won't have to go through the auction."

"I know who you mean. Norton left him in my charge, and mentioned you were to have right of first refusal. He's in the pen with the others. You want to see him now?"

"Let's take a look at the bed first, and then we could use a slice of the pig and the ale you were talking about."

The bed was typical: a wood frame with roping stretched both ways supporting a cushion of straw, which, in turn, was covered with rough cloth made of hemp. It would sleep four adults, but Ignatius had made it clear he wanted no other travelers to occupy it, just Martin and himself. From a bucket of fresh water by the room's window, both men scooped cupped handfuls onto their faces to wash off the road dust. They shook the excess from their hands and proceeded back to the tavern.

Stopping at the table where Isaac Attaway was seated, Ignatius greeted him. "Hello, Isaac. Things alright your way?"

Isaac looked up at his one-time master, and a smile of recognition crossed his face. "Hello, Ignatius. Hello, Martin." Isaac had long ago gotten over the habit of referring to Ignatius as Master and Martin as Mister Martin, and had adapted quite well to his reverse roll as master of his own farm and his own slaves.

"What brings you into town?" asked Ignatius.

"Same as you, I suspect—going to try to buy a slave. I need somebody who's strong and able. Those old men I got do the best they can, but they ain't going to last forever. I got a good crop coming in this year, and I need the help."

"You able to pay money or got some heads of tobacco stored away? Don't think these traders are going to trust you on a future crop."

"I got tobacco from last year I been storing just for this. Thought something might come up where I'd need to use it."

Ignatius looked at Martin, who, understanding the look, gave a slight nod.

Ignatius asked Isaac, "You mind if we sit with you and have our dinner?"

"I'd be honored, sir. You might get some mean looks from others 'round here."

"Ain't none of their business, Isaac."

Both men sat down and motioned to Will to come over. Will's wife, Martha, almost a duplicate of her husband except an inch or two shorter, picked up on the gesture and returned a nod as she was on her way over.

"Hungry or thirsty, are ya? What'll it be?"

"What's the choice, Martha?" Martin said with a teasing smile.

"You know better than that, Martin. We got the boar and we got ale, and there's corn bread. We got some boiled goat, but it don't smell too good. If you want something else, you'll have to get it elsewhere."

"Pig, ale, and bread it is. How about you, Isaac? You hungry?" said Martin.

"I already ate. I don't do the ale stuff, you know that. But if Martha has more buttermilk, I could use a cup."

Martha turned to fill the order, and the table talk continued. First, they covered the usual: weather, crops, and what the king had been doing. They speculated about what the soldiers were doing in these parts. Then they talked more of the specifics Isaac had in mind.

"I'm beating myself to death out there. I used to work for you from sunup to sundown, and on the weekend, hire me out to others from sunup to sundown. Ain't no different now, except I work for myself from sunup to sundown seven days a week, and could use a couple of extra days, if God almighty would just squeeze 'em in for me. I've got to get some help. I don't even get Sunday off now. If I can get two good slaves, I can make it work."

Both Ignatius and Martin chuckled at Isaac's remark, remembering their earlier days.

"Isaac, Martin and Mary are taking over the running of my place, and I guess it's no secret they'll end up with the whole thing after I'm gone. So rather than me doing the talking, I'm going to have Martin do it. I'm a-thinking we're both of the same mind. Martin...."

Martin and Ignatius looked into each other's eyes to make sure they were both talking about the same thing, and read each other's thoughts.

Martin said, "Isaac, you know both ends of running a farm using slaves. There isn't a thing we can tell you about it. But you might be overlooking something."

"What's that?"

"Those slaves for sale all came direct from Africa. You have no history of what they're like; could be alright, but could be trouble. On top of that, they might not even be able to talk English, and you got nobody to translate for you. You might have the money or tobacco to pay for your purchase, but you're just going to be getting more trouble than help."

"I thought about all that. If none of them can't talk English, I'm not going to buy any of them. There is, and you may not know this, another slave for sale. He belongs to Edward Littlefield, and has been a lot of trouble. I was thinking he might respond to me better because I'm black, have been a slave, and would treat him better than Littlefield treats him—or anyone else, for that matter."

Ignatius spoke up. "That would have to be Jim. I didn't know Jim was for sale. I guess it figures. I thought Ed would end up killing him; no one else is going to buy him. Jim's just too much...well...he just isn't going to be a slave. It doesn't matter how nice you are or how much you beat him, he just doesn't want to be a slave, and he's not about to go about it the same as you did. I don't recommend you take the chance."

Martin again took the lead. "Here's what we have in mind. You pick out a slave or slaves you think would make a good buy. We'll take them and train them so to speak. We'll put 'em in that group of slaves we have that talk African—Muslims, they're called. You borrow one or two of our slaves until the Africans are trained and can speak enough English to understand and be understood. Pick out who of our slaves you think will do the job; you know most of them, anyhow. We'll let them know what's happening, and that they can return at night, if they wish. They tend to get nervous if they think they're being sold."

"Why would you do this for me?"

"Because, Isaac, you still have to make payments to us for the land and cattle. This is in our interest as much as it is in yours. Do we have a deal?"

"I thought it might be because you liked me."

Martha brought the food, ale, and Isaac's buttermilk to the table. As she set the food in place, Isaac thought about the offer. He lit his pipe and drew deep, adding a few seconds to the time he needed to organize his thoughts.

"What if this doesn't work out? What if none of them are any good?"

Martin said, "We sell 'em for what we can get out of them, and we go on from there. Isaac, we made a deal with you a long time ago, and we don't want to have to take your place back. One way or the other, this thing is going to work for all of us. Let's not worry about the what-ifs now."

A pause, and then, "Thanks for your offer. We have a deal."

THE BOAR WAS good, and a couple more ales made it seem grand. More than one person was thinking, "That old black woman sure can cook."

Will Bryan came to the table. "Everything alright here?"

"Will, I'd like to see that boy, Andrew," said Ignatius.

"I can take you over there in a few minutes. Be right back."

Will finished what he was doing and took his key ring and a lantern from under the bar counter. Then he removed the chimney from the lantern, lighted the wick, and replaced the chimney. "Follow me," he said, and opened the rear door of the inn. They proceeded to walk the path to the jail.

As always, Will peered through the jail bars to assure himself that the captives were still captive. Satisfied, he unlocked the door, swinging it open for Ignatius and Martin. Once in, the door was closed and locked again.

"Your boy is in the last cell on your right. The next cell is holding that damned nigger, Jim. Watch you don't get too close to him; he's a bad one. You want to go in, or take him out to talk to him?"

"Take him over to the table, where we can sit and talk awhile," Ignatius said.

As Will walked to Andrew's cell, Ignatius and Martin cast a glance at the other slaves: three cells filled with five or six chained slaves in each. There was one cell with a solitary female slave. She looked at the two men with a fearful look, seeming to ask what they had on their minds.

Will opened the cell door as Ignatius and Martin sat down at the table. Andrew stood up, looking past Will at the two men sitting at the table. They appeared well dressed, not dirty or scruffy as an overseer might have been.

"Come on, Andrew. That old man at the table wants to talk to you. If he likes you, he's going to buy you." Then, in a whisper, he said, "His name is Ignatius Attaway, and if I were you, I'd try to make him like you. Ain't too many masters who treat niggers as well as he does."

Andrew nodded that he understood, took Will by his leave, and walked over to the table. Will, said, "I'll wait over at the door while you folks talk."

"Sit down, Andrew. My name is Ignatius Attaway, and…." He stopped talking and stared at Andrew. "I've never seen a slave with green eyes before. You look familiar. Have we seen each other before?"

"Don't think so, sir."

"You ever leave Mister Carter's place?"

"Sometimes, to get stuff."

"In Bryan Town, maybe?"

"Yes, sir. I been here before."

"Well, that's probably it, then. Anyhow, where was I? Oh, yeah, this man is Martin Blackiston, my daughter's husband. Norton Carter wrote to me a while ago saying he had to sell you for reasons I'm not clear on, but I guess he has his reasons. What's your understanding of why he has to sell you?"

"Well, sir, when Miz Jane died, he said he didn't have anybody to take care of the children anymore, and they was just going to have to go to the fields with their mas, and their mas was just going to have to take care of them the best they could."

"What does all that have to do with you?"

"My job was to help Miz Jane take care of the children."

"So why didn't he put you in the fields?"

"I asked him, and he said I was too little for field work."

"How old are you?"

"Miz Jane said I was twelve or so."

"You are a runt, that's for sure," Martin chuckled in the background.

"How smart are you? What else can you do other than take care of children?"

"I don't know nothing else, sir."

"Can you read?"

"No, sir."

"Can you do numbers—you know, count?"

"Oh, yes, sir," Andrew said, his face lighting up and he smiled. "I can count. I can tell you how many children I take care of, how many tobacco plants are in a row, how many horses there are in a team, and I know how to drive them horses, too."

"You can drive a team, or ride just a single horse?"

"I can do both, sir." Andrew was feeling good about being able to tell Ignatius about his ability with horses. "I always was asked to go get this and go get that. If I had to get a lot of stuff, I'd have to drive a wagon. Sometimes, Master Carter let me just ride a horse after my work was done."

"Who hitched the horses?"

"Why, I did, sir!" said Andrew, agitated that Ignatius would think someone else had to do it for him.

"So, you can handle horses, huh? By any chance, can you break 'em, too?"

Andrew lowered his head and admitted he had never broken a horse.

"I suspect not," said Ignatius. "I suspect there isn't a horse that would know you were on him, anyway."

"You give me a chance, and I'll break any horse you can put me on. I can do anything."

Martin chuckled again in the background. *This child has what it takes,* he was thinking, and so was Ignatius.

"Think you can take care of an old man rather than young children?"

"Couldn't be too much different."

With this, Martin no longer chuckled. He let out a loud roar of laughter, and tears ran from his eyes. Ignatius gave him what could best be described as a dirty look, accentuated with a *don't do it again, son-in-law.*

Andrew had decided somewhere along the line he could work for this old man, and Ignatius had formed a favorable opinion of Andrew.

"What old man?" asked Andrew, acting the diplomat.

"This old man," Ignatius said. "Well?"

"Yes, sir, I'll try."

"One more thing. I don't whip or beat my slaves. If a slave gets out of line, I have him work on Sundays. If it's something I really don't like, I'll just up and sell him for whatever I can get. Some folks consider me a nice slaveholder, and I take it as a compliment whether it's meant that way or not, but

I'm no pushover, and don't think I am. You have to do what I tell you to, or I'll get rid of you. Understand?"

Andrew nodded his head yes.

"Alright. I have something else to add. I don't have an overseer. Martin here is as close to an overseer as I have. Whatever he tells you to do, you have to do it without question, even though you'll be working with and for me. Martin is in full charge of all of the slaves on the plantation, and my daughter, Miz Mary, Martin's wife, has as much authority as he has. Clear?"

"Yes, sir."

"Seems as if we understand each other. Will!" Ignatius shouted. "Come back, we're ready."

Will walked over to the table. "Well?"

"We'll buy him for the price Norton wanted—if, and only if, he isn't what I need. Then I expect I can return him."

"Mister Carter did say if you weren't satisfied with him, you could return him to me and I was to give your money back, but it had to be within a month of purchase, and he had to be as good physically as he is now."

"Suits me. You have a sale."

"I'll get to work on the papers when we're back at the inn."

"Have him ready to go in the morning, but we're going to stick around long enough for the rest of the auction."

"The price Mister Carter gave you was the price he wanted for Andrew. As a broker, I have to add five percent commission."

"That's not how I understood it. Serves me right for not asking. Tell you what, I'll pay half of your commission and you can take the rest up with Norton. Either Norton pays you the other half, you forget about the other half, or you can keep the boy. What's it going to be?"

Ignatius was not known for being easy to deal with when it came to money matters. He drove hard bargains and he didn't bluff—at least not as far as anyone had ever figured out.

"I'll work it out with Mister Carter," Will said, keeping a composed look but boiling mad inside. *Odd,* he thought. *Ignatius and Andrew both have green eyes.*

AS IGNATIUS AND Martin returned to the tavern along with Will, the redcoat couriers were posting a notice on the door with the headline, *Stamp Act of March 22, 1765.* The three read the notice as the other patrons gathered around the door and stretched their necks to read over their shoulders.

"King George is getting a bit difficult," Martin said.

"That might explain what happened up in Boston."

"Think I'll give them a message to take back to the king."

"Don't. We're not here to get into it with the king's men. Do something, and we'll be sleeping with Andrew, or worse, Jim."

As the rest of the patrons read the notice, a murmur of contempt could be heard, and several clenched fists shook toward the table where the redcoats had returned to their drinking and laughing, oblivious to the crowd.

ISAAC, PREFERRING TO avoid the morning auction because of the spectacle of a black man buying other black men, approached the traders.

"My name's Isaac Attaway, and I'm a free man. I want to see those slaves you have for sale. If we can settle on a price, I'll take 'em now."

The traders had been at the bar drinking ale most of the evening and were obnoxiously loud, laughing at their own company and what was being said between them. When Isaac spoke, they seemed to sober up. One said, "You buying your own kind?"

"I'm a free man. Own slaves, and need more. You want to do business, or not?"

"Don't get edgy, boy. You know we're going to give you a price higher than you'd pay at auction?"

"I know. But I got my reasons for doing it now rather than at auction. You can't take advantage of me 'cause I know what they're worth after seeing 'em. But if you're reasonable, I'll pay a fair price."

"You got money?"

"I got enough tobacco at the farm and the papers to transfer it to you."

"That means the price will be higher, because we have to transport the heads."

"I'll have my slaves pull it in wagons to anywhere, say...within a hundred miles."

"Alright, Mister Isaac Attaway, follow us." Then he got Will's attention and waved him over to the bar.

"Another ale?"

"Later. Right now, we need you to open the jail."

CHAPTER III

THE CROW OF a cockerel greeted the new day, and soon, the clinging chill of night would give way to another sticky summer day. The cold persisted for the moment, and Ignatius and Martin found a table close to the fireplace to ward off the last vestige.

Martha greeted them with "G'morn'n. You're up early. Couldn't sleep? Mush?"

"Strange bed, I suppose, and the others were moving about, so we just got up. If mush is what you have, then that's what we'll have," said Martin. "A cup of hot tea would be nice, too."

"Did ya hear about them soldiers? Nobody knows where they are. They never went to their bed last night, and nobody's seen 'em 'round."

Ignatius cocked his head. "Strange!" he said.

"Yes," Martha agreed. "The notice ain't on the door no more, so they must've taken it down and left."

Ignatius and Martin glanced at the door where the notice had been posted the night before. Then they looked at each other with looks that said, "Poor bastards."

THE COCKEREL'S GREETING woke the slaves. Some smiled at the sound as if released to freedom, some tried to pray in spite of their restraints, and still others repeated rote phrases in their strange tongue.

Within the hour, the slave traders entered the jail and shouted for their property to get up, even though they had already arisen. Will beat on the doors of his two charges and told them to wake, too. "Jim, I'm going to try to sell you this morning. You look your best, and maybe you'll get someone to bid a penny or two. Andrew, your new owners will be collecting you as soon as they're up and ready."

Will and a couple of his Negroes along with the two slavers had brought buckets of water and the morning food. The food was dumped into the trough on the eating table. It was unrecognizable, but likely consisted of dinner leftovers from the previous night's inn menu mixed with goat milk and meat. It didn't take long after being made a slave to learn not to be particular about what was eaten as long as it didn't smell rotten; what food they received could be the last they would have for days. In many cases, and in this instance, the contents of the food might not hold to their religious beliefs, but their religion also taught them to make exceptions to the teachings in extreme circumstances, as survival was paramount.

The slavers, pistols in hand, opened the first cell and motioned the slaves to come out, still chained together. They hobbled to the table and scooped handfuls of food to their mouths as fast as they could. The bucket of water was drunk from; some bringing the water to their mouth with cupped hands, and others lifting the bucket up in their turn. After the trough was empty, they were ordered back to their cell. The process was repeated cell after cell, with Will's Negroes refilling the trough with fresh food and the bucket of water replaced with new until all of the slaves had been fed. Jim and Andrew were the last to eat by themselves—Andrew first, Jim last. The slavers, unconcerned about Andrew, were more than a little concerned about Jim, and helped Will and his boys watch him with pistols still drawn. The lone girl slave was conspicuously missing, but it was of no concern to anyone in the room; they all knew her fate. Less noticeable was the absence of one of the other slaves who had also been removed during the night.

AFTER FINISHING THE mush and enjoying his first pipe of the day, Martin asked Ignatius, "You still want to stay around for the auction, or just pick up Andrew and get going?"

"Yes, think I want to stick around to see what Isaac buys."

"Suits me. Let's get out there and see what's going on."

The two left the inn. Already, the day had begun to warm. The gathering crowd in front of the jail waited for the slaves to be presented and for the auction to begin. The two took their time wandering over.

"We can get Andrew after this is over," said Ignatius.

They mulled around the others and exchanged the usual greetings. Isaac didn't seem to be among them.

"Where you think he is?" asked Martin.

"Isaac? Don't know. There's Will; we can ask him if he's seen him."

Will was just coming from the jail when he saw Ignatius and Martin walking toward him.

"Good morning. You going to buy more?"

"Don't think so," said Martin. "You seen Isaac anywhere?"

"Isaac! He bought a couple of slaves last night and left with them. He knows the value of property; I'll say that for him. He wanted 'em last night, but stood his ground on the price he was willing to pay. Those traders have a new respect for black boys."

"Well, can't say I blame him for getting out early. It just doesn't seem right for him, buying his own kind. Reckon we'll meet up with him when we get back. You think he made good picks?"

"Not sure. One of the slaves was older than the rest, but from what I could see, he was strong, more or less, and of even temperament. Yes, he was a good buy. The other one, I'm not so sure. She might be a good breeder, but—"

Ignatius interrupted him mid-sentence. "He bought the girl?"

"That's right. Think he paid more for her than the other. Must have had something on his mind."

Ignatius wondered to himself what kind of deal they had made with Isaac.

Martin could see the puzzled look on his face. "Iggy, it might not be what you're thinking, and it might be a pretty smart move on Isaac's part. Let's see what he has to say when we meet up."

"Still, he could've had damn near any girl on my plantation for as long as he wanted just for the asking. Can't figure it."

THE SLAVERS WERE leading two huge donkeys to the auction platform and neither donkey would go up the stairs, despite the physical efforts and verbal abuse the slavers dished out. Will motioned for them to just leave the donkeys where they were, and, turning to the crowd, he said, "Alright, gentlemen, we have first up two slaves of the four-legged variety. Stubborn as they get, and I'm told a whip don't help. These two carried supplies here from the port where the slaves you will soon be bidding for were unloaded from the *Indigo Run*. These gentlemen who bought them have no further use for the critters, and have said they will accept just about any offer. The captain of the ship they bought 'em from said they came from somewhere in the Indies, and their names be Louis and Marie. Looks like they ain't got their wigs on." The crowd laughed, and someone said, "Maybe they should be renamed George and Charlotte." The laughter swelled for a while, then quieted down as Will commenced the auction.

"Alright, who'll start the bidding with ten pounds?" No one raised their hands. "Come on, now, I can't give them away. How about nine? Still no takers? What do you have against donkeys?"

Somebody yelled, "What good are they? They can't plow a field like my plow horse can. They're not half as big."

Ignatius spoke up with a spirited laugh, and said, "Tell you what. You give me ten pounds, and I'll take 'em off your hands. Nobody around here is going to want them. All they do is eat." The crowd laughed even harder than before.

One of the slavers caught Will's attention and nodded his head. Will caught the meaning, and countered back to Ignatius, "Sold, you old cheapskate, and a bargain is a bargain. Before all these witnesses, you have just committed yourself. Come get your property," he said, pointing to the donkeys. Pointing to the slavers, he added, "and your money from these distinguished gentleman."

"Hey! I was just joking, and you know it."

"You know better than to scratch your nose at an auction. Same thing goes about joking. A deal's a deal, Ignatius. Come get your property."

"Martin grabbed Ignatius's arm, laughed, and said, "He's right, Ignatius. You just kind of reverse-bought two donkeys."

"Well, hell," said a chagrined Ignatius.

Martin was still laughing when Ignatius said, "Will, go get Andrew. We have something for him to do. You got those papers to sign for these jackasses?"

"They're right here for the two-legged slaves, but not for the donkeys. They were a late addition, and I got an auction to do. Here," and Will, tossing the jail keys to Ignatius, "go ahead and get Andrew. We can meet at the inn after the auction to take care of the paperwork. I'll have my boys take the donkeys to the livery for you." Will sounded a little like a donkey himself when he laughed.

"C'mon, Martin, let's get our boy."

"I'VE BOUGHT YOU, and you're going to be coming with me."

Andrew stood up as Ignatius continued, "Andrew, we have a situation in which you have advertised yourself as an expert and able to be of help."

Expecting to be chained and led away, he exclaimed, "Huh?! What you mean?"

"We have just purchased two imported donkeys that require the best of care. I have no idea what we're going to do with them, but nevertheless, we're stuck with 'em. I want you to go over to the livery and see to them. Check their hooves, and make sure they can travel. If they seem hungry, and I'm sure they are, you tell the hand to give them hay or oats if he has any, but not too much, 'cause they've got some traveling to do. Check their coats, too. If there's anything crawling around in them, have the hand give you a comb, and get rid of whatever it is. Check if there are any spots on 'em where the hair is missing. If there are, see if the hand has any grease and sulfur—or, if he has it, coal tar. Then rub it on the spots. You understand all I've told you?"

"Yes, sir. I done all that for Master Carter."

Martin opened the cell door and said to Andrew, "C'mon out, boy." The three left the jailhouse, and the bright sunlight caused Andrew to shield his eyes. He tried to adjust after being confined in the dimness of the jail for he couldn't remember how many days.

"Get going, then," said Ignatius. "We're going to stick around here for a while to see how the auction goes. You're on your own; don't let me down. If you do as you're told, we're going to get along fine. You try to run away, you'll be found, and I'll have you back in this cell waiting for someone else to buy you, someone not as nice as I am. Understand?"

"Yes, sir. I understand." Running away hadn't occurred to Andrew, and he wondered why the warning.

"If you finish before we come, you stay there and wait for us. All right, get going."

THE SLAVES WERE ushered cell by cell to the display platform for all to see. Will, as the auctioneer, stood on the platform along with the slavers; the slavers stood guard at each end of the slave lineup.

"Gentlemen," Will shouted to the gathered buyers. "This re-starts the auction. Anybody not inspecting the slaves last evening has missed their chance to see what's under them clothes, but you can come up for a quick look-see inspection if you wish. I suppose you can ask 'em questions if you can speak African." The crowd gave a slight laugh, and Will continued when no one came forward.

"I'm told this batch of slaves were slaves in Africa, so they know all about this business, and you shouldn't have too much trouble working 'em. Fact is, some of these gentlemen may have owned slaves of their own, but their exact history, well…we just don't know. They might have been warriors who got themselves captured and the winning tribal chief, or whatever they're called, sold 'em to the trade, and here they are." Then, reading from a paper the slavers had given him: "This first slave is judged to be about eighteen. He is a sound one, and his teeth are all there. He has all of his fingers and can move them well. He is well built, as black as they get, and should make a good field slave. He was examined by a ship's doctor who found no evidence of disease or frail parts. Alright, who's going to open the minimum bid of a hundred pounds?"

The bidding began, and continued throughout the day. After each sale, Will added the slave number, the amount paid, and the name of the new owner to the already-drawn-up sales forms. Thus, after the bidder had paid the slavers, the ownership of the slave was transferred. One by one, the slaves were sold, then led to an anvil where one of the slavers broke their chains with a cold chisel and hammer. The sold slave was given to the owner, or, most often, to the owner's overseer.

When one of the slaves, a tall, thin fellow, was noted to be missing his right ear, several in the crowd asked what had happened to the ear. Will looked at the slavers for an answer, and they, in turn, shrugged their shoulders. One said, "Who knows? Don't think he speaks English so we can't ask. I'm guessing he lost it in battle. Look at him; he has scars all over his body. This guy may be skinny, but he's tough. Might have taken a few of his capturers down before they got him. He'll just about be able to take anything you can hand out to him. If I was in your business, I'd want this boy."

Big Bull was saying something to his boss, Edward Littlefield. Littlefield nodded his head in agreement and made a bid. Two more bids came from elsewhere in the crowd, and Littlefield offered another. No other bids followed, so Will awarded the one-eared slave to Littlefield. "Come get your one-eared boy, Littlefield." Big Bull proceeded to the platform as the slave's chains were removed.

The slaves Littlefield bought, three of them now, were tied to the back of Littlefield's buggy. Littlefield said to Big Bull, "We have to wait and see if Jim gets sold. If not, we'll take him with us, and then you'll have something to take care of on the way back while we take a break in our travel. Understand?"

"Understood. I'll take him into the woods."

"Make sure these niggers are tied real good. I don't want to have to chase 'em all over the countryside. Keep Jim on a separate rope if we have to take him back."

ANDREW CHECKED THE donkeys over as he had been instructed, and also raised their legs to look at their hooves. One of Louis's shoes had loosened, and a small stone was wedged in it. Andrew removed the stone, and, with a borrowed hammer from the hand, drove the nails back in the hoof. It would have to do until Ignatius or Martin decided what else to do. To be on the safe side, Andrew walked the animals outside and around the corral to see if they limped. His attention went to the auction when the murmur of the crowd became louder as Jim was led to the auction block by the slavers, who had pistols pointed at his back.

Speaking to the crowd, Will said, "This, gentlemen, is Jim. You all know about Jim, and I don't have to say much more about him. Who'll give me a bid?" There were no offers, and Will said, "I'm told by Edward Littlefield that having to sell Jim grieves him, that he would rather sell his mother." The crowd roared with laughter. "And did I mention Big Bull? He's so broken up he cries all night long." Now the crowd was laughing and slapping each other on the back. "Please save this boy from being sold somewhere where no one knows him to be the kind and gentle soul he is. Now, come on. Let's have a bid or two. Come on, now, somebody has to recognize what a remarkable specimen this slave is. Look at the muscle. Why, he could do the work of one of the donkeys Mister Attaway just bought." Someone in the crowd yelled, "He ain't as smart as one of them donkeys, though." The crowd continued to laugh.

Jim knew it was the end, and that no hope remained. He watched for his chance, and took it when it came.

Even though Will had the crowd in a good mood and everyone had put off leaving just to see the outcome of the bidding for Jim, no one offered a bid. Will turned to Jim to say he was sorry, and Jim would have to go back with Littlefield and Big Bull, but he never had the chance to start.

The slavers, looking away from Jim and at the crowd, were distracted. Jim grabbed the slaver on his left, and kneed him in the groin. As the slaver bent over, Jim kicked him in the face, which sent the slaver upward and off the platform. The slaver landed on his head, and lay motionless. Will jumped back and fell off the platform. The other slaver, realizing what was happening, attempted to bring his pistol up to shoot, but Jim had taken the piece of iron bar from his pants and was in mid-swing. Before the slaver could finish his move, the iron bar found its mark.

Confused and bewildered, the trader looked about to understand what was happening. A gash in his neck pumped red, and he felt he had to sit down, but, no longer in control, fell on his side. The light in his mind became dark. Blood pulsed from the wound a few times until the heart understood it was of no use and quit.

It was then, as Big Bull was tying together his newly-acquired slaves, that the slave with the missing ear slugged one of his companions in the face. The slave struck his attacker back. The other slave joined in the fray, and Big Bull shouted for them to stop. Taking his whip, he began to strike them. Big Bull got two or three good punches in his face for his interference, and backed off. He called for help from the confused crowd, but no one came to help break up the free-for-all. Big Bull let the fight run its course.

Jim saw the ruse and understood. He found the broken link in his shackles and opened it. Two small steps and a powerful leap landed him on the ground. With the speed of a deer, he ran toward the edge of town to where he knew there was a swamp and he could make his escape. Even with the shackle chain swinging back and forth on his legs, he was putting distance between himself and his soon-to-be pursuers. One of the crowd, still watching Jim and the action on the platform rather than the fighting slaves, yelled, "Someone get some hounds! Get that damned nigger!"

Big Bull's slaves were subdued without too much effort, and other than a few lumps on Big Bull's face, no one was seriously injured. Big Bull looked at his slaves with anger in his eyes. He saw their smiles of satisfaction and realized what had happened. He decided to let the affair pass for now, but he knew this was a group of slaves he had to keep his eyes on; they were smart, and at least one of them knew English. He would even the score when the timing was right.

Ignatius and Martin were watching Jim running for his life. "Bet a dollar they don't catch that boy," said Ignatius.

"What makes you think so, Iggy?"

"He's headed to the swamp. They'll never pick up his trail, dogs or no dogs. Jim's running for his life. The rest are just running after him 'cause that's the thing to do. They'll give up if the chase gets too hard or it gets dark. Those slavers dead?"

"Can't tell from here. Let's go take a look."

"Forget it. Let's go get Andrew and our rig. We got a ways to go, and I'd just as soon get going. Dead or alive, we don't have to get into it."

They walked over to the livery and saw Andrew. He was holding the donkeys and looking· toward where Jim was headed. As Jim entered the swamp and the crowd still had not become a mob, Andrew smiled, and let loose a whoop and a "Run, Jim!" He hadn't noticed Ignatius and Martin coming up to him.

"What's the yell for, Andrew?" asked Ignatius, knowing full well what it was.

"Nothing, nothing I guess."

"I suppose a guy has to shout just for the helluvit once in a while."

"Yes, sir. I guess so."

"Those donkeys alright, and ready to make the trip?"

"Yes, sir. I checked their shoes, walked 'em, and got 'em to eat some oats. The boy donkey had a loose shoe and a rock under it. I fixed it, but the shoe might come loose again. He'll make it if it ain't too far. Mister Ballard says you owe him for the oats and straw."

"We'll take care of it. You get those donkeys tied to the back of the wagon. You want to ride up in the straw with me, or ride one of the donkeys?"

"You'll let me ride a donkey, sir?" a surprised Andrew asked.

"Sure. You're going to be taking care of this old man and them, so you may as well get used to all of us."

Then Andrew thought of something. "Mister Attaway, I can't ride a donkey with just a rope around his neck. I'd rather have a bridle and reins, and so would they."

"Buying a bridle for a donkey is going to be a little difficult around here. Besides, the donkeys are going to be tied to the wagon, and just have to follow along."

"If I'm to take care of these donkeys, they'll have to get to know and respect me. They can't do that if they think I'm just a load they have to carry."

Martin said, "The boy's got something there, Iggy. I get the feeling he knows what he's doing. I don't know about the donkeys, but you got a good bargain in Andrew."

"Maybe, but I still can't get a donkey bridle around here."

Andrew said, "If I had a few feet of rope and a knife, I could make a bridle."

"You know how to do that, Andrew?" asked Martin.

"Yes, sir."

"Tell the hand, Mister Ballard, what you need, and tell him I'll settle up just as soon as you get the rig and donkeys ready to go. You can use my knife." Ignatius took the long knife he wore from its scabbard and asked Andrew, "Will this do?"

Andrew took the knife and looked it over. It was an old knife, with a blade almost a foot long and nothing more than a wood handle and a hilt made of brass. The end of the handle was oversized, and the steel within had seen many blows from something. The almost razor-sharp blade was worn thin from many years of sharpening.

"It'll do. I've never seen a knife like it."

"My father made it. He used it to dress animals, didn't matter what: cow, deer, bear, you name it. The handle is extra big so it can be pounded with a rock to drive the blade through bone."

JIM RAN, WADED, and fought nature through the muck as he made his way deeper into the swamp. Here and there, his feet sunk into the soft bottom, and he had to stop to pull them out. No stranger to the swamp but never having entered at that point, he knew not where he was or what might lie ahead; what hidden holes he might sink in, submerged remains of trees with their broken limbs waiting to stab a foot or leg, water moccasins, or an Indian who might try to capture him for the ever-present runaway slave reward. Indians sometimes made slaves of captives, to be enslaved again.

Jim paused to figure his best way. As he scanned the swamp, he thought he saw something that did not belong. He took a few steps toward the image, and there, a few feet in front of him, floated a black hat: a soldier's cocked hat. Forgetting for the moment his own situation, he waded over to the hat and bent to pick it up. As he did so, the faint blurred image of a face in the murky water stared back at him. The sight caused him to spring back. Recovering, he reached into the water and grabbed a handful of billowing hair and raised the head. Out of the water, the head and now-visible part of the body revealed the red and white uniform of a soldier. *Wonder what happened to this fellow,* he muttered to himself. Had he looked further, he would have found the soldier's other two companions; but he released the dead man to slip beneath the water, and continued his run for freedom…and his life.

The sun broke through the swamp's canopy and lay low in the late daylight sky. Jim heard the baying of the hounds behind him. He knew the hounds hadn't picked up his trail and the dog handlers were following the easiest route into the swamp, hoping to pick up the scent of a human. Jim knew as long as the hounds were in back of him, he was going on the easiest route in the swamp.

Soon, Jim could no longer hear the sounds of the hounds, and it meant they had given up the chase or had come to where the dead soldier was, and were confused. There were places he had to swim, places where he was able to walk on soft footing, and places he had to crawl through the undergrowth.

The mosquitoes swarmed about him, and spider webs draped across his face. Leaches dined at their pleasure. He came to a clearing where the swamp bottom rose above water, and sat down to rest. As he picked off leaches and swatted at mosquitoes, exhaustion overtook him, and he dozed off.

A stirring in the swamp growth and water startled Jim awake. Four Indians brandishing trade tomahawks emerged from the dense growth. They encircled the runaway slave, and motioned for him to stand up. With the Indians on each side, he stumbled away with them.

"YOU DON'T LOOK at all comfortable in that straw, Iggy. Why don't you just come up in the seat?"

"Think Andrew has the best seat in the house, Martin. Look at him on that donkey. Heck, he's talking to the critter. I don't see any pain on either of their faces. Maybe I should ride the donkey, and let Andrew have this nice soft straw."

"How long's it been since you rode a horse, Iggy?"

"Well, let's see…don't rightly remember. I guess it's been awhile, though. Why? You don't think I can still do it?"

"I didn't say that; I was just askin'."

"Andrew," Ignatius shouted, "trade me places. You come up in this soft straw and take it easy. Let me ride Louis for a while."

"Are you sure, Mister Attaway? He's not all that friendly. Tried to bite me at first. I don't think he likes people riding him."

"Son, I was riding horses at full speed with a pistol in each hand, two muskets on the sides of my horse, reins in my mouth, arrows and tomahawks passing so close I didn't have to shave for a month way before you ever saw the light of day through your mama's legs. Now, get down and give me those reins."

"Yes, sir."

"Oh, jeez!" Martin said, rolling his eyes.

Andrew tried to whisper, "Mister Attaway don't shave."

"You two say something?"

"Nope."

"No, sir."

"Didn't think so."

Martin stopped the wagon so the exchange could take place, and Andrew slipped off Louis. Ignatius slowly straightened up, stretched his back, and rubbed his hips. Martin watched with concern as Andrew waited to give Ignatius the reins.

In the absence of a saddle, Andrew had to cup his hands together to form a step for Ignatius to put his foot into, then hold his weight as Ignatius swung up on the donkey's back. That accomplished, Andrew handed the reins to Ignatius and walked to the back of the wagon.

As Andrew approached the wagon, Louis put his head down and kicked both of his hind legs high in the air. Ignatius instinctively did what an experienced rider would do without thinking about it. His legs tightened around the donkey, and he forced his body to stay erect. Louis tried the routine again, and Ignatius stayed on the donkey's back.

Ignatius shouted, "Look here, you damned jackass, you think you're some kind of mighty horse or something? I've ridden way bigger and more terrible hunks of flesh and bone than you'll ever be. Now, behave yourself, or I'll shoot you right now! You understand me?"

The donkey turned his head around to bite Ignatius on the leg, his lips drawn up showing yellowed teeth. With a clenched fist, Ignatius reached over the donkey's head and pounded him hard between the eyes.

"I'm not kidding, jackass! You hear me?"

They had come to an understanding, Ignatius and Louis. Andrew and Martin looked at one another, realizing that they all, including a certain four-legged creature, had gained a different kind of respect for Ignatius.

"Come on up here," Martin said to Andrew, motioning to the seat. "It's the same as riding back there; jar your brains loose either way."

CHAPTER IV

A SYMPHONY OF crickets, accompanied by the hum of a million other critters, filled the night with their opus as the wagon leading two donkeys and a rider made its way up the long drive. As they moved on, the image of a house—a rather large house—began to come into view as moonlight highlighted its features. Coming to a stop, Andrew looked at the immense structure. It was a manor on an equal scale to Master Carter's. It was a brown or maybe red brick home, and appeared to be two stories high with gabled windows in the roof.

"This is it, Andrew," said Martin. "Get down and help Mister Attaway off that donkey."

"Yes, sir."

As Andrew climbed down from the wagon, Ignatius was already sliding off the animal. Looking around, he saw Andrew coming toward him.

"Don't know as I made such a good deal with you or not. Either way, it seemed to be an awful long trip."

"Can I help you, sir?"

"What I want you to do is take these donkeys over to that barn," Ignatius said, pointing to a barn about two hundred feet from the side of the house. "Tend to 'em and wait there. I'll have someone come and get you, and they'll show you where you can stay. We'll continue this tomorrow. Understand?"

"Yes, sir."

"Alright, get busy then."

As Andrew led the donkeys to the barn, he saw the door of the manor open. A black woman held it as a white lady walked through.

"Martin, Dad, welcome back. Did the trip go well?" she called.

"It did. But Iggy could use a rubdown, a few hot packs, and a shot or two of rye."

"The rye first, if you don't mind, Mary," said Ignatius.

THE BARN WAS dark inside, and not knowing the layout, Andrew decided it best to lead the donkeys inside and let them tend to themselves. If there was hay anywhere, they would find it. Water could be a problem. *No matter,* he thought; he would ask whoever came for him about its whereabouts.

Andrew sat on the ground with his back against the barn until the moon rose higher in the sky. Neither the manor nor the barn could be seen clearly. As he sat there thinking his new situation over, he saw a flicker of light coming from what he thought to be the back of the manor. The light grew larger and larger, and he knew it had to be someone with a candle or lamp coming toward him.

"You must be Andrew," said the approaching voice, which belonged to an older black woman.

"Yes ma'am."

"Well, stand up so I can get a look at you," she said as she came up to him.

Andrew stood up, and the woman held her lamp to his face and moved it about until she had looked him over from head to foot.

"You alone, or is there another boy out here? I was looking for a child about twelve. You ain't but about eight."

"I'm twelve, ma'am. I just don't look it, they tell me."

"You sure don't. They feed you enough where you came from?" she asked in a concerned voice.

"I guess so. I used to fix the food for the other children, and I could eat anything I wanted from it."

"Humph! Well, we're going to have to see what we can do about that."

The woman backed up a step or two and studied the boy, moving her head up and down. Her mouth curved up, and her eyes squinted.

"They tell me your name's Andrew. Is that correct?"

"Yes, ma'am. Don't have a last name."

"You don't?" she said in mocked surprise.

"Well, no matter. My name's Miz Millie. Should be easy to remember."

"Yes, ma'am, Miz Millie."

"I'm in charge of the entire household. Whatever I say goes. Even Miz Mary asks me for my alright to change things around. She don't give orders to none of the house slaves except it goes through me to them. Understand?"

"Yes, ma'am."

"I've known Mister Attaway for a long time. We grew up together on this land. When his wife died giving birth to a beautiful little girl, I'd had a baby a few weeks before, and was called to take her to my bosom and feed her. I changed her soiled pants, and did everything else a mother would do. My baby and husband both died of something a few years later. Miz Mary is as much my child as anybody could be."

Andrew didn't know how to respond, and he lowered his head.

"I wanted you to know how it was around here."

"I understand, ma'am."

"Fine. Now, you hungry?"

"Kinda, I guess. But I gotta take care of the donkeys. Is there water for them somewhere?"

"They in the barn? If so, there's a trough of water in there, and hay is all around."

Andrew nodded his alright that the donkeys would be fine until tomorrow.

"C'mon, Mister Andrew, we're going to get you something to eat."

Miss Millie led him into the kitchen, which contained the usual fireplace with eternal bed of smoldering coals, various pots, pans, and kitchen tools hanging from the walls, a butcher block, and a long table resembling the table in the jail, but without the trough running down the middle.

"You just sit yourself down at the table." Then, looking at one of the other servant girls Miss Millie said, "Did you get Master Attaway and Mister Martin their food, Susan?"

"Mister Martin is eating in his and Miz Mary's room. Master Attaway fell asleep and spilled his rye I fixed him all down the front of himself. That woke him up and he went to his bedroom."

Miss Millie just shook her head to herself and gave a little sigh. "Poor Ignatius," she said in a low voice only she could hear.

She walked over to the fireplace with a tin plate, and from a pot hanging over the heat of the coals, took a ladleful and poured it onto the plate.

Andrew ate the meal, which he thought to be field peas and small chunks of salt pork along with ash bread made in an iron pan rather than in the coals. He washed it down with buttermilk collected fresh that morning.

"When you want to go to bed, you go over there in the corner. There's a pile of mats that should be soft, and you'll be close to the fireplace if it gets a little cold tonight," said Miss Millie.

The stacked mats were not as soft as Miss Millie alluded, but they beat an earthen floor covered in soiled straw. Falling asleep on them without the stench of urine and feces filling the air was a pleasant change from the past few days.

ANDREW AWOKE TO the noise of people shuffling about and talking. They were the house slaves preparing the morning meal. This meal fed both the house slaves and their white masters, and, on many occasions, guests and travelers who had stayed overnight. It was customary for travelers to stay at houses and manors when they traveled, as inns were not always available, and were oftentimes undesirable because of their nature. This morning, there were no visitors. Servants were arranging various food items on trays and covering them with cloths to keep flies off.

"Take those trays to the dining room," said Miss Millie to the servants. "They'll be down to eat by the time you get there."

The servants swung the large pewter trays over their heads and proceed to carry them one-handed into the dining room.

"C'mon, Mister Andrew, sit yourself at the table. We've got to fatten you up some."

As he ate, Andrew worried he'd be in trouble for not eating everything Miss Millie gave him. He knew he could not eat all the food in front of him. He was eating some, but most he just pushed around on his plate, sighing.

Miss Millie sat down beside him. "You eat what you can, and don't worry about it. I just don't want you thinking I'm not feeding you enough."

Andrew looked up at Miss Millie and saw she was smiling down at him. He returned the smile.

"Now," Miss Millie began, "Master Attaway's going to be coming in here when he finishes eating. He wants to talk to you. You done?"

"I'm done. Is that alright?"

"If that's all you can do, then that's all you can do. Now then, Master Attaway told me to get you some clothes. I'll bring you clothes they give to the other slave children. They're about the same thing you have on anyway. You get two sets. You want shoes?"

"I don't wear shoes, 'cept when it snows."

"Well, then, I'll let you worry about that later on, 'cause I know those feet are going to be growing before the snow comes."

About that time, Ignatius came into the kitchen, stopped, looked around, and fixed his gaze on Andrew. "You been fed? Millie! You feed this boy?"

"Calm down, Ignatius," she said.

Miss Millie referred to Ignatius as Master or Mister Attaway when talking about him to others, but speaking face to face, she always called him Ignatius, just as she had done when they were growing up together. She was the only slave who could ever call him by his first name to his face. Both Ignatius and Miss Millie were too used to it to pay any attention to the formalities of proper master-slave relations. When guests heard this kind of talk between the two, they raised their eyebrows and waited for the slave woman to be disciplined, but were always disappointed when nothing happened.

"Certainly, I fed him. That's what you wanted, didn't you?"

"Well…I just wanted to be sure."

"He don't eat much, Ignatius. Maybe you might be able to get him to eat better."

"I wouldn't worry none, Millie. Wait a few years, and we won't be able to grow enough on this farm to keep up with his eatin'. What about his clothing?"

"I was just going to fetch them when you came in."

"Oh! Alright, then. Go ahead with what you were doing."

Ignatius sat down across the table from Andrew and looked at the boy for a few seconds. Andrew was getting nervous, and his thumbs began to twiddle around each other.

"Norton Carter told me he never worked you as a slave in the fields."

"Yes, sir. But I was out there, just not hoeing and cutting like the rest. I was taking care of the children."

"Well, except for taking care of me, we don't have much of that around here. The slaves take care of their own. I don't know how much more time Providence is going to give me. You're going to be helping me until the time comes. But when it arrives, I don't want what happened to you with Norton Carter and his Miz Jane happen to you again. I want you to have something to fall back on. You've got to learn how to work in the field and make yourself useful to others, rather than just useful to a dead man. Do you understand what I'm saying to you, boy?"

Andrew did not fully understand, but he had a faint idea, so he said, "Yes…I think so."

And so it went. For three weeks, Andrew hoed tobacco, potato, and wheat fields along with the other slaves. In the evenings, when the sun had mercifully gone down, he would drag himself to the manor kitchen. His muscles complained, and blisters upon blisters formed on his hands, then popped open. At first, he was almost too tired to eat, but Miss Millie insisted he eat something. He tried, but often fell asleep at the table.

Within two weeks, Andrew was eating twice what he had before he began working in the fields. When Miss Millie woke him in the mornings, he headed straight to the table to eat his meal, and then, as dawn broke, he hurried from the kitchen, carrying a lunch Miss Millie had made and wrapped in a square of cloth with the four corners tied together.

"Don't forget to take care of those donkeys," she hollered after him.

At the end of three weeks, Ignatius was sitting at the kitchen table when Andrew arose and walked sleepily to the table. "Sit down, Andrew," said Ignatius.

Andrew, surprised at the voice, looked up and rubbed his eyes. "Oh! Hello, Master Attaway. What're you doing here?"

"Thought I might have the morning meal with you. That alright?"

"Well, uh, yes. I mean…I guess so." Andrew did not know how to respond to a master asking a slave if something was alright to do.

"Ha! That's alright," Ignatius said to calm him down. "I thought it about time we show you what else you'll be doing. In other words, taking care of me."

A hungry Andrew ate his meal without looking up, and listened passively to Ignatius talking small talk—something about the weather, a good crop of wheat coming in, the tobacco was not looking too good this year, the crops should be rotated next year, and something about a slave cutting another's foot with a hoe. His head jerked up when he heard the word *donkey*.

"Huh?"

"I said I had a set of donkey harnesses made up. After you're through eating, take one of those donkeys and harness it up to my buggy…the buggy with the new springs. I want to see if those donkeys are good for anything else except eating hay and making shit."

Nothing could have made Andrew happier or more exited. He shoveled the last few bites of his meal to his mouth, and his cheeks puffed out as he chewed. Finished, he stood up, and with excitement in his voice, he said, "I'll go do it now." Before Ignatius could say anything else, he was out the door.

"Ignatius, you do know how to make a boy happy," said Miss Millie.

"He's closer to being a man than he suspects, Millie, and he's not going to be a slave forever. It'll take him awhile, but someday, gradually perhaps, but he's going to recognize what he is, what he wants, and how he's going to go about getting it."

In a little more than an hour, Andrew came into the kitchen. "Where's Master Attaway, Miz Millie? I have the buggy ready for him."

"I'll go for him. Just you wait in the buggy."

"Yes'm. I'll wait for him in the buggy."

Ignatius came from the kitchen and climbed up into the buggy and sat in the seat. He bounced up and down a few times. "Ah! These new springs are heaven. Whatcha think, boy?"

"Uh, yes, sir," Andrew said, figuring it was the proper response. "Here's the reins, Master Attaway."

"No, you take them, Andrew. I'll tell you the way."

With a *giddyup* and a flick of the reins, Louis moved ahead.

They didn't go out to the road Andrew had first taken to come to the plantation. Instead, Ignatius showed Andrew an almost-overgrown road leading downhill into what Andrew made out to be a dense stand of trees.

"He's a big donkey, Andrew. Don't think I've ever seen a bigger one."

"I felt sorry for him. Its Marie's time, and he tried to mount her. She wants nothin' to do with him. She kicks and bucks and brays and tries to bite him. He tried biting her on the neck to hold her still, and things just got worse. Now he won't even go near her."

"Gives me an idea."

"What, Mister Attaway?"

"Try one of the plow horses. Make sure she's a young one and has good features. Louis ought to appreciate a real lady. Seems it's the least we can do for the King of France."

"I don't think he'll be able to reach her even as long as he gets."

"You know what a loading platform is?"

"You mean to load wagons with heavy stuff?"

"That's what I'm talking about. Try making one of those for Louis to stand on. Might work. Now, make a sharp turn to your left through that tall grass between those trees. See it?"

"Yes, sir. I can make something out."

They rode another hundred feet or so, and a cabin or maybe more of a shack, came into view.

"This is it. Stop right here, and let's get down."

Ignatius pushed the door of the cabin open, and the top leather hinge broke loose. A musty odor filled their nostrils. Sunlight filled the shack and they entered and cautiously looked around. Ignatius remarked, "Looks as if it could use a cleaning out, don't you think?"

"Yes, sir."

"That's your tomorrow job. Get what you need and take one of your donkeys down here and do a good job. Hitch up the wagon if you need to carry something—that has new springs too, ya know."

"Yes, sir."

"This place used to be where I'd come to get away from it all and relax all by myself. I'd drink a little rye till I felt good. Sometimes, I'd go down to the swamp and fish or hunt. There's a lot of deer and turkeys running around here. They make good eatin'.'"

"Miz Millie cook 'em?"

"Sometimes I'd take something up to her if I was going back. Mostly, I'd cook 'em down here and toss the remains to the wild animals over there. Lots of 'em, you know?"

Andrew didn't answer.

After Ignatius was through looking around, he said, "Follow me."

Outside the cabin, Ignatius took his big knife and cut a couple of small saplings about six feet long. Then he ran the knife down the cuttings to remove the little branches and twigs. "Here, Andrew, take one of these. They're walking sticks—help you get through where we're going."

Then he headed down the overgrown path as Andrew followed close behind. Ignatius stopped and drew his pistol, and Andrew stopped just in time to avoid walking into him.

"You come down here, you always want to have a pistol or a musket with you. Mostly, the only things that'll hurt you are snakes, and they do that before you have time to hurt them. Just watch where you're stepping. If you see something worth eating, you might want to shoot at it. Fishing's good, but you'll probably give up before you bring anything in, as your hook will get caught on something and you'll lose it and the line. If you can find a pool someplace without a lot of tree branches, you can sometimes drop your line there, but keep it close to the surface, or you'll lose it. You ever fish?"

"No, sir. I never done nothin' 'cept work."

"Well, you're going to. We'll be spending a lot of time down here. Make sure when you clean up the cabin you get rid of all the straw and blankets on those bunks. Get fresh stuff. Tell Miz Millie I said to give you new blankets and whatever else you need."

"I thought I was going to work in the fields."

"You are, but not all the time. In fact, you'll be working in the fields three or four days a week, and the rest of the time, we'll be down here or you'll be doing something else for me. I'm…ah…not able to do some things anymore, Andrew. Sometimes I can, sometimes I can't. Sometimes I can't remember why I'm even where I'm at. It's getting the best of me, and I can't do a damn thing about it. There'll be days I don't even remember Mary's name, or even who she is. I won't even remotely know who you are. Then there are times my back and legs pain me so much I just have to sit down until it passes. Eventually, you won't be spending any time in the fields. You'll be with me all the time. But it's important you know how to work in the fields." Ignatius paused and looked down at the floor for what must have been several minutes.

Andrew was not comfortable with the silence and what Ignatius had said to him.

"Damn it!" Ignatius shouted, shaking his fist at nothing specific. "Let's not talk about this now. C'mon, let's go down to the edge of the swamp. I want to show you something."

Andrew had never seen that kind of emotion, and he felt sorry for the old man. Why, he wondered, had Ignatius chosen him, a common slave, to show it to?

They walked single file, and Andrew kept several paces behind to avoid the bent brush swinging back at him as Ignatius plowed through the thick growth. As he waded into the swamp water, he wished he had shoes, as even his callused feet felt the sharp poke of broken reeds and branches.

"See that?" said Ignatius, pointing to a clump of reeds.

"Don't see anything 'cept more of the same."

"Over here."

Ignatius moved closer to a large bunch of reeds denser than the rest. He pushed his arms through the reeds and poked his walking stick around.

"You have to be careful there aren't any visitors inside, such as moccasins. C'mon, put your head in there and take a look around. It's a blind. Big enough to sit in and drink some rye or rum while you wait."

"Wait for what?"

"Deer coming out on their way to eat in my wheat field. Sometimes turkeys, whole families of 'em, will all of a sudden up and fly and scare the hell out of you. Now and then, a wood duck will speed by."

"So you're going to come down here and hunt, and you want me to come along and watch you so nothin' happens to you?"

"That's the general idea. Except...you'll be hunting with me."

"I don't know anything about hunting. I don't even know how to shoot a gun."

"We'll take care of that. Before the next week is over, you're going to be able to shoot just as well as anybody."

Andrew, silent for a second, thought about what Ignatius had just said, then asked, "You're going to teach me, a slave, how to shoot?"

"Just don't tell anyone, alright?"

"Yes, sir. I mean, no, sir. I mean, I won't tell anyone."

"Not even Miz Millie, Miz Mary or Mister Blackiston. Understand?"

"I do and won't. I promise."

"Oh! Before we go back up to the shack, I want to mention something. On the other side of this swamp is a farm belonging to Edward Littlefield. I've always thought him to be of dubious character. I can't say for sure, but he does have an overseer with a bad reputation, and to me, that reflects on Littlefield. He beats slaves for fun, and when there is a reason, he'll almost kill 'em. Just you mind what I've said, and stay away from them."

"Is his name Big Bull?"

"You know him?"

"I saw him kick around another slave in the jail, the one done run off."

"That would be Jim. He's another bad one. Those two are bad boys. Watch out for both. That Jim ran into the other end of this swamp, and could still be in here. I'd guess he's dead of snakebite, or maybe one of those Indians still running around got him."

"Indians!"

"There's pockets of 'em all over. Some of 'em refused to leave the area, and here and there, a few families live together and generally don't cause any trouble. Sometimes they capture runaways for the reward. You'll see 'em on the Potomac in their dugouts, fishing or taking furs to trade somewhere."

"What's the Potomac?"

"Big river west of here," Ignatius said, pointing in a westward direction. "Oh."

"Rich people live on the other side, the rest of us over here."

"I thought you was rich."

"I meant really rich and really powerful."

Ignatius paused for a reaction from Andrew, and when he didn't get one, said, "C'mon, Andrew, its time to get out of here. You've got a lot of work to do down here. You up to it?"

"I'm up to it. Can't wait to finish up and spend time here."

"Good way to look at it. Let's go back. I've got to let Mary and Martin know what we're up to," said Ignatius. Then, as an afterthought, he added,

"Best not to forget to tell Miz Millie, if I know what's good for me...both of us."

"Yes, sir. I know what you mean."

They laughed at Andrew's remark, and were making their way back to the buggy when Ignatius slowed down and clutched his hand to his hip. He sat down on the ground and rolled over on his side.

Andrew, terrified, asked, "What's wrong, Master Attaway?"

"Nothing much, just my hip slipped out. Happens now and then. Jeez, how it hurts! Go get me that bottle that says *Doctor Webb's Elixir* out of the back of the buggy."

"I can't read."

"Well, no mind. It's the only bottle back there. Get it and hurry."

Andrew did, and gave it to the old man, who was already sitting up and turning himself to stand.

"It popped back in, but it still hurts some." With that said, he pulled the cork from the bottle of elixir and took two good swallows. He held the bottle up and looked through the brown glass. "Remind me to get another bottle when we get back."

"Yes, sir. I'll do that."

"Good boy."

Ignatius took his time climbing into the seat, and Andrew stood in back of him just in case. Ignatius had trouble lifting one of his legs high enough to clear the side of the wagon, and Andrew pushed the leg up and over.

"You're earning your way, boy. Think I'm going to be keeping you around."

Up in the seat, Andrew turned the wagon around and they headed back to the manor. They looked at each other without emotion. The old man took another tug on the brown bottle.

Miss Millie was out in back of the manor, wringing the necks of four or five chickens. She looked up when she heard the buggy pull up. She saw Ignatius struggling to get down, and ran over to help.

"Your hip again, Ignatius?"

"Yes, damn thing anyhow. Sometimes I don't know if I've got what it takes to be old."

"You're doing pretty good, if you ask me, Ignatius."

"Thanks, old friend. I do appreciate that."

"Just you watch who you're calling old, mister."

They laughed, and Ignatius raised the bottle again.

"You can do better than drink that stuff. Andrew!" she called. Go inside and get Ignatius his rye, should be some around somewhere in there. Lord knows he's got some somewhere everywhere."

"Yes, ma'am."

Andrew closed the door of the manor, and Ignatius said, "Millie, start teaching that boy to read. When I want him to get a bottle of elixir, I want him to get just that, and not a bottle of rat poison."

CHAPTER V

"YOU'VE NEVER SHOT a gun, that right?"

"Yes, sir."

"You've seen somebody shooting a gun, haven't you?"

"Yes, sir. I've seen Master Carter shooting at trees and things."

"He was probably practicing."

"Practicing?"

"That means he was doing what we're going to be doing, just practicing. The more you practice, the better you become."

"You mean like riding a horse?"

"That's what I mean. Remember when you rode Louis and Marie? You thought you were pretty good at it, and you were. But I'll wager you think you're a better rider now than you were. Right?"

"Oh, yes, sir. I know what you mean. I bet I'm better than anyone at home, I mean at the plantation."

"It's alright to call it home, if that's what you want, Andrew."

One of those lumps came to Andrew's throat. He shook his head slightly up and down without saying anything. "You think I'm going to be able to shoot a gun as good as I can ride a horse?"

"Well, it's not important if you can shoot like an expert. I mean, you're not ever going to make a living at it, and we don't have much call for expert shooters on the plantation. But if you're going to shoot at all, you have to know how. So the first thing you're going to learn is how not to be afraid of the gun you're shooting, and how to be very afraid of a gun you're not shooting."

"Huh?"

"I'll tell you what I mean. When I use the word *afraid,* what I mean is you have to respect a gun and the mighty, almost terrible damage it can do. But let me continue to use *afraid,* as you need to respect it and also be afraid. First about being afraid of a gun: a gun has one purpose, maybe two, but the main purpose of a gun is to kill. The second purpose might be to shoot at targets, like an old tree stump or log, to sharpen your shooting skills, like we're going to be doing today. A mistake or a ball bouncing off something can get you or somebody else killed real fast…or painfully slow. So I want you to be very afraid of a gun; the slightest mistake or carelessness with it can end or change somebody's life in a flash. I want you to remember two things. First, a gun is always loaded, even if you know it's not. Second, never, ever, point a gun at anything or anybody you don't intend to shoot, or at least believe you will have to shoot. Got that?"

"I think so."

"No, the correct answer is, yes. *I think so* is not the right answer. Now, what do you never do?"

"I never point it at anything or anybody I'm not going to shoot or think I'll have to shoot."

"Alright, don't ever forget. If I ever see you pointing a gun at anybody or even an animal just for fun, I'm going to knock your head off and that will be the end of your shooting. Understand?"

"Yes, sir."

"Let's see if you do. Now, is a gun ever empty?"

"No, sir. A gun is never empty."

"Do you know why?"

"Uh...."

"Alright, let me tell you. There have been, and I have seen, people who have sworn they know a gun is not loaded. They cock it and pull the trigger to prove their point. The gun fires even without a charge in the frizzen. Sometimes, somebody gets hurt or killed because of the stupidity of the person who was so sure the gun wasn't loaded. Understand now?"

"Uh huh."

"Next thing is to not be afraid of the gun you're shooting, even though I've just told you to be afraid. Now, you're going to find out a gun kicks back at you, just about like a donkey does if you upset him."

"What do you mean?"

"I'll show you," Ignatius said as he loaded the musket. "Watch how I load this thing, 'cause you're going to have to do it in a while."

In less than a minute, the musket was loaded, and Ignatius looked around for something to shoot. He found his target, a low tree limb on a dead pine about twenty-five feet away.

"Stand to my right about ten feet away and watch me shoot. Don't watch what I'm shooting at—watch how I position myself, and what happens to my shoulder and body in general when I shoot. I want you to see what happens when the gun goes off."

Andrew moved to Ignatius's right and watched.

"Now, do you see anyone or anybody in the area I'm about to be shooting at?"

"No."

"Okay, then. You gotta check, 'cause we don't want to hang somebody up over our fireplace that we shot by accident, do we?"

"No. I guess not," Andrew said with a grin.

Ignatius placed the musket so it pointed in front of him with the butt by his side, set his right leg in back of him, cocked the lock of the gun, placed the butt to his shoulder, and leaned forward a bit.

Squinting to focus his old eyes, he aimed his weapon and squeezed the trigger. Smoke and fire poured forth from the barrel of the gun, along with the ear-splitting sound of a lightning bolt striking way too close for comfort. Ignatius's shoulder jerked backward and the rest of his body followed, causing him to pivot on his back foot.

Andrew didn't see the tree branch fall from the tree. All he could do was yell, "Ow, my ears!"

"Whatcha think of that?" Ignatius asked. "Pretty good shot, huh? Just about the same as shooting Indians and Frogs."

"My ears are ringing," said Andrew, still holding his ears. "I didn't see what you hit."

"Take my word for it, it was a great shot. But did you see what happened to my shoulder and body when I shot?"

"I did. I see what you mean by a donkey kicking."

"Now it's your turn."

Ignatius loaded the weapon again, and again, Andrew watched. "I can do that."

"You'll get your chance in a few minutes." Ignatius finished and said, "Here, take the musket and shoot at something other than me."

Andrew, paying no attention to the humor, took the gun and stood about where Ignatius had stood. He looked at the old man, and Ignatius said, "Well…you going to shoot at something, or not?"

"Alright, yes." Andrew looked around and saw the same tree Ignatius had shot at, and figured he would try to just hit the tree someplace. "I'm going to shoot at that old dead pine."

"Line the sights up so the front sight blade is just about even with the top of the notch on the rear sight. With that picture, move the musket so whatever it is you're shooting, your target is sitting just about on top. Got it?"

"Got it."

"Well, pull back the hammer, raise the gun, sight it, and pull the trigger."

"Now?"

"Yes, now!"

Ignatius stood a little behind the boy, and waited...and waited. Andrew was having trouble sighting the heavy gun, and the barrel moved all around.

"Just pull the damn trigger and see what happens!" Ignatius said with the impatience of an old man.

Andrew pulled the trigger, and the gun barked. The barrel rose out of his left hand, and he lost his balance and started to fall over backward.

Ignatius caught him, and at the same time grabbed the musket before Andrew dropped it.

"My ears are ringing," said Andrew, holding his ears.

"They'll clear up in a while. That's part of the lesson about not being afraid of the gun. First, you've got to be afraid of it. Then you got to respect it and live with it, just like a woman. By the way, if the noise bothers you, roll up a couple of ball patches and plug your ears. Gunfire can cause you to lose your hearing. Lots of those guys in the Indian wars couldn't hear too well when it was over. That's where I learned the patch trick; tar works pretty well, too, but can be hard to get out. Also works pretty well when you don't want to listen to a woman."

"You used to fight Indians?"

"Yeah, I'll tell you about it some time. Sometime when I've had a lot of rye"

Andrew smiled at what he thought was Ignatius's humor, but then seeing Ignatius was dead serious let his smile fade into a reluctant, serious mood.

Without skipping a beat, Ignatius continued, "That, Andrew, is a lesson about guns. Now you have two: they kick like donkeys, and they make a lot of noise. If you're going to shoot a gun, you can't be afraid of either one. I'm going to show you how to hold the gun so it won't knock you on your arse. But you have to get over the fear, and you will."

"I'm not afraid."

"Alright, anyhow, here's what you didn't do when you held up the gun. Give me the gun and watch me again."

As Ignatius shouldered the gun, he said to Andrew, "See what I'm doing? I've got my right leg just a little in back of me, and my weight is shifted to my left or front leg, and I'm leaning into the gun. I'm also holding the gun butt tight to my shoulder. You didn't do any of these things, which is alright, because you've learned something. You do it the way I'm showing you, and you won't end up on the ground and you won't have a shoulder that feels broken. Something else. You get into shooting in the heat of battle, and you don't notice the noise. It's still there, but you're too busy to notice it. Keep wearing those patches. Also, the muzzle of the gun was moving around in circles while you were holding it. You can't hit anything when that happens. There's a couple of reasons for this. The first being when you hold the gun too long, your arm gets tired, and second, because your muscles aren't trained. You've got to train those muscles, and shoot as fast as you can. Of course, the best thing to do is steady the gun by resting it on a log or something, 'cause you don't want to stand up and show whatever or whoever it is that you're shooting where you are."

Ignatius thought a moment to consider what to do next.

"Put the musket to your shoulder again, and position yourself as I showed you."

Andrew faced the supposed target and positioned himself with his right leg in back and his weight on the other. As Andrew brought the gun up, Ignatius said, "Turn your hips to the right a bit. You look like you're going to bow to that tree the way you are. Look at me." Ignatius assumed the stance he wanted Andrew to copy.

"I see," said Andrew as he mimicked Ignatius's stance.

"Good. Now put the gun down and turn around, and do it all over again."

Andrew complied, and his first attempt surprised Ignatius as he studied Andrew's form; there was nothing for Ignatius to correct.

"Good. Now do it again six or seven times."

Andrew did so, and Ignatius was pleased at how fast Andrew caught on.

"That's just about as good as you're going to get, Andrew. Good, boy. Do it again a couple of more times, and we'll get to shoot'n that thing."

Andrew did as he was instructed, and Ignatius, satisfied, said, "That'll do. Give me the gun and I'll load it. You watch close to everything I do, 'cause you're going to load it after a couple more shots."

Andrew, confident, assumed the position he had learned. With the gun butt at his hip, he pulled the hammer to the fully cocked position, raised the gun to his shoulder, looked down the barrel through the sights, and, remembering not to take too long, pulled the trigger. The kick was a little more than he expected, and looking back on it, he had to admit he hadn't heard the gun go off. His ears, though, were still complaining.

Ignatius could tell Andrew had missed, but asked, "Get it?"

"Don't think so."

"Want to go look?"

"I'll just try again."

Ignatius, who had found a fallen log, was sitting on it smoking his pipe. Smoke came from his mouth as he said, "C'mon over here. I'm getting tired of loading. You do it."

Andrew sat on the log next to him.

"Give it to me; I want to point out what's what."

Ignatius proceeded to show and explain the various parts of the gun and what they did. There was the lock, which had the hammer with the flint, pan, fizzen, and spring. Looking closer, the flash hole could be seen. This always had to be checked to be sure it was clear. There was the trigger and trigger guard, the barrel with its sights, and the stock with a ramrod running down the inside. Within the butt of the stock were two small trapdoors. "That's the patch box where the patches are kept," Ignatius said, pointing to one of the doors. "The other door is for tools. I keep a screw driver in it, and a piece of wire to clear a plugged flash hole. Not all guns have those doors."

"The patches are for my ears?" asked an almost laughing Andrew.

"Ha! That, too, but the real purpose of the patch is to keep the ball in place and the powder behind it. Let's get to loading." Ignatius explained in detail the steps of loading the musket. "Don't forget to measure the correct amount of power. Too little, and the ball might not get out the barrel or get to the target. Too much, and the barrel could blow up. Don't let anybody say you don't need to measure the charge, or that you can do it by feel. I've seen the disastrous results of such talk."

Andrew reloaded the musket as he had been taught. "That alright?"

"Shoot it."

Andrew took the position, and once again aimed at the dead pine.

"Missed again," Andrew muttered. "Alright to try again?"

"Hold off a minute. Your eyes alright? I mean, they ever give you any trouble?"

"No, sir. I got good eyes."

"Let's take a look. They walked toward the tree, and on the way, Ignatius said, "If that was your first time, you looked good. But it takes some practice to know just where to aim."

When they got to the tree, Ignatius looked at it and said, "Andrew, look real close. See? See that little nick on the side? That's where your ball just took a piece out of it. You got it, boy! You got it! Thought you said you had good eyes."

Andrew just smiled, and didn't say another word. Ignatius put his arm around the boy and gave him a squeeze. "Nice going, boy. Couldn't have done better myself. Fact is, my first time, I didn't even come close. Nice going."

For the rest of the day, Andrew did most of the shooting and reloading. This boy could, even now, shoot with the best of them. Ignatius wondered how he'd do on a moving target.

"Tomorrow we're going to practice on some moving targets. Let's go back to the cabin, and I'll show you how to clean this thing."

THE FOLLOWING DAY found both Andrew and Ignatius back at the cabin. Their faces were filled with the excitement of expectation. Ignatius hadn't felt this much joy in doing something for…for well, a long time.

They'd smuggled a couple of tin pitchers from Miss Millie's kitchen, thinking she would never miss them. The two looked like a couple of school-boys trying to get away with something. Miss Millie caught the two from the corner of her eye, and just smiled to herself. Seeing Ignatius this happy made her happy, too. She pretended not to see anything or to know anything about it.

"You did get the rope I told you to load in the buggy?" asked Ignatius.

"It's there."

"I want you to get it and climb that hickory over there. See that long lower limb shooting out to the side? Go out on it as far as you dare, tie the rope to it and drop the end down, then climb down. We'll tie one of those pitchers to the end. That's going to be our target for today."

Andrew, having come down from the tree, approached Ignatius as he was cutting the rope at about ground level. Then he tied the rope to the pitcher handle such that it hung about four feet above the ground.

"Watch this, Andrew."

He pulled the pitcher back a few feet and let it swing.

"That's about the speed a walking deer is going to move. We're going to start you shooting at that. Think you can hit it?"

"I hit that pine, didn't I?"

"Yes, but the pine wasn't moving. If you aim at the pitcher the same way, you're going to miss, because by the time the ball reaches that far, the pitcher won't be there anymore. Understand what I'm getting at?"

"Uh huh."

"What you want to do is keep your gun moving at the same speed as the pitcher, but aim in front of it. See what I mean?"

"Yes, sir. Can I try it.?"

"Don't see why not. Just one thing. How far ahead are you going to aim?"

"I don't know. How far should I?"

"That all depends on the speed of the deer and the speed of what you're shooting with. The way you know how fast or slow your load shoots is with experience. This takes a lot more experience than shooting at still targets, as we did yesterday."

"It might take me forever to get that much experience."

"It'll come to you as you shoot. Now, I know that old gun and what it can do, so I know pretty much how much lead to take. You watch me the first time, and then it'll be your turn."

Ignatius stepped back about thirty feet, and had Andrew start the pitcher swinging.

"Run back here fast before the pitcher slows down too much."

When Andrew was back, Ignatius, lightning quick, raised his musket, pointed it toward the pitcher, and fired. The pitcher jumped and danced on the rope until it came to a stop.

"Wow!" shouted Andrew. "Dead deer."

"Not bad for an old man, huh?" said a satisfied Ignatius.

"You were fast. How'd you take aim that quick"?

"I did it a little different than I told you how to do it. You see, had I swung my gun in front of the pitcher to the lead I thought it required, and made sure I was swinging the gun at the same speed as the pitcher, it would have taken too much time. In the case of the pitcher, it would have slowed down, then moved in the backward direction, and I never would have hit it. If it had been a deer, he might have been out of range by that time, or even made it to the brush. So what I do is swing my gun from behind the moving target to the front of it. As I swing the gun and see the target, I pull the trigger, but keep swinging the gun and following through. Are you following me?"

"That's a lot to think about."

"It'll come to you second nature after a bit of practice. Now, reload the musket, and you try it. And whatever you do, keep the musket down until I'm behind you."

Andrew shot and missed four times before Ignatius stopped him and said, "I see what's happening, and you're repeating it every time. Now stop and think about what I'm going to say, and tell me whether you disagree. What I see happening is you're jerking the musket from behind the target, then overtaking it too much. Then you slow down and the target doesn't, and you speed up again. You're not maintaining a smooth speed of your swing. What do you think?"

"I see what you're saying."

"Try it again." Ignatius put the pitcher in motion again, and hurried to get behind Andrew.

Andrew fired the musket and the pitcher kept swinging, untouched.

"You're too worried about it. I want you to walk up to the buggy and check Louis. Walk around the rig two or three times, see if it's alright. Then bring me a ladle of water from the cabin. That ought to ease you up a bit."

Andrew came back with Ignatius's water. "Took a couple ladles myself."

"Alright, take the ladle back and we can try again."

Ignatius set the pitcher swinging again. After reloading, Andrew brought the musket to his shoulder, cocked the lock, aimed down the barrel, synced the motion to the moving pitcher, and became one with it. The pitcher jumped high in the air, coming down to bounce and gyrate about on the rope.

"That's it, Andrew! You've got it all together! Damned if you ain't going to be good."

Andrew repeated his feat a few more times, but then said, "Outta balls. We gotta make more."

"Do it tonight, but we're not gonna do this anymore. You're gonna shoot a deer tomorrow."

ANDREW DIDN'T SLEEP much that night, as he kept thinking about shooting a deer. Maybe it would be about the same as shooting the pitcher, but what if the deer was running? He answered himself by saying he would have to take a longer lead, or move the musket faster. He imagined the deer coming straight at him, and figured he'd just shoot the deer as if it were a standing target. What if the deer was moving away from him? That wouldn't be a nice thing to do. Over and over again, he thought of different scenarios until he fell asleep.

Miss Millie usually shook Andrew's shoulder to wake him in the mornings. It was no different this morning, but when he sat up in bed, Miss Millie was not there. In her place, Ignatius stood over him.

"We want to get out there early while the deer are moving about. Here, eat some of this jerky, and stuff some in your pocket. Get the buggy hitched up, and let's go."

"Where's Miz Millie?"

"Sleeping this time of day. That's what most people do around here."

Andrew had the buggy hitched to Louis in record time, and they soon found themselves hiding in tall grass behind the cabin.

"This early, we'll try it up here rather than down at the blind. We've got the night sky to light up the land enough, and at just about dawn, those deer should be headed back to the swamp from my wheat field."

They'd brought a second musket, so if Andrew missed his first shot, all he had to do was switch muskets for a fast second shot. They sat in the tall grass to wait, with both muskets close to Andrew. All Ignatius had to do was hand him the second musket if needed.

Andrew thought he saw something move, and he touched Ignatius's arm and pointed. Ignatius motioned that he saw it, whispering, "Wait, because there can be several of 'em in a line. About fifty feet behind, a buck may be following them. The buck's smart. He lets the ladies go first, so they get shot rather than him. Tell you something. If you pick off one of the larger ladies, you'll have better meat than if you wait for the buck…your choice."

Andrew picked the doe in the middle. He did not remember anything about the details of what he had learned the day before. Instead, it came to him by instinct, and he squeezed the trigger. The kick and noise he did not notice, but the smoke blanked out his sight, and for a moment, he could not see what had happened. The doe's front legs buckled, and the rest followed to the ground. Ignatius grabbed the musket from him and handed him the spare. Andrew drew a bead on another doe, and it fell. He was about to say something, but Ignatius was up and running toward the back of the string of does; he had spotted the buck. Here was an old man running through the grass with his big knife in one hand and his pistol in the other. He was whooping and hollering like a wild man.

Andrew stood up and wondered what he was doing. He never thought an old man could run so fast, and through tall grass, at that. The buck's head rose and looked at Ignatius. A deer will run under these circumstances, but not this time. He lowered his antlered head and waved it back and forth. Ignatius kept running toward the buck, and the buck charged toward Ignatius. Ignatius stopped, took aim at the charging animal, and fired his pistol. The buck ran another three steps and went down not more than a musket length from Ignatius. Ignatius ran those few feet and jumped on the buck. All Andrew could see was the flash of a knife going up and down, up and down.

It took a while for Andrew to come out of his fixation of watching the display. Then he ran toward Ignatius, and as he came upon him, he stopped short a few feet, as he could hear the sobbing of an old man bent down, his face buried in the deer's coat. Ignatius heard Andrew approach him, and without standing, straightened and looked at Andrew through tears in his eyes.

"I thought it was an Indian. But I killed him a long time ago. Don't know what the matter with me is. Keep it to yourself."

Ignatius stood up and wiped his eyes with his sleeve, then wiped his knife on the deer's coat.

"You and I have a lot of work to do. Shootin' is the fun part. Now we work."

First, Ignatius pointed to a tuft of hair on the inside of the deer's leg, about at the knee joint. "Cut these off first, clear through the skin. Leave 'em on, and the meat tastes kinda strange. Slit their throats next, so they bleed out, and turn 'em to where they point downhill if you can. This isn't too hilly around here, so just slit their throats and let it go."

Now we run a knife up their tummy, starting at about the arsehole and up to the breast bone. Don't cut deep—just under the skin. You don't want to puncture nothing inside. Here, take my knife and go to it. I'll watch."

Andrew did as he was told. The knife would not go through the skin easily, but once in, it slid up the deer's belly with ease.

"Now, turn the deer on its side and roll the guts out. You'll have to reach in with your arms and grab hold and pull. Andrew didn't hesitate, and soon the innards were on the ground.

"Next, split the bone around the arsehole. Here, let me do this, you watch."

Ignatius took the point of his knife, and, pressing it against the bone, hit the handle with a large rock. The bone broke as it was supposed to. He pried it apart with the knife blade and scraped the rest of the anus out along with the rest of the intestine connected to the guts. The deer's penis and testicles were cut off and thrown away.

"Now cut off his head. When the head's off, reach down the throat and tear it out down to the guts. Then we got the other two to do."

They dressed out the does in a similar manner and strung them up, rear feet first on the same hickory limb they had used for the swinging pitcher.

"Now we skin 'em. It's easy. Make a cut around the knees, and run your knife down under the skin, on the inside of the leg to where the belly slit is. Do that on all four legs."

After Andrew had cut the leg skin, Ignatius said, "Now we just peel the skin off. When you get enough skin in your hand, start chopping at it with the side of your hand to separate it from the meat. Watch how I do it. I'll get this one, and you do as I do on another."

It went fast, and Andrew did the third by himself.

"Let's take these critters to the wagon and go back and collect the heads, livers, hearts, kidneys, and anything else you might want to eat. Some people eat the intestines full of half-digested food and think it the best. I've tried it, and it's alright...just not my favorite, so I don't bother. Help yourself if you wish."

Andrew passed.

As they were driving back, Ignatius said, "You give two of those deer to the slaves and another to Miz Millie, understand?"

"Uh huh."

CHAPTER VI

ANDREW WORKED MANY an hour on the old shack, or, as it was properly known, the cabin. Loose boards were tightened and replaced where necessary, and shingles made from oak bark replaced the old ones that had rotted or blown away. He was excited about spending time hunting and fishing with Ignatius, and worked on the project even during his Sundays off. Ignatius, for his part, donated his time supervising while taking tugs from his flask of rye. Once in a while, he went down to the swamp and did what he could do to clear dead and decaying debris from the inside of the blind, replacing most of the reeds that made up the walls.

Weeks went by, and the two spent day and night in the cabin. They talked about all sorts of things, and Ignatius pontificated about his philosophy of life: "You must feed your soul, not only your body." At first, Andrew had a difficult time understanding what he was talking about, and Ignatius took great delight in expounding upon the subject to his captive audience. Asked what he wanted in life, Andrew said he wanted enough food to live, and to stay on the plantation, where he felt he had a home. Ignatius tried to make him see beyond those comforts, and tried to impress upon Andrew that he was a privileged slave, unlike the rest—and that it might not always be that way. Andrew had long understood that he was a privileged slave, but what was Ignatius trying to say?

"Andrew, anybody can hoe the fields and feed the animals, and that I call the maintenance of life, but not life itself. You have to have a self-defined purpose, a goal. I don't think you've met our neighbor, Isaac. He is someone who knows what I am talking about. He used to be one of my slaves, but that wasn't good enough for him. He wanted to have his own farm, so one day, after he'd thought it over for a long time, he asked me if I'd let him buy his freedom. I said I would, but how did he think he was going to go about it? His idea was to work for me and others for wages on his day off. I asked him what he was going to do once he got free, and he said he was going to continue working for wages, either with me or with someone else full-time, and buy himself enough land to live on and live there a free man.

I didn't think he could do it. But that man never took time off. All he did was work. Some days, he walked around as if he was half dead, he was so tired. He never lost faith in himself, and one day, he came to me with a bag of coins, handed it to me, and said he wanted to have the papers showing he was a free man, and could I use him and pay him for working for me. If not, he'd quit working for me and work for others. I told him I would, but as part of the deal, he'd have to start taking care of himself. If he wanted to stay and eat here as he had done as a slave, he was going to have pay for it and anything else he got. You see, being responsible for yourself goes hand in hand with being free. You're never, in truth, free."

When Ignatius thought Andrew could not absorb more of his wisdom, he stopped with the hope that he would consider what he had said, and, either now or later on, bring up the subject again and ask questions—or even offer his own ideas. Maybe Andrew would not dismiss the whole thing as an old man talking just to be heard, perhaps wanting to impress a younger person with his all-knowing, puffed up wisdom.

Andrew understood what the old man was talking about, except the part about *a privileged slave unlike the rest,* and that *it might not always be that way.*

"Master Attaway, what did you mean, I might not always be a privileged slave?"

"What I was driving at, Andrew, is I'm not going to live forever, and therefore your status as my right-hand man will no longer exist. You're going to have to work just the same as any other slave. But there are options for you, the same as there were for Isaac. This means you have to start thinking about what your options are, and that's something I can't help you with. You think about it, and we can talk more when you're ready."

THERE WERE DAYS, more frequently now, when Ignatius did not want to go to the cabin. All he wanted to do was take his buggy around the plantation to see what was going on and spend the rest of the day in his bedroom in the big house, where he slept most of the day and little at night. On those days, Andrew mostly worked in the fields with the other slaves.

Today was one of those days, and Andrew's mind wondered to something Ignatius had said. It had nothing to do with being free, taking responsibility for yourself, or the man he had called Isaac. He had said it the first day as they had made their way to the cabin by the swamp: *loading platform* and *try making one of those for Louis to stand on.*

He did not hear Martin ride up behind him. The horse gave a little whinny, startling Andrew, who turned around to face the horse.

"How you getting along, Andrew? Looks like you're doing pretty good."

"Yes, sir. I just keep working, and the day passes. Sometimes, I don't even think about what I'm doing, just think about other things."

"What things?"

"Well, sir, Master Attaway should get out of the house and go back to the cabin. He likes that, and he seems happy when he's there."

"Wouldn't have anything to do with you preferring to be there rather than here, would it?"

"Well…maybe a little, I guess."

"I'll talk to him and see if I can get him to get out more. It would do him some good, at that."

Martin, about to put his heels to the horse, stopped when Andrew said, "Mister Martin, I'd like to tell you something else I been thinking."

Martin looked down. "What?"

Andrew told Martin about building a ramp for Louis.

"What's he want a mule for, Andrew?"

"Didn't say."

"Hmm, well, let's keep Mister Attaway happy. You got it figured out how to make it?"

"I've been thinking about that, too. I'll just pile some dirt and level it off, put a fence across the long end so Louis can't go forward too far and fall off. Put one of those big draft mares at the other end and see what happens."

"Simple enough. Shouldn't take too much time. Hmm, might work. You pick another boy out, and the two of you start on it first thing in the morning. When it's done, I'm sure Mister Attaway will want to see it in action. I'd like to be there myself."

THERE WERE TWO ways to interpret what Martin had told Andrew to do. He had said to pick a boy. Now, that could mean a boy as in "not yet a man," or it could mean a boy as in "slave," and Andrew, determined to make this undertaking a success, decided to pick the best person for the job. Planning ahead in his own mind beyond just building the ramp, he envisioned some tricky equine handling. From what he knew of the slaves on this plantation, there was only one who had any experience working with equines: the blacksmith, a fellow everybody called Smithy. When the donkeys first arrived and Andrew had asked him to fix the loose shoe on Louis's hoof, Smithy had looked at it. A bit annoyed at the condition of the donkey, he said, "This donkey has a split hoof. He ain't been taken care of since he was first shod, I can see that for sure. I've got to wire it so it don't split anymore, and fit a new shoe. This shoe is all worn out. That goes for the rest of his shoes, and I'll bet his girlfriend's, too."

Smithy's reputation among those who knew him was not good. Though a good farrier and blacksmith, he was thought to be lazy and of a disagreeable personality. Ignatius had often thought of selling him, but finding another skilled slave was not easily done. So, Smithy kept his job.

He was supposed to help out in the fields alongside the other slaves when he did not have any blacksmithing to do, which was often. Along with being lazy, Smithy considered it below him, a slave with a trade, to work with the common field slaves, and he let it be known by being uncooperative. Yet he knew when he was pushing it too far. He did not want to land himself in trouble, so he worked at about half-speed and with half-effort, just enough to stay out of trouble and avoid being picked for a task when someone else was available. Ignatius and Martin had often thought they might make an exception with Smithy when it came to not whipping slaves, but dismissed the idea.

"So," Martin had said, "we're stuck with Smithy. We can't sell him, because we wouldn't have a blacksmith or a farrier."

To which Ignatius said, "I suppose we could have Sam Ballard in Bryan Town come here."

"He'd end up having to live here," said Martin.

"Think I'll let word get around we need a blacksmith and see what happens. Make sure Smithy hears about it secondhand from someone. Might change his attitude."

Andrew approached Smithy and told him about the project. Smithy's reaction to a young boy asking him—in reality, ordering him—to work was a resounding, "Go away, boy. I ain't got time to play with you in the dirt. What do I look like, some kind of playmate?"

"No, you look more like someone Master Attaway or Mister Martin is going to be talking to," Andrew said, surprised he had said it.

Smithy paused a moment within himself and thought about what this young little privileged slave favorite had said and the rumor he had heard about Ignatius and Martin looking for a blacksmith. Mad, but still in command of himself, he took a deep breath and said, "When do we start?"

Morning came, and the two shoveled and leveled dirt as Andrew directed. They dug dirt from one area that measured roughly one rod wide by two rods long; this they called the pit. As they dug the pit, they spread the dirt from it to a similar area at the end, such that it would build up and form a platform with a ramp for Louis to walk up.

Though it had only been a few weeks since Andrew had come to the plantation, anybody looking at him would have noticed he'd grown several inches, and was trading his boyish build for that of a man's. But that did not account for his doing more work than Smithy, as Smithy himself was in top physical condition. Smithy was holding back, and Andrew knew it.

"How busy are you at the blacksmith shop, Smithy?"

"Got more work than I can handle," he lied.

"Ah! That explains the rumor I heard about them looking for another blacksmith."

Smithy gave a nervous "Ha, ha, guess so."

Smithy's pace started to speed up.

The tension between the two was high, and Andrew was determined to break it up. "What you think about Master Attaway's idea of breeding mules?"

"I don't know nothin' 'bout mules. Suppose they're about the same as a horse. You're his favorite boy. What'd he tell you?"

Andrew was starting to feel the resentment, from not only Smithy but from others of the slave population. He'd have to work on that, but he didn't know how, at the moment.

"He told me a mule could outwork a horse, and ate less. And if he could get Marie to accept Louis and make more donkeys, he could make more mules, and he could even start selling 'em."

An idea struck Smithy like a bolt of lightning. It might be of benefit to him if mules were bred on the plantation; he may well end up spending all his time blacksmithing and shoeing, and never have to work the fields again with the common slaves.

Now Smithy was working as hard as Andrew, out-shoveling him and almost leveling the pile by himself. It was Smithy who suggested bringing one of the horses over and leading him back and forth on the piles of dirt to pack it down as they went along. The enthusiasm for the project was now mutual, and Smithy began to ease his resentment of the boy slave. They laughed and joked about what a sight it was going to be to see Louis trying to mount a mare.

"Ever see a smiling donkey?"

"He'll have to rest up for a month after."

"She'll have her own slave from here on."

"Wonder what Marie is going to think? Probably sulk for a year."

"That'll teach her."

WITH THE HELP of Martin's knowledge of horses, a never-serviced young mare was selected that was several hands higher than Louis. Even though the ramp was ready and the mare was cycling, she might not accept Louis. Martin told Andrew and Smithy the mare was like any other lady; she had to be properly introduced to her suitor. Louis and the mare were corralled in separate adjacent paddocks, allowing the two equines to become used to each other. More to the point, this allowed Louis to show when the mare was in heat and ready.

Several times each day, Martin, Andrew, and Smithy walked by the corrals in anticipation of what might transpire. Nor were they the only ones. After word spread around about what was going on, there was not a slave on the plantation, house or field, who didn't figure out a reason to pass by the corral at least once a day. Ignatius himself took an interest, and several times a day came out of the house to see if anything was happening. One Saturday at about noontime, one of the house slaves yelled, "Look at the size of that donkey!" He was not referring to Louis's height. Martin and Ignatius heard it all the way into the kitchen, where they were having a noon meal and talking to Miss Millie about nothing in particular. Smithy ran from the blacksmith shop, his leather apron swinging side to side, holding a red-hot something or other with a pair of tongs. From wherever he'd been, Andrew came at a dead run and jumped the corral fence with two bridles in his hands. Smithy dropped the loaded tongs in the water trough, and they hissed as they sunk. Andrew tossed him one of the bridles, saying, "That's for the mare. Put it on her. I'll get Louis."

Louis kept trying to mount the mare, but with the corral fence between them and his relative lack of height, he was not able. He ran back and forth, around and around, side to side, trying again and again to no avail. Andrew tried to bridle him, but he was irritable and uncooperative. Martin, now in the corral, grabbed Louis around the neck, and Louis reared, trying to throw Martin off—but he hung on, even as the donkey lifted him from the ground. "Smithy," said Andrew, "take her over to the pit, like I showed you. I'll bring Louis after I calm him down." After the mare was gone, Louis still tried to shed Martin, but Martin held on. The donkey settled some, and Andrew managed to slip the bridle on, trying to comfort the frustrated donkey. Ignatius was looking on from one of the corral rails he'd managed to sit on, a genuine grin covering his face. This did not escape a brief glance from Andrew when he happened to look up.

Smithy led the mare to the shallow pit, backing her up until she almost touched the fence across the front of the ramp. Andrew kept an eye on both animals, and when the mare had settled, Smithy, holding the reins close, pulled on Louis's reins and brought him up near the mare's side. Louis nosed around the mare from one end to the other, settling on the mare's rump.

"C'mon, Louis," Andrew said, "follow me." Louis put up some resistance, and Andrew had to pull him with effort, but the donkey soon gave way and followed Andrew to the end of the ramp, where he walked up the small incline and down to the fence. For now, Andrew's job was done, and he jumped off the ramp.

"Smithy!" called Andrew. "You hold that mare steady. Don't let her walk."

Almost before Andrew had finished cautioning Smithy, Louis was mounting the mare and holding her back with his teeth.

"Good going, Andrew," said Ignatius, walking up. "That's going to get you a mule foal, for sure."

Andrew smiled at Ignatius without saying a word, bringing his attention back to the two equines.

"Andrew, I want you to take care of the mare from here on. Make sure she has everything she needs every day, including Sundays. You take care of her even when we spend time down at the cabin."

"I kinda thought I was gonna do it anyhow, Master Attaway."

"Well, now it's official. So now you have to take care of the mare, two donkeys, and an old man."

SMITHY WAS IN his late thirties. He didn't give the appearance of being a blacksmith able to work with heavy metal and equipment, as he was small-framed. While not what could be called short, he was not much taller. His looks were deceiving. On Sundays, Andrew had seen him win many a foot-race when challenged by younger slaves. He was nimble and quick, and could do backflips and other gymnastics no one else on the plantation even thought of trying. He'd developed a skin-tight body free of even an ounce of fat. His arms, out of proportion with his body, were pure bulging muscle, with blood vessels stretched over his biceps and running down around the length of his arms, all the way to his knuckles. He could lift an anvil without straining, and climb a rope hand over hand straight up, without using his legs. Smithy had developed his strength and agility as a result of working as a blacksmith, not because he tried to be a strong man. It was necessary for his small frame if it was to do the work demanded of it. Still, Smithy was of a lazy nature, and, given his druthers, would rather do nothing.

The day came when Andrew asked him straight out, "How come you're so lazy? When we built the pit and ramp, you didn't want to do anything until you saw there could be something in it for you."

"That's just not me to let 'em see what I can do. Ain't going to help me none. All they going to do if they think I can do something is give me more work, and nothing more to eat. Nope, I do what I have to do and that's it. It's not lazy, it's smart."

"Well, it's lazy to me. I guess if you can get away with it, that's your choice."

"I know when to hold back and I know when not to."

They let it go, but Andrew was thinking about what Ignatius had said back when he had expounded about Isaac and setting goals. Smithy was a man with more ability than most any slave on the plantation, and he did not want to do anything with it. He could have been one of the guys others looked up to when in need. Too bad Ignatius hadn't had a talk with him. It occurred to Andrew that Ignatius had thought about it, but understood some people would never get what he was driving at—and Smithy was one of them.

Despite it all, Andrew found himself liking Smithy, and they formed a friendship. When Andrew asked Smithy how he had repaired the ill-fitting shoe on Louis, Smithy told him how he had done it. "The shoe was worn out a long time ago, Andy, and caused the hoof to split because of it. I drilled small holes through the hoof, and ran copper and iron wires through the holes and back again through other holes, twisted the wires together at the ends, and hoped they stayed together. If it don't work, that donkey won't be much good for anything except maybe making donkeys and mules."

"Why both copper and iron wire?"

"The iron's going to rust away. The copper won't, and it ain't strong, but it might hold until I can replace the rusted wires."

Andrew had a natural curiosity about things, and one day, as he was watching Smithy, asked him why he always heated iron before working it with a hammer on the anvil. "Won't the iron bend without heating it?" he asked, remembering when Jim had bent the iron straps in the jail.

"The metal gets brittle and breaks if you don't heat it. Also, you need to get it red hot to weld. And if you take a piece of red-hot iron and dip it in water or oil, it gets real hard. That's how I made those springs for Master Attaway's buggy and wagon."

"Weld?"

"It's when you join two pieces of metal and make it one piece. That's how broken plow blades, among other things, are repaired."

"Here, you try it, Andy." Smithy handed him two pieces of iron strap. "Stick 'em in the coals, and pump the billows. When the straps get almost white hot, take 'em out, and place one on the anvil and hold the other on top of it. Then take that big hammer and beat it hard as you can."

Andrew did as Smithy told him and stepped back, holding what had been two pieces and were now one.

"It ain't pretty, Andy, but you got 'em stuck together."

THE SUMMER MONTHS passed by almost too fast. With the coming of fall, Ignatius seemed to regain his desire to spend time at the cabin, and he and Andrew killed many deer and a few smaller animals, along with turkeys; some they ate in the cabin, but most they brought back to the plantation to be used as Miss Millie saw fit. Andrew learned to shoot shot from the musket, as it was better for shooting turkeys than a solid ball. You had to watch out for pieces of shot when you ate the turkey, though—something Andrew found out about the hard way. He also found out that if he was too close to the bird, he might as well have shot it with a ball; there was not much to eat afterwards.

Andrew had become a busy boy. Every morning, he checked on the mare and the donkeys, even if he had spent the night at the cabin with Ignatius. On the days he was not at the cabin, he and Ignatius spent time with the donkeys, and kept trying to tempt Marie into accepting Louis. Louis, by now, was way past being wary of his female companion, and showed less and less interest. One morning, they came upon the two donkeys to find Marie pushing Louis with her nose. Afraid of this strange aggression, Louis brayed, and backed up to escape. Soon, Marie was pushing Louis with her nose and turning her rump to his side and backing into him. She did this time after time, and Louis, unsure of what to do, brayed and backed away more.

"You know what's she's trying to do, don't you, Andrew?"

"Yes, sir, but Louis sure doesn't get it."

"Give her time. She'll get the message across. That's kind of how women work, you know. When Louis quit trying, that made her mad. Now she's going the opposite way."

"Maybe that foal-carrying mare made her jealous."

"You might have something there."

As they watched, Louis began to grow erect.

"Look, look! He's gonna do it, Andrew!" Ignatius said, pointing at Louis.

And he did.

Soon after, Andrew went over to the blacksmith shop and found Smithy sitting in a chair with his feet propped up on the anvil, asleep.

"Hey! Wake up, lazy," Andrew shouted.

Smithy awakened and jumped up, looking around for Ignatius or Martin. When he only saw Andrew, he relaxed.

"Don't do that. You scared the hell out of me."

"I know. That's why I did it. Guess what?"

"What?"

"Louis just got Marie."

"I don't believe it."

"Bet you'll believe it in about a year."

"Hope it turns out to be a jack."

Andrew had made it a point of going to the blacksmith shop every morning after he finished taking care of his equine duties. It was not so much to see Smithy as it was to see what he was working on. By and by, Smithy let Andrew try his hand at some of the projects. There was always a hinge to be repaired, a broken spring, those darned plowshares finding a boulder no matter how many times the fields had been plowed, and the occasional horseshoe to be fashioned and fitted when one of the horses threw a shoe and it could not be found. There were the shovels and picks, which Ignatius had always preferred to make rather than buy. He thought that as long as he had a blacksmith, he would use him. Miss Millie always needed a new or different pan, and Smithy knew how to make just what she wanted. For the most part, it didn't take a lot of time except when everything broke at the same time.

As things progressed, Smithy let Andrew do more and more work, as Andrew's time permitted. What had begun innocently enough, with Andrew merely satisfying his curiosity, developed into a new way for Smithy to get out of work. It didn't take Andrew long to figure out what Smithy was up to. After a while, Andrew quit going to the blacksmith shop so often. When he did, he always had something else he had to do, and could not stay long. Truth be told, Andrew would have liked to do more of the blacksmith work, but did not feel it was the right thing, nor did he want to get Smithy in more trouble than he already was. Andrew never mentioned it to Ignatius or Martin.

He did not have to say anything. Ignatius may have been old and getting more and more forgetful, but he was not blind, and his wits never failed him. He knew what was going on, but never let on—nor did Martin. The fact was, the whole plantation had it figured out.

One day, while they were taking a break from hunting and were sitting at the edge of the swamp fishing, Ignatius asked Andrew if he liked doing blacksmithing work.

Andrew realized he was not fooling Ignatius at all. He swallowed hard, took a deep breath, looked the old man in the eyes, and said, "I'm sorry for spending time at Smithy's. But yes, it beats working in the fields. Smithy's pretty smart. He knows a lot."

Ignatius nodded his head and said nothing more.

THE THREE OF them had closed the door of the small room they used as a study. Mary sat on a chair and listened to her husband and father, who were speaking in raised, yet civil voices.

"I'm telling you, Iggy, it just isn't going to work having two blacksmiths. We don't have enough work for one."

"It's not costing the plantation anything it isn't already costing. Andrew is more my boy, my helper, than one of the plantation slaves. That's the way we planned it."

"What do you think Smithy's going to do when he hears what you want to do? I'll tell you what he's going to do; he's going to think you're replacing him, and he'll run away."

"Martin, I haven't had ten slaves run away since I took over this place from my father. Those who did weren't much good anyhow. I didn't even look for 'em. Took my loss and considered I came out ahead."

"That might be, but if Smithy ran off, we'd feel it. I know he's lazy, but he's what we got for a blacksmith, and it beats taking our broken stuff to Bryan Town to be fixed, or having that blacksmith come here."

"Dad," Mary injected, "why don't you sit both of them down and explain to them why you want to do this? Reassure Smithy you're not going to replace him."

"Mary, I can't tell him I want Andrew to learn a trade because I'm going to set him free some day. Andrew sure doesn't need to know it, either, because it would just go to his head, and he wouldn't be much good after that."

"Maybe, but I'm not too sure," Mary said.

"What about out-and-out lying to both of them?" Martin said.

"What would I say?"

Martin thought about it for a moment, and said, "As Mary said, sit both of them down together and tell them Mister Blackiston has decided this place needs to be sure it always has a blacksmith available. If Smithy ever got sick, or for some other reason couldn't do the job, there'd be a backup."

"Go on."

"Tell them you've noticed Andrew's interest in both blacksmithing and equines equals that of Smithy's, and therefore, Andrew is going to be the backup. Then tell Smithy it's going to be his job to teach Andrew everything he knows."

"You'll still have to tell Smithy he's not going to be replaced," injected Mary.

"I'd hate to do that, and then decide I have to get rid of him because he just isn't doing the job," said Martin.

"Well, tell him he's not going to be replaced as long as he doesn't give good cause. It's a fair warning, and not a lie."

"Think he'll buy it?"

"I doubt it, but I can't think of anything else. Business-wise, it does make sense."

Later that day, Martin rounded up Andrew and Smithy and told them to go over to the blacksmith shop, where Mister Attaway was waiting. With apprehension, they entered the shop. First Smithy; minutes later, Andrew entered. Their eyes met in a questioning way, and they looked at Ignatius.

Ignatius had thought about how to say everything in the best way, and watched the expressions on the two slaves' faces. However he'd planned on giving his speech, it must not have come out right—at least the reaction of the slaves wasn't as he'd expected.

Smithy looked frightened, and Ignatius thought he saw him almost faint. Andrew looked stunned, as if he'd been selected to be sold.

Both slaves knew better than to ask a master, any master, the reasons why an order was given. A slave took what was shelled out to him, and that was all there was to it.

The friendship between Andrew and Smithy seemed to cool as soon as Ignatius got the words out of his mouth. From that day on, Smithy was a changed man. He no longer dodged work of any kind. He taught Andrew everything he knew, and worked with him as needed. Once Andrew became proficient in the trade, tried even harder to show he was the top blacksmith. But he was always afraid he was going to be sold one day, and that Andrew would end up taking his place when Ignatius died. He was polite to Andrew, but never a friend, and Andrew adopted the same manner toward Smithy.

CHAPTER VII

THE WINTER MONTHS were brutal, and it seemed to snow most every day from November through early April. Icy winds blew from the north. Slaves continuously felled trees for firewood, and took care of the cattle and each other; over half of the slaves were sick at any given time. Frozen ground was cleared of snow in the slave cemetery, and fires built to thaw the ground so graves could be dug. Eleven graves were dug and filled that winter, and another six dug and left open just in case.

Ignatius had experienced winters like this at other times during his long life, and they had impressed upon him the need to always be prepared. As a consequence, it had been his way to consistently overstock on the necessities of life. Root cellars were many, and each was packed to maximum capacity. Slave clothing was stockpiled in excess, and additional items issued beyond the yearly allowance of two complete changes of clothing and one coat.

And then there was Miss Millie. It seemed many plantations had their own Miss Millie, the type who always seemed to know about the almost-magical uses of plants. If she did not have her supply of plants and utensils and somebody died because of it, it was Ignatius's fault, and she would become downright difficult to be around. One of the yearlong duties of slaves was to gather these plants as could be found on the plantation for her use. Ignatius himself felt it was all hogwash, but even he submitted to her remedies if he was sick, if only to keep the peace. Rye was his medicine of choice, and he laid in an ample supply. He had it in the back of his mind to grow and make the stuff one of these years.

Herds of deer, unable to find forage in the deep, snow-covered woods, were hungrier than they were afraid of man. They became aggressive to the point of taking hay from haystacks in addition to browsing fields for anything missed during harvesting. Slaves tried to run them off, and there were a few encounters between slave and hungry deer.

Venison became an easy staple for slaves and whites alike on the plantation. By now it was common knowledge that Andrew knew how to shoot a gun and so, Martin and Andrew became the designated hunters, or, in this case, shooters—hunting not being required. The barn was crowded with the plantation animals; equines, cows, and sheep. Chickens, usually able to endure winters, didn't make it through December. Martin figured foxes had found their way into the coops, or the chickens had found their way into slave's pots—or both.

To Ignatius's chagrin Mary, since her puberty, had always insisted everyone in the household, including slaves, take a bath once a week as she found to do otherwise was extremely offensive to her. Martin learned this early on, when he had first asked Ignatius if he could court his daughter. Ignatius, believing Martin to be of good character and prosperous, gave his permission so long as Mary agreed. So when a smiling and confident Martin approached Mary and asked her if she would take a buggy ride with him, she said, "Yes… if you'll take a bath first, and before each time we ever see each other again." Martin had never heard of such a thing. Why couldn't she just carry a handkerchief doused with perfume and put it to her nose, the same as everybody else? What did she think she was, special or something? Well, Mary may or may not have thought she was special, but Martin did, and thereafter, he took a bath once a week—or more, if Mary mentioned it.

During the winter, any winter, it was impractical if not impossible to take a bath as often as Mary insisted. Water was too cold and too much wood and time was required to heat it for bathing. So, come the winter months, a bath was only rarely taken. Even Mary adjusted to the situation and faced the reality of it. She told herself that as long as everyone didn't take a bath, they would get used to the odor of each other and not notice it so much—and, she rationalized, people did not sweat as much in the winter, and so would not need a bath as often as during the working summer months.

Ignatius never minded winter, and could never figure out people who complained of it. To him, it was just a part of living, and you took care of the situation as need be. If it was too hot, you slowed down some and drank more water; too rainy, drape an oilskin around you; too cold, wear heavier clothing. He dressed in heavy wool pants and shirts, kept his feet in boots made of sheepskin with the wool inside, and draped a couple of blankets around his shoulders. Give him an endless supply of rye and his pipe, and he was a contented man. Ignatius made it through the winter with nothing more than an almost constantly runny nose. At one time, Miss Millie told him to put a little rye in a cup of hot water and add some cinnamon, and it would clear up the runny nose. He did, and he invited Miss Millie to have a cup of her remedy with him.

"Ignatius," she said, "I don't have a runny nose."

"I figure if it will cure it, it will prevent it. So sit down and have a cup with me."

She did, and soon after, they were talking into the late hours of the night about growing up together. Miss Millie did most of the talking, and, Ignatius noticed, most of the drinking of her own remedy.

Ignatius spent many hours talking to Andrew about everything, from what he wanted to do with the mule foal when it was born to philosophical questions of what a man should do with his life. He was trying to show Andrew the road leading not only to freedom, but to accomplishment; freedom being only one part of a full life. If only the boy would want to walk that road with passion, because without passion, nothing could be accomplished.

SPRING CAME AT long last. Patches of snow remained here and there, but anxious shoots of light green began pushing through the warming earth, and buds appeared and unfurled their surprises. Pests of all kinds buzzed around anything with blood in its veins, and ticks began to dig into skin to bury their heads.

Mary ordered everybody, including the slave population, to take their first bath of the year. After the baths, water was boiled and clothes washed until judged to be suitable for a human to wear.

Ignatius ventured out of the house for the first time since it had snowed back in November. With him were Mary, Martin, and Andrew. Ignatius wanted to see the animals first to check their condition. Through the winter, Andrew had given him daily reports about how they looked, and now it was time to see for himself.

Looking at the mare, he said, "Looks as if she's about ready to drop."

"She's big, for sure," Martin said.

"Another three months if it takes eleven months," said Andrew.

"But she's so big," said Ignatius.

"She's a big horse and Louis is a big jack, so she's got a big foal. It's what you wanted, Iggy," said Martin.

ANDREW HAD A tether on Marie, and was exercising her in one of the corrals. He led her in circles and figure eights, had her walk backward, and repeated the routine several times again. He heard Smithy driving a wagon, the same wagon Ignatius and Martin had used when they had gone to Bryan Town to buy him. It was pulled by the same two-horse team. The wagon had been fitted with another seat in back of the front seat. He bet himself that both seats had been fitted with the softer springs.

Smithy parked the wagon by the back door of the mansion and made his way back to the shop. Their eyes chanced to meet, and neither acknowledged the other.

Within a few minutes, Ignatius, Mary, and Martin came out of the house and climbed aboard the wagon, with Martin taking the reins, Mary seated next to him, and Ignatius spread out sitting crooked on the back seat, with his legs propped up on the wagon sideboards.

Martin gave a click of his tongue and a snap of the reins, and the team headed out to the road leading to Bryan Town. Andrew thought it somehow strange that none of them looked his way. It was almost as if their necks were stiff, and could only look straight ahead. He had a slightly uneasy feeling, and when he chanced to see Miss Millie, he asked her where they had gone.

"Well, Mister Curious, if it's any of your business, they had business to take care of in Bryan Town. I don't know what it is, so don't try to get it out of me." She said no more, and his uneasy feeling remained with him.

THIS YEAR WAS different from last year at this time. Whereas last year Ignatius had at first been eager to hunt and fish down at the cabin and spend time teaching Andrew various things, this year, he was lethargic, and did not seem to care about anything except the condition of the foaling mare and Marie the jenny. He was even less inclined to share his philosophy and views on life with anybody who would sit to listen. It seemed he had lost interest in all things, including Andrew.

Knowing Ignatius would not bring up the subject, Andrew took it upon himself to suggest they go to the cabin. He asked Ignatius regularly if they could go to the cabin, and Ignatius accepted more out of guilt about every third time. When they got to the cabin, all Ignatius wanted to do was go to the edge of the swamp and fish in the hole they had discovered—a hole with few snags, and they knew where each snag was.

"You know you didn't put bait on the hook don't you, Master Attaway?"

"Don't care. Too much effort to pull the little devils out when they bite. I'd just as soon drink my rye and watch you pull 'em in."

They'd both give a little chuckle and went on.

"You ever try this stuff?" Ignatius asked, motioning to his flask.

"Yes, sir. Master Carter used to give it out at Christmas to all his slaves. I tried it, and Miz Jane liked to have killed me."

"Miz Jane didn't approve, eh?"

"She said it was Satan's brew, and I was to stay away from it. Smithy gave me some when we were friends."

"I know about that…I mean I knew he was making something in the shop other than horseshoes."

"And you didn't mind?"

"Some have a garden, raise chickens and whatever, why not a little something else? As long as he can work come time to work, it's his business. Want some? Here, take a sip."

Andrew took the flask and took a swallow. It burned all the way down. As he coughed, Ignatius saw the pain on Andrew's face.

Andrew said, "That happens every time I try it."

Ignatius gave a little laugh and said, "Only drunks can swallow it like you did and not react any different than if they were drinking water. Sip the stuff and taste it. Don't get in a hurry. Enjoy it."

"You seem to enjoy it a lot."

"I do. But what the hell!" He paused and looked Andrew in the eye, "Don't you ever like it that much. Makes you a different person than your real self."

"What you mean?"

"Well, there are those who become mean. They'll beat their wives, kids, and slaves, and challenge anybody who looks at 'em. There are those who become funny, or at least think they're funny—but they're really obnoxious and embarrassing to those around them. There are those who become melancholy, and start crying. Some will try things they'd never do otherwise, like riding a crazy horse or trying to fly off a cliff by holding their arms out like wings. I've seen some who take a few swallows and curl up in a corner someplace and go to sleep. Understand what I say?"

"Yes, but I've never seen you do anything you just said."

"Oh, but something does happen. You see, from morning to night, I have a few little sips as I go along. Eventually, something turns off in my head, and I don't feel the pains of the past as much, and I stop remembering."

"What pain? Stop remembering what?"

Ignatius had sipped enough from his flask that he was uninhibited now and he proceeded to answer Andrew's question.

"The pain of remembering: my wife Elizabeth, and all those Indians and Frogs I killed. Those slave girls Norton Carter, Ed Littlefield, and I forced ourselves on when we were just becoming men. I have no idea how many kids I might have running around these parts. We were a wild bunch."

"You did that?!" he questioned Ignatius.

"My father got wind of what we were doing—might have been a slave mother approached my father, and didn't care about her own safety. My father got hold of the other fathers. They tied us to whipping posts on Norton's father's place and whipped us just as if we were slaves, and his slaves were lined up to watch. Twenty lashes each. I've still got the scars, and remember the sting of every one. That's why I never whip my slaves. Since that time, Ed has never spoken to me. Norton and I get along alright, but find it difficult to look each other in the eye."

Andrew took a sip from the flask. Ignatius had been right—that was the way to drink the stuff. He handed the flask back, but Ignatius had gone to sleep.

MARTIN AND MARY were helping Miss Millie take care of a cut on the leg of a little slave girl when they heard the sound of a buggy being pulled at full speed. They watched as it neared them.

"What's Iggy got that buggy going so fast for?"

"That's not Dad, Martin. That's Andrew. I don't see Dad in the buggy."

"Oh, jeez! What now?"

Andrew pulled the buggy to a stop and said, "I can't get Master Attaway to wake up. He looks like he's sleeping with his eyes open!"

"Martin!"

"Stay here, Mary. I'll go see what's the matter!"

"No, I'm going too."

Andrew heard, and climbed in the back of the buggy and held the reins for Martin as they climbed in. They headed back the way Andrew had come, with Andrew giving directions as they went along.

As they pulled up to the cabin, Andrew jumped out before the buggy had come to a complete stop. Martin set the brake, and he and Mary climbed out. Andrew was already on his way down the path to the swamp, and yelling for the two to follow.

Finding Ignatius, Martin said, "He's gone."

BOOK TWO

CHAPTER VIII

IT HAD BEEN five years since Ignatius had died, and things changed as things do; and Andrew was to be counted among them. At over six feet tall, Andrew surprised everyone who knew him. When he had first come to the plantation, most would have bet everything they owned he would not top five feet. Looking at him now, they saw a tall fellow who, while muscular, was not overly muscled, but rather trim and fit. That was not to say he was not strong—but he did not look the part of a strong man, just as his mule did not look strong, but was full of surprises.

IN A MATTER of days after Ignatius was put to rest, Andrew stopped sleeping in the kitchen. It was Andrew's idea, and when he asked Martin and Mary if he could move out because he was not comfortable in the kitchen as a young man, they understood. Young people transforming from children to adults go through many physical and mental changes, and their wish for a certain amount of privacy is understandable.

In reality, Mary only understood part of the problem from her experience as a girl growing through puberty. Martin had a clearer understanding from a male's point of view.

While Mary and Martin had their ideas of the problems of puberty in general, Andrew's understanding of his problem was more specific: it was those skinny little obnoxious girls who used to run around the farm pretending to work with their parents and sticking their tongues out at the boys. They no longer seemed obnoxious. They looked different, and his mind and body reacted differently. To make matters worse, some of the girls now worked in the kitchen, and that contributed to his problem. His penis now had a mind of its own; it was out of control, and never failed to cause him embarrassment at the most awkward times. When he awoke in the morning, those same girls were working about the kitchen. He was unable to make it from his bed of mats to the outhouse without embarrassment. Throwing a blanket over his shoulders and covering himself allowed him to hide his modesty and get out the door, but he always thought he could hear a snicker or a giggle somewhere behind him. This was only the beginning of what he would have to endure for the rest of the day, whenever he saw one of these no-longer-obnoxious girls.

It was agreed by Mary and Martin that Andrew would move out of the kitchen. The problem was there was no other place to put Andrew. All the cabins were full, including the bachelor cabin where unmarried men stayed. The bachelor cabin had eight occupants, all older than Andrew; Smithy being the youngest. Because of the animosity between Andrew and Smithy, as well as the fact that the cabin was full, they had to consider other alternatives for Andrew's housing.

Martin suggested the hunting cabin, but Andrew explained that he did not think it would work, because he would sleep until noon without the noise of others to wake him. Also, he wished to get away from his status of being the privileged favorite among the slave population.

"There's no way you're not going to be thought of as the privileged slave, Andrew," said Martin. That's what you are, and that's that. You have use of the hunting cabin on your day off, because that's the way Ignatius wanted it. You don't have to use it if you don't want to, but we're not going to tell you that you can't."

Andrew had an idea, and was waiting for the right time to mention it. "What if I build a second bachelor cabin for young bachelors? The other one's kinda for older guys, anyhow. I'd do it on my day off, and I'd sleep in the barn till it was done."

"It would solve the problem, Martin," said Mary. "There might be other young bachelor slaves one day. We almost need them now—at least we're going to need them soon, because time is going by, and our slaves are growing older."

"You're right. Andrew, find yourself a place in the barn, and move in as soon as you can. You're not going to have to build it on your own. We have no one who knows masonry to build a fireplace. I'll see if Norton Carter has anyone we could hire to do it…I think he does. Once done, it shouldn't take more than two or three days to build the rest of the cabin if we have four or five other slaves work on it with you."

And so the cabin was constructed. The older bachelor slaves did the cutting of the logs, and fitted them together around the fireplace two of Norton Carter's slaves put up. Smithy seemed to have too much work at the blacksmith shop, so he was unable to work on the project.

On the following Saturday after work was done, Martin told those who had worked on the project to go to the newly-built cabin. Upon entering, they found a venison roast and hot potatoes prepared by Miss Millie. Martin made sure there were several jugs of rum to be passed around. Straggling in a little late were Norton Carter's two slaves.

"Thank you," was all Martin said as he left the men to have their good time.

The following day was Sunday, and it was, of course the slaves' day off. It became clear why Martin had waited until Saturday night to thank his slaves. They woke late, and most held their heads between their hands. When they moved, they moved slowly and deliberately. Martin loaded Norton's two slaves in his buggy and drove them to their master's plantation, just in time for the noon service given by the traveling preacher.

BY AND BY, and after gaining a little personal confidence, Andrew learned to live with his problem. His problem now was to learn how to deal with the looks he received from parents as he and the girls flirted with each other. Parents, even slave parents, could be a force to contend with. Of course, they wanted their daughters to meet a man who would take care of her and have offspring, but their daughter's ideal companion seemed not to have been put in this world so far, so "Mister Andrew Attaway and all you others, move on."

Ignatius had given Andrew some hard-earned advice when he confessed to his wild days when he became a man. He said something to the effect of, "Don't ever feel life is only about you. Others have feelings and emotions, too. Don't force yourself on a girl, 'cause you might get shot, or beat up so bad you won't know who you are anymore—not to mention how the girl ends up feeling. Don't even think about a white girl if you don't want to be hanged. Know when it's right to bed a girl, and when it's wrong. If you just want pleasure, there are girls out there who just want pleasure, too. You'll learn who they are, likely grown women. Ask a girl where she is in her cycle, 'cause you don't want a bunch of little Andrews running around. You understand what I'm telling you, Andrew?"

He said he did, but asked what this had to do with him. A year later, those words came back for him to ponder. His loins told him to do one thing, and his head told him to think about it. The plantation was not big, and the slave population was limited as to choices. Remembering what that slave,

Jim, had mentioned about running away to find his Indian girlfriend, he decided it best overall to find what he was looking for elsewhere.

He remembered that one of Norton Carter's slaves had mentioned that every Sunday, there was a small group that gathered together on Carter's plantation for a church service. Carter had become a religious man after being whipped in his wild-bunch days. He had a circuit minister ride to his plantation every Sunday to give a service to whites and blacks alike. Anybody from anyplace was invited to attend.

Andrew decided it might be time to get religion, and maybe, if he was lucky, a girlfriend, at best—or, at worst, one of those *pleasure* women Ignatius had mentioned. He asked Martin if he could have a pass on Sunday. "Yes, but be back by dark 'cause I don't want to have to get you out of Will Bryan's jail. And watch out for slavers. They'll kidnap you as soon as they see you. You'd be prime meat for those fellows."

He did not find a girlfriend. What he found was that he was prime meat for more than just slavers. Girls, black and white, younger and older, looked at him in a curious way, and talked to each other in their small groups, looking at him and breaking into giggles. A woman he judged to be in her late thirties or early forties and anything but shy approached him. "You're Andrew aren't you?" she said.

"Yes, ma'am. How'd you know my name?"

"Word gets around about the privileged slave who belonged to Ignatius Attaway."

"I'm not privileged anymore. I work same as everybody."

"Sure, you do," she quipped. "Just thought I'd mention I live on Ed Littlefield's plantation...the last cabin in the back, close by the swamp."

Andrew's religious days were over. He had a newfound interest in the cabin, and it was not about hunting or fishing. That was where you could find him any Sunday. Well, sometimes, it would be another cabin—also close to the swamp but on the other side, the swamp being rather narrow, a half mile or so across at this point. Had he forgotten Ignatius's warning about staying clear of Littlefield and Big Bull? True to form, Andrew, fearless as ever, took his chances. Ignatius' other warnings also rang in his ears, but for now, the woman across the swamp was just fine.

WITHOUT IGNATIUS AROUND, and with Marie's jack not having a non-kin prospect to mate with in the future, Martin stopped Ignatius's mule-breeding program. It had been his idea, not Martin's, in the first place. Andrew tried to talk to Martin about how disappointed he thought Ignatius would be if the program were not continued. Martin explained to him that Ignatius had been an old man with time on his hands. Breeding mules was not the business of the farm. Martin and Mary had to run the plantation, and all of their resources and time had to go into it. When explained in this manner, Andrew saw the logic of what Martin was saying, and no more was said about the subject.

BOTH THE MARE—AND, later, Marie—had healthy foals. Not to be out-done by a pair of equines, Mary had one son and two daughters, one after the other and in that order, with, as Martin liked to say, "…another keeping warm in the barn." They named the boy Ignatius, and sometime referred to him as Little Iggy. The first girl was named Martha, after Martin's mother, and the second girl was named Elizabeth, after Mary's mother. Little Iggy called Andrew Uncle Andy. He called a lot of the slaves uncle this or uncle that. It was just his way. Almost as soon as he could talk, he always had a smile on his face and a greeting for anybody he saw. "Hi, Uncle whoever," he'd say, waving his hand. The girls were just the opposite. Martha, though she could talk if she wanted to, seldom did so unless she wanted something. Elizabeth was stone-faced and wide-eyed, and had not yet begun to talk. Her entire world was trying to understand her existence and the things in it.

The kids were a major responsibility, and required a lot of time. Mary had always partnered with Martin in the management of the plantation. Now, Martin found he was running almost everything by himself. He had to do something about it, as there were not enough hours in the day to get everything done and still spend time with his growing family. He had an idea, and talked with Mary about it. She looked surprised and a little startled at the idea, but after thinking about it and talking more with Martin, she thought it made perfect sense.

ANDREW AND SMITHY talked for a while in their congenial way toward each other, but they had not rekindled the old friendship they once had. After five years, and with Smithy keeping his job and Andrew literally working for him part-time, Smithy began to feel more secure, and came to believe that Andrew would not take his job away as long as he was doing well, as Ignatius had promised. But as has been said, things change.

MARTIN WALKED INTO the blacksmith shop and found Smithy shaping a shoe for one of the plow horses. Smithy, upon seeing Martin, put the shoe down. After wiping the sweat from his head and the surface dirt from his hands, he said, "Yes, sir. Can I help you?"

"The shoe you just put down. You're shaping it, is that correct?"

"I am."

"Can Andrew do that?"

"Andrew?! Sure, it's not difficult, once you understand it and have a little practice. Uh, why do you ask?"

"I'm going to come right out and ask you a question, and I want a straight answer and not a question in return."

For the first time in a long while, Smithy had that terrible feeling about losing his job to Andrew, but felt he might as well get it over with. "Alright," he said. "Go ahead." There was no sir, master or mister in his reply.

"Smithy, if you weren't here—if something happened to you, for instance—could Andrew do your job by himself?"

He knew it. Smithy just plain knew it. He was going to lose his job to the favorite of the plantation. *Sonuvabitch*, he thought, but said, "Guess he could. Am I going to lose my job? I've tried for five years to do my best. What'd I do wrong?"

Martin saw that Smithy was agitated, and said, "Take it easy, Smithy, take it easy. No, you're not going to lose your job if you don't want to."

Martin explained to Smithy his problem of losing Mary to other responsibilities, leaving him worn out. "Smithy, you're a good man. Might be the best man on the plantation. You've proven it over the last five years. Before then, you weren't worth anything. But now…well…you're the best we have. I want you to be my overseer. That means you would run everything there is to do with the other slaves. Want the job?"

"What about Andrew? Are you telling me he's going to take this job?"

"Only if you take the job of overseer. I'm not forcing you, understand. It's your choice. Whoever's going to be the overseer has to do it because he wants the job and knows he can do it."

"I'd have thought you would have asked Andrew."

"Too young—not enough whiskers on his chin, if you know what I mean. You've grown into a responsible asset, and I need you in the position."

"Can I think about it? I like being a blacksmith, and don't know if I want to do something else."

"This is Wednesday; I want an answer by Monday morning. If you accept and don't like the job after one month to the day, you can have your old job back."

"Yes, sir. I'll give you an answer Monday morning."

SMITHY, LIKED HIS new job as overseer, as in some ways, it fit his inherently lazy nature toward physical work. Before the trial month was up, he decided the job was for him. Now he was able to use his head and control others to get a task done. Eventually, gained the respect of not only the slaves, but also the whites. Martin considered his advice and ideas for how to make the plantation more efficient to be of considerable value. But Smithy's distrust of Andrew never went away. Those whiskers Martin had talked about were growing, and Andrew could well be the overseer when Martin judged those whiskers long enough.

CHAPTER IX

HE LOOKED AT them: two beautiful wood ducks and a third shot up so bad he thought it not worth bothering with. He would toss it deep into the swamp, and after he brought down one more, there would be enough to cook himself a meal at the cabin: duck on a stick, roasted with a glaze of caramelized sugar and rum.

He loaded the musket and let it rest against the blind's inner wall, hoping nothing would fly by until he finished drinking the cup of hot rum he had heated over a small fire at the bottom of the blind—something he learned from Ignatius. Ignatius used to joke that to keep warm in the blind, one had to hold a hot cup of rum in one hand and stick one's trigger finger in a hot gun barrel, and hope the ducks would wait until the rum had been drunk and the finger warmed. Then it would be time to pick up the musket and wait, and, as a duck was doing its flyby, aim and follow through. Then dinner would almost be ready.

As he brought the cup to his lips, he heard something splashing in back of him. Something, or someone, was walking through the water.

"You in there, nigger? Come out so I can see you, or I'll shoot you through those reeds. I caught myself a runaway."

"What the…!" At the sound of the voice Andrew stood up and turned to see Big Bull, pistol in hand and pointed straight at him.

"I'm not a runaway."

"Come out of there, and I want to see those hands high up," said Big Bull.

Andrew let the cup of rum drop and squeezed out of the blind.

"What're you doing in there if you're not running away and hiding?"

He had to think fast. If Big Bull knew he was hunting, he would know Andrew had a musket, and that would be all the excuse Big Bull needed to shoot him.

"This is Sunday, my day off, and I was hiding in here and drinking rum. Please don't tell anybody. I wasn't running away."

"Damn nigger! I know damn well you were running away and I'm going to turn you in. I can use the reward."

"You don't know nothin'. They gonna tell you I'm no runaway, and I'm gonna laugh at you. I got permission to be here, and you don't. Miz Mary and Mister Martin gonna tell you to get off this land."

Andrew's impertinence pushed Big Bull over the edge. He set a smile on his face and steadied his aim on Andrew. "I don't take that kind of talk from a nigger slave. Think I'm about to show you some manners."

He eased the pistol down, letting the hammer go to half-cock, and slipped it into his belt. He undid the binding holding a coiled whip at his waist. With a practiced motion, he let the whip whistle through the air several times, cracking it loudly with each swing. This was his way of putting fear into whoever was going to feel the bite of the whip. Big Bull unleashed the whip and the tip followed, striking Andrew alongside his left arm.

Big Bull again had the whip in motion, and was drawing back to unleash another. Andrew rolled out of the way of the forthcoming slap of leather. The whip missed its target, and Andrew reached over the blind and grabbed the musket. Big Bull was moving his arm back to swing the whip again when he saw Andrew shouldering his weapon. Big Bull dropped the whip and began to reach for his pistol. By the time his hand hit the pistol's handle, a flash of smoke and fire spewed from Andrew's musket and a mass of shot blew from the barrel, finding its way to Big Bull's chest. His chest exploded red, and the already-lifeless body arched backward and over. There was a splash as Big Bull's back slapped the shallow water. A black snake wriggled to escape from beneath the dead man, and swam to safer cover.

"YOU KNOW," SAID Martin, to Andrew with Mary looking on, "once Big Bull is discovered missing, they're going to look for him. Unless some animal drags him off somewhere, they're going to find him where it's known you spend your time, and it won't take long for them to put two and two together. A black man, even a free black man, has no defense in a court. If someone says or even suggests you did it, you're guilty, and they're going to hang you. At best, you might be able to tell your side of the story, but they're still going to hang you without your day in court."

Mary shook her head in agreement, and her eyes watered. "Andrew, Martin's right. You've got to go away from here."

"But where am I going to go? I don't know anyplace to go; don't know how to get anyplace. All I know is how to ride a mule, and he don't know where to go, either."

Martin and Mary locked eyes, and they talked to each other through those eyes. They each knew what the other was thinking, and their nods were only noticeable to each other.

"I'll get Miz Millie," said Mary.

"Tell her to hurry," said Martin.

Andrew asked, "Miz Millie?! What's she got to do with this?"

"She'll tell you, and you do everything she tells you to do. Understand?"

.

"No. I don't understand."

"You're about to be helped, Andrew. Trust us, trust Miz Millie, and trust Isaac. Isaac is going to arrange things for you to get out of here safely."

"Isaac?" Andrew whispered low.

While they were waiting for Mary to bring Miss Millie, Martin began to explain to Andrew what was happening. "Andrew, you knew Ignatius a long time, and he talked with you about his philosophy of life and how he thought a person should live and grow. But there are some things he never told you, because he didn't think you were ready, and he didn't think other people should know right then."

"I don't know what you mean, Mister Martin."

"I'll tell you. You might not remember that day when Iggy and Mary and I went to Bryan Town; it was the day when the wagon was outfitted with the extra seat in the back for Iggy."

"I remember now, but I never thought about it since."

"We went to Bryan Town to sign papers with our solicitor. Iggy sold you to Mary and me for the sum of one pound—consideration to make it legal. Then, Mary and I signed papers setting you free. You've been a free man ever since."

Sometimes, a person hears something, and the implications are confusing. It takes a little time for the brain to process it, to put it in order. Then it is still not always clear. After a moment or two, Andrew said, "Free? The right time? What do you mean the right time?"

"Iggy wanted you free, because he believed with all his heart that nobody should be a slave to anybody. He'd have set every slave on his plantation free if he thought it would do any good. He couldn't do it, because if he had, he'd have been ostracized by every other plantation owner for miles around; there could've even been violence. Slavery is a way of life here, and there is nothing we can do about it…at least not now. On a small scale, he was able to help a few slaves gain their freedom, and you're one of them. He didn't do it just because you were his friend and he loved you as a son, but because he believed you had it in you to do something with your freedom. He also confided in me that while you had great possibilities, you were too satisfied. He had to find a way to wean you, to get you on your own. Freedom was the first step. Being independent was the second, and something he didn't get the chance to…well, get you to understand. That's why he was always talking to you about developing responsibility…planning your path, and so forth. If he had told you that you were free, he thought it would go to your head. Now, you don't have a choice, and you're going to either swim or drown. All I can say is to remember what Iggy told you, and swim."

"Loved me like a son?" Andrew asked, shaking his head side to side. "He treated me well, and I guess you could say we was friends, but I don't think he thought much more of me than that."

"Next time you see your reflection in a mirror or pool of water, take a good look at yourself. Iggy looked at you hard the first time he saw you at the jail waiting to be sold. He saw faint traces of himself in you, and it almost caused him to panic. He thought you were probably his grandson or maybe great-grandson. Ever notice he had green eyes like you?"

"Those wild days he told me about?"

"Yeah. Those wild days."

"Damn!"

Mary returned with Miss Millie, who looked around and saw Andrew in conversation with Martin.

Martin, seeing Miss Millie, looked up and said, "Miz Millie, Andrew's got himself into a situation, never mind what, and we're going to need Isaac's help. You know what I'm talking about."

"Yes, sir. I know what you're talking about. You want me to go to Isaac's and tell him what's happening."

"Tell him he's got another candidate, and I said it's alright."

"I'll leave now."

"Thank you, Miz Millie. Be careful."

"Always am."

"Andrew," said Martin, "hide in the cellar until it's dark. I'll let you know when, and then run around the edge of fields as low as you can, and go see Isaac. Don't worry about anything else—not the mule, the donkey, not us, not anything. Leave your clothes and everything else. Tell Isaac what you told us. You don't know it, but he's your only chance. Don't say goodbye to anybody, not even your mule. Keep your eyes and ears open for anybody you might run across, and avoid them at all costs. Don't go close to a road. It's important no one sees you. Are you sure you weren't seen coming here?"

"I don't know for sure, 'cause I was busy running, but I knew I had to keep low and out of sight."

Martin added, "Take the musket with you. It might just save your life again, and we don't want it around here. Too many conclusions could be drawn by anybody seeing it."

"WONDER WHERE HE'S going," Smithy said to himself. He returned to the bachelor's cabin with a smile across his face. He was thinking about the woman on the other side of the swamp.

ANDREW CREPT UP on Isaac's house. A wide oak hid him from the view of anybody who might be outside. There was movement on the front porch, and the moon and stars highlighted a figure just short of recognizable. It could be one of Isaac's slaves, or it could be Isaac. How was he to know? He waited, and looked around. There was light coming from one of the structures at the rear of the house; Andrew knew it to be the slave quarters, if his memory served him right. Though he had been to Isaac's place before, he had not paid any particular attention to the layout. All he had been concerned about was the horses and oxen, as he led them to his shop to be shod and returned the same way.

The front door opened, and another figure stepped out. It was the unmistakable silhouette of a woman. She sat down next to the other figure and put her arm around his shoulders. "She has to be Isaac's woman," thought Andrew.

Andrew watched for a while, and decided to take his chance. "Mister Isaac, Mister Isaac," he called in a low voice.

Isaac didn't move, because his hearing was bad, but the woman did. She straightened her body, and looked past Isaac toward the tree. She tapped Isaac on the shoulder and pointed toward Andrew. Isaac stood up. Motioning for the woman to do the same, he led her into the house. He came out again holding his musket, and the inside lights dimmed.

"Who's there?" he demanded. "I said who's there? If you don't want to be shot, come out from that tree."

Andrew left his musket standing against the tree, raised his hands, and stepped out into view, hoping he wouldn't be an easy target.

"It's me. Andrew Attaway. I need to see you."

"You armed?"

"My musket's behind the tree."

"What you want to see me about?"

"Mister Martin and Miz Mary said you could help me. They sent Miz Millie to tell you."

"You keep those arms of yours about your head and come over here."

Andrew looked around to be sure no one else was nearby, and walked to Isaac's porch with his arms straight up.

"What you got on your mind, Andrew? Miz Millie came earlier to tell me I'm to help you go north, but I need to know why."

Andrew related the events of the day, and when he got to the part about shooting Big Bull, Isaac interrupted him. "Stop right there. It's time for you to come into the house. Put your arms down. You look like you're trying to hold up the sky or somethin'." He motioned Andrew toward the door of the house.

Inside, the woman stepped back against a wall and pointed a musket directly at Andrew. Isaac motioned for the woman to put the piece down, indicating that this visitor was alright.

She was pregnant, and there were signs of other children scattered about the room. Andrew thought he had seen the woman before, but could not remember where; somewhere in the distant past.

Without an introduction or explanation, Isaac said, "Continue with what you were telling me outside. I want to hear it from you."

Andrew finished his story.

"And they told you to come to me, huh?" Isaac asked.

"Yes, sir, they said you were my only chance."

"If I help you, you're going to make promises. I'm talking about prom- ises you swear to keep. Promises that mean you won't tell a living soul. If you ever say anything about what I'm talking about to anybody, that's anybody, Andrew, you're going to be just as dead as if Big Bull had torn your head off. Are you willing to go ahead with this? Because if we go any further, you will have promised your soul, and I'll see to it you no longer take a breath if you go back on those promises. This is serious stuff—what you want to do?"

"Mister Isaac, I don't have a choice. I don't know what you're talking about that I can't talk about, but…alright. Whatever it is you say I shouldn't talk about is what I won't talk about."

Isaac felt an angered hot flush come over him, and wondered how this scared, meek, could-be coward had ended up on his doorstep. Annoyed, he raised his voice and said, "Wake up, Andrew! Quit playing the obedient slave. As of now, you are no longer a slave, with or without papers. Quit calling me *sir* and *mister*. Quit being the young, stupid, obedient slave boy. Your life has changed now—forever changed. You're going to be a wanted man, and getting caught is going to mean you're going to be hanged as soon as they can throw a rope over a tree limb, and they will go after everybody who helped you. If you can't understand what I'm telling you, I don't want a damn thing to do with you. You've grown from a skinny runt into a man's strong body, but you never became a man. That's something you've got to do now! I mean right this minute! Do you or don't you understand?"

Andrew was looking into the intense, almost flaming eyes of Isaac, and he heard every word. He reflected upon his life in one moment, and felt almost ashamed; Andrew the privileged slave was what he was called.

Isaac waited, and he saw Andrew's inner reflection and realization of self. Andrew's face was like looking into a clear, calm pool of water that had just been disturbed by a rock thrown in. Waves of water radiated out until the pool became calm and clear once again, except now, the image in the water had changed into something that had not been there before, the ripples in the pond having washed aside the sediment to reveal its true bottom.

"What's it going to be, Andrew? Are you a man? Are you ready for what's ahead? Mind you, if caught, you might be threatened with being killed if you don't reveal who helped you or where you were helped, but even then, you can't reveal a thing. If you say yes, I'll help you. Otherwise, you're on your own, and good luck. If you say yes, from here on out, you're locked into that agreement. Ready?"

Andrew didn't answer; he was still in his epiphany.

Again, Isaac prodded him. "Andrew?"

Andrew looked at Isaac and said, "I'm ready." There was no *yes, sir;* there would be no more yes-sirs, no more masters, no more, no more, no more. Andrew was his own man, his own master.

"That's what I had to hear. That's what I had to see, and I see it in you. Take a deep breath. You're on your way to a new beginning. Hang on. It's not going to be easy. But life isn't easy, leastwise a life that's worth living."

Had not Ignatius and Jim said something similar?

"Get that musket you left by the tree," Isaac said. "Then go 'round back to where you see the light coming from one of those slave quarters—there'll only be one cabin lit. The man inside will tell you what to do. I'll go ahead and fill you in on what you can expect."

Andrew set himself down to listen to Isaac.

"The man, we call him Raymond, is going to take you to a hiding place. You're to remain there for maybe a week, maybe more. It all depends on how we feel about who's watchin' what's happening around here. You might be there a couple of weeks, don't know for sure. It just depends on what the patrollers and other busybodies are up to."

"Then what?"

"Then we take you north. Maybe we take you south first, and then west, and then south again before going north. Not many make it going directly north. Gotta be smart and watch all the signs about what's happenin'. Now go and do what I told you."

Andrew gave a nod to Isaac, and his journey began.

HE APPROACHED THE cabin slowly and with caution, trying to look through the window to see what and who might be inside. This was of no avail, as the window was draped with cloth of a kind, and only shadows could be seen. He knocked on the weathered door, and it shook and moved with each rap. "Moment," said the voice inside.

The door opened, and the voice from within said, "You Andrew?"

"I'm Andrew. Isaac said for me to come see a Raymond. You him?"

"I'm Raymond. Come in."

Andrew entered just enough to look side to side. Raymond looked to be older than Isaac but younger than he remembered Ignatius being. Satisfied, he stepped in further so Raymond could close the door. It was a typical family slave cabin with a fireplace at one end. A steel pot hung over glowing coals. A crude bed close to the fireplace and a small table with a single chair made of split wood completed the furnishings of the small cabin.

"On your way to freedom, huh? Well, good luck. It's going to be a hard journey. You're going to work your black butt off…maybe even get it shot off. You sure about this?"

"I'm sure."

"Rumor has it someone done in Big Bull. You hear anything about that?"

Surprised by the comment, Andrew tried his best to look unaffected. "No. What happened?"

"Don't know any details. C'mon, ain't got time for this kind of talk. Just thought you might know something 'bout it. Raymond went to a box, removed several candles, and put them in a bag. Andrew noticed the man walked slightly bent over and placed a hand into the small of his back. "Follow me, Andrew."

As they left the cabin, Raymond said, "Watch where you're going. We got to move fast, but don't want to look as if we're runnin' away from anything. Don't want to be exposed any longer than we gotta."

They turned left out of the cabin. The moonlight was only enough for Andrew to make out objects, and he noticed that Raymond seemed to be having difficulty seeing.

"You see a root cellar somewhere up front of us about a hundred feet?" Raymond asked.

Andrew stopped for a second, looked ahead, and moved his eyes from side to side. "Yes. It's almost straight ahead. Hard to see for sure."

"Thought so. These eyes ain't so good anymore. I do better in daytime."

At a hurried walk, they came to an earthen embankment with doors to the root cellar.

"This is what you're going to call home for the next few days."

"What? In here? If anybody's going to be looking for me, this is going to be one of the first places they'd look."

"That's what we want them to do. You'll see. Open one of those doors while I light a candle."

Andrew raised the door closest to him and let it swing open and down to the ground. The two descended the short flight of wood stairs, and Raymond took a look in back of them to see if there was any movement. "Now, Andrew, close the door." After the door was closed, Raymond set the candle in a candle holder on the wall. In front of them was a pile of potatoes stacked to the roof.

Andrew was about to ask Raymond what was going on when Raymond said, "We've got to move all those potatoes from where you see them to where we're standing. In back of them is another door that leads to your hiding place. Let's get to moving them, and after you get into the other room, I've got to move all of them back. Wish I was a younger fellow."

A good hour went past as the two moved the potatoes. As they worked, Raymond replaced burned candles with new. After most of the potatoes had been moved, a small, maybe two-foot-square door was uncovered, and after a few more minutes, enough of the tubers had been moved to access it.

"Open that door, Andrew. Here, take a candle and look around. There might be a spider or two, but there won't be anything else."

The door swung inward, in case whoever was inside had to get out for some reason without the help of others. It would not be too difficult a task to move potatoes from the outside to the inside of the hideout, thus allowing an escape.

"Go ahead. Look around," Raymond repeated. "Crawl in, and I'll show you around."

Andrew got down on his stomach and inched his way through the door. Raymond followed. The room was not more than four feet high, and maybe ten foot square. Looking up, Andrew saw that the ceiling was braced with timbers covered with planking. The floor had a thick layer of straw. Iron pots with wood covers, piles of corn still on the cob, and bunches of carrots, cabbage heads, and squash lay in neat piles along one side of the dirt room.

"Can't build a fire down here, so eat 'em raw. I've never heard of rats or mice or any other critter getting in here, but if it does happen, think of them as food, and invite them to dinner." Raymond laughed at his own joke, and Andrew just tried to accept what fate had dished out.

"There's drinking water inside those iron pots, except for that last one. It has a smoked deer hindquarter. Ain't nothing better than chewin' on the stuff. Just take your knife and cut off a slice and chew on it. Hope you don't smoke, 'cause that or a cooking fire wouldn't be good in here. You can light a candle for a short time, only long enough to give your eyes a bit of exercise. There's fresh air entering through a hollowed-out log that runs from over there, see? In the corner, up through a few feet of dirt. Outside, it can't be seen. I don't think anybody will ever find it; I haven't been able to, even when I'm looking."

Andrew was trying to understand everything Raymond was telling him. At any other time, he would not want anything to do with this situation. He was going to be in a trap.

"Don't smell too bad down here—guess the lag's still working. As you breathe, you let out bad air, and it has to get out of here, or you're going to die. It finds its way out the cellar door and that hollow log. Stand under the log, and you can feel a breeze; long as you can feel it, you're alright. Oh, by the way, that there wood slab over in that other corner is where you do your business. Just pull it back and let it go in the hole below. We've never cleaned it out, and probably never will. I guess nature just takes care of those things. If you look up through the hollow log, you should be able to tell if it's day or night. That's about all I can tell you. We had one fellow down here who told us he spent just about all his time looking up through the hole."

"What happened to him?" inquired Andrew.

"Far as I know, he made it north. We took him out of here, and the first thing we did was give him a bath. After that, his handlers took him, and I never heard any more."

"His name wasn't Jim, was it?"

"Don't know his name, but Jim don't sound familiar. Why you ask?"

"I just knew a fellow by that name once. He ran away, and I never heard anything more about him."

"You know, I do remember a runaway named Jim. You're not talking 'bout that slave who was up for auction years ago, and killed a couple of slavers getting away? Why, 'course you are. He was a slave under the overseer you got in trouble about. Uh oh! I wasn't supposed to let on I know 'bout that. Tell you what, Andrew. Let's not talk about it right now. But no, that Jim never went through here."

CHAPTER X

BEING CONFINED, BEING in solitary, or being buried alive is one of the most difficult, horrible situations in which any person could ever find himself. There is no stimulus, no interaction, and no focus; there is nothing to allow you to find your bearings. A day? Sure, anyone can do it for a day. Three or four, and it starts getting bad—real bad. You think over and over again about everything that ever happened to you. If you didn't believe in a god before, you do now, and you keep praying, "God, get me out of here, and I'll do anything you want." That doesn't help; your god doesn't answer. How each individual copes with this seemingly eternal loneliness differs from the next person, so to each his own on how to keep from going insane.

Andrew could always open the door, move the potatoes aside, and make it north by himself. But he never considered the idea. In Andrew's case, he thought about what Isaac had prodded him on. What was it he had said— something about being a man? At the time, he was thinking about what he hadn't done. Now he had time to think about what he *would* do.

How many days had it been? Andrew didn't know. He thought five or six, but had lost track, and was unsure. He heard a noise coming from the direction of the door. *Did they catch me, or is it time to leave?* Looking up the pipe, he did not see a hint of light, and supposed it was night. He picked up his musket, and, hoping the old charge of powder would still go off, waited.

"Andrew!" he heard someone call. "Open the door and help us. It's time for you to leave."

His heart beat hard and fast as he lit a candle. Andrew unlatched the door. Potatoes fell into his prison, and he pushed them aside. A hand and an arm reached through the entrance. Then a face looked in.

"You had enough of this, or do you want to stay a while?" asked Isaac.

"Get me out of here," Andrew said as he pushed himself through the door and into the root cellar proper. Before going outside, they piled potatoes back over the hidden doorway.

Outside, Andrew stretched and looked up. It was a totally black night, except for the billions of stars shining throughout the clear sky. He stretched again, and Isaac said, "No time for that. Raymond, take this man to the stable, and get him cleaned and dressed. Make sure he takes a bath in the watering trough. Polecats smell better than he does."

Raymond grabbed Andrew by an arm and led him to the stable. There, Raymond guided Andrew toward the watering trough and motioned for him to get in. The water was cold at first, but it was refreshing. "Oh, but to lay in it for an hour or so," he was thinking. That was not to be. Raymond told him to use the lye soap next to the trough, and to hurry up.

Out of the trough and dripping wet, he stood and looked around. Raymond pointed to a pile of clothes. "While you put those on, I'll explain what's going to happen next, and how you're going to get out of here."

Andrew picked up the clothes and whistled. "These are pretty fancy. I'll stand out like a...what I heard white men say...a dandy."

"That's almost how we want you to appear. Those are driver's clothes. The kind drivers wear when they take wealthy masters and other white people from one place to another. You're going to be driving a white man down the south road."

"I'm going to what?" Andrew questioned. "That don't make no sense at all."

"It does when you consider this white man is your friend, and he's gonna get you out of this place with the two of you pretending he owns you, and you're driving him."

"Where'd you find a white man to do that?"

"Just get dressed and let's get going."

While Andrew dressed, he wondered what was taking place. Was he getting himself out, or was everything going to come to an end, a bad end? A white man who would risk getting a slave out of this situation was rare.

"You look good enough," Raymond said. "Let's get going."

They walked over to the back of Raymond's cabin and came upon a one-horse buggy, except it was not a horse. It was a mule—Andrew's mule. He glanced at the man in the passenger seat, stunned.

The man said, "C'mon, Andy. Climb up in the driver's seat, and let's get going. I'll fill you in on the details after we're on our way. We gotta get going fast."

Still stunned, Andrew said, "Mister Blackiston!"

"I said let's go, Andrew," Martin said, returning Andrew's surprised look with a smile. "We've got to get you out of here."

As soon as they were on their way, Andrew asked, "You do this all the time?"

"Now and again, when everything's right—and now when everything's wrong."

"That's my mule, isn't he, Mister Blackiston?"

"You can drop the mister and master stuff, Andrew. Just call me Martin…please. I believe you and Isaac already went through that. There may be appropriate times to use those titles, but not with me. Save it for some other time and place. Yes, he's your mule. Thought you might like to drive him one more time. Here, take the reins.

"After we get down the road about fifteen miles, we're going to meet another man. He's going to take you by a route he knows going north. Then I'll return to the farm, and you'll do whatever's in your destiny."

The morning star was visible in the east, and soon it would be dawn. Martin reached into a pouch attached to the buggy's dash and pulled out an envelope. "This is the document Mary and I signed granting you complete freedom. There are four exact copies, and Mary and I each have one. Our solicitor has the other. This one is for you. You shouldn't have any trouble going about your business as a free man. Your problem is going to be going about your business as a wanted man. If you can go far enough north, you may be alright." Andrew put the document in his pocket.

"Thank you, Mist…Martin. I owe you my life. Thank you again."

"You were always good for the Attaways and Blackistons, Andrew. We thank you."

THE SUN WAS high and the shadows short when they noticed two riders coming from behind. As the riders came abreast, Martin tipped his hat, and the riders tipped theirs in return. Rather than overtake them, the riders fell back behind.

"Neither of them is the man we're to meet, Andrew. Just keep going."

Andrew chanced a glance over his shoulder at the two riders. "Those two are following us, Martin. You think something's wrong?"

"Don't know. Just keep going."

Martin removed his pistol from his waist belt and cocked the hammer. "Steady, Andrew. Just keep going."

The riders increased their pace and came about on each side of the buggy. Both took out pistols and pointed them at Andrew and Martin. Martin held his pistol under his cape, waiting for the next move.

"Hold those horses up, boy," commanded one of the riders. "We've a few questions."

Martin motioned Andrew to pull up, and Andrew did so.

"What's the meaning of this?" Martin asked the pair.

"Your driver looks like a runaway we've been tracking, and you could be a passer. We're thinking this man is the runaway, and you might be, too."

"You're out of your mind," Martin said, raising his pistol.

The bounty hunter on his right and a little behind had his pistol already pointed at Martin, and let loose a shot that caught Martin just behind his right ear, scattering blood and skin over Andrew. Martin slumped to the dash and fell from the buggy, caught in the traces and rigging.

At the sound of the shot, Andrew's mule raised and started to run, but the second bounty hunter was quick to ride in front of them, grabbing the leathers and calming them.

"Get down from there," said the first bounty hunter to Andrew.

Andrew climbed down, looking at Martin and hoping to see some sign he was alive.

"Pull your friend out of there to the side of the road."

Martin's head laid on the ground, covered with mud and blood; his body hung down and was held by his legs, caught and twisted around the reins and traces of the buggy.

Andrew untangled Martin and pulled him clear of the rig. Martin's eyes were filled with mud, and his tongue hung out of his open mouth. Andrew wiped Martin's eyes and was trying to see if Martin was alive or dead when one of the hunters said, "Leave him be. Get in the back of the buggy, nigger."

Once in the buggy, he was chained so he could not escape or reach the bounty hunters in the front seat.

"We've got to get rid of that dead whatever he is. Wonder if there was a reward on him, too?"

"Don't know, but a dead runaway isn't going to bring a reward; he don't look much like a nigger, anyhow." They dragged Martin's body deep into the underbrush and let him be.

They then tied their horses to the back of the buggy and slapped the reins on the mule's back, shouting a command for the mule to start out.

"Add the reward money and what we can get for the mule and buggy, and I'd say we done pretty good."

CHARLES CRAMMER, HEARING the approaching buggy, came out of his modest house and onto the porch to await the visitors. Seeing Crammer on the porch, the bounty hunters pulled up in front of him. The first of them addressed Crammer, and said, "We've got your escaped slave. Had to kill his buddy, but here he is."

"What buddy you talking about? There was no one else I wanted, just the goddamned slave that ran away."

One looked at the other as if to say, "You talk too much."

The other tried to cover his verbal mistake, and hoped Crammer would not dwell on it. "Probably somebody was trying to beat us to it. Nothing to worry about. Anyhow, here's your nigger. Now that reward."

"Let me look him over," said Crammer.

Crammer looked Andrew over, and, scratching his head for a moment, looked at the bounty hunters. He said, "Gentlemen, I've never seen this man before. I'm afraid you've got the wrong one. Don't know 'bout the man you killed. Afraid you've got yourself a problem."

"This ain't your runaway?" asked the first bounty hunter.

"Nope.

One bounty hunter looked at the other with a silent question about what they were going to do. Crammer picked up on it.

"Tell you men what I'm going to do. My reward for the runaway was a hundred pounds. I'll buy this slave from you for half that, and that's all any of us hears about any of this from now on. That okay with you?"

"Got to talk to my partner," said one. "Give us a minute."

"You've got just a minute, or this poor man and the dead man are your problems, and I'll send all of you out of here."

The two bounty hunters turned and spoke low to each other. They seemed to be discussing what to do. They turned back to Crammer and said, "We'll take the deal, Crammer."

"Thought so," said Crammer as he gave the coins he already had counted out in his hand to the bounty hunters.

The bounty hunters took the coins, and with no more conversation, got into the buggy and turned it toward Bryan Town. As soon as they were out of sight of the farm, one said to the other, "We didn't do too bad when you consider we got fifty pounds, a buggy, and a mule."

"Wonder what we can get for this rig in Bryan Town?"

"Want to go after Crammers slave now? That hundred pounds would come in handy."

"Too much trouble. He won't be on the road same's the other nigger was. We'd have to chase him through hell to catch him. I don't want to work that hard."

SOME SUMMER NIGHTS can be cold or on the chilly side, while others can be hot and humid; this night was hot and humid. Mosquitoes swarmed, poking at Andrew and sucking his blood as he lay on the ground, chained to an old wagon wheel. He was a strong and able man, capable of lifting the wheel and running with it. But where would he run? Again, he thought over his options, and the only one he could think of was to wait and see what developed. Thinking through his situation, he looked about and saw a boulder that would serve his purpose. He decided it would do no good to show the document to the man who would hold him captive. He stood up and carried the wheel to the rock where he removed the document from his waistband, stuck it under the rock, returned to where he had been, and slept as best he could—which was not much.

Come morning, he woke up when he felt someone kick his leg and say, "What do we have here? What's your name, boy?"

"Name's Andrew. Got here last night."

"I know about that, and that's all I want to hear. I'm the overseer. What you good at doing?"

He noticed the overseer was a white man, but he had faint characteristics typical of someone with black blood in their veins. "I'm a blacksmith, and do a fair job of horseshoeing."

"We've got someone to do that. Don't need another. You do anything else?"

"No."

"Guess you're going to be working the fields. You get Sunday off if you don't mess up during the week. Understand?"

"I understand."

"Good." He turned to the wheel, and with the heel of his boot, smashed the spoke Andrew's chains were wrapped around. "Spokes or slaves, that's how I take care of problems. The woman here will show you where to go."

An older chestnut-colored woman behind the overseer stepped forward. "Mister," she said to Andrew, "follow me."

"Get him out there before long," said the overseer. "We've got a lot to do today."

"I'll get him out there when I get him out there. Things take time to do it right."

"Well…hurry it up."

Andrew stood up and took a long, unhurried stretch. The old woman led him to a cabin and motioned him inside. "Don't take too long to look around. This is where you're going to live. Take a look, and follow me to the field."

He entered the cabin and found it to be the same as the usual slave cabin. This one had beds for a half-dozen slaves. A couple of beds had personal items scattered about on them, while the others did not, so he figured he would be sharing the cabin with two other men. With no other clothes than the fancy clothes of a driver he was wearing, he turned and motioned to the old lady that he was ready to go.

The old lady led him to the field and stopped. She said, "You're to wait here until the overseer comes." In a whisper she said, "I'm sorry," and left.

As Andrew watched the old lady walk away, he heard a horse approaching from behind. Turning to look at the source of the noise, he saw the overseer.

The overseer dismounted and approached Andrew. "You took too long. I'm going to teach you to obey my orders if we're to get along." With a signal of his hand, a dozen or more field slaves approached and circled Andrew. "You're going to learn that what I say is the law, and you don't have any friends to help you. Hope you get it right, 'cause there ain't been many who get a second chance." The slaves surrounding Andrew moved closer to him. Afraid, and not having thought it through, Andrew threw punches at the pack of slaves. He landed lefts and rights, and blood flowed from their mouths and noses. One slave went down holding his side; another gasped for breath and held his throat where his wind pipe was smashed. It was not to last; the overseer crashed his pistol down on Andrew's head, and Andrew sank to the ground.

"You're one tough nigger," the overseer said to Andrew, who was unconscious. "You're more trouble than you're worth. You just killed a good nigger, 'cause he ain't moving, even when I kick him. We didn't gain anything by getting you. Master Crammer ain't going to be happy when I tell him about this."

Crammer, hearing the commotion, was already on his way. He came up on horseback, looked at the dead slave on the ground, and asked what had happened. The overseer told him, and Crammer cursed and ranted for what seemed like hours. In reality, it wasn't that long, but it was long enough that everyone there knew he was mad as hell, and hell would soon break out.

"Give him ninety-nine. Let's see if the black bastard can take it." He turned his horse and galloped away to the house at full speed.

The overseer motioned to the mob of slaves, who were already mad enough to draw and quarter Andrew for killing one of their own. They grabbed Andrew and dragged him to two oak trees, where a felled branch had been tied across to make a gantry. The overseer had a few silent words with one of the slaves, who nodded his head in understanding. He took off at a run, and soon returned with a block and tackle, which, in turn, was fixed to the cross branch. After stripping Andrew of his clothes they hoisted him up, by his tied wrists, until his feet barely touched the ground.

"One of you get a bucket of water and toss it on him. No use wasting a good whipping on someone who's not awake to feel it. Hope he ain't dying on me."

The overseer untied a whip hanging from his saddle. He let the whip out full length and walked toward Andrew, doing a few practice swings along the way, the tip snapping with each one. Paying no attention to whether or not Andrew was conscious, he said, "You get in trouble again, and it'll be two hundred. This time, just ninety-nine."

He pointed to one of the slaves, and the slave came over to him. He gave the whip to the slave. Speaking to Andrew, the overseer said, "Slaves do the whippin' 'round here. You ain't got no friends. Nobody is friends to nobody. You plan on running, and you're going to get turned in." The overseer nodded to the slave.

The first hit was unbelievably painful. Andrew had never felt anything like it, and was dazed. By the time he understood what was happening, another strike had fallen across his back.

"Slower," barked the overseer. "He's got to savor each one."

By the sixth or seventh, Andrew began to wretch, and he threw up, with most of the vomit running down the front of his body. His legs became weak, and he couldn't support himself on his toes as he hung from his bindings.

Almost ten minutes passed until the overseer said, "Fifty. Take him down and get him dressed. He hasn't felt the last twenty, and he'll never make it to ninety-nine. Lower him, and throw water on him whenever you think of it. If you see him move, take him out to the field and give him a hoe. If he don't move by morning, he never will, and you can bury him."

Despite Andrew's size and strength, he had passed out long before the whipping was over. After the other slaves lowered him, he was still unconscious, and lay crumpled—nothing more than a pile of beaten-down humanity. The clothes that had been stripped from Andrew were brought over to him by one of the slaves, but he stopped, not knowing what to do next, as he had never dressed an almost-dead man.

The old woman whispered something to the slave, who motioned to the others. They all went back to the fields. Not caring about what the overseer could do to her, she tended to Andrew. She grabbed Andrew's legs and turned him belly down on the ground, stretching his legs as far as she could. She left him for a few minutes and returned with a bucket of water. The water pouring over Andrew's back caused him to awaken and grimace in pain.

"You're hurting, but that means you're alive; you can still go on. This ain't nothing compared to some of the whippings I've seen. Don't make him mad 'cause he'll do much worse. This was just showing you what he can do if he gets to being mad."

THE REST OF the day, until the sun went down, the fields were worked. The overseer rode about, handing out a slap of the whip whenever he judged that someone was lagging behind. He came to Andrew, who was not working as hard as even the slowest of the others, and thought, *It's a wonder he's out here at all.* The overseer rode on.

The day came to an end, and the slaves walked back to their cabins. Andrew, weak, tired, and in pain, made his way to his cabin and stumbled in. Inside were two other slaves, a man and a woman, fornicating on one of the straw beds. The woman screamed and moaned, and her face wore a smile combined with an expression of pain while the man's head fell backward and his rump set a steady, almost frantic, oscillating pace.

Andrew, too tired to pay attention, fell face down on one of the straw beds. His wounds had stopped bleeding, but remained open, and his own sweat was making them sting. He lay in agony, tired but unable to doze off, thinking, *Got to get out of this somehow.*

A hand touched his arm. "Mister, mister," he heard a voice say. "Let me put some of this on your back. It will make it feel better." He opened his eyes and saw the woman he had seen when he first entered the cabin.

"What is it?" he asked.

"Don't know, but it's what we put on cuts on horses. It works for us, too."

She used her fingers to apply the ointment to his open cuts. He recognized the odor of the greasy substance as something he had used before on his own animals. It felt cool, and eased his pain.

The man spoke. "Sorry about the whipping. He didn't pick me to do it just because I happened to be there. He knew you were staying in this cabin." Andrew looked at the face of the voice, but didn't recognize him; at the time, he hadn't thought to look at the man the overseer had picked to whip him. "I had to do a good job on you, or I would've been next. Maybe even Clare here would've been picked to whip me."

Clare went across the room, opened a wooden box, and retrieved something. She brought it to Andrew. "This is salt pork. Eat it, and don't forget where you got it, 'cause you owe me some when you get your allowance." Andrew swallowed it almost whole as Clare gave him a tin cup of water. "There'll be ashcake in the morning. It's about all we get around here, except what they let you grow or raise in back of the cabin. We got mostly beans, some squash, and a few chickens. So maybe you can have an egg in the morning if you help gather 'em and clean the coop."

"I'm called Thomas. What you want to be called?"

He thought about using a different name because he was a wanted man, but decided it would be better to be caught and brought to justice than to work as a slave in these conditions.

"Andrew Attaway."

"Oh!" said Clare. "He's got two names. You must be important, huh?"

"Just the name my master called me. Don't know why."

"Can we call you Andy?"

"I answer to that, too."

"You from around here?" asked Thomas.

"Not too far, I don't think. I belong to the Blackistons and Attaways down the road going to Bryan Town."

"Never heard of those names 'round here."

"How'd you get to this place?" Clare asked.

"I was driving master Blackiston when a couple of riders came on us. They killed him, and I was taken. Your master bought me from them."

Clare looked at Thomas, and they both just shook their heads. "Welcome to the farm," said Thomas.

Clare changed the subject. "We gotta get to tendin' the garden. I'll hoe weeds. You help Thomas."

Andrew wanted to close his eyes and sleep away the pain, but understood that sympathy was not something handed out here, and if he wanted to eat, he had to work. Ignatius had always told him that a man can do a lot more than he thinks he can, and all he has to do is do it. Picking up chicken poop and gathering eggs would be easier than anything else he had been through that day. He got up from his straw bed and followed the other two.

By the light of the moon, they found their way to the back of the cabin, where a small plot of land had been converted to a miniature farm. There were beans growing up dead vines stretched from stakes in the ground to the cabin eaves. On the other side of the plot was squash. The chicken coop and roosting hens were at the end of the plot, almost touching the adjacent cabin's garden.

As Clare hoed, Thomas said to Andrew, "Let's get those eggs first." They opened the coop door and searched for eggs. "Six hens, six eggs. Not bad," Thomas said. The two men dragged the coop along with the hens to a clear space next to the where the coop had been, gathered up the old straw, and put it back in the coop. "We go back an forth every time we clean the coop. Help me pick up the chicken shit." They shoveled the poop with flat planks Thomas had fashioned into something resembling a shovel blade, and dumped the poop where Clare was working. She, in turn, spread it around the beans and squash.

"One more thing," said Thomas. "I'll be right back." He went back into the cabin and came out with a cloth sack. "This is grain for the chickens. Crammer gives it to us in return for eggs."

"Good arrangement."

"Good for Crammer first, and good for us second. Crammer lets us have this garden and chicken coop 'cause that way, it don't cost him as much to feed us, and he gets eggs and vegetables whenever he wants."

Clare joined in. "He don't even buy us clothes. Jus' gives us cloth and we make our own; least they fit that way."

"Don't cross him or the overseer. You already got a taste of what happens if you do."

"How come the old lady gets to talk back to the overseer?"

"The old lady's his mother. Crammer's his father," said Thomas.

"I'll bet his wife is hard to live with 'cause of that."

Clare said, "Crammer doesn't have a wife. I've never seen him with a woman other than the old woman. He doesn't believe in it. He won't let any of his slaves marry, either. Says if any of us end up having babies, he'll sell 'em as soon as they're old enough. Thomas and I've had two, and they was taken and sold as soon as they came off my breasts."

"I'm surprised he gives you Sundays off when he could work you."

"Nope, no work on Sundays. Crammer's got religion, and goes to church every Sunday. They say he's some kind of important person in the church. Don't know what he does, but I've heard he gives 'em lots of money."

"Do the slaves ever go?"

"No, he never lets us leave this place, but every so often, a preacher makes the rounds of the farms and stops here and we have to listen…no exceptions. Tells us if we want to get into the Kingdom of Heaven, we got to believe in somebody called Jesus and do what our masters tell us to do."

"We listen," Clare said. "After the preacher leaves, some of us laugh, and others start saying they believe and want to get to Heaven. Thomas and I take our weekly bath and come back to the cabin and climb in the straw." She paused, and giggled, "Sundays ain't the only days, as you know."

THE FOLLOWING MORNING, some miles south on the road where Martin and Andrew had been stopped by the bounty hunters, seven men camped just off the road in a break in the forest. Of the seven men, one was black and the others were Indians. From the appearance of the Indians, they looked to be Piscataway, a semi-peaceful people, but one never knew for sure what they would do if they had a mind to. The Indians talked to the black man, and he answered in their tongue and shrugged his shoulders. He pointed up the road toward Bryan Town, and the Indians nodded their heads in agreement. They kicked dirt over the campfire and collected their grazing horses. Mounted, they headed toward Bryan Town.

After riding a few miles, they came to a narrow road branching off the main road. One of the Indians pointed to tracks in the road. The tracks were those of a buggy and several horses. The black man read the meaning, and said, "I'd say those tracks came and then returned from the direction of Bryan Town. We'll follow them, and see where they turned around." Following the tracks, they soon came to a farm where slaves were working the fields and an ever-present overseer sat on a horse, keeping watch. Not wanting to be seen, the black man signaled the Indians to fall back. Grouping together, they exchanged words, and after a few minutes rode off in the direction they had come. They settled down in the clearing where they had spent the previous night.

As soon as they arrived, they attended to their tired horses. It wouldn't be long before they would ride the same route from which they had just returned. Someone lit a fire signifying it was time to eat, and after cooking meat of unknown origin, they settled down to make plans for the coming night. There was laughter and discussion, with some becoming exited and loud when they expressed their views on what to do with the supposed enemy. The black man tried to calm them down, saying this was not a raiding party to kill and collect scalps. The Indians were not happy, but after much talk and reasoning, the black man was able to win his point of view; there would be no unnecessary blood spilled.

As the sun began its descent, the party once again prepared their mounts to be ridden. Back they rode to the farm, and to the spot where they had turned around earlier. Leaving one of the Indians to tend to the horses, the black man and Indians crept low onto the farm, heading toward what they figured were slave quarters, where candlelight shone through windows.

There were slaves walking around outside the cabins. The black man knew from experience what it meant; slaves were taking care of their gardens.

Might as well go to the closest one, thought the black man. He signaled the others to stay back, then waved for them to follow as he crept closer to the slave community, looking for his target. The man he chose was old and bald-headed, with a full white beard. An old woman with a head of hair matching the color of the old man's beard worked alongside him. *They'll do*, the black man thought.

He crept up to the old couple. "Psst. Old man."

The old man didn't hear him. The old woman turned at the sound and saw the black man. "Tag," she said. "Someone's callin' you."

"Huh? Where?"

"Over there," she said pointing.

"Who's there?" he asked.

"I'm a slave, same's you. I work for someone else. Just want to ask you a question."

"Hey?" said the old man.

The woman said, "He wants to ask you a question."

"What's he want to know? How to plant somethin'?"

"I don't know. Ask him."

"Where are you? Come on over."

The black man stood up and walked to the old man and woman.

"My name's Jason," the black man said, not telling them his real name. I'm looking for a brother of mine. His name is Andrew. Did he happen to come here in the last day or two? He might be using a different name."

"We ain't supposed to talk about that stuff. I don't want a whippin', ya know. What you gonna do if he is here?"

"Just want to talk to him to see if he's alright so I can tell his mam."

"Tag, we did see that new boy here yesterday, or was it the day before? His name is Andy, or something like that."

"Ain't a good worker, if you ask me. Don't think he's used to workin'."

"Tag, the man just wants to talk to his brother. That's not bad, is it?"

"Guess not. Alright, youngster, I'll tell you where he is, but if you get caught, you're on your own. Understand?"

"Yes, sir, I understand. I didn't talk to you or anybody else."

"You follow me. Act like we do this all the time. Shouldn't be anybody watchin' us this time of night. We all take care of our gardens this time anyhow. Sometimes somebody's got to borrow something from somebody else or help them with something. So if we're amovin' 'round, ain't nobody gonna think nothin' of it."

They walked, and the black man kept to Tag's side as if he knew the way without him.

They came upon one of the shacks, and Tag knocked on the door. Clare opened it. "Tag! What brings you around? You need some help with something?"

"This man needs to talk with his brother. Says his name is Andy. That new man is the only Andy I know of 'round here."

The black man stepped out of the darkness and into the light from the cabin door. He said, "I'm Jason, Andy's brother. I need to talk with him."

She was thinking about how many lashes they'd get if they got found out, when from around the side of the cabin appeared Thomas and Andrew.

"What you need, Tag?" asked Thomas.

Tag looked at Jason and said, "You tell 'em, mister."

"That's my brother," Jason said, indicating Andrew. "I need to talk to him."

Brother! Andrew thought. *What's he saying?*

"Alright, Tag," Thomas said, "I'll handle it from here. You go back to your place and forget everything, understand?"

"I may be old, but I ain't crazy. I forgot it all already." He turned and left, saying, "Good luck, young 'uns, whatever you're up to."

Once in the cabin, Andrew glanced at the man who said he was looking for his brother. His short beard did not grow smooth, but rather knurled on one side of his face. Andrew thought he could make out a branded "R" through the tangled beard, and it came to him. He was older and more grizzled than the last time he had seen him, but he knew it was Jim. As far as Jim was concerned, he thought it a little spooky the way this guy was staring at him, and turned his eyes away.

"What'd you say your name was?" asked Andrew.

"Name's Jason."

"You look just like a damned nigger I used to know, branded *R* and all."

A bit dazed by Andrew's remark, Jim looked for a long while at the tall slave. The dim memory of a little boy came back to him. *It can't be,* he thought. *No way could it be. This can't be that Andrew. This ain't no runt. But the same green eyes.*

Thomas looked at the face of the man he knew as Jason. "He's right. You do have the brand. We don't need your trouble. You'd best leave here."

Jim spoke to Thomas. "I'll tell you the truth, if you want to hear it. Either way, this man's going with me, and I'm not alone. So please don't give me any trouble."

"What's the truth?" asked Clare.

"I guess this man is who I was supposed to meet, along with someone else named Blackiston. Blackiston was to bring him to me so I could escort him up north. Don't know what happened to the plan, but I and some companions tracked him here. I understand him to be a free man, but that don't mean anything hereabouts, and even if he were a slave, I'd be doing the same if I was asked."

Thomas and Clare exchanged a brief glance, and their eyes rejoined Jim's.

"You get going," said Thomas. "As far as we know, this here Andrew fellow just went out to take a piss and never returned, and we don't know a thing other than that. You owe us, 'cause we're taking a chance and could get a whip'n."

"Oh! How do I owe you?"

Thomas moved closer to Jim and whispered something in his ear.

"You sure?"

"I'm sure," responded Thomas.

"I'll see what I can do. It'll take a while."

They shook hands. Jim turned to leave and said, "Let's go, Andy. We gotta go."

They made their way from the cabin to the meadow, and were almost to the road when Jim heard the zing of a musket ball go past his ear.

"Hit the ground!" he yelled at Andrew, who had heard the musket's report and was way ahead of him.

Someone shouted from the front porch of the big house. "You come back here, you niggers. I'll kill you if you don't."

Five Indians laying ready in the grass fired their muskets toward the porch.

"Jesus Christ!" was the last thing heard from the man as he disappeared inside the house.

They ran to their horses, where Andrew jumped up behind Jim and the group rode at full gallop down the road and to the forest clearing. Dismounting, Jim said, "We don't dare stay here long. Just want to let you know what's going to happen from here on. We're—"

Andrew interrupted, "Your name is Jim, isn't it? You're that goddamned nigger I ran into in jail a long time ago. You've changed."

"Well, you sure don't look nothin' like that skinny little boy that used to wipe baby's butts, either. What the hell they feed you? You're taller than me, and could pick up ten times what I can."

AFTER RIDING SLOW and careful for three days to avoid being found, they arrived at an Indian village on the bank of a wide, slow-moving river. Barking dogs ran around the horses' legs but received little attention from horse or rider. Jim motioned to his Indian companions, and they went their way. Raising a leg over his horse's neck, he jumped off, and Andrew followed. No sooner was Jim off the horse than he was surrounded by half a dozen kids competing to give him hugs and shouting words that Andrew didn't understand. An Indian woman carrying a baby made her way through the crowd of children, and Jim took the baby in one arm. With the other, he bent down and placed his hand on the woman's buttock, pulling her to him. "Mine," Jim said in explanation to Andrew.

"It does look that way."

"C'mon. Follow us, and we'll talk a while. Hungry?"

Andrew entered the Indian longhouse and looked around. It had been constructed from two rows of saplings placed into the ground, bent toward each other, and tied together to form an array of arches. Animal skins and mats made of grass and reeds were placed over the arches, and the ends of the house were closed off with the same. At one end, hides were tied back to form a closable entrance tall enough for a man to walk through, but Andrew had to duck his head. In the center of the house, the hindquarters of a deer cooked on a spit, slow and even over smoldering coals as smoke swirled its way up through a hole in the roof.

The woman and children followed Jim into the house. She glanced Andrew's way. Jim followed her glance, and spoke to her in her language mixed with a bit of English. She motioned to Andrew in a way anybody could understand: *Welcome, friend.* He thanked her by bowing his head in return.

"Her name's Awinina. I was captured in the swamp not long after I escaped from that auction—you remember, don't you?"

"I do. I was hoping you'd get away before anybody got you."

"Well, I got away from the whites and more or less ended up running straight into a bunch of Indians, instead. I tell you, Andy, I thought I was a goner for sure, or they were going to turn me over to the whites for a reward. I learned later they planned on holding me as their own slave until they could find out if there was a reward for sure. They marched me across miles of forest, keeping out of sight all the way. We got to their settlement, and I knew I'd been there before. Awinina ran out of nowhere and grabbed me and kissed me all over, at the same time yelling at the others to let me go."

"That was fast work on your part. I never thought of you as much of a ladies' man—too damned ugly, if you ask me."

"It wasn't fast. This was the Indian girl I kept running away to spend time with, and kept getting into all the trouble about. Seven kids later, and here we are."

Awinina yelled out the door, and children began coming in. Each took a mat and sat on the ground. Jim helped Awinina serve their children the venison along with wild onions and squash, and as he did so, he caught a slight smirk on Andrew's face. "According to the Indians, I'm her slave, because I was captured and I have to do whatever she tells me. In reality, if I didn't help, she'd cut me off in a moment."

"From what I see, that might not be a bad idea."

"Hmm."

After dinner, they, including Awinina, smoked pipes; and Andrew and Jim brought each other current on what had happened since they had last seen each other. Conversation turned to more urgent matters. "This is what's going to happen from here," said Jim. "I'm guessin' you know a nigga by the name of Isaac?"

"Think I might know who you're talkin' 'bout."

"Well, he set this thing up. We've worked for some years now doing this kind of thing." Jim lit another pipe and took a couple of puffs, enjoying the feeling of the smoke as it filled him. "He figures who the candidates are, and I take 'em north. Ain't no guarantee life's going to be better up there, but at least they got a chance. And any chance is better than none. Let me tell you who we figure is gonna make it. People who just plain hate other people tellin' 'em what they can and can't do. In other words, those who want freedom, and ain't afraid of what they've got to do to get it. But if you're the one gets picked to go, it's just like taking a paying job. You do what the boss tells you, or you can go someplace else. So while you're being helped by us, you do what we say; no exceptions. You still interested?"

"I've gone this far, and can't turn back now. Tell me more."

Jim said, "I don't tell you anything until you need to know. That way, if you get caught, you can't tell much 'cause you don't know much. Andy, it's gonna be a tough and dangerous trip. Even a big boy like you is gonna wish he hadn't decided to do it at some point. If you change your mind, let me know by morning."

"I'm not changing my mind."

"Hope not. Let's get a good night's sleep, 'cause it's gonna be the last good one for a long time."

CHAPTER XI

ANDREW WOKE AS Jim and Awinina were talking. She held her suckling baby in one arm while preparing dough patties one-handed with the other.

Seeing him move, Jim said, "Andy, you're up! You ready?"

"For what?"

"Prepare for the trip. We won't be leaving until later, maybe even tomorrow morning. This is where I let you know more about what's happening. There's going to be another person going north. She should be here sometime today."

"She?! A woman? She going to slow us down?"

"I'm told she can take care of herself. It's somethin' I insist on before accepting anybody. The more people, the slower it goes, and the more chance there is of being caught. But I've run three and four before, and we made it."

Awinina motioned toward the fire pit. Jim said, "Morning meal, Andy. Let's eat." On the hot rocks surrounding the pit were what appeared to be rolls or bread. Awinina gave one to Andrew. He bit into it and found it was a bread not unlike ashcake, but tougher; inside was meat he thought to be squirrel.

Jim, sensing the questioning look on Andrew's face, said, "She makes dough out of ground corn, flattens it out, spreads chopped meat on it, rolls it up and cooks it on those rocks. Tastes like squirrel or rat, maybe both."

"Good cookin'," Andrew said.

"Help yourself to another. She'd be mad if you didn't, and you don't want to get that Indian mad at you."

Andrew helped himself to another, and then one more, and ate them standing. "This'll do."

"See those skins over there?" Jim asked, pointing to a stack of deerskins against the far wall of the longhouse.

Andrew nodded.

"There's guns and powder under 'em. Check 'em, and make sure they're ready to go. I'll show you what to do with 'em after I finish making these packs." Turning his attention to the task at hand, he began loading buckskin bags with jerky and dried apples. These he twisted closed and tied with strips of rawhide.

Finished eating, Andrew wiped his mouth on an arm and his hands along the sides of his pants. He walked toward the hide pile. Awinina stopped him, and, kneeling down, held a buckskin hide against one of his legs. "What's she doing?" he asked.

Jim looked up, and before he could answer, Awinina started pulling on Andrew's pants and shirt, saying something in her language.

"You're not going to go far in the outfit you're wearing," Jim said. "She's making leggings and shirts for you, and wants you to take your clothes off so she can use them as a guide."

"But, ah…"

"Don't worry about it. Wrap a hide around you if you're bashful. Won't take her long."

Andrew expected Awinina to look away, but she only backed up enough to give him room to take his clothes off. Seeing this, Jim said something, and

Awinina turned around and rolled her eyes upward. Andrew took his clothes off and walked toward the pile of hides. As he did so, Awinina gathered his clothes, catching a fast glance at Andrew as he walked away.

She went to her mat where she would cut and sew, displaying a noticeable smile. A few of her gathered children, having witnessed the incident, laughed and giggled.

Without looking back, Andrew took a hide off the top, wrapped it around himself, and tucked the ends under each other. He pushed the stack aside, exposing the muskets and pistols.

Andrew inspected each of them, making sure they were unloaded, barrels clean, and vent holes clear. He checked the flints by dry-firing each gun two or three times to ensure a good spark and strong, secure stones.

"They're in good shape. Where'd they come from?"

"Don't know. Stolen, maybe donated. Don't know. A white man gives 'em to me. The same man who'll be bringing the woman."

"Who?"

"Couldn't tell you his name if I knew it. Best we not know anything about each other. This way, nobody could force us to say anything if we're ever caught. But I think he's from south of here. He don't look like a farmer. Think he works in a town. Could be a merchant or solicitor, or maybe even a preacher. He dresses in clothes like you were wearing. Been doing this for a couple years. That's about all the guessing I'm going to do. You'll meet him when he brings the woman. Best not ask him anything."

"I follow."

"Sorry about Blackiston."

"Me, too. He did a lot for me."

Jim sensed Andrews's mood, and left him to his thoughts. He was about to ask Awinina if she needed anything when Andrew, motioning toward the guns, asked, "You expect we'll have to use 'em?"

"If we're stopped…well…we do what we've got to do. We'll need to shoot game along the way 'cause this food won't last till we get to where were going."

"Hope nothing else 'cept food. What you want me to do with the guns?"

"As soon as it gets dark, we'll take all but three pistols and some powder flasks and bags of balls down to the river and hide them in the dugouts. We'll cover 'em with skins so they'll still be easy to get to. We want to look as if we're trading hides when we go up the river."

"We're going on the river, huh?"

"Not far. Just a little way, and we'll be walking the rest of the way. That's all I'm going to say now."

By nightfall, the woman and her escort had not shown up, and the sun had gone down. Jim was silent, and said little except, "Hope nothin' happened to 'em. Not unusual for 'em to take the extra day. I kinda expect it. But if they're not here tomorrow, we take off the following morning without her."

Andrew didn't say anything, but nodded that he understood.

"C'mon," Jim said, "let's get those guns and skins down to the dugouts."

They walked the path leading down to the river's edge.

THE POTOMAC IS a wide tidal river, and as such, rises and lowers with the tides. When the tide is low, the banks of the river reveal debris of all sorts. By far the most common are dead branches, and here and there, a whole tree. At the bottom of the riverbank, as it flattens out and disappears under the river, are several inches of shells of all sorts: the oldest of which have been laying there since before man came to the continent, and others so new they still have remnants of whatever lived in them only a short time ago.

THEY MADE THEIR way down the path, and from the high edge of the riverbank, Andrew looked out over the river. The reflection of the moon bounced off the water. Far across and downriver, lights could be seen. Andrew stopped a moment to look.

"Those lights are from the house of a planter," Jim said. "I hear they're important people. They own lots of slaves. As long as they stay on their side, they can be as important as they want. The dugouts are hid in the overgrowth along the high edge. You can't see 'em, but they're just a few feet from us."

Jim led Andrew through the growth until they came to the dugouts, and said, "Cut branches long enough to reach from side to side of the dugouts; about six for each boat will be enough." They laid the branches across the top of the boats, trimmed them to fit, and secured them with rawhide straps laced through holes in the gunnels, which had been used for this purpose several times before.

"We'll lay a few skins over those branches so it looks like a boatful, but under 'em, there's room to hide the guns, and the dugouts won't be heavy and hard to paddle. We want to look like everyday Indians taking skins to trade. That way, there's nobody going to want to try to stop us."

"We'll keep the food in the longhouse and bring it when we go. Don't want any dogs or other critters chewing down on it."

"Go ahead and start putting those muskets and powder in the dugouts—you know, split 'em up between the three dugouts. We'll load 'em later." It took several trips to take the guns and hides to the dugouts before the job was done.

"What now, Jim?"

"We wait for what's-her-name. You like whiskey?"

NOISE WOKE ANDREW, and he sat up. Whatever or whoever it was hit him square on top of his head—at least it felt that way. He wrapped his arms over his head and fell sideways. There he remained, trying to remember what happened. It came to him, and he swore it would never happen again. He sat up and focused on his surroundings. Awinina was busy with her morning routine: feeding her children. She glanced at him, picked up one of what she had cooked, and waved it at Andrew to ask if he would like one. The thought of food made him queasy. "Please, no," he said. Awinina smiled and gave it to one of her little ones.

By the looks of Jim, he had been awake for a while. He was sitting on a mat with his head held between his hands. The children were playing with one another, running around and making noise—normal children. Jim, cranky and not tolerant of the kids running and playing around him, shouted at them to keep quiet. Awinina intervened, shook her finger at him, and said something less than angry but stronger than normal. Andrew, not knowing a word of the language, understood every word she said.

Jim managed to stand and said, "Let's go, Andy. See if there's anything out there."

"Not now, maybe later."

"C'mon. It'll do you good."

"No, it won't."

"It'll only get worse in here. Let's go."

It reminded Andrew of having to clean chicken coops and gather eggs after he had been whipped. They walked around the outskirts of the village, listening for sounds of someone approaching.

Hearing nothing, they returned to the longhouse. They had already brought each other up to date on the happenings of their lives. Andrew was more up to date with news of the colonies, and told Jim the latest.

"I don't care what those people in Boston are up to." Jim said. "It's their country, not mine."

Andrew wanted to add that it didn't make much difference to him either, seeing as how it didn't have anything to do with him. "The Colonials want freedom for Colonial white men, and don't care anything about us niggers. They've already got it good. What're they complaining about, having to pay their share of expenses to the British? Why should I care about them?"

They agreed on the subject, and with nothing else to say, fell into silent boredom and dozed off.

A commotion from outside woke them. Children shouted, and the dog welcoming committee barked their usual greeting as strangers entered the village.

"C'mon. They're here," Jim said.

Two riders, a white man and a young black woman, had entered the village, and the Indians had taken their reins and were leading them. Both were well dressed, though covered in trail dust.

Jim looked up at the couple. "You're late."

"Couldn't help it," the man said.

"You're here," said the man to the woman. He pointed to Jim and said, "This man's name is Jim. He's going to take you the rest of the way. He's good at this. Do what he says."

"Why's that?"

"Oh, never mind. Forget I said anything."

"Uh oh," Andrew thought.

Awinina approached the woman's horse to help her dismount. She was dressed in a long dress similar to something a house servant might wear—plain and gray.

Once the woman was off the horse, Awinina tugged at the woman's arm for her to follow. The woman looked around at the man. "It's all right," he said. "Follow her."

Then he asked Jim, "You get those guns I sent you?"

"I did. Andy here checked 'em out, and they're in good condition."

"Don't want to know his name. Knowing yours is enough…too much."

"Awinina'll fix you up with somethin' to eat if you'll get down and follow me."

"Can't, I've got to be going. I'm overdue to get back as it is."

Jim handed him the reins of the horse the woman had ridden.

"I wish you all good luck," the man said, and rode back the way he had come.

Andrew and Jim entered the longhouse. They saw Awinina trying to talk to the woman, but the woman couldn't speak her language. Awinina was pointing to the woman's dress and shaking her head from side to side. "She's trying to tell you the dress you're wearing isn't fit for the trip we're going on," Jim said.

"Well, I didn't have time to shop before they came and got me. What was I supposed to do?"

"Awinina'll think of something."

THE WOMAN LOOKED around the longhouse, and at the two men, who stared back. She looked at Andrew, who was wearing nothing but a deerskin, and thought, *I've got to get out of here.* Instead, and with no place to go, she said, "Something wrong?"

Jim said, "What's a good-looking nigger like you doing going north with a couple of beat slaves like us?"

She was biracial: tall with long, firm, muscular arms and legs. Her skin was golden and smooth, uncommon for a slave of the field. There was never a smile when she spoke, and her tone was dead serious and sure in every word, authoritative and aloof. When she spoke, you had best listen to what she was saying.

"Don't even think of touching me, or you'll be cut up as bad as a dog fighting a bear."

"Uh oh! Look, this trip isn't supposed to be…uh…sociable. When they said I'd be taking another with us, I had no idea they were talking about some woman who was going to make life miserable, and had no sense of humor. I'm a married man, to an Indian, and I'm not about to come home all scratched and torn to shreds 'cause she'd never believe I ran into a bear.

What she'd do to me would be much worse. If you don't want to come, go back now."

Andrew stood up and tried to break up the confrontation before it got a chance to build into something ugly. "Hey, hey! Stop it, you two. Jim, she can't turn back now, and you know it as well as she does. Lady, relax. Jim here sometimes says things he thinks are funny, but aren't. He's a good man, and there's nothing to worry about from me, either. I'm just interested in getting out of here." While he was saying all this, he was thinking to himself, *you are about the most gorgeous woman I've ever seen, but I'll bet you are hard as hell to get along with.*

Jim, as a younger man—during the time he used to leave the plantation without permission—had fallen into the hands of Indians more than once. He had a quick mind, and a natural ability to pick up other languages. The native language spoken locally came to him naturally. Very rarely, he'd substituted an English word when he had forgotten or did not know a word. Awinina, on the other hand, didn't speak more than a few words of English, and was content the way life was. However, she still had a sense of what was going on between people speaking in a different tongue. Seeing what was taking place, she smiled and shouted something out the door. Within minutes, six children came into the longhouse, the oldest carrying a baby; they circled around Jim.

The young woman felt somewhat reassured, and told herself to take her chances. But she still had to clear the air. Again, she looked Jim in the eye, and with hands on her hips, said, "Let me tell you something else, Mister Jim. I am not a nigger. I'm a white woman."

"White! You ever look in a clear lake, lady, and see who you are? Because if you did, you'd see you're a nigger just like me. You may be light, but you're a nigger."

"My mama was black, and I had a white father. I'm half and half."

"Makes you a nigger."

"No, it makes me a white woman with black blood, and it makes as much sense as calling me a black woman with white blood. I choose to be a white woman with black blood."

"The law says you got more than ten percent black in you, you're a nigger."

"It's a slave owner's law, and that's why we're here. I choose to make my own law, and my law says I'm a free white woman. You say anything different, and you and I are not going to get along together, and this trip is going to be one miserable time for both of us."

"Lady," said an exasperated Jim, "you can be any color you want to be. Ever think about the color of fire?"

She let the comment go. In a way, it was a compliment. "Furthermore, I don't care for the word *nigger*."

"What's wrong with it?" asked Jim. "What else they gonna call us 'cept niggers?"

"To me, it does not sound...what? Dignified. Yes, dignified. That's what is wrong with it. It sounds derogatory. Call a Negro a Negro, or maybe just black, but comport yourself."

"Huh?"

"Be dignified. Speak up for yourself and others. Don't lower yourself."

"You got a lot of high ideas. Don't think you face what—"

Interrupting to put out the burning fuse between the two, Andrew asked, "What's your name?"

She looked at Andrew, and a strange feeling came over her; it puzzled her.

"Branwen. And you would be...?"

"Andrew, Andrew Attaway. What's your last name?"

"No last name. Branwen is what I call myself."

Andrew and Jim looked at each other, remembering when they had first met, and Jim had asked Andrew what his last name was. They nodded that they both remembered.

The nuance was noticeable. "What?" she asked.

"Nothing," said Andrew.

She was quick to understand it was not worth pursuing. Perhaps another day.

"Don't think I've ever run across a person with your name. You run out of ideas for a last name, or are you like me, and don't think it means anything?" asked Jim.

"I named myself; and yes, a last name is meaningless. And I'm not about to name myself after somebody who owned me. He wasn't a bad person and treated me fairly well, but he owned me, and I don't like being owned, not by anybody."

"How'd you come up with it?" Andrew asked.

"I read a story once, and Branwen was the name of a lady who married a king."

"You read?" asked Andrew.

"Yes, I read. Do you find it surprising to find a slave who can read?"

"Yeah, guess I do. Not many of us can."

She cocked her head to the side. "Us! You read?"

With a laugh and a smile, Andrew said, "Now who's surprised? Yes, I do. And it was that damned nigger over there," motioning to Jim, "who let me know how important it was."

"That damned...what? What is it you two know about each other? There's another story here someplace, isn't there?"

Andrew related the story of how he and Jim had first met, of how they were thrown together to await auctioning, how he had been lucky enough to be bought by a considerate owner, and how Jim had not been as fortunate, and of the events following. He told how they had reconnected after Andrew had found it necessary to become a fugitive—not a fugitive slave, but a fugitive wanted by the law for something else.

"Quite a story, Andy," said Branwen, comfortable calling him Andy from the first time she saw him.

"We shouldn't be telling each other stories," said Jim. "It's time we move on. We've got a long way to go. It's going to be a long, hard trip, Branwen. It won't be long till you're gonna wish you hadn't started."

"Whatever's in front of me is better than what's in back of me."

"Did anyone tell you what to expect on this trip?"

"They just told me you would fill me in on the details."

"You're one trusting person."

"I wasn't worried. I'm tough as a bear," she said, and a smile crossed her face for the first time.

THERE WAS AN easing of tensions now between Branwen and Jim. They seemed to relax, drawn together in a common understanding.

Andrew glanced at Branwen, and the glance turned into a stare. He followed her form from head to brogans, much in the same way a man appraises a horse. His trance broke when she turned her attention to him and their eyes met. Caught, his eyes looked to the ground.

Branwen thought, *who or what is this man Andrew? He seems to let others do most of the talking, but when he has to, he takes the lead. Interesting man, this Andrew, and he's not bad looking, and not dumb. He has the silent intelligence of…what are you thinking, Branwen? This is not you at all, Branwen. Wake up!*

Jim caught the silent conversation Branwen and Andrew were having with themselves. "As I was about to say, this trip isn't going to be fun. You'll wade through swamps, swim across a river or two, and be drenched by cloudbursts. And while you're in those swamps and rivers, don't worry if there are snakes and other things around you. Set your mind at ease, 'cause they're all around you. Rattlesnakes warn you not to go near 'em. Copperheads don't say a thing, they just come up and bite you. But both of those snakes will try to get out your way if you make enough noise. Moccasins, on the other hand, they go out their way to attack you from far away, and they travel in bunches. Those the ones you got to watch out for, nothing else to be afraid of. Spiders and things get in your face and sometimes bite you, but ain't going to hurt you. Mosquitoes will drive you crazy if you let 'em.

I know a guy who got bit so bad he swelled up to twice his size, and they had to cut him out of his clothes. Mosquitoes got to be the worst thing out there. If you get to where they're driving you out of your mind, grab as much mud as you can, and rub it all over you so they can't get through to bite. If we had bear fat, it works, too. But we don't. Keep it in mind, though."

"You trying to scare me out of going?"

"Just telling you the way it's going to be. You make up your own mind if you're still going or not. I don't want you changing your mind half way through and doing something that'll get us caught. I just might strangle you to keep you quiet, and that's not a threat, it's a warning. Well…maybe I'll just knock you on that white chin of yours and put you to sleep for a while."

"Jim's trying to make a point. It's going to be tough. If you've any doubt about how tough it is, or if you think Jim's stretching it a bit, you'd be better off going back and taking your medicine and getting it over with."

"If I die of all those things Mister Jim was trying to scare me with, it would still be better than going back."

"They whip you a lot?"

"Not once. I worked in the house ever since I can remember. They told me I was the overseer's daughter, and brought me into the house so I didn't have to be around him. But mama told me when I was about ten that I was the master's child. The overseer story was to keep the truth from the master's wife. No, my work was pretty easy and I didn't mind it at all. I made clothes for Master and the family, as well as the slaves. Mama taught me what she knew about potions and cures, and I used the knowledge to take care of almost everybody when they got sick. Master never had to call the doctor for man or animal. He taught me to read, told everybody I needed to know those things to help him with his work inside. His wife didn't think he should do it, and in some ways, he treated me better than he treated her. He ruled the house with an iron fist, and what he said was the law. She cried a lot."

"So why you running away? You had it good."

"Master had a son about five years younger than me. We got along pretty good as children. Then, when he got older, and his voice dropped he changed. He tried to throw me down and tried to…well…you know. I fought like hell, and got away more than once. I didn't dare tell him he was my half-brother. But as he got older, he grew stronger than me, and he succeeded. Soon, I no longer resisted, as I knew it was hopeless to fight, and it would be hopeless to tell either my master or his wife. I gave up. One night, about a month ago, I ran away, ran north. I was hungry, my feet hurt, and I hadn't had a drink of clean water for a week. I saw a black man riding a horse on the road. The only black men riding horses I know of are free. I decided to take a chance, and came out of the woods and hailed him. He stopped, and I asked him to help me. His name was Isaac. You know him?"

Remembering the promise, Andrew said, "No."

"Anyhow, he hid me in a cabin with an old man, who took care of me until I was feeling better. Then I was taken away by the man, who just brought me here. He told me he would arrange for an escort to take me north, and here I am."

Awinina said something to Jim. Jim raised his voice responding, and in turn, she raised hers.

"She has informed me that there is no one in the village as tall as Branwen, and therefore, there are no clothes that'll fit her."

"And…?" Branwen asked.

"You're about my size. My clothes should almost fit."

"You mean wear leggins and a breech cloth?!"

"Uh huh."

She made no further comment and said, "Thank you."

A slight trace of a smile appeared on Andrew's face, and it did not escape her notice.

"Andy, why are you only wearing an animal skin?"

He looked down at himself, and realized how he must look. "I'm waiting for my clothes to be returned by my servants," he said, straight-faced.

"Oh!" was all she said.

CHAPTER XII

SAM WATCHED THE two men as they left his stables. The pair said they were going to the inn. He watched until they entered the inn and followed, except he branched off and went to the jail rather than the inn.

"Will!" said Sam. "Glad I found you."

"I been telling these people how I want this jail cleaned up. After an auction, this place is downright hard to take a breath in. What's on your mind? Something wrong?"

"Don't know. Two fellas came in and asked me to take care of their horses and a mule-pulled buggy."

"Well?"

"They asked me if I knew anybody who'd buy the buggy and mule."

"And?"

"The buggy is Martin Blackiston's. I'd know it anywhere. I never saw the mule before."

"Martin's?! Hmm, guess I'd better ask 'em a few questions, huh? Where are they?"

"Said they were going to your inn."

"Point 'em out to me."

Turning to the cleaning crew—some slaves, some not—Will said, "I've got to leave for a while. Finish cleaning this place. We've got a new batch coming tomorrow or the next day. I don't want 'em getting sick. They ain't any good if they don't look good."

Closing the main door and locking it, Will led Sam to his inn.

The old hound dog was in his usual place at the front entrance. His ears twitched to shoo flies, and as the two men stepped over him, he opened an eye and closed it again.

It was early, and less than a handful of people had arrived at the inn. "Don't point, Sam. Just tell me if they're in here, and where."

"Those's the two, at the table where Martha's serving 'em drinks."

Will put his arm around Sam's shoulders and led him to the bar. "Make like we're old friends going for a drink. Got it?"

"Got it."

They sat down at the bar, and seeing them, Martha said in her shout-across-the-room voice, "Don't you two go getting drunk on me now. It's morning, and I'll not have it. Will, you get your own. I may be your wife, but I'm not going to wait on you."

"I know, Martha, I know. Don't get that way. We're not going to get drunk."

"Well, you best not!"

"I've seen those two before, Sam. They're bounty hunters. They've brought runaways to my jail before, to hold until their owners come with the reward."

"What you gonna do?"

"Put 'em in jail and ask questions. You armed?"

"No."

"Me neither, but I will be."

Will served himself and Sam a couple of small mugs of ale from behind the bar. He reached under the bar and took a loaded pistol from beneath. "Martha!" he yelled. This barrel's leaking all over the place! Didn't you notice?"

"Watch your tone with me," she snapped as she hurried to Will. "Now, where's this leak?"

Kneeling down below the bar he said, "Here. Where else would it be?"

"Will, what's the matter with you? You talk to me in a civil tongue!"

Will whispered, "Get down on the floor. There might be some shooting going on in a minute or two."

She stooped down. "Those two I was serving?" she whispered back.

"Yes."

"You're not doing this alone," she said. "Give me the gun at the other end of the bar."

"Take this one. I'll get the other as I go 'round to the front of the bar. You sure about this?"

"We've always done things together, and that's the way I want it."

He gave her a quick kiss on her cheek and looked in her eyes a moment.

The few people in the inn were all trying to look at what they thought was a husband-wife confrontation.

"Get me those rags at the end of the bar, Will," Martha said, just loud enough to be heard by all.

He stood up and went to the far end of the bar, reaching underneath, taking the gun, and cocking the lock. Without hesitation, he stepped out from behind the bar, and walked toward the two bounty hunters with his arm raised, pointing the gun at the pair. "Keep your arms on the table, and don't even wipe your mouths!" he said.

At the same time, Martha stood up and pointed her weapon at the two. Sam walked to Will's side, ready to jump at them if necessary.

"What's this about?" asked one of the bounty hunters.

"You've got some explaining to do about how you got the buggy and mule."

"We bought them."

"You got a bill of sale?"

"Well, ah, not on us. It's in the buggy."

"I don't think so. We'll take a look later. In the meantime, you're going to be Bryan Town's guest in my jail." The two hunters exchanged a *what-now* glance.

Will shouted to the rest of the people in the inn, "You other folks leave for a while. Don't want any of you hurt."

He spoke again to the two slave hunters. "Now, you two take any weapons you have—guns, knives, and the like—and put them carefully and slowly on the floor."

They surrendered their pistols, and one dropped a small knife to the floor.

"That all?" asked Will.

They shook their heads yes.

"Take your clothes off."

"Take our clothes off! Why?"

"Just want to make sure you didn't forget something. I mean it, now. Do it, and don't give me any trouble, 'cause I'll shoot you dead."

"But, but, the woman!"

"She's seen it all before. Get to doing it!"

"Look at the size of that knife strapped to his ieg! That blade must be a foot long," Sam said.

"Go through their clothes, Sam. See what else they got."

"Here's something." He removed a small gun from one of the pants pockets. "The other guy had one, too."

"Look at the size of 'em. I've never seen pistols that small. What'd you plan on shootin', fleas or flies? Hope you aren't on the up and up, 'cause

I'd like to confiscate 'em for my babies to play with," said Will, laughing. "Martha, you alright?"

"Oh, I've seen little boys before. Don't worry."

"You gentlemen put your clothes back on, and march out the door with your hands high over your heads. Sam, if you'd take a look in the buggy for the bill of sale, I'd appreciate it."

One of the hunters said, "Ain't necessary. There isn't one."

"Thought so. What happened, and how'd you get it?"

"Shut up, Lenny. Keep your mouth shut."

"What for?"

"If you say anything else, I'll break your neck when we get out of here."

Will interrupted. "Hold it down a while. Let's get you two over to the jail. Start walking, and keep those arms up."

Will opened the tavern door and motioned for the two bounty hunters to proceed. One of them dragged his foot over the resident hound, and the old dog snapped at him.

"You ought to teach that dog manners, mister. What's he doing there, anyhow?"

"He's lickin' his balls, waiting for something better to come along. He just might've found it. If you don't want to end your days as dog food, I'd suggest you get movin'."

Inside the jail, Will said to his cleanup crew, "Make way. These men need a couple of cells. Those two on the end been cleaned?"

"No, sir," said one of the workers, "but we'll get 'em right now."

"Forget it. These two don't need clean cells." Will pushed the two into their cells.

"This is how I've got it figured, fellows. Something bad has happened to Martin Blackiston, and you know what. That means you're both going to hang out there on the auction block, soon as the judge says for me to buy a rope." He paused to watch their faces, which he noticed were now sweaty and drained of blood. "Now, I'll tell you what I'm going to do. One of you is going to tell me what happened, and I'm going to guess it's the one who didn't do the actual killin'. That man might, just might, get a lesser sentence. Don't know what it'll be, but I don't think you'll hang. It'll be up to the judge."

"Don't say a word, Lenny. He don't know a thing, and he can't prove anything. He's just trying to scare us into confessing something he can't prove."

"Don't listen to him, Lenny," said Will. "I told you straight up how it will be. He's just trying to save his hide. He did the killin', didn't he?"

Lenny was not a fast thinker, and his friend stood out as the leader of the two, so Will concentrated on questioning Lenny. It didn't take much more talking on Will's part until Lenny spilled his guts. He confessed to what had happened and where, with his partner screaming in the background for him to shut up.

"Sam, get us three horses and ride with me. I've got to find Martin and let Mary know what happened. She's got to be beside herself wondering."

"Three horses? Sam asked.

"We'll need one to carry Martin."

"THIS IS ABOUT where that Lenny guy said it happened," Will said. "Plenty of track. Mostly horses. Can't make out buggy tracks, 'cept here and there."

"He said they dragged him off the road into the woods," said Sam. "That's what we got to be looking for—signs of something being dragged on the side of the road."

"Right. You go down the road, and I'll continue on. If one of us sees anything, fire your gun."

It was Sam who ended up firing his gun, and Will came galloping at full speed.

"You find somethin'?"

"Yes. Take a look. Something was dragged from the road. The weeds are still bent down leading into the brush."

"I'm not an Indian, so I don't know much about tracking in the woods. 'Bout all we can do is get in there and start lookin' 'round."

They tied their horses to trees and waded into the underbrush.

Sam heard it first. "You hear that?"

"What?"

"Listen."

They stopped talking and stood still.

"I hear it. I'd guess a deer. Hope not a bear. You reload your gun, Sam?"

"No, damn it."

"Well, reload it. Don't want to face whatever it is alone if it comes bust'n out."

"Hope it goes the other way."

They remained still and listened.

"Something's going through the brush, and it's coming this way," said Will, raising his pistol.

"Whatever it is, it keeps stopping and starting, as if it's having a hard time of it," said Sam.

"That's no animal. C'mon, let's go in there. I'll bet it's...."

Martin burst from the brush.

"Jesus, Martin! You're alive!"

"Where's Andrew?"

"God, man, your ear is hanging down by a thread," said Will.

"I guess it is. Feels like it. Can't hear a thing on that side. Head aches. Don't know what happened. Just riding with Andrew and woke up back there. Heard something. Guessed it was people and walked your way."

They helped Martin mount a horse, and the three rode toward the Blackiston farm. Will was thinking, "Damn, I was looking forward to hanging those two bastards. Might still do it."

CHAPTER XIII

BRANWEN TRADED HER gray dress and ill-fitting brogans for a pair of moccasins and a set of Jim's extra clothes: a buckskin shirt and leggings, complete with breech cloth. She thought herself ridiculous dressed in such a manner, but hid her thoughts and convinced herself it would be worth it in the end.

She tied her bedroll and a filled water skin, tying it to her pack and carrying it to the longhouse entrance to await the others. Pushing aside the skins covering the entrance, she stepped through. Eastward, the bright fireball of the sun still hid below the horizon, but was casting its rays into the blue sky. A smattering of orange clouds with wisps of gray woven through hung motionless, as if waiting further instructions. The air was fresh and clean, and a slight breeze blew toward the Potomac.

Branwen looked at Andrew with a quizzical look as he emerged. "You growing a beard?"

"Don't think shaving's too practical on this trip we're going on."

"Don't know if I like that."

"Well, excuse me, lady! You'll just have to get used to it. You gonna be bossy?"

"When I feel like it."

They looked at each other, wondering the other's thoughts. Andrew, remembering what he had been doing before Branwen brought up the subject of the beard, said, "Here, this is yours."

He handed Branwen a pistol, a flask of powder, and a pouch of balls. "Those balls will fit either the pistol or the musket. You might have to wrap the ball for the pistol with and extra patch, 'cause they're a little small."

"They're heavy! How do you get them in the barrel, just drop them in?"

"You're telling me you don't know about guns? I guess we all just figured...well, no worry, I'll teach you as we go along. For now, just shove it in your belt and.... Forget it. Put it in your pack. The important thing to remember is not to point it at me or Jim...especially me."

She smiled one of her rare smiles, and turned to watch as Jim said his goodbyes to Awinina and the children. They were in a family embrace. Jim said something to Awinina, and held her with both arms. After giving her a drawn-out kiss that made the kids giggle, he turned to the others. "Let's go." He picked up his gear, and Andrew and Branwen did the same.

"Braween!" Awinina called, trying to pronounce Branwen's name. Branwen stopped and turned as Awinina approached her. She held up a buckskin dress in front of Branwen, placing it against Branwen's hips. Awinina said something, and Jim translated. "She said she made this for you last night, and you shouldn't have to dress like a man."

Branwen went to Awinina, hugged her, and kissed her cheek. She turned to her companions, saying, "Now, if you two will excuse me for a minute—just turn around now—I'll change, and we can go."

"Hold on to the breechcloth and leggings. They may come in handy later on," Jim added.

The trio walked single file down the path leading to the Potomac and to where the dugouts were hidden—Branwen in the middle and Andrew bringing up the rear. He was thinking, *she's carrying a heavy load and doing alright with it. Not even bent over. She's going to do all right. But a few hundred feet isn't a few hundred miles.*

They paused on the riverbank and looked across. Andrew's eyes focused on the area where he had seen the lit house the night before. He could make out the house now, surrounded by cleared forest, plowed and turned into a slave of man—like the people who worked it. He thought he could see people moving around the fields. They looked like ants busy on a mound.

Goodbye, slave life, he thought. *Hello, freedom.*

"We better load those muskets," said Jim.

After the muskets were loaded, the Indians began to drag the dugouts down the riverbank, far enough into the water that the fronts floated while the back ends, still on land, held the boats from floating away. Next, they motioned for the threesome to climb into their respective dugout.

Once the travelers were seated, the Indians dragged the dugouts further into the water until they were afloat. With a jump, they lay across the boats from gunnel to gunnel, then twisted to settle on the bottom in a kneeling position, motioning for the travelers to do the same. With paddles in hand, the crews turned their dugouts into the current and began to paddle upriver.

If anyone were to look from afar, they would see three dugouts, each paddled by four Indians, carrying a load of hides upriver to be traded. Through a spyglass, they would see that two of the paddlers were not Indians. Branwen's coloring, a close match to the Indians, would take a keen eye to discern from afar. This would be the first of several calculated risks Jim and his refugees would take in the upcoming months. The current risk was considered minimal, as any supposed observer would have to intercept them at some point, and this would be difficult to undertake with questionable results.

Through the day, they paddled upriver, beaching the riverbank for short spells to rest. Come dark, they would again find a place along the riverbank to sleep, pulling their boats from the water only far enough to be stable. As uncomfortable as it was, they slept in the boats, as the overgrowth ashore and uncertainty of what could be waiting for them or crawling about nearby was too much for the travelers to contemplate. Jim preferred to continue through the night, but overcast skies made it difficult to see.

Come daybreak, they again paddled upriver. A constant barrage of bugs clouded around them. With every breath, the tormentors got sucked up their noses, landed in their ears, and crawled through their hair. Branwen pleaded they go further toward the middle of the river, thinking the attackers would be fewer when further from shore.

"Current's faster there, and you'll tire out. Just pay no attention to 'em. They ain't biting. Just hav'n fun with you," Jim said.

"They're in my eyes and ears."

"I know. Try cutting holes in a food bag to see out of, and pull it over your head. We might move out of their range as we go."

Jim took his own advice, as did Andrew. The bags were effective, and they paddled steadily on with a new determination. The Indians seemed to pay less attention to the swarm of critters, but laughed and pointed at the hooded passengers.

After a couple of hours, Jim shouted something in the Indians' language, and pointed ahead. They headed to where Jim had pointed and ran their dugouts aground, wading ashore and pulling the dugouts from the river. There, they unloaded their packs, guns, and gunpowder. What they could not carry—about half of the heavy lead balls and gunpowder—they left with the Indians, taking only enough for a few shots at whatever needed shooting, man or beast. Carrying fifty pounds on your back soon becomes a hundred pounds and gaining.

They watched the Indians with the three dugouts leave as they stood on the riverbank. Jim said, "Pick your gear up, and let's find the trail. Anyplace we go, we have to be careful about being in the open any more than necessary."

"You think we might get caught?" asked Branwen.

"There's always the chance, but I haven't come close to it so far. I have nothing but grateful clients."

Andrew and Branwen said nothing more, and waited for Jim to continue.

"We'll be going a long way north. It'll take us a couple of months. Our destination is a plantation run by a Quaker family. They're antislavery, and though some of those who work on the farm are slaves, they can buy their freedom. These Quakers are good people, and they'll see to it you go to some destination I don't know about. Branwen will go somewhere, and you, Andy, will go somewhere else. I'll return to my village. Once you two are relocated, you should be able to find work and live free."

"You don't know the terminus?" she asked with some alarm.

"Huh?"

"Where we're going."

"No. You'll learn where you'll go when we get to the Quaker farm."

"Jim, I don't have papers to show I'm free like Andy has."

"You will. Be patient and trust me."

As they picked up their packs and muskets, Branwen said, "Jim, I didn't like you at all when I first met you. But after seeing how you were with your family and what you're doing for us, I take it back. You're a good man, and even if we don't make it, I won't change my mind about that."

Jim was not a man who knew how to accept a compliment, and he had no idea of how to respond to one. He looked at Andrew for some help, but Andrew had turned his head to avoid having to help Jim out of the awkward situation. He settled on, "You might change your mind by the time we get where we're going…but thank you anyway. Guess I'm just a mouthy nigger. Sorry about what I said."

"Don't change."

There followed a brief silence, and Jim resumed being Jim.

"There's still a few hours of daylight. Up this riverbank about a hundred yards is an animal trail. We'll walk it until the sun goes low, and stop for the night. We should be far enough into the woods by then to build a fire without drawing attention."

They walked along the bank for a few minutes, and Jim stopped to look around.

"Here it is," Jim said, pointing here and there on the ground. "See those animal tracks going to the river? They come out here to drink. We just follow 'em north, more or less."

Jim took the lead, and Andrew said to Branwen, "Let me carry your musket. It won't help you much if you don't know how to use it."

"I can carry it," she said.

"I know. But I'd just feel better if I carried it."

She did not protest, and handed the gun to Andrew, relieved not to be carrying the extra weight. "Thanks, Andy."

"After you," he said, motioning Branwen to go in front of him.

They spoke little as they single-filed along the path that had been traveled for centuries by animals and man: animals looking for food and water, and man looking to explore the unknown in the hopes of finding his dream. When the Indians, the first inhabitants of this land, discovered the well-trodden paths and trails of animals, they found them a convenient way to further discover it. Later, settlers—the white men from across the water—made use of the same trails for their wagons and horses. Those paths became primitive trackways for travel, exploration, and commerce. They would be turned into roads and developed in the centuries to follow as main arteries throughout the land.

As the sun began to set low in the western sky, Jim turned around, and as he removed his pack, he said, "This is far enough. We'll stay here for the night."

He looked around and up, and with a side-to-side motion, kicked dirt aside. "This'll do for a fire. You two start gathering wood. Big and little pieces of anything that'll burn. I'll get the fire going. Mind you, watch out for snakes."

While the other two were scavenging for wood, Jim opened his pack and removed a small leather pouch. Kneeling by the place he had picked for the fire, he opened the pouch, pinched a bit of something black, and placed it on the ground, shaping it into a loose pile. Next, he removed a chunk of flint several times larger than the flints used on muskets. This he placed next to the black matter, and struck it several times with the back of his long knife. Sparks flew from the blade. One spark stayed lit as it settled on the black stuff. Jim bent low, and blew a gentle puff of air onto the small flame as it began to burn brighter and higher.

Andrew and Branwen dropped their armfuls of gathered wood, and Jim fed the smallest pieces to the fire. As it grew, he added larger pieces until he had to step back from the heat.

"Spread your bedrolls around the fire. This won't keep you warm tonight, but it'll give us enough light to eat by while it burns."

"Any chance of somebody spotting the fire?" Andrew asked.

"Always a chance, but we're in this forest pretty deep, and the fire is small. Not much chance of anybody seeing it. 'Course, there's always the chance we'll run into Indians coming the other direction, but not here. We're not far enough north. We should be out of the woods by tomorrow and coming to farmland. We could walk the trail almost all the way to where we're going, but it's the long way to get there. We'll walk around the open areas, and keep in the surrounding brush as much as we can. You'll see slaves working the fields and their masters and overseers watchin' over 'em. We want to be sure they don't see us. Slavery doesn't stop as you go north, it just gets thinned out."

A week went by as they made their way through the growth separating one cleared field from another. Now and then, turkeys, deer, and all sorts of other small birds and small animals bounded out in front of them. A wild boar rutting the ground and not paying attention to the rest of the world stopped as the travelers came within a few feet. The boar, surprised, jumped and grunted. Andrew and Jim halted, cocked their muskets, and aimed at it. For a moment, it was a standoff: Andrew and Jim not wanting to shoot as it might draw the concern of others close by, the boar through its own unknown reasoning deciding to charge or not to charge. In the end, it turned around, running into a thicket and grunting its disapproval of the whole affair.

As night fell, they settled in a clump of woods between fallow fields, which were less likely to have anybody about. The week's journey had worn on them, and they were tired, dirty, dusty, and not in a good mood. There was none of the usual storytelling or question-and-answer sessions. They ate jerky and dried apples again. Andrew looked at a dried apple and shook his head. "I'm not hungry enough to eat this stuff anymore," he whispered, putting it back into his pack. He took a bite of jerky and decided it didn't taste any better. He swallowed what he had, and returned the rest of it to his pack.

Branwen saw him, and knew without asking what was wrong, as she felt the same. In a low voice, she asked the two, "You think there's anything esculent in one of those fields?"

"Huh?" they asked.

"Something we can eat that didn't get dug up from the last crop."

"Oh."

"Could be," said Jim. "Looks like they grow more than just tobacco around here."

"I'm more than willing to go out and look around. There's enough moonlight to see by," said Andrew.

"Me, too," said Branwen.

"Let's wait a while," said Jim, "then we can all go out and root around."

Slaves worked the fields from sunup to sundown, and the long summer days meant hard hours of backbreaking labor. But their labor was working for their masters, and tired as they may have been, they still had to take care of their own business. There was cooking meals for the family, washing clothes, and tending to their own private gardens and livestock of one kind or other, alongside or in back of their cabins. Depending upon their masters, slaves were able to sell their produce, meat, and eggs to others. The income derived was legally their master's, and the masters distributed it according to their own rules.

These were the lucky ones. On some farms and plantations, slaves weren't allowed to grow or raise anything for their own profit or use. Smart masters allowed it, as it cut down on what they had to supply their slaves to keep them alive and healthy.

This night, candlelight still shone through windows, and here and there, a moving light pointed out a slave as he tended his personal garden. The lights went out one by one, and the voices that once floated over the fields fell silent; figures of people retired to shelter and rest.

"It should be about time," said Andrew. "I could go to sleep myself, 'cept I'm so hungry."

"Whatever we find out there, we eat raw. Ever eat a raw potato?"

"I'd eat a raw rock right now."

Avoiding two of the fields they remembered as having nothing but tobacco stalks, they concentrated on the other field. It had been plowed, and the turned ridges and furrows exposed unharvested tubers. They plucked the potatoes and devoured them raw, much the same as children might eat candy. Wild onions, hot as peppers, were found growing at the edge of the field, and were eaten as they were pulled.

Days went by as the travelers made their way around farmland from one farm to the next, staying hidden in the heavy growth of trees. When fields were being worked during the daytime and sufficient cover to travel unseen was unavailable, they backtracked to previously encountered trees and shrubs, and there, they waited for night. After darkness came, they once again continued traipsing, with only the night sky to light their way.

It was one of those days of hiding and resting when the noise of someone making their way through the copse of trees in which they were hiding caused them to stiffen in alarm. A woman, a slave, had made it to within a few feet of Andrew, and there, she squatted behind a tree to relieve herself; Andrew had hidden in the brush just ahead of her. The woman was unconcerned, talking to herself and looking everywhere but in front of her. She began to sing and praise the Lord, and her eyes rolled toward the sky. The overseer, hearing the noise, called, "You stop entertaining yourself and get your business done and get back out here."

"Yes, sir. I'm doing as good as I can."

"Well, you get it done fast as you can."

"Yes, sir."

As her head turned back, from out of the side of her eyes she caught sight of Andrew, did a double take, looked straight ahead at him and gave a shriek. "Ehhh!"

"What's wrong, May? You alright?"

May's eyes were as big as full moons.

"I said, are you alright? Want me to come in there?"

She blinked several times, and it came to her as a great enlightenment: this was a runaway she was looking at.

"I'm coming in," said the overseer.

"No, no. I'm almost done," she called back. "I just saw a snake, and it scared me. Ain't nothin' but a big black snake. Boy! Is it ever big."

She looked at Andrew, and, as if she were still talking to herself, she said, "You be careful. Hope you make it, big black snake." She stood up, and as casually as she had come, she walked back to the field, singing her song.

WITH THE FARMLAND in back of them and again in the woods, they picked up the trail. It was now safe to build small fires. Being out of both dried apples and jerky, and with scavenged crops not always available, they fed themselves on grubs roasted on flat rocks in the fire. Sometime snails were found, if it was wet enough, and an occasional unlucky snake. Frogs were always a choice find, but their cousins, the toads, were passed over. Branwen knew about mushrooms, and which ones were good to eat and which should be avoided. "It's time to do a bit of hunting for whatever comes along," said Andrew. Nobody argued.

"This where you're going to show me how to handle a gun, Andy?"

"Afraid not. We don't have enough balls and powder. What we've got, we've got to make count. Can't waste it on practice or on a bunch of small animals like squirrels. Deer and bigger is what we're after."

"I haven't seen anything you could shoot at since...well...I haven't seen anything."

"That's partly 'cause you've been looking at where you're going, and not at what's around you. Stop once in a while, and look around yourself. That in itself will cause an animal to run. Turn around and look where you just came from, and you might see something come out of the trees to look at you."

"True, but we can't count on that happening. We're going to hunt 'em," Jim said.

"Look, boys, I'm hungry, sore, tired, and am in no mood to guess about this. Tell me what to do, and let's get some meat."

"Woo! Sounds like the lady ain't happy, Andy. You take it from here."

"You can go through the woods all day trying to scare up something to shoot at. But all you're doing is telling the animals where you are. They'll freeze and won't move, or they're way ahead of you and moved to other parts before you ever get close. I've stepped on animals and didn't know it. Ignatius once bought a dog was supposed to be the best bird-sniffing nose in all of Maryland. Well, we took her out for the first time when she was little more than a grown pup, and she ran a few yards after we let her go and then she just sat down. Now, if this dog spotted a bird, she was supposed to point to it. You know what I mean—erect with neck out, snout pointing ahead, and tail straight as a rod. I wasn't happy, and told Ignatius this dog was no good. He said he agreed, and he'd take the dog back to the man he bought it from. I went over to the dog and petted it on its head, and told him to come on. He just sat there. I got a bit mad and kicked his rump. Damned if a grouse didn't get up from under that dog and fly away before either Ignatius or I could even think about shooting him."

Branwen laughed, and had to wipe her eyes. Jim had a smile on his face as if he hadn't enjoyed a good story for a long time. Their laughter was contagious, and Andrew sat down and joined in.

Soon, the mood faded away. Branwen said, "So, the crux of the story is what?"

"If you're going to hunt, you've got to understand the animal you're hunting. You can't hunt on your terms; you have to hunt on theirs."

"I don't feel like looking for something in woods I can't even see through. It would be futile."

"You're right. And I'd bet within the area you can see right now, there is at least one animal: deer, rabbit, raccoon, or whatever, frozen in its tracks waiting for us to go away. You could be looking right at 'em and you wouldn't know it unless it moved. Then you'd pick 'em out in a second."

"So we make 'em move?"

"Na, they'll never move. We use another plan. Let them do the work. This is an animal trail we're following north. Animals use it to hunt their food at night, and we can't see 'em then. We'll get off the trail and hide in the woods, as deep as we can and still see the trail. Animals look for food from just before sundown to just after sunup, and you can see 'em as they're returning to their hiding places. They lie low until it's time to eat again, and they may not eat every day. They're not like us—we need food all the time. We'll go off in the woods and hide ourselves, get a good night's sleep, wake as the sun starts to light the sky, and watch the trail. Chances are good something will come walking by, and we can get it. This is a good spot, 'cause we haven't seen a human being or anything else for days."

"You learn all about hunting from Ignatius?" asked Jim.

"Yes. I miss him the old guy."

Branwen saw a side of Andrew she liked. With genuine concern, she asked, "What happened to him, Andy?"

"He just died one day when we were fishin'." His eyes welled with tears, and he wiped them away with his arm. He felt Branwen touch his shoulder, and her hand slid down until it rested on his forearm. He looked at her. She didn't smile often, but when she did, it was from her soul. This was one of those times. He shook his head and said, just a bit embarrassed, "Anyhow, where were we?"

"We shoot a critter in the morning," said Jim. "Let's move off the trail, find a place to make camp, and get some sleep."

They stopped, and Jim poked around for places that looked as if they were clearings waiting just for them. "Hey," said Jim. "Here's a fire pit. This'll do just fine."

"Someone's been here before, Jim?" asked Branwen.

"Animal trails have been used for hundreds, perhaps thousands of years before by others. No use doing over what they've done before. This spot has been used by more people than there's hairs on your head."

"What you think about a fire, Jim? Start one or not?"

"Might as well. Nothing to cook now, but come morning, I'll bet we take care of that."

SOMETHING WOKE ANDREW. He lay on his back and looked around as much as he dared without moving his body. He saw nothing, heard nothing, and soon forgot about it. His gaze settled on the sight above. The sky was clear and moonless, and it shone with stars, beautiful stars: yellow, red, blue, and white ones, some twinkling and others content to glow in beauty without showing off. An occasional star streaked across; others tried, but disappeared before completing their journey. Branwen purred, and Jim snored loudly enough to shake pinecones from trees. "Careful, Jim," he thought, "We don't want to scare tomorrow's food."

He closed his eyes and turned on his side. A twig snapped, and then another. It woke Jim and Branwen. Each lay in silence, trying to figure out what it was. There, they heard it again—something at least as large as a man walking about. It would stop and start again, walk around, and again stop and after a minute or so to resume its roundabout way. It stopped again; Andrew thought it was just beyond his feet, and that he could sit up and reach out and touch it. Slowly and with deliberation, he reached for his pistol and pulled the hammer back, covering the action with his other hand to smother the noise. Jim, in a loud whisper, said, "Don't shoot, don't shoot."

They stayed frozen in position, scarcely daring to breathe. The walking continued, going past Andrew until it could no longer be heard. They lay there for several minutes before Branwen asked, "Is it gone?"

"Maybe," said Jim. "Hope so."

"Why didn't you want Andy to shoot at it?"

"You don't shoot at something not knowing what it is. It might have turned and charged us."

Andrew said, "Might have shot my toe off, too…or yours."

"He probably would have," Jim said, and laughed.

"Oh, you…! Can we go back to sleep now?"

"If you think you can," said Andrew, "with whatever it is walking around out there."

Andrew turned over, laughing to himself for having set Branwen up to where he knew she would be unable to close her eyes, let along fall back to sleep. Jim soon settled back to rocking the trees. By and by, he heard Branwen return to her purring, and he wondered how she could fall asleep with Jim snoring the way he was, and while something was walking around in the black of night. He fell asleep still wondering.

Something bumped Andrew on his back. He thought it was whatever had been walking around earlier. As he reached for his pistol, he stopped when he realized it was Branwen. She had rolled out from under her bedroll, still asleep. Propping himself up on his elbow, he reached over her to grab her blankets and pulled them over her. She continued to move in her sleep a little; she raised her arm, and it fell across Andrew. Her kitten snore began again.

Andrew thought, *that's nice. Wonder if she knows? Na, forget it.*

He awoke to Branwen shaking his shoulder, and he sat straight up. He wiped his eyes, and stretched long and hard. It was daybreak, a dark daybreak in which the sun struggled to shine through the overcast sky, the complete opposite of the night before.

In a whisper, she said, "Sorry about last night, Andy. I move around sometimes when I'm sleeping after something's happened, like those footsteps."

He didn't know quite how to reply, though he knew how he'd like to. Instead, he said, "Don't know what you mean. Where's Jim?"

"Out there somewhere."

"Must be after meat."

A slight drizzle of rain began to fall.

"I've got to pee," Branwen said.

"Me, too. Aren't you afraid of our visitor?"

"Na, bad dreams only walk at night."

They stood up and brushed themselves off.

"I'm going over there," she said pointing, meaning Andrew was to go someplace else. She didn't walk straight away from him, but instead side stepped a little too close to his back, rubbing against him as she passed.

He felt her breasts brush against his back, and a feeling went through him. It was a sensation he would remember not just the rest of the day, but the rest of his life—and something he would, years into the future, wonder about; had it been an accident, or on purpose?

They rolled the bedrolls up and set out to find Jim in the increasing drizzle.

After walking a few minutes along the path, they saw him crouched behind a fallen tree overlooking a clearing. Jim, hearing the two, turned around and put a finger in front of his mouth, meaning for the others to be quiet. Looking past him, they saw a deer about fifty feet ahead and broadside to Jim. It walked slowly, dragging one of its back legs. The deer attempted to lie down, but fell over.

Bringing his hand down and over his musket's lock, Jim pulled back the hammer and shouldered his weapon. The tip of the barrel made a circular motion, then stopped and held steady. Blue smoke and a loud report issued from the gun. Jim's shoulder jerked straight back, and he had to catch his balance as he rolled backward. Recovering, he shouted, "Got it!" Looking at the other two, he said, "We eat real meat now."

By the time Jim had stood up, Andrew and Branwen had reached him, and together they walked to the deer. Jim's shot had been true, right through the heart. Sticking out of the deer's rear leg was an arrow broken off about six inches from the hoof.

"I saw she was hurt. After she fell, she looked at me. I could see her eyes weren't the usual brown. Instead, they were almost black, and I could swear I saw a yellow light coming from them."

Branwen and Andrew looked at each other and said nothing.

Jim said, "Enough. Let's get to making meat. Back leg won't be good to eat, and the heart is shot to pieces."

"We're not going to try to go on in this rain, are we?" asked Branwen.

"No, this rain is coming down pretty good now, and I've an idea it's only just beginning. We'll clean the deer out, and then we'd best build a lean-to and stay. Afterward, we can tell tall tales till it lets up."

Andrew said, "How about cutting out a few steaks, and we'll eat 'em today. We'll dry and smoke as much of the rest as we can over a fire if we can get one going.

The fire was not difficult to build. By placing the deer hide over four upright stakes, they were able to shelter the fire, and it began to smoke just the right amount. They hung the meat above the fire and turned their attention to making a lean-to. By now, they were drenched, and the rain held steady.

It was afternoon when they finished. With a little over four feet of headroom, they crawled into the structure.

"Just what I needed," said Jim. "A bath."

"I'm changing into those dry leggings, breechcloth and all," said Branwen. "Turn your heads."

She dug around her pack and found that little water had made it through the buckskin covering. Finished changing, she said, "You can turn around now."

Andrew and Jim also changed. Jim looked the same, but it struck Branwen as funny when she saw Andrew in his fancy clothes. She refrained from laughing aloud, but had to turn her head away for a moment.

With the rain coming down, they had not had time to even the forest floor or make a bed of pine needles on which to unroll their bedrolls. The lean-to was cramped, and allowed no space between the three as they tried to get comfortable. Branwen was in the middle, and though cramped for space, would be better protected from rain blowing in.

"You've got the best spot in the house, Branwen. Two guys on the outside to protect you," said Andrew.

"Don't go getting too protective."

"I heard you."

"Yes, well, I'm caught in the middle of two snoring animals. You can be heard from here to where we came from to where we're going. There's not enough room in here to turn over and cover my ears."

"What got her going, Andy? You do something I didn't see?"

"Probably, but I have no idea what, and I don't care. I'm closing my eyes, and gonna try sleeping through this. Wake me when you want to cook those steaks." He turned on his side, back toward Branwen.

"You touched me," she said.

"Uh, jeez."

"ANDY, ANDY," BRANWEN said, shaking his shoulder. "Wake up."

He sat up and rubbed his eyes. "What's the matter? You ready to eat? I'll put the steaks in the fire."

"Take a look at Jim. Something's wrong with him. It's anything but too cold or too hot in here. He's rolled up in his bedroll and shaking. He's sick."

She sat up so Andrew could look more closely at Jim.

"He don't look good at all." Andrew felt Jim's head. "He's hot enough to cook on."

Andrew opened his pack and took out the empty food bags. Knocking over the oak bark slabs covering the open end of the lean-to, he looked around and set the bags out in the rain.

"It's let up some. I've got to put more wood on the fire."

The food bags he had placed outside the lean-to were soaked now, and he placed inside each one of them a hot rim rock from the fire pit, then put each at the lean-to's entrance. As he entered, Branwen said, "We could watch him better if he were in the middle of us. I'll move my stuff out of the way, and you can drag him and his bedroll over."

They each grabbed an end of Jim's bedroll and dragged it to the middle of the lean-to. The hot rock bags were placed around Jim, close to his body.

"They should help keep him warm. When these get cold, I'll switch 'em out with others," said Andrew.

Jim threw off his bedroll, his chills being replaced with hot spells. Branwen moved the hot bags away just enough.

"Andy, cut some meat and boil it to make a broth. He needs nourishment. Then make a tea of pine needles and the outside part of hickory bark. I'll try to get it down him."

"Pine needles and hickory bark! What—?"

"Fights pain and fever."

Andrew was going to ask her more questions about how she knew all this, but wisely decided against it. No use getting her going. He did as he was asked.

FOR THREE DAYS and three nights, Jim tossed and turned. His talk was incoherent, and he alternated between cold and hot spells. Branwen and Andrew took turns trying to get liquids down him; sometime successfully, sometime not. Andrew changed his breech cloth when it became necessary, and both took turns wiping him down when his body became drenched in sweat. They wondered where all the sweat came from, as he had not drunk much liquid.

On the fourth day, Jim was nothing but hot without sweat. If he had cold spells, they were known only to him.

"He's not going to make it, Andy."

"Let's get water in him."

"He won't take it. He won't swallow."

Andrew said, stern and determined, "Sit him up. I'll get water down that god damned nigger if I've got to push it down with my gun barrel."

He almost had to. Branwen helped him up, and Andrew jammed a water skin as far back in Jim's throat as it would go, and pushed it down more with his fingers.

Jim gagged, but Andrew put his hand over his mouth and held it tight. He squeezed the water skin with all his might.

"Andy! Be careful! You might fill his lungs and drown him."

"He's dead either way. Help me push on the skin."

She closed her eyes and turned her head, not wanting to see what was happening, but doing as she was told.

"That's done. It's either in his stomach or his lungs. He's not trying to cough it up, so far. Either he can't, or it's in his stomach."

She let Jim down and put her hand by his mouth. "He's breathing."

"I don't want to do that again. But I will if he doesn't start drinking."

They watched him for a while, until, exhausted, they both fell asleep.

IT WAS BRANWEN who woke first. She looked at Jim, and once again placed her hand by his mouth. He was still breathing. It was shallow breathing, but it was still breathing.

Andrew woke next and looked at Branwen. "Well?" he asked.

"I don't know."

"He still hot?" .

She felt Jim's forehead and down his neck. "Doesn't feel as hot as he was. Maybe the water worked."

The sun came up, and Andrew moved a bark slab from the front of the lean-to.

"Hey! It's stopped raining."

Branwen looked out and pushed more bark slabs aside.

"Let's get going," said a weak voice in back of them.

IT WOULD BE a week and a couple of days before Jim was able to travel and once again lead the others. Andrew shot two more deer, and rigged a snare to catch rabbits. He never quite figured how the loop should be made so it closed before the rabbit ran away. He tried several ways, and for his efforts, he was rewarded with what he called "one lousy rabbit." The rabbit was not enough to feed one of them, but they shared the little critter and finished the meal with more venison.

On the trail again, Jim lowered his head and slowed down. Stopping, he looked around.

Andrew and Branwen saw them, too; footprints of moccasin-wearing feet.

"What are they, Jim?" asked Andrew. He had also seen the footprints.

"Indians, for sure. I've run into 'em around here before. They're peaceful now the Indian and French war is over, but they'll take whatever they want from you. You've got to be firm with them, and make a show of your guns. They figure what you've got ain't worth dying for. I'd take your pistol from your pack, Branwen, and at least pretend you know how to use it."

She did, and Andrew took it from her.

"This is a quick lesson on how to load and shoot, just in case. We don't have time or powder to practice. Just try to remember just in case."

He loaded the pistol and went through the routine—too quickly, he thought, for Branwen to understand. "You think you can do that?"

"Yes."

"If we get to where we actually use these things, I'm going to give you your musket. All you gotta do is pull back the hammer all the way and pull the trigger. Then switch to your pistol."

"And after that?"

"Use your guns as clubs, use your knife, stick your fingers in their eyes, bite 'em like a rabid dog, 'cause other than that, there is no after that."

"You sound like you've done this before, Andy," said Jim.

"Nope, I asked Ignatius the same question, and that was his answer. It was experience talking."

At the sudden realization of the possible danger looming ahead, there was silence as each accepted the fact.

Inside of himself, Jim was worried. He'd experienced the Indians before without any problems, but he'd never seen this many footprints before.

"Cheer up. Our—what did you call it, Branwen?—is just a day or two ahead."

"Terminus is the word you're thinking of."

"That's the word. I like it."

THE DAY WORE on, and Jim, still not up to full strength, slowed a little.

Andrew noticed, and looked at Branwen. As she looked back he could see she had noticed the same thing.

"Jim, I'm getting a bit tired. Think we could rest for a while?" he asked.

"Not a bad idea. Guess I'm still not my old self."

They found a small clearing, took off the packs, and sat. Branwen cocked her head a little; she was trying to hear something.

"What's the matter, Branwen?" Andrew asked.

"Is that a creek or river I hear?"

"It is," said Jim pointing at the trees in back of them. "It's just through those trees and down a little hill in a ravine."

"Think we could go down there? It sounds refreshing."

"Don't see why not. Take your guns. Those Indians might be thinking the same thing. Hide your packs in the brush."

The sound of rushing water grew louder as they approached. A little further on, they could see the splash and mist of water as it pounded against boulders, smoothly gliding over and around others.

Branwen waded in first.

"Oh! That's cold."

She splashed water on her face, and the shock of it made her draw in a deep breath. "It feels so good."

Jim and Andrew followed her in, repeating her ritual.

They climbed out and sat on a large boulder, just looking at the creek. Fire and water have a mesmerizing effect on people; they can stare into them for hours on end. "Look!" Andrew said. "It's a fish."

"You pack fishing line, Jim?" said Andrew.

"There's some in there someplace, but we don't have time. We'd best get back and get going again. I'm feeling fine."

They trudged up the hill and through the trees and brush.

"They got our stuff," said Jim.

"Indians?" asked Branwen.

Jim nodded his head yes.

"Now what?"

"We can be at the Quaker farm by tomorrow afternoon, if we hurry. Think you can do without food that long?"

"What about water?" said Branwen.

"That creek pretty much runs alongside this trail all the way."

"Travel at night?" Andrew asked.

"If there's enough moonlight. Otherwise, sleep on the ground, and hope it doesn't get too cold. We'll be alright."

"Ya know," Andrew said, "we might've been lucky. I mean, those Indians taking our stuff and moving on. If we'd been face to face, no telling what would've happened."

Travel by night they did. Jim seemed reinvigorated at the thought of an end to their journey the following day. On his mind now was the return trip he would have to make alone. The Indians seemed a larger danger now than they had in the past. He knew of a couple of other trails leading from his home to this place, but he had never tried them, only heard of them. He thought he might try one on his way back.

THEY WERE ABOUT to emerge from the forest into an opening. Jim put his arm out and stopped the others. He took a few careful steps forward to get a clear view. The white house was situated at the top of a swell in the land, and shone brightly under the lights of the heavens. It was a familiar sight, and had not changed since the last time he was here. Though not clearly visible, set well in back of the house were cabins, which could not be mistaken for anything else but slave quarters; a few coloreds were still up and tending their gardens.

"We'll wait here till they quit, and then make our way to a shelter over yonder in those woods, just to the right of the house. That's where my part of this journey comes to an end. I'll go back to Awinina and the kids for a while."

"A while!" said Branwen.

"Yes, just long enough to get on Awinina's nerves, then I got something to do I promised somebody."

"A promise to a couple you owe a debt?"

"I already said enough. 'Sides, it's you two who owe 'em."

CHAPTER XIV

THE HOUSE, STANDING alone and dissolute on top of the land rise, looked inappropriate for what would normally be expected of a wealthy farmer. It was simple and functional, lacking ornamentation of any kind. An exception to the apparent austerity was a garden of flowers and shrubs winding around the house—possibly the sign of a feminine presence.

In contrast with the exterior, the interior would strike a visitor as antithetical décor: walls painted in gay colors, furniture made of carved woods, and overstuffed chesterfields and chairs tastefully placed. Figurines adorned tables. Tapestries and oil paintings hung from the walls. Feminine presence confirmed.

In spite of her husband's frugality and her Quaker ways, the lady of the house wanted—demanded—a few luxuries. Her philosophy and, therefore, the question she often asked her husband was "Why do we have wealth if we do not use some of it for pleasure? You would get more pleasure out of life if you ate from the finest silver, drank from crystal, sat on overstuffed chairs, relaxed in front of a fireplace, and smoked a fine meerschaum pipe with a couple of hunting dogs by your side." She did not understand that her husband's pleasure came from wealth accumulation. This had almost ended the man's marriage early on, but he was cursed with the affliction called love, and would do anything for his wife.

There was one other exception to his frugality: he used a great amount of his wealth to back various schemes to free slaves, and to influence certain individuals in the colonial legislature to pass slave-friendly laws, with few favorable results.

"WHAT'S THE FARMER'S name?" asked Andrew.

"Williams, Thaddeus Williams," said Jim.

"So if these people are such good people, why don't they set their slaves free?" asked Branwen.

"I ain't got no understandin' of these people. All I know is they help those I bring 'em. You might do better to ask him when you see him."

"I will," she said, matter-of-fact. "You mind?"

"No."

She said nothing more.

"What now?" asked Andrew.

"Stay here and look at the stars for a while. When we're sure no one will see us, we'll go on. Williams has a hunting shack about a half mile into the woods from the opposite side of the clearing. He'll know we're there when he sees smoke from the fireplace. We get to it by following the clearing around the edge of the woods."

Sometime past midnight, Jim tapped a dozing Andrew on the shoulder. Andrew's sleep had not been a deep sleep; it had been more like one of those in-between states in which dreams meet reality. He sat up and shook the cobwebs from his mind. Likewise, Branwen woke up and looked around, stretching as if trying to touch the sky.

"Next stop is the shack in the woods," whispered Jim.

They had come a long way, had a few close calls, encountered or per-haps barely missed encountering Indians, experienced hunger, sickness, bad weather, and a multitude of other things which, at the time, had made them question what they were doing. And now, it was almost over. Just a little way to go in the direction this man, Williams, was to lead them. Could he do as well as Jim?

Jim took the lead, following the edge of the forest around the clearing until a wooden structure came into sight. "That's the smokehouse. There's a path in back that'll take us to the hunting shack." They walked around the back of the smoke house, and Jim pointed to an opening in the woods, say-ing, "This is the way. Let's go."

The trio walked along the path, and now and again, one of them tripped on a vine growing just off the ground or ran into a low branch. Somewhere close, a rustling in the trees was heard, and a high-pitched shriek sounded throughout the forest. *An owl got his dinner of rabbit,* thought Andrew.

"Well, there it is. Don't look like much, and it isn't. But it serves its purpose."

They were safe for now. Jim had used this cabin for the almost-final destination for refugee slaves in the past.

While slaves were *en route* with Jim or others like him, arrangements were made by Williams through his likeminded friends to arrange for lodg-ing, jobs, and the necessary documents to prove the colored person in ques-tion was a free man, either by birth or by manumission. A refugee slave could stay until he received documentation and transport to his destination. Some refugees were destined to work in factories, on fishing boats, or in shipyards, and others would do fieldwork or serve as house servants—not much differ-ently than they had done as slaves, but they would be doing it as free people.

Jim walked over to the fireplace at the far side of the cabin. Firewood had been placed in a neat stack next to it. Beside the stack was a wooden box with a few sticks of firewood spilling over the top. A smile came to Jim's face as he hesitated a minute to look. He took some firewood off, placed it in the fireplace, and proceeded to light a fire. He no longer had his flint, so he stuck a splinter of wood in his pistol's flash hole, poured a bit of gunpowder on a log, and fired the gun with the flint close to the log. The powder flashed with a bright light, and the log caught fire. Jim removed the top from the box. In it was a covered clay pot. He picked the pot up and removed the top.

"Ah, bless them people. It's full to the top," Jim said.

"Of what?" said Andrew.

"Drink, Andy. Cider, it smells like."

Jim brought the pot up to his mouth and took a small sip. "Yes, sir, it's cider, and still a bit bubbly."

"I am kinda thirsty. Pass it over when you're done," Andrew said. "You want some, Branwen?"

"No, I don't. I've seen what spirits do to people, and I'd just as soon not be that way. I use it to clean wounds and make potions. Nothing else."

"Not everybody gets that way, girl," said Andrew. "Some of us just likes to drain the tensions from working at life."

"Nevertheless, you fellows do what you will. Just remember, I can be a bear if I need to."

Jim took another swallow, and another. He wiped his mouth first on one shoulder, then on the other, and handed the pot to Andrew, who took a couple of gulps. Branwen was rolling her eyes at the two, and decided to change the course of what was happening. "Well, Andy, you still hoping to get work as a blacksmith?" she asked.

"Wouldn't mind, but don't know if it'll happen right off. I know I was set free, but no one else does. I can't tell anyone to check with Martin or Mary, because Martin's dead, and there's that other thing about me being wanted for killing Big Bull. Those papers Martin gave me won't do any good, slave or free, as long as I'm wanted for killing Big Bull."

"Williams might be able to help you out," said Jim. "We'll talk to him in the morning 'bout it." What Jim hadn't said, but was thinking, was that Williams might not want to do anything if Andrew couldn't convince him he had murdered Big Bull in self-defense.

"I've been thinking about something else on the way up here. Suppose Williams doesn't want anything to do with me? You know what I mean. Suppose he doesn't want to get involved with a runner running from a serious crime? I wouldn't blame him if he told me I was on my own, and to leave him out of it."

"Oh, no, Andy! I don't think that'll be the case," said Jim, wondering if Andrew had somehow read his mind.

"I've been thinking on the way up about going west as far as I can go, and taking my chances. They say if you go far enough, you'll run into another ocean. Nothing but Indians out there. If a black man went out there, he might be able to do what he wants. You know, cut down trees and plant what it takes to live, shoot deer to eat, and make clothes. Get an Indian girl for a wife, and spend the rest of your life living the way you want."

"Your scalp would be quite unique hanging from some Indian's long-house," said Branwen.

"Huh?"

"Not many other scalps like it."

"Oh. Anyhow, watching out for Indians shouldn't be much worse than having to look over my shoulder everywhere I go, and someday maybe being shipped back to Maryland, or even hanged by a bunch of whites, just so they could see a bulge-eyed nigger hanging from a tree, kicking his legs and wetting his pants."

"We're all taking the same chance, Andy. I'm taking a chance just like all those before me, and all those after. Jim's taking a chance just taking us. Even this white man, Williams, is taking a chance." Then Branwen thought, *first man I even thought was a nice person, and he wants to run away and take up with some Indian just because it worked for his friend. Well, there's more around than just him.*

"I'm not just a runaway. I'm wanted for more than stealing something from a white man. I'm wanted for killing a white man. Nobody's going to give me a trial or listen to my side of the story. If I get caught, I swing."

"Let's see what Williams can do, Andy," said Jim, "then you can make up your mind."

They passed the pot around again and talked about other things that made no sense to anybody not drinking. Andrew's eyes kept closing until Jim said something, and Andrew would wake just long enough to ask what Jim had said. Jim would repeat himself, and Andrew would make a comment as his eyes closed about halfway. Branwen, disgusted with the two of them, curled up on a bearskin rug next to the fireplace. The sound of a purring kitten indicated that she was asleep.

A POUNDING ON the door woke Branwen. She sat up and looked around. The fire in the fireplace had burned low, but was still putting out enough heat to take the night's chill off. Looking around, she remembered where she was, and there, sitting on the floor with his back propped against the side of the shack, was Andrew, his head bent down on his chest. Jim had collapsed in an awkward position resembling more or less the bearskin rug she had fallen asleep on.

Again, someone pounded on the door. "Who's there?" she demanded.

A voice from the other side of the door said, "Mister Williams saw smoke coming from the chimney, and wants to know who's in his hunting shack."

Without identifying herself, she said, "Mister Williams is expecting us. Please tell him we're here."

"Yes'm," was the answer.

In a raised voice Branwen said, "Alright, you two, time to get up. Williams knows we're here. Jim! Get up, get up!" She walked over to the prostrate figure and nudged him in the ribs with her foot. "Get up, Jim. William's going to be here in short order."

"Oh, my head!" was all he said.

"You deserve it. Did you hear what I said? Williams knows we're here. He's going to be here any minute."

Andrew didn't say a thing. He knew there would be no sympathy from this woman. Instead, he got up and went outside to attend to nature. Jim, holding his head, got up and followed in Andrew's footsteps.

Andrew tossed more wood in the fireplace while Branwen straightened the place. Jim was of no help at all. He sat on the floor against the woodpile, trying to focus on anything that didn't move.

"Last time I do that," he declared.

"Sure, it is," Branwen said. "You'll never touch a drop again. Right?"

"Ohhh!"

"Better make yourself pretty, Jim," said Andrew, "or you'll mess the whole thing up."

"It don't mean nothin' to Williams. He's come to expect this of me. He might be a tad suspicious if I wasn't in this condition."

"Hell of a password," said Branwen.

"There should be some tea on one of those shelves. Would one of you make a pot? Please!" said Jim.

Branwen stepped up to the task. Not finding a tea infuser or strainer, Branwen tossed a handful of tea into a pot and boiled it, and before long, Jim had his hands curled around a hot cup of tea. He had no problem straining the leaves through his teeth, except when he went to spit them out on the floor, he caught Branwen's evil eye telling him he'd better not. Instead, he spit in the fireplace, and swallowed a bit at the same time.

The sun was almost overhead before they heard a rap on the door followed by, "Jim, you in there? This is Thaddeus. Open up."

"I'm coming." He made his way to the door and opened it.

"Hello, Thaddeus."

"Ah! I see you're in your usual condition, Jim. I should introduce you to my wife someday."

"Please don't, Thaddeus. Come in."

Upon his entry, Jim introduced Andrew and Branwen.

"Unusual name, Branwen. I was told you preferred not to take a surname."

"Doesn't mean a thing. People know who Branwen is without a middle or last name."

"I see. But now Branwen is a fugitive slave, with a reward for her return. As of now, there is no Branwen. She's gone, and that's all there is to it."

"This has something to do with a new identity for me, doesn't it?"

"It does. I suppose I should've asked how your trip was, but it's just as well we get to the business at hand. Time is important, and there is little of it. Let me get to the specifics."

Jim said, "You want me to stick around, or can I get to going back?"

"You've done your job, Jim. You can go now, or stay here and rest for a day or two, if you wish."

"I'll rest and leave first thing in the morning."

"Thought so."

"I'm going outside and get some air while you talk to these two."

The others watched silently until the door closed behind him. Then Williams spoke. "First let me talk to this young man. You're Andrew, am I correct?"

"Yes, sir."

"A letter arrived for you. Can you read? If not, I'll read it to you."

"I can read."

"Ah, good."

"It arrived about a month ago. You should read it before we discuss anything more. The sender also sent me a letter which I have read, and it filled my heart. Hope yours does the same for you."

Andrew took the letter and looked it over. It was sealed with the wax stamp of the Blackistons. He took the letter and excused himself to sit on the bearskin rug in front of the fireplace. There he opened it.

"While you read the letter, I'll talk with Branwen."

Andrew gave a quick motion of his head and began to read the letter.

Williams turned his attention to Branwen. "Branwen, I have here documents indicating you were born a free girl child of a white man and his black slave, who he set free prior to your birth. The name on the document is Bonnie Miller. It's not a fake document. Unfortunately, the real Bonnie Miller died of pneumonia caused by consumption. You fit her physical description in all ways. The real Bonnie Miller passed away two years ago, while under the care of a doctor she also worked for. The doctor thought her papers might be of use to us. Now you have come along, and Bonnie Miller continues to live."

"Bonnie Miller! I like it. What was she like?"

"I don't know. I do know she helped our doctor friend, and was taking care of people inflicted with the consumption when she caught it herself."

"She must have been a nice person. I'll like carrying on her name."

"You may do more than just carry on her name. Our friend has agreed to take you in as a helper; you'll be doing the same work Bonnie Miller did."

"I could get the consumption, too!"

"Yes, you could. You don't have to take the job. We might be able to find another job for you. But under the circumstances of him donating the identity, I thought I'd ask. Either way, the identity is yours."

"You'll have to excuse me for sounding so selfish, but I was afraid for a moment. Yes, I'd like to work for the doctor. I have some experience in helping sick and injured, though a real physician might not approve of some of my methods."

"That's settled. You'll leave tomorrow morning."

Williams and Branwen—now Bonnie—looked toward Andrew and saw a man's man weeping to himself. Bonnie moved to Andrew and knelt in front of him, putting her arms around him and drawing him to her. "What's it say, Andy?"

He was too choked up to say anything, and handed the letter to Bonnie. She read it to herself.

My Dear Andrew,

I hope this letter finds you as well as Martin and me. Yes, Andrew. Martin is alive. The ball fired at Martin's head did not kill him. He has lost his right ear and the hearing in that ear, but otherwise, he is the same hardheaded (as he proved) man we both love. He was found by Will Bryan after he caught two bounty hunters attempting to sell Martin's buggy and mule. The farmer who bought you has also been brought to jail for trial.

That is all good news, as I am sure you will agree. However, it does not stop there. Mister Littlefield, who employed Big Bull—you do remember Big Bull, don't you?—found his decomposed body in the swamp down where you and Ignatius used to hunt ducks. He had fired Big Bull, because Big Bull almost killed one of the slaves with his whip. Big Bull had hit Mister Littlefield with his whip, helped himself to Littlefield's supply of rum, and took off toward the swamp, swearing at Mister Littlefield and everybody else he came across. After a week of not hearing anything of Big Bull from anybody, he decided to go into the swamp to look for him. He took along several of his slaves to help him search, and one of the slaves found his bloated and decomposing body in the reeds.

Mister Littlefield and the constable decided the official cause of death as just plain too drunk to save himself from drowning.

I have enclosed an additional copy of the manumission document made out by Martin and me showing we set you free, as I suppose there is a chance your copy may have been lost or destroyed with your ordeals. There is an additional testimony from both Martin and me testifying to the authenticity of the papers, and any reader may contact us or our solicitor to confirm.

We love and miss you, and want you to know you are welcome back, should you decide to return.

Our love,

Mary and Martin Blackiston

"That's wonderful, Andy. I'm so happy for you. Are you going to go back?"

"Guess I could go with Jim. But I want to think about it a bit."

Williams, overhearing Andrew and Bonnie, said, "If Jim's leaving tomorrow, you haven't much time to make up your mind, son. Better hurry it up."

"Did you have a place for me to go if I stayed?"

"We did, but that was before I received a letter about you being a free man. We don't usually place a free man. It's up to a free man to find his own place."

"Mind telling me where and what it was? Maybe I'll just go there and take my chances."

"If that's what you want to do, I'll consider the position filled, and won't offer it to anybody else. But you have to be the one who asks for it. If it's any help, I'll give you a letter of recommendation to the extent I know you and know of you."

"What and where?"

"There's a blacksmith in Lexington who needs a helper. Lexington is a small town not too far from Boston."

"How do I get to it? Can you draw me a map and give me directions?"

"I can, but it's a long way from here. My idea would be to take you with me when I take Bonnie to Boston, and you can get off there. Lexington's less than a hundred miles from there, and you're used to walking."

"That's good of you."

"My wife would say it was the Christian thing to do," Williams said with a self-satisfied look on his face.

The Christian comment resonated with Bonnie, and her face came alive with the realization she had something to ask Williams. "Mister Williams, I hope you don't mind if I ask you a question you might not like, but that I've been thinking about for a long time."

Williams' smile vanished, and his face became serious. "Go on. What's on your mind, girl?"

"I know you're a Quaker, and I know Quakers don't approve of slavery. Why do you have slaves, and why don't you let them go or make them free?"

"Oh, well! I thought you were going to ask me about drinking cider and giving it to Jim there, and that you didn't approve of such things. Jim was pretty bad this morning, wasn't he?"

"He was, and I don't, but that's another subject."

"I'll tell you after I address your first question."

Williams found a chair and sat down. He stretched his legs out and folded his arms in front.

"When I first came to this country from England, I was an ambitious lad and wanted to have a plantation and make a lot of money. It seemed easy enough, what with all the land available. All a man had to do was swing an ax and grow crops. Well, I soon found out one man can't do it all by himself. Oh, maybe a small place just big enough to survive and raise a family; there's plenty of those around. One bad winter, though, and they're done for. They have to go into town and get jobs doing whatever they can. Not much different than the jobs we're getting for you runaways. I wanted more than that. The only way to get help around here was to have slaves. So, I bought slaves with what little money I had. Things were going pretty good for me. One day, I was in town to buy another slave, and I saw this pretty young girl. We were instantly in love, and I began to court her. But her parents didn't approve of me because I wasn't a Friend, and to top it off, I had slaves. They said I couldn't court the girl anymore."

Williams sat back and lighted a pipe. He inhaled deeply two or three times, and blew a series of smoke rings high in the air.

Bonnie said, "Well, Mister Williams, what happened?"

"Well, I'll tell you. That girl was not the type not to go after something she liked. Ha! She must have thought I was quite the catch. Never could figure that out. But anyway, she up and told her folks she was in love with me and she was going to marry me." Williams inhaled another lungful of smoke.

Bonnie, who had entered this conversation with a chip on her shoulder, was now a completely captive listener.

"Go on, Mister Williams," she said.

"Now, bear in mind I had never asked her to marry me; it was her idea. Oh, sure, I was thinking about it, but I knew her parents would never have me. Then she walks right up next to me and puts her arm through mine, and announces I am going to become a Quaker and free all my slaves. I don't mind telling you, I had to sit down real fast. I didn't know what to do. I wanted to vanish like a genie going back into a bottle. I saw the looks on her parents faces. Two people with jaws dropped down to their laps. They'd never heard their little girl talk that way before." He paused and looked to the ceiling, but was looking way back in his memory.

"Anyhow, I said to her, 'I'd like to talk to you outside for a minute.' Her parents didn't even notice us leaving. They were still trying to close their mouths. Outside, she said, 'Thaddeus, you know yourself these slaves have been difficult to handle. Just give them the option of working for you for pay, or you'll have to sell them. They cost more now than if you could hire the work done anyhow. This way, they'll have to take care of themselves.' Well, you know something? That made sense to me, and then and there, I asked her to marry me. She was on my side. Since then, we've had to modify that policy a little. I now give my slaves the option of buying themselves from me. I give them Saturdays and Sundays off, so they can work for pay from other people, and if they work for me on their days off, I pay them. There's a few of the older ones who just don't want to be on their own, and want to stay with me the way they were. So I don't sell them, and we get along pretty good. I've never used a whip on any of them, though sometimes I might have been tempted."

"The ones like this goddamned nigger." Nobody noticed Jim had come in and was listening to Williams.

"Yes. Exactly as you must have been. I wish there were ten of you."

"Bonnie might not ask," said Andrew, "but I will. What about the drinking cider thing?"

"Friends aren't against drinking. Like anything else, we believe in controlling yourself. But in my case, my wife is personally against it, and doesn't want it in the house. That's not too much to ask of me, considering all she's done and what she means to me. But I drank before we met, and there's nothing I like better than to relax once in a while with a cup of cider or even something stronger. And now and again, I like to get together with some of my old friends and talk about old times with a little cider being passed around. So I had my people build this hunting cabin away from the house. When I tell my wife I'm going hunting, she knows what I'm talking about, and doesn't say a word except 'Good hunting. Don't be gone too long.' It's kind of our understanding. I don't think I've ever taken a gun out to this place since I've had it."

There was silence around the room, and then Williams said, "Enough of this talk! Are your questions answered?"

There was silence for an answer. and he said, "Do what you have to do for the rest of the day, or just talk. Bonnie, you come back to the house with me. My wife will get you cleaned up, and she has a new outfit for you. I don't think it would do having you dressed as an Indian when we get to Boston. Andrew, when Bonnie returns, she'll be bringing you two changes of clothing. One will be for everyday wear, similar to what you have on, but new; and the other will be for work. Suggest you go down to the stream in back and clean up. Frankly, you're a little ripe. Wouldn't hurt you to go with him either, Jim. We'll see you bright and early." He got up and tapped his pipe on his heel, and the ashes fell to the floor. Williams closed the door behind them as they left. A few seconds later, Bonnie came in again, swept the pipe ashes into the fireplace, and said, "Men!" before leaving again.

When Bonnie returned, she was dressed in a plain gray dress, wore a bonnet, and carried another bundle of clothes, which she explained contained a change for her and two sets for Andrew. In place of her moccasins, she had on a pair of shoes not too different from the brogans she had worn before, but finished much more nicely.

A FAMILIAR POUNDING at the door woke Bonnie and Andrew. It was the same person who had awakened them the day before. "Mister Williams told me you got to be ready to leave in two hours, and for you to get ready. Eat as much as you can, so we don't have to stop. I'll pick you up then." He left a basket with them which contained hot biscuits, butter, and milk. After the man left, Andrew said, "I guess this is it. Where's Jim? Must already be up and taking his early morning."

"Don't think so, Andy. Look at what he wrote on my nice clean floor with a burnt piece of wood."

It read:

Always glad to help a friend.

You two get to know each other.

Maybe see you sometime.

That damned nigger

"He went his way," Bonnie said.

"We'll see him again. I know it for sure. Don't know when or where, but we'll see him again."

IT WAS EXACTLY two hours later that Williams and his driver pulled up in a coach. "You two ready? We've got some traveling to do. I don't expect us to be stopped by anybody along the way, but just in case, I brought a brace of pistols if do get stopped and they don't like our answers, or maybe they're road bandits."

"We've got pistols and muskets, too, Mister Williams. Don't think we'll have any trouble we can't handle."

"Does the fact that you never showed me how to use them mean anything?" asked Bonnie.

"Bluff it," said Andrew.

"I'd like to kick you sometime."

"Ignatius used to kid, 'Never show a woman how to shoot unless you know she loves you more than anything in the world.'"

"Guess I'll never learn."

REACHING BOSTON, THEY rode through the city. It was the first time either Andrew or Bonnie had seen a city, though Andrew had been to Bryan Town, but it had not looked anything like this. Bryan Town was only a small collection of stores, a few houses, the inn, the jail, and the livery—and that was all. Here, there were streets made of flat stones, which produced an odd sensation through the carriage as they drove over them. There were rows and rows of houses and stores and offices and crowds and more crowds of people. People, some dressed in their finest, others selling newspapers, people pushing carts loaded with vegetables and freshly-butchered livestock and fish piled high as a haystack and chickens and ducks and buckets of milk. Tars flirted with girls who showed a little leg. And as all this went on, soldiers dressed in their handsome red and white uniforms kept watch over the populace, with particular attention to the young girls.

Williams ordered his driver to stop so they might look at the activity. "They're certainly flippery," said Bonnie.

With a questioning look, Williams questioned, "They're what?"

"You know, the soldiers dressed in their pretty uniforms, ruffles and all."

"Oh, sure. Some of them, I suppose."

"Why are they looking at everyone?" asked Andrew.

"Who?"

"The soldiers."

"I'm not sure. I understand some of the people are unhappy with some of the taxes and other rules imposed on them. I've heard there have been crowds protesting, and in a few cases, they've thrown rocks and garbage at the soldiers."

"That's no way to act. There must be another way. I'd say there were just a couple of troublemakers inciting the others," Bonnie said.

"You sound like my wife. You have good insight on what may be happening."

A soldier with his musket at the ready came to the side of the carriage and spoke to Williams. "Excuse me, sir. You can't stop your carriage here. You'll have to move on."

Andrew dropped his hand closer to his pistol.

"Can you tell me where we could find a doctor named Warren?" asked Williams.

"Yes, sir, I know of him." The soldier proceeded to give directions.

They drove on, and Bonnie commented, "He was polite, but he was frighteningly polite. I had the sense he might have hurt us if we had given him cause."

"I don't know, Bonnie."

"I saw what you did, Andy. Would you have used your pistol?" she asked.

"Don't know. I just reacted to the situation. I felt as uncomfortable as you did. Glad we're out of there."

"If it's any comfort," said Williams, "I don't think he was concerned with fugitive slaves, and though he didn't show it, he noticed Andy's musket and pistol. Odds are he was as scared as we were."

"You're a Quaker, Mister Williams. Would you have fought if we had been attacked?" asked Andrew.

"I'm a Friend because my wife's a Friend. That was our understanding from the start. I'm completely devoted to her and the Friends. But when it comes right down to it, yes, I'd have been in the fray."

They pulled up in front of a house set back from the street with a path leading to a small set of steps and the front door. "Andrew, you may as well stay here. I'll be back in a few minutes after leaving Bonnie with the doctor. Bonnie, come with me."

Bonnie turned to Andrew and said, "You may as well keep my guns. I'm going to help put people together, not the other way around." She gave Andrew a hug and began to say something. Andrew put his arms around her and tried to kiss her. She pulled away and turned her head and Andrew settled for just kissing her cheek. "Maybe some other time, Andy. Goodbye and good luck."

"You, too," was all he said as he released her.

Williams and Bonnie walked to the door, where a small sign stated it was the house of Doctor Joseph Warren, and to please knock loudly.

Williams knocked on the door several times before it was opened. A young man, smartly dressed, stood before Williams and Bonnie. Andrew couldn't hear what was said, but Williams said something and motioned toward Bonnie. The young man extended his arm and asked them to enter. They did so. The door closed.

"She got away from you," said the driver. "I had been wondering about you two since the first time I knocked on the door of Mister Williams' hunting shack. The way you kept looking at each other without the other knowing. I just thought it would have a different ending."

"What's your name?"

"I'm Sam. I like to think I'm Sam Williams. Haven't asked Mister Williams if he'd mind me using his name."

"Are you one of his slaves?"

"Yes, sir, but after this trip, I should have enough money to finish buying me."

"Then what're you gonna do?"

"I want to keep working for Mister Williams."

The door of the house opened and Williams stepped out, turning back and to shake the hand of the man who had opened the door. Andrew lowered his head to see further into the house, but to no avail. She was not to be seen.

Not a word was spoken as they drove through Boston. Williams observed the people at work and the ever-present soldiers. There seemed to be an awkward peace—but, nevertheless, a peace—between them.

Andrew, on the other hand, was lost in his thoughts. He hadn't noticed they had left Boston until Williams said, "Lexington's less than half a day down this road. It'll make my trip a little longer, but Sam here could use the extra pay. We'll take you."

It was not more than four or five hours after leaving Boston that they came upon a tavern. A sign identified it as Munroe's Tavern.

"What'll it be, gentlemen?" asked a man. "Name's John Munroe."

Williams said, "I'll have a pint."

"And your two boys?"

"Nothing for me," said Andrew.

"Milk, if you have it," Sam said.

It occurred to Williams that Andrew didn't have any money, and had nothing to eat.

He took Andrew aside and said, "Andrew, order yourself something. You might need a little money. We give a refugee enough to get him settled, anyhow, and I think you still qualify."

Turning toward the man again, Andrew said, "I'll have milk, too."

"How'd you like some chowder to go along with those drinks?" asked Munroe. "Just made it this morning."

The chowder and drinks were brought to them, and Williams asked the innkeeper, "How far is it to a blacksmith named Harrington?"

"You're just about there. You keep going down the road, and you'll come to the town green. Harrington's on the far side."

It was not difficult to find the blacksmith's shop on the far side of the green. They drove their carriage up a short dirt road and stopped. The clanging sound of a hammer striking an anvil came from inside the shop to greet them. They peered inside a doorway large enough to drive a wagon through. The shop seemed dark, lit only by sunlight beaming through the door and a few windows here and there. At the other end of the shop, coals glowed from the forge.

"Wait here. I'll have a few words with Harrington. He still thinks I'm bringing a refugee rather than a free man." He disappeared into the dimness of the shop.

"What you going to do if he don't want a free man?" asked Sam.

"I have a backup plan."

"What's that?"

"Go west and see what the rest of the plan has in store for me."

Williams came out. "He wants to talk to you. Follow me in. Sam, you wait here."

Williams led Andrew through the shop to where Harrington was quenching a piece of iron. Upon their approach, Harrington turned and looked at Andrew, studying him. "You know what and why I'm doing what I'm doing to this piece of iron?" he asked Andrew.

"Don't know for sure, 'cause I don't know what you're trying to make. But I'd guess you might be annealing the steel so you can cold work it, and you're just cooling it down, or you might be trying to give it a bit of temper."

"Take a close look at it. What do you see?"

Andrew came closer to the work, and could see the slight irregularity where two pieces had been joined to make a longer piece. "I'd say you just welded the piece from two shorter lengths, and were cooling it down."

"You can weld?"

"I can. I'm a pretty good farrier, too."

"We don't get much shoeing business other than making a few shoes. Most of the farmers 'round here do their own. Williams tells me you're a free man."

"That's correct."

"The reason I wanted a runaway, other than I don't believe in slavery and thought I could help, is that I don't want to pay a big wage. I thought putting on a runaway would cost me less."

"I've never been paid a wage before. Just had what I've needed given to me. I'd be willing to work for whatever you think I'm worth, as long as it's enough for me to buy food and a place to live."

"I've got an office in the back I don't use all that much. Would you be willing to stay there? I'd pay you enough for your food, and enough more to take care of your other needs."

"That would do me. But I want you to know I'd want to improve my lot in life. I'd want to see what else I can do, and how far I can go."

"Meaning what?"

"I may want to venture at something else."

"You thinking about something else in particular?"

"In the back of my mind, yes."

Williams had the feeling Andrew had just dashed his chances with Harrington.

"If I take a chance on you and you're as good as you seem to be, will you give me a year of honest work, and after that, three months' notice if you decide on seeking your fortune elsewhere?"

In his mind, Andrew was thinking this was a deal that would allow him time to figure out what he wanted to do, and what direction he wanted to go. "If that's an offer, I'll take you up on it."

Harrington extended his hand, and they shook. He said, "Name's Daniel Harrington. Just call me Daniel."

"Come get your guns and clothes from the coach," said Williams.

"Guns! You have guns?" asked Harrington.

"A couple of muskets and pistols."

Harrington was thinking about something, but kept it to himself until he knew Andrew better. *Better have a word with John*, he thought.

"WHERE'S DANIEL?" THE man asked.

"Scared the devil out of me. Didn't hear you come in," said Andrew.

"Sorry. I've got a broken plowshare. Need it welded soon as possible."

"Let me take a look at it. Daniel's in his house." Andrew looked at the two pieces of plowshare the man held in his hands. "Shouldn't be a problem. I guess I can do it now." Andrew plunged the broken ends of the two pieces in the glowing coals of the forge.

"Daniel told me he'd taken on a helper. You must be him."

"That's right. Andrew Attaway's my name."

"I'm John Parker. How long you planning on staying here?"

"Don't know for sure, but at least a year. That's the deal I made with Daniel."

"He did mention that. Did he tell you anything else about life around here?"

"Nothin' except the people are pretty good people, and most have known each other all their lives, and many are related one way or another."

"Did he mention the militia?"

"The what?"

"The militia. You know what a militia is?"

"I've heard about 'em. So, what about it?"

"The provincial congress has recommended that each town have a militia, and every able-bodied man should be a member of it. I've been elected by all those in our militia to be their captain."

"I've a feeling what you're about to say."

"Uh huh, 'you look more than able-bodied to me, and since you're living here, you can consider yourself a member…if you want.'"

"I've overheard Daniel talking to others about it, but didn't pay much attention to what was said."

"Simply put, the British are giving us a difficult time about taxes, and we're giving them a difficult time right back, saying that they have no right to tax us without our consent."

"Don't know much about it."

"I guess I should ask you—do you have any feelings for or against the British?"

"They've never bothered me."

"That's an answer you might expect from half the people anywhere but here. Here in Lexington, we all feel pretty much we'd just as soon the British went back home and let us run own lives and govern our own affairs."

"If you're part of a militia, it means you're willing to fight, and, if necessary, die for the colonies. Now, I can't force you to be in the militia if you have sympathies for the British, but here in Lexington, people aren't going to get along with you too well."

Andrew was being pressured, and he knew it. His immediate thinking was he could get out when his agreement with Daniel was up—a good time to look westward once more. Chances were, nothing would happen before then. "John, you want me in the militia, I'll be in the militia—and if it comes to fighting the British, I'll do the best I can."

"That's what I wanted to hear. Ah, Daniel said you had some guns, right?"

"A few."

"Keep 'em ready at all times from now on."

"What else?"

"We meet once a year on the green, sometimes more. We muster, and then we go over to Buckman Tavern. Most of the boys would just as soon skip the muster and go right to the tavern…you'll like 'em…great bunch of boys."

BOOK THREE

CHAPTER XV

AFTER TIGHTENING THE cinch, he was about ready to lower the stirrup when he felt her press up against his back. He knew it was her by her unique scent. "Where you going?" she asked, whispering in his ear.

She left no room for him to turn without brushing against her. He took a chance. As he turned, she stayed pressed against him, and it was wonderful, and she was wonderful, and he was in love, and—

"What the hell's all that noise?" Andrew said aloud to no one but himself. "Wake a man from hell. It was so real. Wonder what…." He swung his legs out from his new feather bed and put his head in his hands. Andrew listened, and his ears focused on the noise. It was horses again; those goddamned pounding horse hoofs, running hoofs, all night long. They seemed to be going to and from the reverend's house. *Reverend Clarke's place had more visitors the last week than there are horses in Lexington* he was thinking. *But tonight, it's been nonstop. Why can't they just walk, and let a man sleep?*

The drummer beat his drum as the belfry rang out. Talking to himself, he said, "The militia call. This better not be a training session, 'cause I'm not in a training mood. I've been doing this two years now, and it's the same old thing: nothing." He stood up and stretched, walked over to the paraffin lamp, and turned it up just enough to see. Finding the chamber pot, he urinated and tried to clear his head.

Andrew dressed in a hurry, grabbed his pouch of balls and powder flask, slung them over his head, and let them hang down his backside. Picking up his musket, he opened the frizzen and made sure there was no gunpowder in the pan before closing the frizzen again. His canteen he let hang down from his left shoulder. On the way out, he grabbed a half-loaf of stale bread off his table and chewed on it; it would have to do for now.

Out in the street, he could see other figures moving toward the common. Windows were lighted, and silhouettes of people were looking out, filling the frames. Dogs barked as men ran toward the common, and a cur tried to bite Andrew's legs as he ran. He swung the butt of his musket at the dog and felt it strike home; the dog gave a yelp, changed its mind, and backed off, content to sit and watch the hurly-burly.

Arriving on the common, Andrew saw Sergeant Munroe pacing back and forth as he waited for his company of men to arrive for muster. There were several men coming from Buckman Tavern across the street, but most were coming from other directions. Coughing as he had been for several weeks, Captain Parker arrived and went straight to the sergeant. Andrew heard the sergeant ask Parker, "You alright, John?"

Captain Parker replied the same as he always did. "I'm fine. Let's get these men formed."

The militia was made up of Lexington's able-bodied men; most were farmers, a few were tradesmen, and some, like John Parker, were a bit of both. There were older men who had been in the British army during the French and Indian war, including Parker and his older cousin, Jonas Parker. These experienced men knew something about the commands of a regimented army, but the other younger men gathering on the common had little or no knowledge. When they were ordered to muster, it was about all one could expect from these men to be quiet, listen with attention, and answer when the clerk of the company, who just happened to be Andrew's boss Daniel Harrington, took roll.

Standing in back of Andrew was Prince Estabrook. He was a slave belonging to Benjamin Estabrook. It was presumed by all that he was in the militia as a substitute for his master, Benjamin, but as Benjamin sometimes showed for muster, no one knew for certain what the arrangement was.

"Hi, Andy."

Andrew turned around to see who the voice belonged to. "Hello, Prince. What's this about this time?"

"The usual, I guess."

Sergeant Munroe yelled, "Listen up, men! Come to some kind of order! Answer when your name's called!"

The roll was called, and somewhere in the neighborhood of a hundred and twenty men answered as a few stragglers continued to come from here and there. Afterwards, Sergeant Munroe turned the militia over to the captain.

Captain Parker addressed his men. "Sorry to wake you men, but we've been notified by riders from Boston that British troops are on the march to Concord to find and destroy hidden stores of arms, munitions, and food for use by militias, us included. They are also to arrest a couple of visitors lodged at Reverend Clarke's house. If you don't know them by sight, you know them by reputation: they're John Hancock and Sam Adams, and are considered rabble-rousers and troublemakers by the British. And, I might add, that's a fact we've come to support."

"Here! Here!" most of the men shouted in unison.

"Sergeant Munroe here posted armed guards, of which some of you were a part, around the reverend's house early this morning just prior to the alarm to assemble was sounded. The sergeant has also sent a rider to find out how far away the British are." Interrupting himself, he coughed several times.

Prince turned his head toward Andrew and said, "The captain doesn't look good. Bet he's lost twenty pounds in the last month. I heard he has the consumption."

"I think you're right," said Andrew, nodding his agreement.

Captain Parker was well aware his militia was made of old Indian fighters who fought on their own terms, and undisciplined younger men who did not take to orders. For this reason, he led his militia by consensus of opinion, offering his own opinion first rather than strict military commands.

"Boys," the captain said, "We're here to consult with one another on what we should do, but let me give you additional information I've been given so we can come to a consensus. By all reports, we're outnumbered by several hundred or so. Also, the provincial congress and the safety committee, of which Adams and Hancock are leaders, have given an order for the militias to not, I repeat, not take aggressive action unless the British start it first."

From somewhere in the ranks came, "We can't just turn tail and run, John. We have to stand up to those redcoats and let 'em see we're not afraid." Several others sang out in agreement. Some expressed the opinion they should take cover behind the stone walls or hide in the woods, so the British would be sitting ducks and easier to fight should they start tearing up the town or harassing the people.

Others, considering the odds, voiced their opinion that it was best just to clear out and see what was going to happen. Later in the day, when it was warmer, they could regroup and work out a plan of action.

In the end, it was agreed between Parker's men that they would form up on the common and let the British see that they were not welcome, but no one was to interfere with the British march or do anything that could cause hostilities to break out.

"And if they want something else?" asked Parker's cousin.

"Well, Jonah, listen for my command. I know you'd like to get a couple more scalps for your collection, but let's not put us in jeopardy." Some of the men laughed at the reply as they remembered some of the happenings in the last war, and knew Jonah had been a fearless fighter with notches on his tomahawk. They understood there were several others present who had fought alongside him, not a coward among them.

"Gotcha, cousin. We'll wait for your command," Jonas said with a knowing smile.

"What now, captain?" asked another. "We gonna just wait here for 'em? It's getting a bit cold." Several others seconded his comment.

"None of the scouts we've sent out have returned, so we don't know where the British are. They were expected soon, but none have shown. I doubt if they all could have been stopped and captured by the British, but I just don't know. Makes me think they had to ride all the way to Boston, and the redcoats haven't left. It's safe to bet they won't be coming anytime soon, if at all. All those who want to go home can go, but don't get too comfortable. Be on the alert for a recall. I don't know what time those redcoats are going to be here, but we have to be ready. Those of you who would rather wait around can wait at the Buckman. I'll be there waiting to see what else is going to happen. This cough is getting to me, and I could use something to clear my throat."

The militia broke up, its numbers going their chosen ways. Andrew and Prince remained on the common after Andrew said, "Hold on, Prince. Before you leave, I'd like to talk with you a minute."

"Sure, Andy. What about?"

"I've never quite figured you out. I know you're a slave, but I can't figure out why you're so willing to take a ball for Benjamin."

Prince gave a slight smile and a hint of a laugh. "No, that's not the way it is. Benjamin and I pretty much grew up together. He inherited me when his father died. We're more than just master slave. We're friends. He counts me as a possession for his worth and knows he can do with me what he wants, but he still asks me; he doesn't tell me. I've served with him before in a few skirmishes, fighting Indians, and we both came out alive. I'd do anything he asked of me."

Andrew thought back to his days with Ignatius. He had been one of the few blacks who could look back at a master with fondness, but he also remembered when he had been made a slave again with a not so kind master. Though the scars from the whippings had faded, the sting of the whip would never leave his memory.

Continuing with Prince, Andrew said, "I guess each of us has his reasons for doing things, but why would you, or any slave, be willing to fight the French and Indians, and now the British, when you'll still be a slave? Only the white man has profited from these wars. I'm not even sure what I'm doing here, right here on this ground, right now, waiting to be shot and maybe killed. I'm free, but I don't know how long. If somebody takes a mind for me to be their slave, they could find a way to make me no longer free."

"I can't speak to what you're saying, or for any slave other than myself. But Benjamin told me a long time ago he'd set me free anytime I wanted. I said I was fine the way I was. Now, things are looking a little different. Benjamin says this, this—whatever you want to call what's happening in Boston—is going to lead to a war with Britain, because in a way, even the white people of the colonies are slaves to them. He says if we win a war for freedom, we'll all be free, including Negroes, and I can have a regular job with him."

"Maybe so, Prince. I hope you're right. Might be true up here, but where I come from, well…I just don't know. They're a different people down there. They're always going to have their slaves. Even the British don't have slaves anymore."

JOHN HANCOCK AND Samuel Adams had left the Reverend Clarke's house along with the reverend to listen to the militia's discussions. By the time they arrived on the common, most of the men had departed. The reverend said, "Parker's probably inside the tavern," pointing in that direction. They made their way to the tavern and found the captain at a table talking with Sergeant Munroe.

"William," said Captain Parker to Sergeant Munroe, "We need to send out another scout. Take care of it."

"Will do, but it looks as if the reverend and his friends are on the way over here."

"Let's see what they have to say."

Parker began a coughing spell, but managed to quell it, and looked up at the approaching trio.

"I believe you know these gentlemen, John," Reverend Clarke said.

"I've seen them around, and know who they are."

"We'd like to talk to you."

"Didn't think you came here to play cards, Reverend. What can I do for you?"

The reverend, together with Hancock and Adams, told Captain Parker, with Sergeant Munroe listening, that it was important to mention again not to engage the British for any reason, and should the British look as if they were going to take action or even approach the militia, the militia was to disperse as quickly as possible.

"I understand, and the men and I have already discussed what we should do, and pretty much agreed upon the same action. "We're going to show the British we stand together, and nothing else."

"John," said the Reverend, "We're all in agreement on how to handle the British. Now it's time for Samuel and John to go elsewhere, and I believe Sergeant Munroe knows the way."

"Send the scout first, William, and then go to the reverend's house and take care of what he requests."

"Until then, we have other work to attend to, John," said Adams. "You'll excuse us."

"As you will," Parker said.

NOT LONG BEFORE sunup, one of the scouts returned to give Parker a report: the British were fast approaching, not more than half an hour away. "It was hell, John. I saw the British stopping and questioning everybody they came across. Took their horses and set them on foot. I just barely managed to get away and outrun them on my horse."

In turn, Captain Parker had the call to arms sounded by way of the drummer and the belfry. As the militia was forming on the common in some semblance of a military formation to wait for the British, Captain Parker waited until the bulk of the militia had arrived, or at least those who were going to arrive. It was clear the number of militiamen present at the first muster would not be able to arrive by the time they were now needed. Perhaps half of them were present when the captain gave them his order, "Do not shoot, I repeat, do not shoot at the British, no matter how much you'd like to. Don't heckle them; don't take a threatening stance, but rather take a ready stance. Don't forget we're outnumbered, and if even one of you takes an aggressive action, you could well be dead, as might also the men next to you and several others."

Once again, Jonas Parker spoke up, "And if they start shooting at us, we're still to wait your command?"

"Jonas, if they start shooting at you, save your skin. Shoot back, if that's what you think. Run, take cover, do anything you feel is necessary. Remember how it was when we were fighting Indians and did the same thing."

"That's what I wanted to hear, John. I'll be quiet from here on."

Parker said, "Make sure your muskets are loaded and ready."

Andrew usually carried his gun with the barrel loaded and the pan empty to prevent an accidental discharge—something Ignatius had taught him. *Don't put powder in the pan unless you're planning on shooting.* Andrew remembered what Ignatius had insisted upon. *It's too easy for the stuff to go off, or get wet and never go off.* The pan now loaded, Andrew gave his attention to Captain Parker once again.

Captain Parker had just finished addressing his men when down the road coming from Boston appeared the British troops. As they came closer to the common, the end of the column could not be seen, confirming the troops were high in number, vastly outnumbering Parker's. There were several British officers at the head of the column. As the British came close to Parker's men, one of the officers shouted something to the gathered militia.

One of the men asked, "What'd he say?" directing his question to no one in particular.

Andrew said, "I think he was telling us to drop our arms and go away."

The men were confused and looked to Parker for an order, but before he was able to give it, the British officer shouted a command to his troops and they rode towards Parker's group. Parker, alarmed by what appeared to be aggressive action on the part of the redcoats, shouted, "Don't stand your ground, don't fire! Disperse and get out of here!" But with the British troops riding toward the militia, both the British officer and Parker's orders were not clearly heard by Parker's men.

"Members of the militia were asking each other what the orders were. Still others didn't wait to know what they had been; it was clear enough the British were coming at them, and they weren't about to wait around and find out why. Most, but not all, of the militia tried to disperse and run for safety... but not fast enough.

"C'mon, Jonas," prodded Daniel Harrington.

"Think I'll stand right here, Daniel. I don't want to get a ball in the back from one of them redcoats."

Andrew and Prince had joined Daniel to try to get Jonas to go with them, to no avail. Daniel said, "Let's go boys. His mind's made up."

It was about this time that someone let loose a shot. Andrew looked up at what he thought was the source of the shot: the Buckman Tavern. Daniel looked at the British troops, and Prince looked all around to see anything that would indicate where the shot had come from—smoke in the air, for instance. The question of where the shot had come from was forgotten as the British troops, believing they had been fired upon, opened fire on the militia. They did more than just respond to what they perceived as firing by the patriots by firing back; they became crazy and wild. They fired at the militia on the common as the militiamen were running for cover. As the militia ran from the common, some of them stopped long enough to return fire at the British. Jonas Parker lay wounded on the ground, but, having gotten a shot off, was reloading when one of the British soldiers ran up to him and used his bayonet to finish him. Prince grabbed his own shoulder and went down. Andrew fired a shot, but knew he'd missed without even looking, and tried to reload as he ran toward a stone wall to take cover.

From his vantage point behind the stone wall, Andrew could see British officers riding into the frenzied maze of troops, shouting orders and commanding them to cease firing. Andrew watched, and when he was certain the troops were pulling back, he ceased any further thought of firing at the troops; it had to end somewhere. Little by little, the troops stopped their mad act of aggression.

Andrew knew little of the bars and stripes on uniforms indicating rank, but it was clear that one of the British officers was above the others in rank. He shouted orders at other officers, and they, in turn, began to yell what Andrew thought to be commands to the troops. Little by little, the British soldiers regrouped to form up in ranks. Once formed and awaiting further orders, one of the lesser officers shouted something to the troops, and they—at least the ones within sight and earshot of the officer—cheered while firing a round of shots in the air. Without further hesitation, the column of troops moved out, marching on the road to Concord without ever stopping at the reverend's house.

Upon seeing the troops move on, Andrew came out from behind the stone wall. He began to go toward the common, but stopped and turned around to go behind the wall again, leaning his musket against the wall. *No use looking like a target,* he thought as he ran to where he thought he had seen his men fall. There was the old man who had kept referring to Captain Parker as his cousin, doubled over and no longer moving. He was dead for sure, as were a couple of others not so far away. Prince was there, too, clutching his left shoulder and grimacing in pain.

"Hurts like hell, Andy," Prince said as Andrew went to him.

"Let's take a look at it," was all Andrew could say as he cut away some of Prince's shirt. After examining the wound, Andrew said, "Doesn't look too bad, Prince. I don't see any blood pumping, and no bones sticking out. Can you move it?"

"Don't try," said a voice. "Let me take a closer look at it."

Andrew turned to look at where the voice had come from. It was Dr. Fiske. The doctor stood behind him. At the same time, he saw other militiamen and town residents coming to the common. The reverend was among them, doing what a reverend does at such a time as this. John Parker was walking about looking at the wounded and the dead. All he could do was shake his head. He paused when he came to his cousin, kneeled down, and straightened the dead man's crumpled body. He bent down and whispered something in Jonas's ear. A tear rolled from his eye and dropped from his nose. After a moment, he resumed his walk among his men. The last Andrew saw of him was his back as he walked across the street to the tavern. *The tavern!* thought Andrew. *The sound of the shot! I saw someone, a heavyset man, in an upper-story window as the window was being closed. I'd swear he had a pistol in his hand, but I don't recall any smoke.*

In the tavern, Captain Parker was alone. Everybody else had gone to the common. He could have served himself a drink, but it was the furthest thing from his mind. His eyes were fixed with an almost hypnotic stare at the fireplace as its flames twisted and turned up the chimney. Could he have done something, anything, differently to have prevented the slaughter of his men? This was the question he asked himself over and over. It was not supposed to have happened this way, but he knew better. The only way it could have been prevented would have been if he hadn't had the militia there in the first place. Adams and Hancock could have left Lexington for another hiding place, and the British would have searched the town over and not have found them, and then they would have continued on to Concord. On the other hand, the British may have done more to the residents of the town than just searching their homes. He wouldn't put it past them to have killed complete families, raped whoever they had a mind to, and burned houses, shops, even the churches. No, he convinced himself; he had done the right thing, and so had his men.

"John," Reverend Clark said upon entering the tavern. John Parker turned his head and looked up at the figure without saying anything. "John, you had best come out to the common and give your support to your men and the people. They need guidance."

"Had to think a few things through, Reverend. I'm going to count on you to take care of the wounded and the dead and the people. I'm giving the men a couple of hours of rest and time to prepare themselves, and then we're going to go after those bastards." He was overtaken by another coughing spell.

THE MILITIAMEN WHO had not had the time to return to the green to meet the British had, by now, been dribbling in, and they looked in disbelief at the carnage. Captain Parker returned from the tavern with Reverend Clarke, and as they reached the common separately, each had his work to do. Parker went from one militiaman to the next to tell them there would be a muster at the same place about noontime. The purpose was to go after the British and do them damage. "Spread the word among any militiamen you can find, and then outfit yourself for a couple of days."

Andrew did his part to spread the word, and when the replies began to confirm they had already heard the order, he set out to go back to the shop to pack essentials in his haversack, including dried meat, a small pack of cornmeal, and a pan that would serve to cook and eat from, thinking, "If that doesn't do it, I'll just have to live off the land. Grubs are pretty good when you're hungry." As he walked off the common, a commotion of sorts caused him to look up the road toward the Reverend Clarke's house. He stopped to look. *That's Sergeant Munroe,* he thought. *Those two men with him look like Adams and Hancock.* One of the men was dressed as if he were going to church, and the other, a heavier, blowzy fellow, was dressed almost the opposite. *Damned if he don't look like the man I saw in the tavern window. Well, no business of mine. I've got to get going.* He left his thoughts and continued walking to his room in the shop.

It was close to noon when Andrew returned to the common, and most of the militia had already returned. Captain Parker was trying to gain the attention of his men, but was having a rough time of it because of his coughing spells. Had Sergeant Munroe been there, he would have brought the militiamen to attention. The drummer, a young man, perhaps even still a boy, sensed the captain's dilemma and beat a roll on his drum, which got the message across for the men to listen up to the captain. The members of the militia stopped what they were doing and gave the captain their ear.

Captain Parker addressed his militiamen. "Men, we're marching Concord way to give those good people a hand with the British. I have no idea what the situation is, and I don't want us to just barge in and start shooting if there isn't any shooting already going on. I know you'd like to take your revenge, and by God, I hope the opportunity presents itself, but if we start anything, things could get a lot worse. Now, if they're already shooting in Concord, find something to hide behind, and join the fun. My favorite targets are going to be officers—especially any officer I recognize as one of those we ran into this morning." There was a wave of agreement and a raising of muskets from his men.

Parker continued, "Now, as I see it, those British troops have to return to Boston, and the only way they're going to be able to do that is by backtracking on the same road they came in on. Whether there's action in Concord or not, there's going to be action when they return. We're going to disperse in the woods and take shots at 'em as they come back. Fire your musket, find another spot, reload, and fire again. Keep it up, moving toward Boston, until what's left of 'em have to swim back to jolly old England. A word of caution: those of you who fought the French and Indians know how to do it. Keep moving, keep out of sight, and keep 'em guessing. They'll be so scared, they'll have to change their britches."

The men again raised their muskets and cheered. "Just be careful, especially you younger men for whom this might be the first action of this kind. Be careful of where you're shooting and where you're shooting from. It's fine to get the British in a crossfire, but if one of us misses his target, that shot could hit one of your own men on the other side. Keep well hidden behind something that can stop a ball, because you don't want to be shot by the British...or your neighbor." A few of the old timers nodded their heads in silent agreement while the younger men listened for any hint of how to stay alive.

The captain said, "Drummer and fifer out front!"

Andrew found himself somewhere in the middle of the column, marching on the road to Concord. He could hear the drummer and fifer playing something he had never heard. It was easy to time your stride to the cadence of the beat. He thought, *we're all taking like steps, but few are in step.* He smiled at his thoughts and laughed to himself. His thoughts turned to serious matters.

On the common the fight had not been expected. He had let loose a shot without aiming; just pointed his musket in the general direction of the commotion while taking cover, and it was all over. This time, it was going to be different. Was he going to cower and take cover without doing anything, or was he going to expose himself long enough to get a good shot, then duck behind cover as the Captain had said to do? He remembered the time he'd had the run-in with Big Bull, and had done what he had to without thinking. There was no remorse at any time after he had killed Big Bull; the man was bad, and Andrew had been fighting for his life. But killing some British boy soldier he didn't know anything about and had no real argument with—not even after what had happened on the common earlier in the day—would he be able to live with himself afterward? Yes, he would. After all, the British wanted to control people just as much as the owner of a slave wanted to control his property. *So, what's in it for you, Andrew?* he asked himself. *You know damn well whatever comes of this fight or any others isn't going to help you or your kind, regardless of what Prince said.*

Parker's company had been marching for what seemed a long time. The talk among them had died down to silence and the monotony of marching. A few of the men heard it; others did not. They exchanged glances and talked with one another. "You hear something?" one said. Another responded, "Hear what? I don't hear anything." Still another said, "I think I do." The sounds increased until most could make them out; it was shooting. Captain Parker shouted his command as best he could in between his coughing fits. "Take cover in the woods! Could be the British coming back!" What Parker and his men didn't know was that other companies of militia from nearby communities had joined in with the Concord militia, and had the British on the run in full retreat.

There were other companies of militia clustered in the wood on both sides of the road, both behind the Lexington boys and in front of them.

Andrew ran to his right and almost collided with a man who had decided to take cover on the other side of the road. They brushed each other off and continued running in opposite directions. Andrew found a fat oak tree to hide behind and checked his musket. Damned if he hadn't forgotten to load it. With the gun loaded and with powder in the pan, he strained around the oak to see the road: clear shot. Anything or anybody coming within his view would be a goner. He had a sight picture with enough room to lead his target.

The sound of gunfire travels, but it's not always easy to tell how far away it is. Andrew let himself relax and turned his back to the oak, slid down it, and sat on the ground. Looking around, he saw two squirrels chasing each other, jumping from tree to tree. *Wonder if they're in love or if one stole the other's nuts?* Similarities between people and animals had always intrigued him. He thought, *push a mule too hard, and he'll stop. Push a horse too hard, and he'll keep working until he drops. Some men are mules; others are horses. Captain Parker's a horse.*

Off to his right, the sound of musket fire increased until his ears rang. Gun smoke filled the air until the woods looked as if they were on fire. He glanced at the road and saw nothing but redcoats—some running, some stopping to fire and reload. A soldier came into his sight path, running. Andrew took a bead as the soldier slowed down to reload. Andrew adjusted his lead and fired. The soldier never knew a ball had passed through his neck, and fell over silent. Another redcoat stopped to help his fallen comrade, and he himself was cut down by another of Parker's men. A rustle in the brush to Andrew's right, and he turned to see his own men running to keep up with the British retreat. They'd run, find new cover, and fire again at the retreating British. Andrew left his cover and advanced with the rest.

An animal being chased will run and try to evade its pursuer, even if wounded, until its heart stops or runs out of blood to pump. The pursuer will run after its game until it is tired, even if hungry. One has no choice; the other can try again tomorrow. And so it was with Parker's militia. Some tired; others ran out of balls or powder, and still others needed to get back to their families and farms. That was the militia way of thinking and fighting. In Parker's case, he was in pain, and suffering coughing spells from overexertion. Enough! Andrew had been wrong. Parker was a mule—stubborn, but still a mule, able to outwork a horse but knowing when to stop. As Parker's militia pulled back, the British troops were still running the gauntlet, the militia following at an easy pace.

AFTER RETURNING TO Lexington, Andrew went to the Estabrook house to see how Prince was doing with his wound. "You should have heard it, Andrew," said Prince. Those redcoats had reinforcements coming. They stopped up the road and shot a cannonball at the common. It went straight through the meeting house. "When I heard the cannon go off, I jumped out of my chair and looked for cover. Benjamin kept telling me to be calm or I was going to open my wound. He said they weren't going to shoot at us. I wasn't too sure, but he was right."

"Good to see you doing alright, Prince. I'll be getting back to the shop." Andrew turned to leave, and Benjamin Estabrook opened the door to let Andrew pass. Andrew nodded his head at Benjamin, but Benjamin put his hand on Andrew's shoulder and stopped him.

"Thank you for fighting for us, Andrew. You're new here, and I know the story of how you happened to be here. Come by anytime."

As Andrew left the house, he thought, "Not many like him. I understand Prince's thinking a bit better now."

ONCE AGAIN, CAPTAIN John Parker had the alarm sounded for his militia to muster on the green. Having worked at the forge all day, Andrew was hot and sweaty as he carried his musket across the street to form up. He was one of the first to arrive, so he sat down on the green to await the others. They dribbled in one by one, or in groups of twos and threes as they met coming from all directions.

Is that who I think it is? Andrew thought to himself. The figure came closer, and Andrew stood up and waved. "Prince! What you doing here with that arm of yours?"

"Doctor Fiske says I'm not going to get much better than this, so I can get back to work." He moved his arm around to his back and scratched between his shoulders. "See? If I can do that, I can do anything."

"Scratching is one thing. You try knocking someone's head off, and that's another."

"Let's hear what the captain's got to say. You got any idea?"

"Ain't heard a word. We been getting lots of people in the shop, and none of them have said anything." Andrew looked at another man sitting a few feet from him. "You know what this is about?"

"Don't know. Hope it's just a meeting, and we can go over to Buckman's and have a pint."

"I'll drink to that," Andrew said.

The gathering men sat or walked around. Some dozed, some talked with each other, and a few went over to Buckman's.

An hour had gone by before John Parker left the tavern, followed by the men who had wandered in.

Sergeant Munroe mustered the militia, and Parker stood in front. Interrupted several times by his coughing spells, he said, "We're going to Cambridge to await further orders. As you may know, we have the British in Boston sealed off by land. It's expected they're going to try breaking through our lines. Our job is to help reinforce where we expect them to come through. Be ready to march in the morning. We'll meet here at sunup. Dismissed."

Some of the men went home; others remained to talk, and a few went to Buckman's Tavern. Among those who stayed, the talk was about the upcoming possibility of another fight with the redcoats, but also, almost to a man, about how bad Captain Parker looked.

CHAPTER XVI

CAPTAIN PARKER'S MEN marched into Cambridge looking bedraggled and out of step. They stopped at Cambridge Common, where they were to camp until receiving further orders. Shouts and gestures from the already-gathered troops—some encouraging, some downright vulgar, and others more or less humorous—were yelled at them. Not to be outdone, Parker's men returned the greetings in kind.

"Never thought I'd see this many of us gathered in one place," said a boy of about seventeen standing next to Andrew. "Must be thousands."

Picking up the conversation, a fifty-something man said, "Wish they'd been on our green when them dirty redcoat bastards came through. This war'd be over."

Andrew could not stop thinking, *what the hell am I doing here, about to fight a white man's fight?*

THEY'D BEEN CAMPED on the common for a couple of weeks with nothing to do except play cards, arm wrestle, and occasionally fight with men from other militias for no other reason than getting on each other's nerves. A few of the gathered men would go to the tavern, but after a while, they ran short of money. Captain Parker had spent some time at the hospital to see if there was help for his condition, but nothing seemed to work. In order to be able to think more clearly, he had chosen not to take the medicines.

The men in Parker's company, as well as the others on the common, were talking about being gone from their families and farms too long, and said they had best start going home. Before many left, orders came out for the Massachusetts militias to proceed to Charlestown Neck, with no other explanation given. One of the officers, a General Putnam, while giving orders to the militias, noticed Captain Parker's coughing spells. Approaching Parker, he saw how sick Parker was.

"Parker, you're in no condition to lead these men in a fight. I want you and your company to stay here at Cambridge and help guard General Ward should the fighting come this way."

Captain Parker gave no argument, but turned to his company and said, "If you didn't hear the general, he said we're to stay here and help guard General Ward's headquarters. This is where the Committee of Safety and the new Continental Army will be headquartered. Check your equipment, and be ready."

Andrew had found one of the few trees on the common that had a side open for one more man to sit and lean back against. His view was of the street, and he watched the various companies of men march toward Charlestown Neck: officers on horses first, followed by the rest. He noticed one of the riders going in the opposite direction, and thought he had seen him before, but was not sure. There was something else—not about the man, but about the horse. It had a slight limp.

Andrew sprang to his feet and ran after the horse and rider. Catching up with them, he shouted at the rider, "Hey! Get off this horse. Don't you know he has something wrong with him?"

"Get away from me!" came the sharp reply. "I've got other things on my mind than this horse!"

Andrew paid no attention to the man, running in front of the horse to grab its bridle. "Whoa, there, girl," he commanded the horse.

"If you don't get out of my way, you're going to be in big trouble, mister," said the rider.

"Well, then, I'm going to be in trouble. Let me take a look at what's wrong with this girl. It'll only take a minute. Otherwise, you're going to hurt her bad."

Not waiting for the man's reply, Andrew patted the horse's neck and slid his hands down the horse to the hoof. He raised the hoof and looked at it, then up at the rider. "Your horse has a rock in her shoe. Give me a minute, and I'll take it out. You stay there."

Andrew took his long knife from its scabbard and dug in the space between the shoe and hoof. "Got it!" he said. Then, with the handle of his knife, he pounded the nails of the shoe back in. "This ought to get you by until you can find someone to replace a couple of nails with bigger ones."

"You know about horse things, mister?"

"I'm a pretty good farrier and blacksmith."

"You come over to that building in about an hour," the rider said, pointing to one of the school buildings. "I want to talk to you."

"How'll I know where you are?"

"Just ask for General Putnam. They'll direct you." The general rode on.

I've a bad feeling about this, Andrew thought, *and it ain't 'cause I shouted at a general.*

"DAMN IT, PUTNAM, I don't like you going around me to the Safety Committee. I can't afford those two hundred men you're sending to Charlestown. This is headquarters for the new Continental Army, and it has to be protected along with Charlestown Neck. I have no idea where the

British are going to attack. We know they planned on occupying Dorchester Heights, which would allow them to attack from the south. If you have troops digging trenches around Charlestown, they'll never be able to intercept the British, even if they aren't too tired to fight."

"Artemas, if I don't have those men, I'll guarantee the British will be overrunning this place. I know they don't want us to command those hills on the peninsula, because they're fighting too damn hard to get us off. That's where they'll attack you from, not Dorchester. We can turn 'em around if we have enough men."

"I still don't like it, Israel. It's cutting it too thin. Well, it's out of my hands, and I've said what I had to say."

A thought came to Putman's mind. "If it's any help, there's a small company of men, maybe fifty or so. Their captain is John Parker, the John Parker and his men who were at Lexington. Parker's sick—I think he has the consumption. I ordered him to stay here to guard headquarters, as he's unfit for fighting where I have to go."

"Have him quarter his men in these barracks. Not much of a trade, two hundred able-bodied for fifty with an unfit leader. But he's got guts from what I've heard, so it'll help."

"Excuse me, sirs," said a private entering the room, "but there's a black man outside who said General Putnam ordered him to come here."

"Oh! I'd forgotten about him. He's one of those independent types who don't respect authority well. But he knows something about taking care of horses. He took a stone out of my mount's shoe; fact is, he wouldn't let me continue riding the horse until he took care of her. Thought you might be able to use him."

"Ha! Someone stood up to you, Israel? Well, by God, I'll have him moved in now. We'll be in need of someone who has a way with horses and not generals." Addressing the private, he said, "Private, show the man where he can stay. Put him up somewhere around where you bunk, so you can show him around. Tell him I'll talk to him later."

"DON'T KNOW IF this is punishment for bumping heads with that officer or if it might be good," Andrew said to Harold, the private who escorted him. "I guess it's a whole lot better than sleeping on the ground in a tent. Wonder what these buildings were used for?"

"I understand they were occupied by students, but they were all sent home because of what's happening."

"This is a school, and the students sleep here?" a surprised Andrew asked.

"It's a university, from what I know. Only the smartest students come here."

"Well, how about that? This bed might have been slept in by some future important man with a hundred slaves working for him some day."

"I don't know about that. About all I know is how to farm, and my parents don't have any slaves...they can't afford to buy and feed 'em. Were you a slave?"

"Yes, more or less. I was set free."

"You mean so you could fight the redcoats?"

"For other reasons. I'd just as soon not talk about it, if you don't mind."

"You're not a runaway, are you?"

"No, but I'd say the same thing if I were, wouldn't I?"

"Guess so. I don't know much about slaves. Don't know much about black people. You different from whites, other than your color?"

"I got thick lips and wiry hair."

"I can see that, but that's not what I mean. I mean in other ways."

"Other than what you can see, I don't know of any other. Maybe these smart kids who go to this school can answer your question better than I can."

"You don't like to talk about this kind of stuff, do you?"

"I don't know how I feel about it. You're the first person I've ever talked with about these things. You're the only white man who ever asked me, or wanted to know. Most blacks just figure the white man is smarter 'cause they're the boss, and they have the whip. But you know, I met a black lady a couple of years ago, and I'll bet my musket she is smarter than most of the students at this school."

"What does she do?"

"I'm not sure what she does, but she works for a doctor in Boston."

IT WAS THREE days before General Ward remembered about Andrew, and then only because he had cause. He didn't go to Andrew directly, but sent Harold to have him come to the stable.

"So, you know something about horses, eh?"

"I know something about 'em. I'm no horse doctor, though."

"See what you can do with my horse. He twisted his leg or something. He's limping and keeping the leg up. I know it's not broken."

"I'll see what I can do. Where is he?"

"Harold will show you. I've got to get back. Report to me after you know what's wrong."

Harold led Andrew to the horse's stall, and Andrew examined the horse. He slid his hand down the leg, picked up the hoof, and forced it to bend up and down. "This horse is done for, Harold. He has a snapped ligament, and that's as bad as a broken leg. I'll go tell the general. How do I find him? I'm lost in this maze of buildings and hallways."

Andrew and General Ward returned to the horse's stall. The general wanted to see for himself. He looked the horse over and also ran his hand down the horse's leg. He repeated the motion on the other leg. "I see what you mean. Nothing can be done, private?"

"Nothing I know of, General."

"I thought that might be the case," General Ward said to Andrew, "but I wanted to be sure. Put him down, and have him butchered for rations."

"Anything else, General?"

"That'll be all." The general stopped for a moment, then turned around and said, "Don't know if you've heard this or not, but we've had to retreat from those damned hills on the Charlestown peninsula. Our forces are now mostly concerned with protecting this place."

"That's pretty bad, huh, General?"

"Right now it is. But that's not what I'm getting at. What I'm telling you is this place in Cambridge, right here in these buildings, will be the head-quarters for the new Continental Army."

"I've heard something about that."

"What you may not have heard is there is now a commander over all of our forces. He'll be coming tomorrow or the next day, from what I understand. His name is General Washington. The second Continental Congress has appointed him as the Commander in Chief of the Continental Army. He'll head everything from now on."

"How does that affect me?"

"Washington doesn't like militias. He believes it's too easy for a militia to retreat to the comfort of their farms when they want to rather than fighting the enemy when times get tough."

"…And?"

"You'd fit in well in a regular army, with your knowledge of horses. That would be your assignment, if you would join as a regular. What do you think?"

"I'll have to go back to Lexington to talk with the man I work for. We had a deal, and I still owe him some time to fulfill my obligation. I can't give you an answer right now."

"Do what you have to do, private. Hope to see you around." The general turned and walked away.

RIDING TO LEXINGTON, Andrew thought over what the general had asked him. *What do I think?* For some time now, especially since joining the militia, Andrew had been questioning himself about whether he was for or against the cause the militia was so willing to give their lives for. He thought there were only a handful of militiamen like Jonas Parker, who would be willing to put their lives in danger. But as a group, and with a few strong-willed individuals to stir the pot, they fed off each other, and had built up a difficult-to-stop group bravado.

There was never talk among themselves about freedom for black people in the new government, should it come to be. There was only talk about freedom for them, and how they would show the king a thing or two if they had the chance—talk that grew louder pint after pint at Buckman's.

He tried to talk to Prince about his concerns, but Prince evaded the subject. It occurred to Andrew that Prince was more afraid of not being a part of the group. And with his lifelong arrangement with his master, Benjamin Estabrook, Prince was comfortable with being a slave.

He rode past Buckman's and went directly to the blacksmith's shop. Daniel Harrington looked up from his work to greet him. Andrew skipped the small talk. "Got to talk with you," he said.

Harrington listened as Andrew told him of General Ward's offer to join the regular army. Daniel was as patriotic for the colonial cause as any man, yet he needed Andrew in his business. Then, when Andrew mentioned the distrust this new general, General Washington, had for the patriots, Daniel seemed to sour on the subject. After much thought, he told Andrew he would like him to stay until he could see how the now-declared war was faring. For if the war was a lost cause, there would be no use for Andrew to join and perhaps be killed. Also to be considered was the fact that the war could either increase or decrease the blacksmithing business, and this would determine the necessity of keeping Andrew. Andrew felt relief at Harrington's answer, as there was now no pressure for him to make an immediate decision.

GENERAL GEORGE WASHINGTON arrived at Cambridge in early July and issued orders not to recruit slaves into the Continental Forces. By November, he had issued orders not to recruit Negroes, free or slave; old men; or young boys who were not able to bear arms. Those Negroes already enlisted could stay in. These orders were the result of his personal views as well as those of the Continental Congress. The reasoning around the exclusion of Negroes, Andrew had heard, was that white people didn't want blacks to have guns, as they were afraid there could be Negro uprisings.

Early in November, following on the heels of Washington's orders, the British governor of the Virginia colony, Lord Dunmore, issued the Dunmore Proclamation, which had as its purpose the recruitment of all bondsmen and slaves, regardless of color. In return for their service with the British, they would be set free. The result was twofold: first, slaves were running away faster than the British could sign them up, and second, Washington and the Continental Congress had rescinded all orders to not enlist Negroes.

In Andrew's mind, the question of whether or not he would become a regular or even stay in the militia was settled. After Lexington, Andrew could not even consider joining the British. He was already a free slave, so he could see no reason to fight for either side. He would stay with Harrington until spring and then go west, unless Daniel changed his mind and wanted Andrew to go ahead and join the Continentals as a regular; in which case, he would give his three months' notice and head west.

CHAPTER XVII

AUTUMN LOOKED AS if it might come sooner than usual this year. Maple leaves turned red without an early frost, and rain brought them to the ground; the usual display of vibrant autumn colors was not to be seen this year. Fruits of nut trees littered the forest floor, with squirrels dashing about to take their pick. Deer enjoyed an assortment of wild plums, persimmons, and crabapples. The air had cooled, but was not yet cold during the day. Come nighttime, it was a comfort to have an extra blanket.

Andrew had become skilled as an all-around blacksmith, having picked up tricks of the trade from Daniel—tricks Smithy never knew. The day before, he had finished making a wagon wheel of oak, and around its rim, he fitted an iron tire. Smithy had never made the wooden innards of a wagon wheel, although he was good at fitting an iron tire to an existing wheel, if the wheel was in at least fair condition.

It was close to noon, and time for his supper. As he washed his hands in the quench tank, he heard a wagon pull up in front of the shop. Instead of going into his room to eat, he walked through the shop and out the wide door. The sun blinded him for a moment, and he tried to shade his eyes with his hands to see the wagon. He barely had a glimpse of another horse tied to the back of the wagon before Daniel blocked his view by walking up to the driver to exchange greetings.

The wagon belonged to a farmer who had come to the shop to pick up the wheel. As he and Daniel talked, Andrew, whose eyes had now adjusted to the daylight, rolled the wheel out of the shop and eyed the tethered equine. He stopped, and the wheel rolled on its own until it bumped into the wagon and fell over. He looked at the horse, which was not a horse. "By God, damned if that isn't a mule and he looks like…I'm sure of it. He's my mule!" Hearing Andrew, Daniel and the farmer turned to look.

"You say something, Andy?" said Daniel.

"That your mule?" asked Andrew of the farmer.

"It was. Not anymore. I traded it to Daniel for the wheel."

"Let's get that wheel in the back of the wagon, Andy," said Daniel. "Then you can take the mule and we'll see what we're going to do with her." He could see the look in Andrew's eyes.

"How did you come to have him?" asked Andrew.

"I don't see it's any business of a nigger."

Daniel, surprised at the answer, changed his expression from the courteous smile he reserved for customers to a blank face displaying a touch of anger. "Don't talk that way, Eli. He's human, just the same as you and me, and deserves better. He's one of the best blacksmiths I've ever run across, and you'd best appreciate it, 'cause he made that wheel for you, and it'll give you good service as long as you don't run into another boulder and smash it up like you did the last one."

"Well…maybe," Eli said, embarrassed at having been told off.

"Well, go ahead and answer the man, Eli. I'd like to know myself. I don't want to trade for a mule if I don't know where he came from."

"Don't know where he came from, so I don't know his breeding. But—"

Andrew interrupted, "I know where he came from. We want to know how you got him."

Daniel turned his head to look at Andrew with a questioning look. "How do you know where he came from?"

"I bred him."

That made more questions than it answered, but Daniel figured it would all come out, so he continued with Eli.

"Now, Eli, where'd you get him?"

"He pulled up a load of slaves from Maryland. I was going to buy a couple, because the one I have ain't worth nothin' anymore. I guess he's beyond his time."

"So how'd you get the mule?"

"The man said I if bought the two slaves, he'd throw in the mule for two dollars Continental, 'cause he didn't want to have to take him back."

"You got a bill of sale for him?" asked Daniel.

"Not on me, but yes, I've got one."

"You bring it in tomorrow, understand? Leave the mule here as long as you're taking the wheel."

"I'll have my boy bring it by tomorrow for you to look at, but I want it back."

"Why're you getting rid of him?" Andrew asked.

"'Because he ain't no good pulling a plow. I've had him a year or better, and he just stops plowing. Can't push him, pull him, or give him the whip. He just won't move until he's ready. I can hitch up a horse, and he'll plow until he drops dead."

Daniel looked at Andrew, who didn't say a thing. Eli wouldn't want to know what Andrew was thinking.

Silence fell over the three same as a fog covers low land.

Daniel broke the silence. "Take the mule, Andrew. I'll talk to you after a while."

Andrew untied the mule and let the rope end drop on the ground. The mule took a step until his muzzle met Andrew's shoulder. Andrew looked the mule in the eye, and the gentle animal nudged him. Andrew raised his hand to the mule's head and stroked him, turned, and walked around the shop to the rear. The mule, without being coaxed, followed a few feet behind.

"I'll be," muttered Daniel.

BARTER WAS ONE mode of paying for goods and services, and sometimes, it was the only way. Daniel Harrington had a constant supply of meat, vegetables, chickens, and eggs because of it. Much of his house furnishings had come from bartering. It worked both ways—if he needed something, he'd work a deal to repair or make something out of iron, and sometimes copper or brass, in trade. Andrew's pay consisted of his room in the shop, food from Daniel's surplus, and some money in pounds sterling. Now, pounds had been replaced with the Continental dollar. However, since the war had begun there were times when Daniel ran short of currency, and Andrew had to wait or accept something in trade; the new Continental dollar was in short supply, and was not always accepted.

Andrew knew he would move on in the not too distant future, and did not want to accumulate anything he would have to carry with him; therefore, he preferred money. Other than a five-year-old gelding named Henry and the items he needed for daily living, his possessions were a feather bed and a comfortable cushioned chair which he thought he owed himself, and could sell when the time came. He was also able to acquire a fifty-caliber Pennsylvania-type long rifle, which, so the story went, had belonged to a lieutenant who died of the smallpox. The lieutenant and the rifle had belonged to one of the new Continental rifle companies. How the rifle had found its way to Lexington was a little cloudy. Ask somebody how, and you'll always get an answer to match the situation. The rifle had somehow found its way to the blacksmith shop as payment, and Daniel was pleased to transfer ownership to Andrew after he showed interest. Now, Andrew was showing an interest in this mule.

"So it's agreeable, the mule for a month's pay?" asked Daniel.

"And oats to feed him for a month."

"Done."

TIME PASSED, AND Andrew worked with the mule, whom he named Gage. Why did he name him Gage? He remembered the two donkeys he had worked with when he was a young boy, Marie and Louis. Someone else had named them before Andrew entered the picture. The story he had heard was that they were named after the rulers of France, who were enemies of England and the colonies. So, it was appropriate to name asses after asses. Now, it was about time to give his mule a name, and he thought he might carry on the tradition. Though Andrew's mule was only half ass, that was good enough, and he thought it described the general and governor of Boston. So the mule came to be named Gage, after the man who had planned the raid on Concord, putting Lexington in the middle.

PRINCE INTRODUCED ANDREW to people he knew, mostly other blacks. From this social circle, he met Scap Mason, a free man who hired himself out to do anything if it paid in currency, gold, silver, or something of value in trade. Scap had a large family, and his children were in their teens. When Scap got a job of some kind, the entire family except Mama Mason would help; Mama tended the home. Lila was sixteen, and somewhere in the middle of the age group of offspring. She and Andrew took a liking to each other and spent considerable time together. Scap did not have so many children that he did not notice what was going on between the two. He also noticed Andrew was a well-built man, able to work hard, and had acquired a bed, a chair, some pots and pans, a horse and mule, and some fine guns. He also had a job, and it was rumored he knew how to read and write.

One evening, Andrew rode Gage over to see Lila. He was thinking of asking her if she would take a ride with him, but when he knocked on the door and asked to see her, Scap opened the door and said, "She's here, but I want to talk to you first. Just me and you, man to man."

Uh oh! Andrew thought. *I know what's coming.*

They walked out to the front yard of the house, where Scap turned to face Andrew.

Andrew got the first word in. "Look, Mister Mason. I haven't done anything with Lila. You can ask her."

"No, no, no! Not what I'm saying. I'm not accusing you of anything. I just noticed you two seem to like each other. You spend a lot of time together, seem to have fun, and Lila floats around in a dream land when you're not with her. Now, where I come from, that means there's got to be something there."

Andrew felt beads of sweat all over. The slight breeze in the air gave him a chill down his back.

When Scap could see that Andrew was not going to say anything, he said, "What I'm saying, Andrew, is you'd make a fine man for Lila, and I'd like you to be part of this family. I know she has it on her mind."

Andrew didn't know what to say, and just stood there trying to think of something.

"I said the wrong thing didn't I, Andy?"

"Yes, I'm afraid you did. Does Lila know you're talking to me about this?"

"We had a talk about it. Yes."

"Well, then, I guess I'm going to have to talk to her."

"No, Andy. It's my place to do the talking to her. It would be best if you just left. It would be the right thing to do if you didn't come back."

"HOW'S IT GOING, Andy?"

Andrew turned from hammering a piece of red hot iron on the anvil, and there stood Prince. "Prince!"

"I stopped by to tell you I was leaving to go back with the militia. This new general, his name is Washington, has a job for us to do."

"What is it?"

"Don't know, but it's supposed to take several months."

"You don't have to join the regular army?"

"No, I'll be back after the job is done. You interested in going along?"

"Don't think so, Prince. You know my views on the war. Most of the guys in the militia have guessed, too. Don't think I'd be too popular."

"Well, suit yourself. I'll be seeing you."

"Hope so."

"What was that all about?" asked a knowing Daniel. "I overheard something about the militia leaving again."

Andrew explained what he knew to Daniel. "Sorry, can't tell you more. Must be some kind of secret."

"It won't be for long. There isn't anybody in Massachusetts who can keep a secret after they meet the next person."

Andrew gave a chuckle, and turned to beat on the piece of iron.

"That brings up something, Andy."

"What, Dan?"

"You said something about the militia knowing your views, which made you kinda unpopular."

"Yes."

"Well, something else is making you unpopular around here."

"Go on."

"I've heard rumors about you and the Mason girl, and how you done her wrong. Any truth to it?"

"Depends on what you mean by done her wrong. She expected more than I wanted to give, and I told her father so. He wouldn't let me talk to her, and didn't want me coming around his place no more. Anything else has been made up."

"That's not quite what's been going around. Want to know what I've heard?"

"No. Anything other than what I just told you isn't the truth."

"I believe you, but I'm not others. Then, throw in your views on the war, and you're someone people around here want to stay clear of."

"What do you want me to do, Dan, leave?"

"It would be the best thing to do."

"I'll be gone come morning. You can have the feather bed and chair. Should take care of any time you figure I still owe you for the mule."

"Sorry, Andy."

"Me, too."

Andrew had a lot going through his head, and sleep didn't come easy. He had just had a good dose of how people could be. He figured it was another lesson learned. He was thinking back about all the good people he had known; Ignatius, the Blackistons, Isaac, Miss Millie, Jim, and Branwen. Those were real people, the kind who wouldn't let you down. After a couple of hours and as many cups of cider, he fell asleep.

The morning sky was mottled gray, threatening to snow or drop freezing rain. The cold made Andrew's nose drip as he slipped the bridle over Henry's head. Gage was going to be the packer, and Andrew had already loaded his possessions.

"Andy!" Andrew turned to see Daniel a few feet away from him.

"How're you going to ride Henry without a saddle? Bareback's fine if you're an Indian, but you're not. Take the one you've been using and call it a bonus. I don't mind telling you, I don't feel good about this. Didn't sleep much last night."

"Well, hell. Here I went thinking a bunch of bad thoughts about you and just about got comfortable with it, and you do something nice like this."

"Want to talk about it?"

"Probably should, but I had to make a decision like this some time ago when I left the South. When I was almost here, I found out I didn't have to leave, and could go back to what would have been a comfortable life. I made the decision to continue northward, and haven't been disappointed. I've had my eyes opened to many things, but I haven't been disappointed. Just 'cause a man's comfortable is no reason not to see what's down the road. So, no. Think I'll go down the road. Thanks for the saddle. I and my backside appreciate it."

AFTER HE LEFT Daniel Harrington's blacksmith shop, Andrew had in mind to find the old Braddock Road going west to the Ohio Territory. Rather than following the Post Road in the direction Harrington had told him to go, he found himself going the opposite way, toward Boston. Here he was going east, because he was thinking of a certain somebody named Bonnie. If she was sealed off in Boston, how would he be able to go in and find her? He needed to see her, even though the chance of finding her was a longshot.

As he rode past the Cambridge green, he saw several militia companies, mixed as one and ready to go wherever General Washington was sending them. There were also the regular uniformed Continentals; each company was keeping to themselves. He saw the school buildings, and wondered if Ward and Putnam were still there. He thought about seeing if that private, he thought his name was Harold, was still around. *But why?* he asked himself, and decided to keep riding toward Boston.

"Clear the way, clear the way!" soldiers were shouting.

Andrew pulled up on Henry, "Whoa, boy, whoa. What's going on?" Down the street came a carriage with what appeared to be two Continental officers driven by a private. The officers were dressed in blue and white uniforms, and wore cocked hats. One, a rather big-looking fellow, sat ramrod straight, and the other tried his best to do the same, but didn't show the same stature as his companion. As the carriage came near Andrew, the larger officer gave a sidewise glance in Andrew's direction. Then he did a double-take at Andrew, and gave a firm command to his driver to stop.

Looking at Andrew, he said, "You there, with the pack mule!"

"You talking to me?" Andrew said.

"I am, indeed. Come over here closer so I can talk to you."

Andrew gave Henry a gentle nudge in the side and a click of his tongue. Henry, with Gage in tow, walked to the carriage, stopping on his own when he came close.

"That, son, is a fine specimen of a mule. Where'd you get him?"

Andrew was thinking he should turn and run and get out of there as fast as they could go. He didn't want some officer commandeering his mule. Instead, he said, "He was pay for my services as a blacksmith."

"Blacksmith, hmm?! You know anything about that mule's sire and mare?"

"I do."

"I'd like to talk to you more about him. Would you meet me at the stables—we shouldn't be but a few minutes? I'd like to look him over. You know where the stables are?"

Andrew answered that he did, and he would meet the officer there; but he had an uneasy feeling.

"Fine, fine. I'll be there as soon as I can."

The carriage resumed.

Andrew was about to turn Henry and Gage and make haste toward Boston, when an onlooker asked, "Do you know the general?"

"I don't have any idea who he is."

Surprised, the man said, "You don't know about General George Washington?"

"Think I did hear the name, but didn't pay much attention. Must be important, huh?"

"About as important as anybody there is. He's the commander of all the Continental forces."

"Well now, guess I'd better go see what's on the general's mind."

At the stables, Andrew halted and looked around. Nothing had changed since he had last been there, except maybe more horses.

"I know you," said a voice from the dimness of the inner stable. As the voice emerged, it said, "Can't think of your name, but you were here talking to General Ward."

"Hello, Harold. Yes, I was here telling General Ward the bad news about his horse. Name's Andrew. Remember?"

"Yes. You come'n back?"

"Not if I can help it. Another general wants to talk to me."

"We got a lot of 'em 'round here. There's the big man himself coming this way. He ain't the one, is he?"

Andrew turned to follow Harold's gaze, and saw the two officers he had seen in the carriage walking toward him. As they approached, Andrew saw General Washington, walking as erect as he had sat his horse. He appeared to be about the same height as Andrew. He didn't have the paunch most of the officers his age seemed to carry.

"He's the man."

They watched the two officers approach. Harold stepped backward a few steps to be sure he would not be too close. He wanted to disappear, as being this close to officers made him nervous.

Washington stopped a few feet in front of Andrew, and the shorter of the two officers walked another couple of paces, stopped, and said, "I'm Major Mifflin, General Washington's aid de camp." Motioning to Washington, he said, "This is General Washington. And your name, sir?"

"Andrew Attaway."

Washington asked, "Are you in the army or militia, perhaps?"

"I was in the militia, but I'm moving on now."

"What militia?"

"Out of Lexington."

"Lexington! Were you there when the British attacked?"

"I was, and we chased 'em all the way to Concord and back. Got at least one of 'em. And I was also right here in these buildings helping guard against them while we fought the British on the Charlestown peninsula."

"I wanted to talk to you about your mule. Now I want to talk to you about other things. Would it be possible for you to meet me in my quarters at three o'clock?"

"I suppose. I'm not in any hurry to go anyplace, but I don't like to leave my animals and guns."

"Good. Don't worry about your belongings. Your friend there will take care of them."

Washington, seeing Harold in the background, said, "Private, have this man's possessions taken care of, and put them under guard. See to it he's able to freshen up."

It seemed to Andrew that the General was not a man with whom to curry disfavor, so although he had little appreciation of authority, he made sure he was waiting for Washington at a little before three.

A corporal led Andrew into an ornately decorated room, and there, behind a large desk made of carved and polished dark wood, sat Washington, writing. He looked up at Andrew, and put his quill down; a courtesy to Andrew and a trait of the general.

"Sit down, please. Would you care for a brandy?"

"I don't think I've ever had brandy."

"Well, allow me to introduce you to one of the finer things." Washington stood and went across the room to a small table holding several bottles and glasses. He pulled the cork from a decanter and poured a rich brown liquid into a large round glass with a short stem. It seemed an unusually large glass to be used for such a small amount of drink. "Here," said Washington as he handed one of the glasses to Andrew. "Before you take a sip, swirl the brandy around a bit, and inhale with both your nose and mouth. Take some in, and let it roll over your tongue as you taste it. You'll find it agreeable…at least I do, but then, I've been drinking it for a long time."

Andrew did as he was shown, and found the drink both smooth and rough at the same time. He felt warmth from his throat down to his stomach as he swallowed. "I guess you have to get used to it. I've been drinking whiskey and cider most of my life."

"Now, what I wanted to see you about was the mule. I've an interest in mules, but I've never been able to breed any big enough to do the work I had in mind. I always had to have more mules in the team than I would have liked. They're good, just not good enough. Again, after the war's over, and if I'm not swinging from a British gallows, I'm going to continue experimenting with breeding them until I get what I want. Tell me what you know about this mule of yours. He's about as big as I had envisioned a good mule to be."

As they drank Washington's brandy, Andrew related Gage's history and that of the jack named Louis who had sired him. The brandy was not to Andrew's liking, but he noticed Washington had drunk his, and could be waiting for Andrew to finish so he could offer another round. With an effort, Andrew swallowed the rest of his glass as Washington turned his head for a second.

"You know, when I first saw you on your horse, I saw this big black bearded man with two pistols in his belt, a big knife, and three muskets on his pack mule. I was thinking you were trouble for anyone who got in your way. Are you?"

"I don't cause anybody any trouble."

"Where're you going, and what're you planning on doing?"

"I want to see someone I know in Boston. Thought I'd try to get in."

"Can't be done, son. If we don't shoot you, the British will. Don't even try it."

There was a pause in the conversation as Andrew digested what the general had said.

"You're not turning into a loyalist, are you?" the general added.

"I don't think much about either side."

Washington rose and prepared two more brandies. Sitting down again behind his desk, he asked, "Mind telling me why?"

Andrew told him from beginning to end how he felt about both sides, and the general listened to every word without interrupting or asking questions, even for clarification.

"There seems to be the American side, the British side, and your side, wouldn't you say, Andrew? You're almost another country aren't you?"

"I hadn't thought about it that way, but yes, I'd say you might be right, except I'm just one of many in that other country. We don't belong to either white side."

"Interesting. We should talk in more depth about it at some future time…and we will do so. In the meantime, consider this: fight only one war at a time. To divide your enemy is to conquer your enemy. Choose which side you want to be victorious, so you can fight it next. A man has to believe in something, and, if necessary, fight for it."

There was a lull in the conversation before Washington said, "Knowing you can't get into Boston without dying trying, what are your plans?"

"I'd like to go west, cut a farm out of the land, and maybe have a family."

Washington picked up the quill and absently rolled the tip back and forth in his fingers. Neither man said a word. Andrew took a sip of brandy, and Washington set the quill down and picked up his own. As he raised the glass, he noticed the ink on his fingertips. He put the glass down. "Andrew, I've a proposition for you. Want to hear it?"

Suspicious of what was to follow, Andrew said, "A proposition! Sure, I'll listen."

"I mentioned to you that after the war, I intend to go back to my farms, and, along with the usual, try breeding mules and growing different crops. I've a lot of farms and a lot of animals. They're on the Potomac River. I believe it runs all the way west to at least the Ohio Territory. The Ohio Territory is where this country, American or British, is going to expand. If you're thinking of going west, that's the way to go. If you'll work with me on my farms, we both might be able to find out more about it."

"You have slaves, don't you?"

"Yes, I have slaves."

"Are you going to set them free?"

Washington's face went from congenial to introspective. "I can't. They're my property, and they represent a major part of my fortune—and, I might add, my wife's."

"Then I can't work for you."

"I can understand your position, but I wonder if you understand mine."

"I think I do."

"I wonder if you really do. Let's for a moment say I set my slaves free."

"You end up having to hire what slaves do for free."

"Free! Free my arse!" Washington almost shouted. "Do you have any idea of what is involved with owning and using slaves?"

Andrew did not reply, but sat there looking intently at Washington.

Washington continued, "I have something like three hundred slaves. The old ones can't work so do a little farming for themselves and take care of children. Even though the too old and too young can't work I still have to take care of them; provide food, shelter, clothes and so on. Maybe a third of the slave population can work if they're not sick or have some other kind of problem."

Washington poured himself another brandy, passed the bottle Andrew's way. Andrew waved it off.

"If I freed the slaves where would they live and work? What would the old slaves unable to work do? Who would take care of the children? Frankly, I'd like to get rid of them and hire the work done, but it's not possible. Martha would never agree with the idea. We've talked about it before."

Andrew had heard the argument before. It was one of his recollections of talk between Ignatius, Mary and Martin.

"Anyhow," Washington continued. "I have a war to fight right now. You and I can continue this conversation some other time. I'm a little busy at the moment."

Andrew put his glass down and shook his head at the general acknowledging what he had said, but not agreeing.

Washington understood the silent gesture and said, "Still, I ask you to think about what we have spoken about, about working for me."

Andrew rose, and seeing this, Washington did the same, walking to Andrew and extending his hand. The two men shook hands and then as Andrew turned to leave the room Washington said , "If you change your mind, remember what I offered. And should you change your mind before I get back to Mount Vernon, I'm going to advise my manager of my offer to you. All you have to do is find your way."

"I'll keep it in mind. Good luck, Mister Washington."

Andrew was about to open the door when Washington called after him, "Just a minute. Come back for a minute, if you would."

Andrew stopped. He turned and looked at Washington, but said nothing.

"You're still going to try to get into Boston aren't you?" the general said. "Made a plan?"

"I'll find a boat and row over when there's no moon. That's about the only way I can think of at the moment."

"As long as you're determined to get yourself killed, would you mind if I suggested another plan? It might keep you from getting shot by our troops and by Gage's marines as soon as you put foot on shore. Of course, you'll be shot or hanged later, but at least you'd get to see some of Boston first."

"You didn't get to be commander for nothing. I'll listen."

"I'll give you a letter signed by me authorizing you to pass through our barricade unmolested. Then you can go down the Boston neck and up to the gate guarded by the British. I'd tie a white flag on one of your muskets and ride your horse right to the gate. The guards will either shoot you or let you approach to speak. Assuming they didn't shoot you, state your case about what you want to do, and see what happens."

"You think it'll work?"

"No, but it's about the only way you might get in. I'm fairly sure you'll be allowed to go in, but you won't be allowed to look for this person you know. What will happen is you'll be taken and questioned about everything you know about our side. They might decide you're a spy and execute you on the spot, or they might figure you to be just crazy and toss you in jail. I favor the latter. However, I don't believe they'll let you leave to go out the gate because of possible information you might take with you. If you're lucky, they could set you free, and like other citizens, you would not be allowed to leave Boston. Then you might locate your friend."

Washington sat down and took a sheet of paper from a drawer and began writing. He paused, looked up at Andrew, and said, "Mind if I ask you who this friend of yours is?"

"A lady I met some time ago."

"I thought that might be the case. Do you have any idea where she is in Boston?"

"I believe she works for a doctor."

"There are several doctors in Boston. Do you know which one?"

"No, it never came up."

"I hope it isn't Doctor Warren. He was able to get out of Boston to fight on Breed's Hill. Unfortunately, he was killed, as I understand it."

"The name doesn't sound familiar. As I said, I don't remember hearing the name of the doctor she works for."

Washington completed the letter, dusted it with talc to dry the ink, and handed the document to Andrew. He said, "This should get you through our barricade. Then it's up to providence and the British. Good luck to you."

Andrew thanked the general and turned.

"Keep your eyes and ears open, and advise me if you happen to get out."

"Would that not make me a spy working for the Americans?"

"Enough talk," Washington said, and sat down to find where he had left off in his work.

ON THE WAY back to the stables, Andrew thought over Washington's plan. It could work, or he could end up dead. It was, however, a better plan than rowing a boat; he hadn't thought about the posted marines around Boston, ready to capture or shoot anything they saw.

"How'd it go with the general, Andrew?" asked Harold.

"It satisfied my curiosity, but I don't think General Washington got out of it what he wanted. He said…"

"I don't want to know anything more. I've been a flunky all my life, and I know it doesn't pay to know things that could get you in trouble. I'll get your things."

"I'll leave Gage and everything that was packed on him, and one musket. Keep looking after 'em for me while I'm gone."

"Huh? You don't want them now?"

"No. I've got something else to do first. How do I get from here to Boston?"

"You're not right in the head, Andrew. The place is closed off. Unless you want to swim, there's only one way into Boston."

"Harold, find me a piece of white cloth, about the size of a small flag."

CHAPTER XVIII

THE AMERICAN TROOPS looked at Andrew as he rode past. None tried to stop or question him. He was no more than a curiosity to most, a big, bearded black man carrying a small arsenal. No one wished to tangle with him.

It was different when he arrived at the Boston neck. The road was barricaded and guarded by a lieutenant and his men. The lieutenant challenged Andrew and his men surrounded him, muskets at the ready.

"What business do you have here?" asked the lieutenant. "You're not thinking of going into Boston?"

"I'm gonna try," he said, and handed the lieutenant Washington's letter.

The lieutenant unfolded the letter and read it. "You know General Washington, huh?"

"In a way."

"That's not going to help much in Boston. You have next of kin we can notify?" The rest of his men laughed.

"No, no one."

"If you're crazy, go ahead. I'm not going to stop you. Hope it's worthwhile."

The lieutenant had his men step aside.

"Can I have the letter back?"

"If the redcoats find it on you, you could very well be hanged at sunup. Best leave it with me."

Andrew didn't argue, and coaxed Henry on.

Looking down the road, he could see a blockade of men, out of musket range but well within the range of cannon. On both sides of the road, he saw a no man's land. Nothing moved except the trees as the wind blew their leaves, which were deepening in color. He tied the white rag Harold had found for him to the barrel of his musket, and the thought occurred to him that it might be the last he would ever see of his guns and Henry. What was it Branwen had said when he had tried to kiss her in front of the doctor's house? "Maybe some other time." Maybe! Was it worthwhile, as the lieutenant had asked? Perhaps he was crazy.

Looking ahead toward the blockade, he could see activity increase the closer he came. The red and white uniforms were unmistakably British soldiers, and they moved to position themselves in a line across the road the closer he came. One of the soldiers in the middle withdrew his sword, holding it at the carry. As Andrew approached within twenty yards, the soldier raised his sword over his head and shouted a command, upon which the soldiers raised their muskets and trained them on Andrew. Andrew pulled the reins, and Henry stopped. "Too late to go back, boy. Wonder what we'll do now that won't get us killed."

"Dismount your horse," yelled the soldier with the sword. Leave your weapons on the horse, and come forward ten paces."

He stuck his pistols under his bedroll, leaving his musket and knife tied to the saddle, and climbed off Henry. He proceeded to walk the ten paces, and stopped. One of the soldiers next to the one who had been giving orders gave his musket to the man next to him, and advanced toward Andrew. He searched Andrew and backed off to the side. When clear of Andrew, he called to the man with the sword, "He has no other weapons, sir."

"Escort him in, private."

The private motioned for Andrew to proceed to the line of soldiers.

"I'm Captain Bailey. Who are you, and what do you want under your flag of truce?"

"My name is Andrew Attaway. I've come to find a friend of mine."

"For what purpose?"

"I'm concerned about her welfare."

"Ah, a lady friend! She must be something special for you to risk your life. Are you with the American militia, or possibly with their army?"

"No."

"Then you're a Loyalist?"

"Neither one."

"So, if you're not with the American forces and you're not a Loyalist, you're feelings are for…?"

"Myself."

"Hmm. Where do you come from?"

"Way south of here."

"Corporal," the captain said to one of the men, "keep this man under guard until I return."

"Yes, sir."

The captain mounted his horse and road into Boston. The corporal ordered the rest of the soldiers to come to order arms and then to parade rest. Andrew stood still for a while, and then took a chance and sat down on the road. Henry wandered up to him and nuzzled his hair. A few redcoats grinned and gave a slight laugh. "Better stay sitting on the ground," said the corporal. "And don't try reaching for those guns." Andrew nodded his head in understanding.

By the position of the sun, Andrew figured it was about noon, and judged that he had been there close to two hours. A horse and rider followed by several marching soldiers came into view as they marched out of Boston and through the neck toward the barricade. As they drew nearer, it was clear that the horseman was a captain, but not the same captain who had left Andrew waiting. This was a changing of the guard.

"You there!" said the new captain, addressing Andrew, "I assume you are the person looking for his friend?"

"I am. I'm Andrew Attaway."

"Corporal, take the musket and knife from the man's horse and prepare to lead him after me. Andrew Attaway, after the corporal has taken the reins of your horse, mount up."

Andrew noticed the corporal didn't look under the bedroll where the pistols had been placed, and hoped they were far enough under so they would not fall out. As they rode down the neck, the corporal took Andrew's knife from its scabbard and tested its sharpness by stroking his thumb across the blade. He held the knife up and looked it over, returned it to its scabbard, and placed it inside his own belt.

I won't be seeing my knife again, thought Andrew.

"GENERAL HOWE, THIS is the fellow who wants to find his friend," said the captain.

"Come in and have a seat, young man."

As Andrew entered the room, he saw two other officers he presumed were also generals, as they were dressed in similar uniforms. The captain clicked his heels together, did an about-face, and left the room. Andrew thought, *why do I keep running into generals? I'm nobody.*

General Howe rose and introduced Generals Clinton and Burgoyne, then said, "We understand you're looking for a friend—a female friend, from what Captain Bailey told us. What relationship is she to you?"

"I met her some time ago when coming north. We traveled together."

"And…?"

"And I know she came here to work."

General Burgoyne asked, "Are you runaways?"

"We're both free, and have papers."

The general stroked his chin and ran his hand down his beard; his face showed a certain amount of doubt. "Well, I suppose it doesn't matter what she or you are. We had assumed you were a runaway slave, and had come to join us because we would set you free."

"I didn't know you freed slaves if they joined with you."

"We do, but I guess that's not important right now."

"Who is this woman, and do you know where she is?"

"Her name's Bonnie Miller, and she works for a doctor."

"Which doctor? Boston has several doctors."

"Don't remember his name, if I ever knew it. But I know where his house is."

"Describe it."

"It's a two-story house set off the street. It doesn't face the street, but is set back and turned sideways."

"That would be Doctor Warren's house. The rabble-rouser's dead and gone. We killed him on Breed's Hill. He was one of the troublemakers who caused the riots, and this damned situation we find ourselves in. He got out of Boston before we could arrest him."

"This woman," said General Howe, "I'm assuming she's also a Negro?"

Andrew said, "Father was white, and mother was black."

"I know of a woman who is of mixed race and does, or did, work for Doctor Warren. I went to the doctor to have a cyst lanced." Howe didn't mention he could have lanced the cyst himself, but used the visit as a ruse to observe the doctor. In turn, the doctor feigned being busy to avoid Howe. "He and his colleague were busy, so she cut it open. She's as tall as I am.

Her hair is straight, not like yours, and she keeps it tied in back. Would that be her?"

"That could be her, yes. Can I see her?"

"We can't allow you to roam the streets of Boston looking for her," said General Clinton.

"For that matter, you yourself could be suspect with regard to why you're here," injected General Burgoyne. "You may be a spy, for all we know."

"I'm going to have you escorted to a waiting area down the hall while I discuss this matter with the generals," Howe said. "We shouldn't be long. We have other matters more pressing than this."

Andrew and his escort, an armed corporal, entered a room where a sergeant was passing time at his desk daydreaming. In the corner of the room was a single jail cell. *Must be the holding area,* he thought.

The sergeant looked up when they came in. The escort spoke to the sergeant, and the sergeant got up and opened the cell. Andrew was instructed to go in. It had been a long time since he had seen the inside of a jail cell. This time, there was no Jim and no rusty iron straps to make knives from.

There was nothing in the cell except a single plank bed without mattress or covering, and a couple of wood buckets under the bed. He slid the buckets out and discovered one had rags in it, and the other was empty. It occurred to him these were meant for nature's calls; much better than the hole in the dirt floor he had experienced with his first encounter with jail cells as a boy.

The sergeant sat down at his desk as soon as the escort left. Andrew glanced around the room, and saw his musket had been brought in and stacked in a corner of the room next to the sergeant's desk. Other than a coat-rack and a bulletin board, the room was bare. A large window in the front of the room looked out to the street. He saw Henry tied to the rail. How he wished there was a rusty iron strap somewhere. There was nothing to do but stretch out on the bed and take it easy.

Andrew dozed off, only to be woken by "Hey, you." He woke, sat up, and turned about. It was the corporal who had escorted him. "I'm to tell you General Howe has sent someone to the doctor's house to find your friend, and they will get back with you as soon as they find her."

"What then?"

"I have no idea. I've told you everything I was told to tell you. But if I were to guess, I'd say you're going to be our guest for quite a while."

"In here?"

"No, we have regular accommodations for prisoners," said the corporal, and left. The sergeant looked at Andrew and said nothing, turned around, and continued dreaming.

Andrew knew it was time to make a plan, and he didn't have much time. Things were going to happen fast. He settled back and thought about the if-this-then-that scenarios.

After a few minutes, he stood up, and with one of his feet, slid one of the buckets from under the bed to the side of the wall. The sergeant turned his head to look. "Just got to take one, Sarge."

"Leave it under the bunk when you're done. We'll take care of it after you leave."

While he relieved himself, he studied the bucket, and saw what he hoped would be there: the bucket's bail was of stout iron rod, connected through holes in the side. As he finished, he looked at the sergeant, who paid no attention. Stooping down, Andrew grabbed the bail with both hands, forcing it inward and disconnecting it from the bucket. He hid it in his pants as he buttoned them, and proceeded to slide the bucket under the bunk.

The sergeant got up to leave the room. Stopping a moment, he looked at Andrew and said, "My turn. Don't go anywhere, boy." Pleased with his own sense of humor, he laughed as he left.

Andrew turned over on the bunk facing the wall. He pulled the bail from his pants. Holding it in one hand, he wrapped it around his fist with the other, and straightened the rest of the bail as best he could. The business end of the weapon was not sharp, but it would do the job if it had to.

Coming back into the room, the sergeant held tin cups in each hand. "Thought you might be thirsty. This water doesn't taste good, but at least it's wet." He handed one of the cups through the cell bars to Andrew.

"Thanks."

"Hate to see a man suffer. If you want more, speak up."

Andrew thought, *Nice man. Hate to see him hurt, but....*

IT WAS LATE afternoon, and the sun cast long shadows. Soon, night would come. General Burgoyne walked into the room, and the sergeant snapped out of his dream world and came to attention. The general, not paying attention to the sergeant, walked past him to Andrew's cell. "We sent someone to Doctor Warren's house to find the girl. He reported back that the girl went with Warren when he escaped from Boston. Therefore, we have to assume she sided with Warren and his warped political thinking. You, being a friend of hers, probably think in the same way. You'll remain in our custody and under guard in the stockade until we figure out what to do with you." The general turned around and left without allowing Andrew a word.

Andrew looked at the sergeant, and the sergeant looked at Andrew. "What now, Sarge?"

The sergeant shrugged his shoulders and sat down.

Within minutes, a captain followed by two corporals entered the room. Again, the sergeant snapped to. "Release that man, sergeant. We're to take him to a more secure residence."

The sergeant opened the cell door and motioned Andrew to come out, whereupon the corporals took him by the arms and guided him to where the captain was waiting. "You will follow me," said the captain to Andrew.

Andrew had other plans. Wind-milling his arms backward and around and breaking the corporals' grips on his arms, he made his break. Grabbing the two by the backs of their collars, he slammed them together hard, as if they were a pair of cymbals. Andrew let go, and they fell to the floor like two fresh dung patties. Withdrawing the bucket bail weapon, he made a dash to his musket. The sergeant moved to follow Andrew's motion, and Andrew pointed his makeshift weapon at him; the sergeant sat down at the desk. Shrugging, he motioned that he wanted no part of this.

Andrew dashed, grabbed the gun, and bounded toward the captain, who was un-holstering his pistol. He was on the captain before he had time to cock the lock, smashing the butt of his musket square in the officer's mouth. The captain crashed against the doorframe and fell to the floor. Andrew slung the musket across his back as he looked about him, making sure the two corporals and the sergeant were not going to be a problem.

He entered the hallway with caution and looked both ways. There was nobody in sight except an old black lady on her hands and knees scrubbing the floor. She looked up with curiosity in her eyes, and returned to her task. Running would draw attention. A person walking and appearing to be doing nothing out of the ordinary is rarely noticed or questioned. So he walked with authority to the tall entrance door. Outside were the figures of several men standing around talking, most of them soldiers. As casually as he could, he walked toward Henry, thinking nobody was paying attention to him—but a bearded black man with a musket slung on his back tends to draw the looks of others. As he untied the reins from the hitching post, he glanced around and noticed most all of Boston looking at him.

"Hey, who's that?" someone yelled.

Andrew swung his leg over the saddle as another voice called out, "Stop right there! This is General Burgoyne, and I command you to stop!"

"Let's go, Henry!" Andrew shouted. Henry began to run, and at the same time, the gathered men ran in front of him, trying to grab his reins and yelling for him and his rider to stop. Henry stopped only long enough to rise up on his rear legs. He did this several times while Andrew held on, trying not to fall off. Each time the horse came down, he tried to hit somebody, anybody. He succeeded, and the head of one of the men spurted blood from the forehead.

A gunshot sounded from behind Andrew and Henry. General Burgoyne or one of the men in his group had fired, and the sound of the concussion as it passed close to horse and rider caused Henry to jump. The men in front backed away from the mad horse. Henry burst into a full gallop, with Andrew hanging on. Scattering to get out of the way, some men tripped and fell over each other. Others were not as fast, and felt how it was to be brushed by a horse and rider at full speed. More gunshots passed by the pair as they made their way around the first corner. Andrew was guiding Henry toward the neck, hoping he remembered the way and wouldn't run into a dead end or take the wrong turn.

The barricade of guards, alerted by the gunfire, stood ready, but unsure of what was happening. Their standing orders where to stop and question anyone attempting to leave Boston. But here came horse and rider full speed. The captain, sizing up the situation, ordered his men to open their line in the middle. "If he doesn't stop, let him pass, and shoot as soon as he's clear."

They were dead ahead—the barricade of guards spread across the road. Would Henry stop? He hoped not. "C'mon boy, just keep going. Don't stop on me now." As horse and rider approached the line of guards, the guards separated, leaving a space between them large enough for Henry to run through. As they ran through, Andrew glimpsed the guards lifting their muskets.

The guards reformed their line, and the captain gave the order to fire. A volley of musket balls chased the fleeing pair. A lead ball aimed at the middle of Andrew's back dropped too low in flight, and though it was off, it still found Andrew's leg. He grabbed at his right leg. Pain more intense than that of the whip shot up and down his leg, and a fire as hot as his forge smoldered beneath his hand.

He clenched his teeth and continued to run Henry through the neck and past the American barricade. From the side of his vision, he vaguely saw some of the Americans shoulder their muskets, then lower them again after seeing but a single rider and no red uniform. Would they shoot? Did they shoot? He didn't care, and didn't think about it. All he wanted to do was get away, and he ran Henry until he thought he was safe. He slowed to a walk. The pain in his leg eased a bit, and he continued to go ahead. But where? He didn't want to go to Cambridge, but it was his best chance to have his leg taken care of. Then he could figure out his next move. Cambridge it was.

Sometime and somewhere before reaching Cambridge, Andrew either passed out or fell asleep hunched over the saddle, his head against Henry's neck. It was dark, and Henry walked without guidance. A few soldiers and militia walked the streets. Two soldiers approached to take a closer look at the man Henry carried. He gave a whinny, turning away from the curiosity seekers and kicking with his rear legs. The whinny and sudden rise of Henry's rump woke Andrew enough to gain control of his horse. He asked one of the soldiers where he was, and where he might go to have his leg looked at. One of the soldiers pointed to a road at Andrew's side and said, "Right down that road a mile or so." Andrew turned Henry and walked him in the direction the soldier had pointed.

"That's not the way to the hospital, Frederick. Why'd you send him the wrong way?"

"The hospitals are full up from that Bunker Hill scrap we got into, and since we're not fighting with 'em right now, he didn't get hurt in any battle. Plus, didn't you notice he's a nigger? I don't want any of them around. Got enough of 'em down in Maryland. I'll bet he got caught stealing something."

"He's still hurt!"

"What of it?"

HENRY CONTINUED TO walk even after Andrew had once again passed out. Eventually, a farmhouse came into view. Henry continued to the gate leading up the drive, where he stopped with his head against the gatepost and Andrew slumped over his neck. Henry dozed and waited.

CHAPTER XIX

SHE FOLLOWED THE boy up the stairs, down the hallway and through a bedroom door. "He's in there," said the boy.

Two women turned and looked at her as she entered the room. They had the same look she had seen so many times before: the look from people, white or black, when they saw black instead of the expected white.

"I'm Bonnie Miller. I came in place of Doctor Warren. I assume you're the Whitakers?"

"I'm Anne Whitaker. This is my daughter Lori White, and the boy is her son, Billy. Where's Doctor Warren?"

"Doctor Warren was killed during the fighting on Breed's Hill. I was his assistant, and am trying to help where I can. With doctors in short supply, I'm about all that's available. Is that him over there in the bed?"

Lori said, "Yes. He doesn't move much—just seems to sleep, and talks nonsense sometimes. Sometimes he wakes and looks around, but I don't think he sees or can understand where he is or what's going on around him.

We can give him water then if we put a cup to his lips. I don't think he'll last the night. He's your kind. I hope you can save him."

My kind even from a Quaker! she thought as she angered within. "Let me take a look at him."

He was on his side with the wound from the ball covered over with rags. There was a wet cloth draped across his forehead to ease his fever; his nose drained into his beard, and his body glistened with sweat, His mouth, half open, allowed only shallow breaths.

The oldest woman asked, "You think he'll live?"

"I'm not a doctor, so I can't tell for sure."

"Are you going to be able to help him?" Anne Whitaker asked.

"I have experience assisting a physician, and know pretty well what to do with wounds such as this."

The musket ball had broken his leg about halfway between the knee and the hip. She opened her bag and selected the necessary tools.

"You have all the tools a doctor has. I thought you weren't a doctor."

"I more or less inherited this armamentarium from the doctor I worked for. His mother asked me if I could use them."

"What's an arma...what you said?"

"The necessary doctoring tools."

"Oh."

Bonnie cleaned one of the instruments with a clear liquid from one of the flasks she carried in her kit, then probed the hole in Andrew's leg, whereupon Andrew winced as his leg jerked. "Take it easy, fellow. Here, I'm going to give you something to drink. It will ease the pain." She reached into her bag and brought out another flask, offering it to the man's lips. He drank it and flinched, but Bonnie followed his mouth with the flask and forced him to drink. "We're going to wait while it takes effect."

"What's that?" asked the older woman.

"It's something my mama taught me to make. She used to make it and other potions to use on the..." She almost said plantation, but caught herself. "The farm. She could make stuff that would make you feel better, no matter how sick you were. We used it on animals as well as people."

"What's in it?"

"This is made from spirits, poppies, honey, and mint leaves."

"You mean liquor?" the older woman said with an air of disapproval.

"That's what I mean. Call it liquor, alcohol, whiskey, or whatever."

"I'm not sure I approve of its use," the older woman said.

"I don't think you'd approve of this man dying, either," Bonnie said, annoyed with the woman's self-righteousness. "There are bone fragments in there, and the ball is next to the break. I don't see where it's starting to rot, no sign of blood poisoning. I'm going to try to save it."

The younger woman asked, "What if it starts to rot?"

"I'm going to try to prevent that right now." She reached into her kit a brought out two small leather bags. "Here," she said, handing one of the bags to the younger woman, "one of you make a tea out of this, and we'll try to get him to swallow it. I'm going to put the other bag in the wound."

"What is it that it will stop rot?"

"More stuff I've learned about. This is made from purple daisy, moss, and garlic."

The boy spoke. "Are you a witch?"

Bonnie laughed with the other two women. "No, son. I just know about some medicines, same as a doctor does. But I'm not a doctor."

"What's the difference?"

"About three more years of working with a doctor and a couple hundred more patients."

With the boy's curiosity somewhat satisfied, Bonnie continued with her patient.

"I'm going to remove the ball and clean out as many bone fragments as I can. Afterward, I'll set his leg and tie it to a board to keep it as straight as it can be. I'll stuff a rag in there after dipping it in spirits, and remove the rag to look at the wound a couple of times a day. If I see any rot starting and I can't control it, I'll have to take his leg off."

"You know how to do that?" asked the oldest woman.

"I've seen it done, and it isn't much different than sawing a ham in half. Tie the leg tight with a rope to keep the blood from draining out, then put a red hot poker to it to clot the blood."

"What if the rot continues?

"Make him as comfortable as possible and let him die."

The younger woman broke in, "That's it?! We just let him die as comfortable as we can? Nothing else can be done?"

"The only thing I know is what I've seen done. As I told you, I'm not a doctor. You might say a prayer. Do you have any spirits?"

"You again mean liquor?"

"Yes."

"No!" the younger woman said with indignation. "We wouldn't have it anywhere around here."

The older woman interrupted, "Why do you ask?"

"I use it to help clean wounds, as it works better than water. I have a small flask of it, but not enough."

The older woman said to the younger, "You know where your dad, bless his soul, kept a bit for health purposes. Go fetch it. It's still under the front porch."

The boy who had escorted Bonnie spoke up. "Grandpa made a lot of it out in the shed. It's in barrels."

"Well, the family secret is out. You always were your grandpa's favorite," said the older woman.

"We'll need rope, too, enough to tie him down. If he doesn't sleep through this, he's going to be screaming something terrible. In his fever, he might try to do just about anything. We also need a lot of clean rags and some boards—like bed boards, but cut as long as his leg. I'll use the boards to tie to his leg to keep it straight."

While the younger woman and the boy went for the items, Bonnie removed the rag from the man's forehead, wrung it out, and dipped it in fresh water. Before placing it back, she cleaned the drained mucus and other matter from his beard. As she did so, she studied the man's face, and smiled just a little. She lifted one of the man's eyelids. "I'll be damned," she muttered. "Green eyes".

"What?" exclaimed the older woman.

"I know this man. It's been a while, but I know him."

"From where?"

Ever careful, even among Quakers, she said, "It was a gathering of family a long time ago; a reunion of sorts."

"He's a relative?" asked the older woman.

"Sort of a distant one, as I remember. Think he might have married one of my cousins."

This satisfied the older woman for the moment, and she settled back to watch. The young woman and boy returned with the items Bonnie had requested. "This here's what Daddy used to use." Neither woman went into detail.

Bonnie pulled the cork from the bottle and passed it under her nose to whiff. *Good stuff,* she thought.

They proceeded to tie Andrew to the bed frame. Bonnie hoped, and the Quakers prayed, that her medicine would keep him asleep, or at least still enough for her to do what she had to. Next, with a rag soaked with spirits, she cleaned dirt from around the wound, then spread the wound and poured the liquid in. Andrew groaned and tried to move, but then settled back. The spirits and blood spurted back out in a pinkish color, which she wiped away.

Next, Bonnie took various hemostats and additional probes from her kit. She splashed them with spirits and laid them on a rag next to the leg.

An hour and more went by as Bonnie used her tools in the wound and picked out pieces of bone. At the same time, the women kept watch over Andrew, and when he seemed to be feeling the pain, they would make him swallow more of Bonnie's medicine.

"Got it!" Bonnie said as she withdrew the musket ball. "Just a few more pieces of bone, and…." She laid down her tools. "One of you take hold of his ankle and pull the leg. We're going to try to align the leg bone."

The younger woman did as she was asked, and Bonnie grabbed the leg around the broken area. She guided, and felt the bone moving. "That's about right," she said. "Alright, ever so gently, stop pulling. That's where we want it. Gentle, now."

She spread the wound with hemostats and poured the remaining contents of the leather bag as deeply into the wound as she could. Next, she stuffed a rag soaked with spirits into the wound, and tied three boards around the leg. "We'll keep him tied down until he comes around. It's important he doesn't move the leg, and if it needs to be moved, one of us is going to have to help. That's about as much as I can do for him."

In the morning, Bonnie removed the spirit-soaked cloth from the wound, and was satisfied with what she saw; she did not see rot, and the wound no longer bled.

She joined the other two women for a morning meal and tea. Anne and Lori were curious about how Bonnie had come to work with the doctor in Boston. Bonnie never confided the real reason or how it had come about, but what she told the two was close to the truth. She said she passed the doctor's house one day, and there was a *maid wanted* sign on the fence surrounding the property. She needed a job, so decided to knock on his door and ask.

When the doctor questioned her about her qualifications and experience, her knowledge of natural medicines came to light. The doctor's interest soon turned to the remedies she knew of, and he forgot about hiring Bonnie as a maid. Instead, he offered her a job assisting him in his practice. Soon after, he referred to her as his nurse, and Bonnie liked the feeling it gave her. After giving the explanation, she said, "I never knew he had slaves, and when I found out, it was a complete shock to me. I didn't quite know what to do."

"I gather that was quite offensive to you," said Lori, "but not enough to quit and go elsewhere."

"I thought about it, but there are times to fight and times to plan your strategy. Besides me, Dr. Warren had two other black boys, and soon after, a white maid. At first, I thought the boys were paid, because none of us were treated differently. I noticed he was a little gruffer with the boys, but thought it was because they were boys and needed a little more motivation. It wasn't long before I had my suspicions, though.

One day, I overheard one of the boys saying he hoped the doctor wouldn't send him back and get his money back. I knew then they were slaves, and I asked them if they were. They told me they were slaves just like me. I told them I wasn't a slave, and they couldn't believe it. I decided then and there I was going to learn all I could from the doctor, and then leave him. I guess that's being hypocritical, but it was what I thought best at the time. As I learned while I was there, Doctor Warren was a complex man. He spent about as much time planning strategies against the British and making speeches as he did doctoring. His apprentice and I did much of the doctoring. Did you know he was elected president of the Provincial Congress? Did you know he joined the fighting on Breed's Hill as a volunteer, but was offered a position as an officer? He said he wasn't qualified to be an officer. Either way, he took a chance of being killed, and he was."

Over the course of the next two nights, Andrew came in and out of consciousness, and experienced bouts of delirium brought about by the combination of his high fever and Bonnie's pain medicine. At times, he saw a boy painted red and white pointing a toy musket at him, while a black and white striped woman tried to push the boy out of the way. With the stern look of a mother, she commanded the boy to go home, and for Andrew to go back to sleep. As the effect of Bonnie's medicine wore off, Andrew felt more pain, and he sometimes groaned and grimaced while trying to move. Bonnie allowed him only a small amount of her medicine, as she knew what happened to a person as they started to depend on the potion more and more.

The women, taking turns and sometimes working together, continued to attend to Andrew's bodily needs, and the boy kept himself busy supplying clean rags and disposing of soiled ones in addition to his other chores. Bonnie filled a large pot with water, and added honey and a bit of salt for Andrew to drink in place of plain water. She had him drink broth made from whatever meats and vegetables the Quaker family had on hand, saying her patient needed to build his strength to get well. She continued to change the dressing and splash the wound with spirits, inspecting it for rot; so far, all looked well.

The fever continued late into the next morning, but by late afternoon, it had broken, and Andrew began to wake and focus on his surroundings. This was not a place he knew. He surveyed himself under the bedcovers, and saw that he was naked, and had a great number of towels and rags about his body.

"Hello, Andy. You look better. How are you feeling?" Bonnie asked.

He was still trying to figure out where he was and what had happened. "What happened?" was all he said, to no one in particular.

"Look at me, Andy. Do you know me?"

He looked where the voice had come from, and felt overwhelmed. "You're the black and white woman! Damned if you ain't Branwen!"

"Not so loud, Andy. I'm Bonnie Miller around here, understand?"

Remembering the name she had taken, he said, "Ah, yes. I remember. Bonnie it is." He paused and looked around, then back at Bonnie. "What happened? Why am I here? How'd I get here? How'd you get here?"

"I don't know how you got shot. I assume it had something to do with the war."

It came back to him when he heard the word *war*. He thought better about admitting how he got shot. He was a little embarrassed about it, and didn't want to tell Bonnie he had been trying to find her in Boston. She might find him foolish for thinking she cared for him. "I don't remember what happened," he said.

The older woman spoke. "My grandson heard a noise in the front of the house while it was still dark. He woke us, and we went outside and found you there, bent over on your horse and oblivious to anything around you. How you stayed on that animal is a wonder."

"Let me take a look at your leg," said Bonnie, pulling back the covers from Andrew's leg.

Andrew, aware of his nakedness, reached for the covers to pull them back, and felt pain from his leg. He let out a groan and lay back again.

"Sorry, Andy. I get the same reaction from a lot of the people I work with. I'm used to naked people, but naked people aren't always used to me... not when I first start working with them. Now, let me look at your leg." She spoke with the stern words of a military commander rather than words of a beautiful woman. She was still the Branwen he had met when they were on the run: sure of herself, and not afraid of others. She didn't take guff from anyone.

"I'd just as soon have the doctor do that, if you don't mind," said Andrew.

"Me, too, but I'm the closest thing there is to a doctor around here, so as far as you're concerned, I am the doctor. That's my work on your leg, and you're damned lucky to still have it. If you give me any trouble, I can still cut it off and wrap it around your neck."

"You remind me of a woman I used to know named Branwen, tough as horseshoe nails and all business. Do what you have to, and I'll grit my teeth and bear it."

She gave Andrew a warning look that said, *You talk too much. Shut up.* She removed the dressing and wiped the wound with a cloth wet with spirits. Andrew gritted his teeth and tensed. "Relax, Andy," she said. "This is going well. There's is no sign of rot. Guess I can't beat you with your own leg. Let me put a new dressing around your leg. I promise I'll be gentle."

She finished dressing the leg and pulled the covers over Andrew, saying, "I'll be leaving for a while. I've got other people to tend to."

"Other people?"

"The ones I regularly take care of. They aren't hurt as bad as you, but in some ways, they are worse than you. Some are old and need things done for them. Some are sick. Some have the pox."

"What if I need something?"

"The ladies will bring you something to eat. Now, listen to me. I don't want you moving your leg, no matter what. The bone has to grow itself together and that won't happen if you move it. If you have to pee or poop, do it. They'll tend to you. Don't be embarrassed; just cooperate and you'll get better."

"How long before I can get up and do things for myself?"

"I would think a month; it's a bad break, so we'll just have to see. It'll be another four to six weeks, maybe longer, before you'll be able to walk around with a crutch, and even then, still with the boards on your leg. I don't know how much longer they'll have to stay on. We'll have to see how you're getting along. You in a hurry to go somewhere?"

"Guess not."

She took his hand and squeezed it. "I'll be back tomorrow or the next day. You'll be fine till then."

As he watched her turn and leave, Andy wondered what the squeezed hand meant—if anything.

The older woman, Anne, said to Bonnie, "It's late. Please stay another night and get a good rest."

Bonnie realized how tired she was, and the invitation came as a relief. "I will. Thank you."

Andrew had been sleeping an hour or two when he was awakened. "We got another!" cried out the older woman as she hurried through the door. He tried to sit up, but his leg reminded him to stay down. Two men in British uniforms followed Anne, carrying—more like dragging—a profusely bleeding man whose arms they had placed around their shoulders to keep him upright. The men let him down on the floor and stepped back. They looked at their companion with blank stares, not knowing what to do next.

Raising his head just enough to see the man, Andrew saw he was no man at all. If anything, he was fourteen, sixteen maximum. "What happened to him?" Andrew asked.

"We were delivering a message to General Washington in Cambridge under a flag of truce, and we were ambushed by militia who paid our white flag no attention. Robert here got hit in the back."

"We knew of this place and brought him," said the other soldier.

From down the hallway, Andrew heard, "Clean bandages and boiling water! I need them now!" Bonnie ran into the room carrying her doctor's kit, and looked around the room. She chanced to glance at Andrew, but her eyes fell upon the wounded redcoat. She kneeled down to inspect him. "Goddamned war!" she exclaimed. "This isn't anything but a child. What's he doing so far from home?" she asked nobody in particular. "He should be home milking cows."

The young woman came into the room carrying an armful of rags. "The water will be ready before too long."

"Forget it," Bonnie said. "He's dead. I'm not Jesus Christ, and I can't bring people back from the dead." She crumpled to the floor over the dead boy-man, lowered her head, and cried.

"Bonnie," Andrew said to her. "Come here."

Looking up, Bonnie could see Andrew through her tear-blurred eyes, holding his arm out to her; but still, she continued kneeling on the floor, crying.

"Bonnie," Andrew said. "Please come to me."

Bonnie raised herself and went to Andrew. When she got to him, she took his outreached hand and sank down alongside of him. She lowered her head on his chest, and cried as loud as she could. Andrew put his other arm around her, hurting as he did, and raised his head enough to kiss her on the forehead. She raised her head just enough to look him in the face. He kissed her along the side of her tear-covered nose. She did not pull away, and he went no further.

"You care about people, all people, don't you?" he asked, knowing there would be no reply.

ANDREW WAS SITTING up in bed reading the Cambridge newspaper Branwen had left. There was news about the Boston siege, as well as several articles about who had come to visit whom in Cambridge. Some farmer was building a barn, and neighbors from all around came to help. In comparison with the last, there was nothing new in this edition about the Boston siege; there was mention of a few sniper shots from both sides, but otherwise, no news. Winter had slowed war activities down. The last edition told about the cannons General Washington had set in place overlooking Dorchester Heights, but had not used so far. This week's edition did not mention anything about them.

He thought he heard a horse outside the house, and the sound was soon followed by a knocking on the front door. In a few minutes, Lila walked into the room and asked if he felt like having a visitor.

Guessing it was Branwen, he said, "Bonnie usually just walks in. Why so formal now?"

"It's not Bonnie. It's a soldier named Harold."

"Harold! The only Harold I know is…yes, I want to see him. Where is he?"

"Come in, Harold," Lila said to the man just outside the entrance.

Harold walked into the room wearing a smile. "Heard you got shot up a little. Serves you right. Didn't the general warn you?" Harold walked over to the bed, and the two men shook hands.

Lila backed out of the room and disappeared to continue what she had been doing. The two men continued with their pleasantries until Harold asked what had happened. Andrew related the story to a point, then said, "… and after I got shot, I don't remember a thing…have no idea how I got here. Ol' Henry must be smarter than I give him credit for. How'd you find me?" He paused a few seconds and looked Harold over; somehow, he had changed, and before Harold could answer, Andrew noticed the stripe on Harold's arm. "You made corporal. How'd that happen?"

"It's part of why I'm here. I found out General Washington is a real smart fellow. He knows more about what's going on around here than anybody thinks. He found out some crazy black man crashed through the Boston barricade, and from another source, a wounded black man was headed here. Seems one of his soldiers pointed you in this direction so you could get help. Why he didn't point you toward Cambridge is something he couldn't answer right off…just said he must have got confused."

"I don't remember any of what happened."

"Well, anyhow, there's been a lot of activity around Cambridge. Lots of horses and cannon coming in. I don't know, but I think something's about to happen. The general and his troops may be moving out. Anyhow, the general remembered I knew you, and he sent me to ask you to reconsider joining the Continentals to work with the horses. You could either do it willingly, or he'd do it the hard way and conscript you if you looked to be recovered. I can see you're in no shape to go into the army, and that's what I'll tell him. By the way, sorry I couldn't bring Gage, but I brought the rest of your stuff, including the musket and rifle. I left them downstairs with the young lady."

"He took Gage, huh? I never thought he'd…never mind. Gage will do a good job for him. You got promoted just because you knew me?"

"The general said it was because I was doing a good job with the horses, and would be working with you. You were going to be a private, and needed someone over you other than him. He said you don't respond to authority well, but you might respond to friendship."

"Tell the general I'd desert before being a slave again, and have to fight for something that ain't going to help me or my kind."

"You sure you want me to tell him that? How 'bout I just say you're a long way from being able to even walk?"

"Suit yourself, Harold. Whichever you prefer, but don't give him the slightest idea I might be available later on."

"That would be his idea, and I'm sure he'll have it in the back of his mind. Try to keep out of his sight."

"It's not easy not being inconspicuous when you look like me. The general said something close to that himself."

"I might mention one other thing. It's known a certain woman has been taking care of you, and she learned her skills from a Doctor Warren of Boston. Because she came from Boston with the doctor, she is suspected of being a spy for the British, and is under investigation to determine her history. The general told me to tell you not to mention anything to the lady that might help the British, including our conversation; and if you do help her, she and you would both be hanged."

"It's time for you to leave, Harold! Tell the general to get out of my life."

CHAPTER XX

SITTING ON THE front porch of the farmhouse with his leg propped up on a stool, Andrew gazed across the barren fields waiting to be worked and seeded by the season's new hands. This was a small farm, unlike the ones growing mostly tobacco in Maryland, in fields sometimes stretching as far as one could see. In comparison, even Isaac's small farm made this one seem like a slave's small back-of-cabin garden. You could almost throw a stone across these fields. There were a few cows raised for milk and meat, and a few head of sheep with their fleece grown out, waiting to be sheared. Chickens were out and about, pecking the ground. A few hens began to lay eggs again in secret places known only to a few—Billy being one of them.

Billy's dad and grandpa had died two years previously when the barn burned, and neither was able to escape the flames. It was difficult for the women to work the farm, but by faith and determination, and the fact that there was not much else they could do, they bent to the task. They were strong and determined women, but the work required more labor than they could provide by themselves. They decided they would have to hire a few hands to help out full time rather than only at harvest time. Some were black, and some white; it had never made a difference to these people. If a hand could do the job, and was honest and of good character, that was all they required. During harvest, some slaves belonging to others were hired, but the two Quaker women never entertained the idea of owning slaves.

Hands ate in the farmhouse along with the rest of the household. Anne and Lori prepared meals on an iron stove and in the stone fireplace. Meals were served on a long table. Come mealtime, hands sat at the table, and Anne always asked one of them to say the blessing. If the chosen hand did not know how to say a blessing, Anne or Lori would patiently say a few lines, and have the hand repeat what they had said. In this way, the hand would learn, and would be called upon again at another meal to try it once more.

After the blessing, the two women brought bowls and platters of food, placing them at intervals along the table. Arms belonging to hungry men darted for the food and quickly brought it to their plates, where it was devoured almost in a single mouthful. Manners, at best, consisted of not stabbing another's hand while reaching for food. Pitchers of milk and buttermilk seemed to never stop moving up and down the table. After a long day's work, some hands returned to their homes, and others, who had no homes, slept in a small cabin similar to the slave cabins Andrew remembered in Maryland.

He thought about the two Quaker farms; this one without slaves, and Thaddeus Williams', which had slaves but allowed them to buy their freedom by working toward it on their own time. Thaddeus had proven himself a friend of the slave, and in his own way, tried to right the wrongs of slavery by offering help to escaped slaves, as he had done for Andrew and Branwen.

A horse and buggy almost hidden by the cloud of dust it stirred up was making its way up the long drive leading to the farmhouse. He had a feeling he knew who it was, and the excitement of anticipation went through his body. The driver came into view, and, as he had hoped, it was Branwen. He looked at himself as best he could, and hoped he looked somewhat presentable. The trousers he wore, with one leg cut off to fit over his splinted leg, had belonged to Lila's husband, and fit except for the fact that they were too short. The man must have been shorter than Andrew, but heavily built. Lila's husband's shirts were way too small, so he wore his own, which, after a good washing, were not bad at all.

Branwen pulled the reins, and her horse stopped at the path leading to the farmhouse porch. After setting the brake on the buggy, she climbed down and took off the coat she wore to keep the road dust off. She reached inside the buggy, took out her doctor's bag, and walked up the path. Branwen wore black, as was her custom; it was suitable for her practice. The image of her in the form-fitting buckskin dress she had worn on the trip north flashed across Andrew's mind. He much preferred the girl he remembered in buckskins, but he would have liked her whatever she wore.

"Hi, Doc," Andrew called as she climbed the porch stairs.

"Well, look at you," she exclaimed. "Is this the Andy I know, out in the sunlight and taking it easy? Why'd you shave the beard? I was just getting used to it."

"Figured I might get that illusive kiss if I shaved it off. What you think?"

She evaded the question, "Let's take a look at that leg."

"Rejection makes it hurt."

"If it slips off the stool, it'll hurt a lot more. You should be more careful. I don't want to have to set it again, and you don't want me to, either."

She set to examining the leg.

"How does it feel, Andy?"

"It feels fine. I just wish I could walk on it. It feels all cramped up; it wants to bend. You know, like a scratch you can't itch."

"We'll give it another week, and then let you try walking on a crutch. How'd you get down to the porch, anyway?"

"Billy and his mom steadied me, and I kind of hobbled down the stairs and out here."

"Be careful, you're still too unsteady. A zephyr could blow you over."

"Huh?"

"I said a little wind could blow you over."

"What I thought you said. When can these boards come off?"

"It's going to be another couple of months before you'll be ambulant again."

"You mean then I can be my old walking self again, I guess."

"Almost, Andy, but not quite. You know, your leg is shorter now. You're going to walk with a limp for the rest of your life. A thicker sole on your boot will help a little to even you out when you walk. How much depends a lot on you, and how much you want to work at it."

"I don't care about the limp, as long as I can get around. Hell, you could've cut the leg off, and then where'd I be? Even then, I'd just tie a stick on the stump and keep going. But I'm damn grateful for what you done."

"Are you going back to Lexington to do blacksmithing again, when you're able?"

"Thought about it, but no, I wouldn't fit in anymore. They know my feelings about things, and it wouldn't work out for me to go there. I already talked to Daniel about those things before I left."

"He was the man you worked for?"

"Yes. He and the rest of the whole town are so…what should I call it… patriotic. I'd have a hard time of it if I showed up again."

"That bad, huh?"

"The whole town thinks the same as a beehive. They don't see beyond all the talk—what's his name?—Sam Adams is always going on about. He gets everybody all fired up about taxes without representation, and all that stuff. They believe they're under the king's thumb. They've never considered the whys of what the king is doing. Not one of them can think for themselves. I've had enough. Not one of 'em knows what being under the yoke means. They should try being a slave."

"You don't even know what it's like, Andy. You were privileged. Sure, you had your moments when you were kidnapped, but they were just that, moments, compared to others who live their whole lives that way."

"True. I've been whipped, and Ignatius had me work in the tobacco fields to pay my way, so to speak. So I'm damned lucky. I can compare my limited real slave life with others, and I can appreciate how much more they have suffered. But no, ma'am, I can't get into any life where I'm oppressed. Those fools in Lexington can't see it. They were born free, and are blind to that sort of thing."

"So what are you going to do?"

"First thing is to pay back Misses Whitaker and Lila. There's a lot of things around this place that need fixin'. I'm going to start just as soon as I can get on them crutches you were talking about. After that, I guess I'll go west, where I've wanted to go from the start."

"How you going to get that kiss if you go out west?" she teased.

"I've just about given up on it. And if I stayed, what would I do? There's nothin' 'round here I can make a livin' at."

"There might be, Andy."

"What?"

"I said there might be. I sometimes take care of a woman in Watertown. Her son and a few of his friends joined up with the army in Cambridge. They had all been working in the mills. I think she said they repaired them and did other things; I'm not sure just what. The owners need to find people to replace them. You might fit in. Could be something to look into."

"So I should get a regular job for a maybe kiss?"

She looked straight ahead without expression, and did not answer his question.

"Then again, maybe not. What you have against a kiss? I'll bet I've kissed more women just to say hello than most people shake hands. Ain't no big deal."

"It's a big deal to me. I don't take it lightly, and frankly, I'm afraid."

"Afraid?! Afraid of what?"

"Afraid of what it'll lead to."

"What it'll lead to?"

"You know why I'm a runaway. What you don't know is that the experience I ran from was so terrible, I don't want anything to do with men anymore, at least not on that level."

NIGHT CAME, AND a highway of stars paved its way across the sky. Now and again, a shooting star flicked down to earth. One came so close it left a trail of black smoke before it burned out. Andrew had never paid much attention to constellations, because he could never picture in his mind what they were supposed to represent. The dippers he could see, but lions and scorpions, no. Maybe if he had a couple of swallows of the stuff stowed under the porch, it might help. It might help him understand what Branwen—no, Bonnie—had said about why she ran away…but it was under the porch, and he was on top, and with his bum leg. It looked as if that was the way it was going to stay.

The door opened, and from the sound of the walk, he knew it was Lori. She walked to his side and said, "Are you going to sit out here all night? You haven't even come in to eat."

"Wasn't hungry."

"We'll help you in when you're ready, but don't stay too long, because we've got to get to bed before long."

"If you don't mind, I'll stay out here tonight. Look at those stars. Maybe I'll just try to count 'em all. If you'd bring me a blanket, I think I will. Got something to think about, and this seems a good place to do it."

"Something you'd like to talk about?"

"Thanks, but it's kind of personal."

"I'll bring you a blanket and a plate of food, too, if you'd like."

He thought this would be a good time to ask the question. "A couple of biscuits would be fine. But would you think me a bad person if I asked you to bring me that jug you have under the porch?"

"You're a lot like my dad was. I loved my dad, even if he did drink. I don't care for drinking, because I know what it can do to a person. Then again, my dad also used it medicinally to relax after a long, hard day, or when he had problems he had to think over, and I suppose that's what you might be needing it for."

"Pretty close to what I had in mind."

"This has something to do with Bonnie Miller, doesn't it? I know there's more between you two than a broken leg, and I know it has nothing to do with a family reunion."

"How you know that?"

"I'm a woman."

"You know about those things, huh?"

"I said I was a woman. Men can't understand things about women, and you just have to accept what you see. If you try to understand us, you'll just go out of your mind. Don't take anything personally. We can make you feel you're the greatest thing God ever created, or we can make you feel like a pile of pig poop. You're feeling like a pile right now, aren't you?"

"I must have a hole in my head."

"How so?"

"You're reading my thoughts."

"That's because I'm a woman. Now, you want to talk about it?"

"It's best if I work it out myself with a couple sips of that medicine."

"Only if you eat something with it."

"What's on the menu?"

"Tongue, beans, and cabbage."

"That's a change. Yesterday, it was beans and cabbage with tongue."

"You want what's under the porch, or not?"

"I'll take the meal with my medicine."

"Wait right there," she said, and backed into the house.

He had thought about talking to Lori about Bonnie, as Lori knew her; but it would betray a trust. The less anyone knew about Branwen, the better it would be. He'd work the problem out on his own.

BUDS OPENED, AND spring's bright green began to wash over nature in its rebirth. Two hands stayed through the winter to do whatever was needed. The fields would need plowing as soon as the land dried, and the Whitakers would need to hire more hands. The winter hands had built a new barn as time and weather permitted. Since the old barn had burned down, a make-shift shelter had been constructed of upright logs embedded in the ground and covered with smaller branches, not unlike the longhouses Indians used. The days grew warmer, and Andrew's leg grew stronger. With a crutch, Andrew had been walking for a couple of weeks. In that time, he had replaced a wheel on a wagon, nailed down loose porch boards, learned to milk cows, and repaired the weathered window frames and shutters around the house.

Eventually, Bonnie removed the splint from his leg. She continued to come by to take a look at his leg, and the visits had become routine. He could almost count on her coming on Fridays around ten in the morning. Other than Bonnie checking his leg, they didn't talk much about anything other than the weather and news of the war. Both avoided talk about their relationship. She would then slip away to spend time with Anne and Lori, talking about the things women talk about. He wondered if they ever talked about him. It occurred to him she need not come as often as she did to check on his condition, as the leg had long since healed. This gave him hope she was interested in more than just his leg. Then again, maybe she came for the camaraderie of women.

IT HAD RAINED the night before, and the sky was still overcast; one of those mornings that casts a gloom over a person's mind, making him feel not up to doing anything. Added to that, Andrew felt he had been cooped up on the farm too long, and needed to get away for a while. Branwen had said something about a fulling mill in Watertown. Maybe that would give him somewhere to go, if for no other reason than to see what she was talking about. He saddled Henry, and the two plodded by the porch where Anne was standing looking up at the sky, likely with the same feeling Andrew was experiencing.

"Where you off to?" she asked.

"Thought I'd see what there was to see in that Watertown place."

"Not much to see there. But guess it's worth the ride to cure cabin fever."

With the previous night's rain and the early spring season, the road was muddy and slippery, so Andrew kept Henry to an easy walk. It was a slow journey, but what was he in a hurry for? It gave him time to think—about what was ahead of him in his life and what he really wanted, where he was going, and with whom.

That must be the mill, Andrew thought, catching sight of a large stone and wood building dead ahead. Alongside the mill ran a river, and between the river and the mill was a waterwheel, filled by a long wooden trough that entered the river several hundred feet upriver. *Now, that's clever. Wonder who thought that up?* he said to himself. *Wonder what it does?*

A thin man, perhaps a little over five feet tall, approached Andrew as he entered the mill. The man asked in a loud, squeaky, high-pitched voice, "What do you want?"

"I understand you might need some help keeping your machines running."

"Don't know where you heard that. You somebody's slave?"

"I'm free," answered Andrew, without saying anything else.

"Well, we might need somebody when the looms come. You know about that stuff?"

"Don't know anything about looms. I'm a blacksmith."

"Well, looms are made mostly from wood. Can you work with that?"

"I've done some work with wood. I can repair wagons and buggies, and even make wheels from scratch."

"Excuse me," the man said, and ran over to a group of what Andrew saw to be women and children. He picked up a switch and let it fall on one of the children. The child didn't cry, but rather straightened up and continued doing something with his feet.

Returning to Andrew, the man said, "You've got to watch 'em every minute. He fell asleep. Can't work when you're sleeping," the man said, laughing in the high-pitched voice that sent a chill up Andrew's spine. He backed away from the man a step, and would have liked to stick his fingers in his ears to cut the noise of the man's voice.

"You have children and women working! What do they do?"

"They do the fulling. I think we're going to have machines do that as soon as they work well enough, and we get the water wheel finished and connected, but we're going to wait till the looms come for that. Then they can work the machines."

"What's fulling?"

"You don't know much about this, do you?"

"No."

"Fulling has to do with making wearable wool cloth. The individual farmers around here shear their sheep, and their wives and daughters spin it into yarn and weave cloth. They could do the fulling themselves, but it takes a lot of time, so they bring the cloth here, and we full it. Fulling more or less tramples down the cloth so it's soft and wearable. That's what those workers are doing, stomping on cloth with their feet. As I said, it takes a lot of time.

We work long shifts here since the war started. That's probably why that lazy boy fell asleep."

"How long does he work?"

"Most all day every day, about sixteen, eighteen hours. They get Sundays off."

"You pay and feed 'em, right?"

"Feed them?! You nuts. They bring what they eat, if they have anything to bring, and eat it as they work."

"What if they get sick, and can't work?"

"There's always somebody waiting to take their place. You've never worked like this, have you?"

"No, not like this. I was a slave once, but it wasn't noth'n like this. I'd rather the slave. Think I'll go now."

Andrew turned to leave, and the little man said, "Well, not so fast, there. You know that new general, Washington I think his name is. He didn't want any blacks fighting for him, but now he's changed his mind. I was thinking you could always join the cause. But I see you've got a problem with one of your legs, and even if you were white, you might not get in. What's wrong with that leg, anyway?"

"I did my time fighting the redcoats already."

"One of 'em got a clean shot, huh?"

"Something like that, yeah."

The man continued, "Already, there's not many white men around. When those looms come in, we'll be needing someone who can help us get them going and keep them in repair, and finish connecting the water wheel to 'em. You be interested? Where can we find you?"

"You might try looking for me out west somewhere, but I don't think I'll be interested."

A WHITETAIL DEER darted out in front of them and tried to run across the road. It had almost made it when one of its front legs went down in the mud. Thrashing about and trying to stand was of no use; the leg was broken. Soon, it seemed to accept its fate, and quit trying. It looked up at Andrew, then turned its head to the other side and waited for Andrew to place his pistol to the back of its head.

After dressing the deer, Andrew tied it across Henry's rump. He looked at himself, and found he was covered in mud and blood. Even his boots were full of mud.

THE OLD OAK tree next to where the barn used to be was a strange sight. When the barn had burned, it had never completely caught fire. Only the side of the tree toward the barn had burned; the other side was scarcely singed. Now it looked as if it were half a tree: one side dead, the other alive and well. The big, high branch growing out of the living side had always been used for swings for kids, and for dressing cows and sheep.

Andrew hoisted the deer onto the limb to where he could work on it. He cut the head off, and thought for a moment about saving the brains and using them to make buckskin from the hide; but he was tired, and his leg had started to bother him, and one deer hide was barely enough to make a pair of gloves or moccasins. So he skinned the deer and wrapped the head in the hide and carried it to the edge of a field, where he placed it in the forest undergrowth. Come morning, it would feed a den of fox or coyote pups.

Anne and Lori saw him coming to the back porch with the deer carcass over his shoulders. They opened the door, and Andrew set the deer down on the floor. "Glory be," said Anne. "That critter is going to taste good after we're through with him."

"Want me to cut him up out here, or take him into the kitchen?"

"You leave him right where you are. Don't you dare come in covered with half of God's creation all over you. Just leave him right there as is," Anne said. "Lori and I'll take care of him. We'll spit him in the morning, and he ought to be done by dinner. Now, go get yourself cleaned up."

The next morning was Friday, and the two women were up earlier than usual. They set to work on the deer. "Should we wake Andy?" asked Lori.

"Let the poor man sleep. We can manage."

They washed the carcass, removing the ever-present loose hair. Dragging the carcass into the kitchen, Lori at one end and Anne at the other, they hefted the deer onto the table. Anne shoved the spit, a long iron rod, down the deer's throat and out the other end. The rod was square, and over it, two large, double-pronged, fork-shaped devices at each end would cause the carcass to turn with the spit. The forks were pushed into each end of the deer, and the legs were bound with buckskin strips along its body.

"Ready?" asked Anne.

"I guess."

The two women lifted the spitted deer and placed it over the fire, sliding a handle onto the spit so it could be turned.

"Add some wood to the fire and stoke those coals, Lori. I'm going to wake those boys in the cabin. We're not turning this thing ourselves all day."

Lori gave no argument. A hand, still groggy, came in and sat down by the fireplace. Lori fixed him a plate of fried potatoes and eggs, some of the first the hens had laid this spring.

Soon, Andrew and the other hand were sitting at the table, eating the morning meal.

"Bonnie should be coming soon for her usual Friday visit," said Anne. "Think I'll ask her if she'd care to stay through till dinner. What you think, Lori?"

"That would be nice. I'm sure Andrew would agree, wouldn't you?"

With a mouthful of biscuit and milk, Andrew looked up to see the women and hands looking at him. He swallowed and took another sip of milk. "Think she would," he said. He lowered his eyes back to his food, smothered another biscuit with butter, and stuffed it into his mouth. He kept his eyes fixed on his plate, avoiding the smiles and smirks.

Anne gave Lori a look that said, "Lay off. You're embarrassing him. Stop pressing."

Lori shrugged her shoulders and turned away. The two hands followed Andrew's lead, and turned their attention to their biscuits.

"Boy! Those biscuit are good," said one of the hands, trying to defuse the moment.

"I'll take second shift turning the spit," said another.

"Think I'll take care of a few things in the cabin," said Andrew, and he brought his dishes to the sink and pumped water over them to rinse them off.

"Leave them, Andrew," said Anne. "I'll take care of them. How about turning the spit for a while?"

"HOW LONG UNTIL this is done?" Andrew asked anybody who'd venture an answer.

"Maybe a little after the sun's gone down. This deer isn't a big one," said Lori. "Where's Bonnie, I wonder? She should have been here by now."

By early afternoon, Bonnie still had not shown up, and it was generally agreed she likely had another patient to look after. There had been other times when she had not shown early on Fridays. Most incidences were of a medical nature, to take care of someone who had fallen ill or had an accident. Once, she herself was so sick she just wanted to sleep until she was better. As it was, Dr. Warren's mother was able to take care of her, and applied her own remedies.

Andrew was back on spit duty, and thought he heard a rider approaching the farmhouse. Lori heard it, too, and went to the living room and looked out the window. It was not a carriage she saw, but rather a horse and rider, and they were running hard, even in the soft mud. They stopped short of the front porch, and the rider jumped off his mount and ran up. He pounded and shouted for somebody to open the door.

"I've got to talk to Mister Andrew!" the boy said.

"Andrew!" Lori yelled. "Someone here wants to talk to you. You'd best come quick!"

Andrew came to the door and saw the boy, but didn't recognize him. "What you want, boy?"

"It's Miz Bonnie! She's been taken!"

"What you mean?"

"They said she was a runaway, and took her!"

"Who took her?"

"I don't know. Some white men. Miz Bonnie and I were loading her buggy at Miz Warren's, and they walked up and grabbed her, saying she was a runaway and they were taking her back. She yelled at me to run and find Mister Andrew at the Whitaker farm, and that's what I done."

"How many white men?"

"Three or four. Don't remember, and couldn't see, 'cause some were movin' around and around."

Taking the boy's horse and riding after them would be the fastest thing to do, but the horse was old and swaybacked, so he'd have to take the time to saddle up Henry.

"Which way'd they go, boy?"

"Don't know. I was getting my horse when they left."

In less than thirty minutes, Andrew had Henry ready to go, and they were riding toward the Warren farm. Andrew had pistols in his belt and the musket slung over his back, all loaded and ready.

Missus Warren was waiting for him when he rode up. Though they had never seen each other before, each knew who the other was.

"I've been waiting for you. They took her. Said she was a runaway."

"They have a buggy?"

"No. They tied her on a horse."

"How many?"

"I saw two, but there could have been more. They went south," she said, pointing down the road.

"Headed toward Maryland," he said, mumbling to himself. He turned Henry. "Giddyup! Let's go, Henry!" Henry maintained a fast walk just short of breaking into a trot. They could have a long way to go, and there was no use in tiring both of them.

According to his reckoning, they had a three- or four-hour head start on him. The sun was just now getting low in the sky, and it would set in less than an hour. The bounty hunters couldn't travel at night, as they had to sleep sometime. Staying overnight at an inn would be risky, because others might get the idea they themselves could take the runaway for the reward. They would have to stop overnight by the roadside, and would have a campfire burning. If they were smart, they would take turns sleeping; but smart or not, Andrew knew not to underestimate his enemy.

It was now dark, and a somewhat overcast sky made it difficult for horse and rider to see. Henry walked slow and steady, stopping when he couldn't make out the road surface. Then Andrew would have to climb down and lead him onward for a while, get back on, and try again. It was slow going, and more tiring for both of them than if it had been daylight.

The stars said it would be morning in a couple of hours. In front of him, Andrew thought he saw a firefly, but only one, and in the same place. He kept watching until he was sure of what he was looking at. It was the flickering flames of a campfire, flashing on and off through the trees as Andrew and Henry walked along.

Andrew climbed off Henry, tied him to a tree, and removed the musket. He walked along the road until the campfire was directly off to his right side. They were camped along the river he had been hearing for several miles.

"Too dangerous to just run into the woods without being able to see anything," he thought. "I'll wait till dawn and get 'em when they come out. Hope it's who I think it is." He hid himself in the trees on the opposite side of the road, and sat down against a tree to wait. The day had worn him out, and he knew he would fall asleep. The sound of the bounty hunters breaking camp in the morning would wake him. He slid down on the ground and lay on his side so he would not snore.

He was awakened by a scream, and sat up and looked about. It was still night. He heard the scream again.

"Get away from me, you bastard!"

"Shut up, you black bitch, and spread those legs!"

"For God's sake! What you doing?" said another voice.

"Just go back to sleep or get in back of the line."

"Ha! Is that all the longer you can get?" I don't think you could do it if you was invited. Let me show you how."

"Just you shut your mouth!"

Andrew was well on his way by now, with his musket out in front of him, breaking through brush he could not see. He bounced off trees, paying no attention to the branches digging into his body.

"What was that?" one of the voices asked.

"An animal," said the other.

"Don't sound like any animal I ever heard."

Andrew burst out of the trees into the small clearing, yelling and shouting. He fired his musket, hitting nothing. There was a man on the ground with his bedroll turned down, and another man desperately trying to pull his pants up.

Turning the musket around, Andrew took hold of it with both hands and brought it down hard on the partially-clothed man's head. The man went down, blood spilled from his head, and an eye bulged from its socket.

Branwen yelled, "In back of you!"

Turning as he drew a pistol from his belt, Andrew saw a knife coming down on him. He brought his arm up just in time to deflect the man's swing, pushed his pistol into the man's stomach, and fired.

The man curled on the ground, crying in pain. He knew he would soon be dead.

Branwen stood naked, trying to put what was left of her dress back on. "Andy, there's another one. I think he went down by the river." Andrew looked around and motioned for Branwen to be silent. He listened, but couldn't hear a thing.

"He's hiding 'till we leave. Let's go. Be careful where you step. Those trees don't move out of the way."

He led her through the trees while looking over his shoulder toward the fire. They emerged on the road in time to see the dim outline of a figure leading a horse down the road. Andrew pushed Branwen back into the woods. He saw a flash of light, and an instant later, something hit him hard in the side, knocking him off his feet. Confused for a second, he realized he had been hit by a ball.

Andrew drew his one remaining loaded pistol, feeling the pain in his side. Switching the pistol to his other hand, he tried to aim toward where he had seen the image of the horse being led. He could not see anything, but heard a horse running at a full gallop down the muddy road. "He's gone. We won't have trouble with him again."

"You alright, Andy?"

"I'm alright. Let's get their horses. They'd be by the river. Got to get what's left of the musket. Think I broke it."

"You sure you're alright?"

"I'm sure."

Andrew helped Branwen onto one of the horses and tied the rest of them in back of Henry. The sun was coming up, lighting the landscape. Dew began to drop from the forest leaves, making a sound like rain.

They'd been riding for about a half hour, neither one saying a word—Andrew because he was starting to feel the increasing pain in his side, but not wanting to admit he was hurting. Branwen's silence was strange for her, but Andrew didn't mind, as he didn't feel much like talking.

Henry stumbled in the mud, and Andrew let out a moan. Branwen looked over to see a grimace crumpling Andrew's face. She fell back just a little, and saw the red stain under his arm. "Andy! You...you're bleeding."

"It'll be alright."

"How do you know? You a doctor?"

Against his will, she made him stop so she could see the wound. She looked him over, murmuring, "Hmm," which she had heard Doctor Warren utter so many times that it was now becoming something she did without thinking. "That ball hit a rib, and it's broken. Might have glanced off. We've got to brace it somehow before you drive it through a lung."

There were no medical supplies of any kind. She looked around to see what she might use. "Horse blanket," she said. She removed the saddle from one of the horses and wrapped the blanket around Andy's rib cage as tightly as she could, and tied it with rope. "That'll do for now. Should keep you upright and lessen the pain."

Continuing their journey to the Warren farm, Branwen continued her strange silence. She didn't say a word, except to ask Andrew from time to time if he was alright, and he would always answer that he was. When Andrew spoke to her, she would sometimes look at him, but wouldn't reply; at other times, she wouldn't even acknowledge him.

When they arrived at the Warren farm, Branwen climbed off the horse, and without looking at Andrew, she walked into the house.

Missus Warren came outside and approached Andrew still atop Henry. "What happened? She went straight to her room and closed the door without saying a word. I don't think she even saw me standing there."

"Her kidnappers were trying to have their way with her when I upset their plans. I killed a couple, and another got away. She's been pretty much silent the whole time. Something's on her mind."

Seeing Andrew was hurt, she asked, "Are you alright, Andrew?"

"I'll make it. Let me know how she's doing, by and by. I'll try to check on her when I'm feeling better."

He didn't want to leave Branwen in the condition she was in, but knew it was useless to approach her now, and his own condition needed attention. Anne and Lori did a fair job of tending to his wound, applying their own remedies handed down for generations.

In a couple of weeks, Andrew had recovered to his old self. The ultimate test was swinging the ax and cutting down a big maple. Sure, it hurt a bit, but he could tell he was on the mend, and there was no excuse for not doing work. He thought about going to the Warren place this coming weekend. As things played out, Doctor Warren's slave boy came by on his old swayback to give Andrew the message that it would be best if he didn't try to see Bonnie now. They would let him know when it was the right time.

CHAPTER XXI

THE NEW BARN was up, the fields were planted, and the farmhouse looked as if it could go a few more winters before needing attention. Andrew felt he had repaid Anne and Lori for their help and hospitality. The time was right to move on.

He thought about going to Cambridge to see if Gage was still there, but it was something close to a half year ago when he had last visited, and chances were slim that anyone, including Harold, would still be there. Then, too, he did not want to place himself in a situation in which he might find himself back in the war. Because of his interest in mules, he thought Washington would take possession of Gage and have him well cared for.

Henry was ready to go, and the pack horses, liberated from the bounty hunters, were carrying their share of supplies for a long journey.

Andrew had not heard her approach as he swung himself up on Henry's back. "Where you going?" Branwen asked.

His head turned toward her voice, and there she was in her inquiring look that he had so often seen. "Don't know."

"Poor answer."

"I know. But it's the only answer I've got."

"You're planning on going to you-don't-know-where without saying even a goodbye?"

"Easier this way, I guess. Didn't think you cared."

"That's it, huh? You're just going to take off, and everything behind you will be gone and forgotten?"

"They told me not to try to see you until they let me know you were up to it. Never heard a word. I figured you didn't want anything to do with me, or any other man. You said something close to that. Remember?"

"I remember, but that was then. I've thought things over, and...and, well...I think I've figured things out, and I can get on with life. I rode out here myself to tell you it's alright now...I mean, I've thought about a lot of things, and I want to talk to you."

"About?"

"Let me tell you, Andy."

"Go on."

"My past experiences with men were with poor excuses for men. They were nothing. They were all about themselves, and nobody else. My white father showed some empathy by moving my mother and me out of the field and into the house. His wife was not pleased, and let him know about it. She treated us badly, but stopped short of beating us. He treated us as well as he could under the circumstances.

"It was a difficult situation to live with, but we managed. It was my half-brother who became the problem I could not stand. He was nothing but a disturbed, sick, self-serving excuse for a human being. He'd have had his way with me whether he knew I was his sister or not. I saw overseers grab girls in the field and force them down anytime they had the urge, and when they were through, get up and whip her for not doing enough of whatever she was supposed to be doing. Some even forced themselves on little boys while their mothers looked on, unable to do a thing about it. I thought all men were that way. You saw that side of me when I first met you and Jim. Remember?"

Andrew nodded his head yes, and said, "Oh, I remember, alright. I couldn't imagine going all that way on the trip north with you."

Continuing, she said, "When I first went to work and lived in Doctor Warren's house, I was more frightened than if I had stayed at the farm with my crazy brother and the overseers. I thought I'd be his daily reward for a good day's work. I was wrong; he proved himself a perfect gentleman, and after a while, I didn't worry about it anymore. His apprentice assistant proved the same. That's when I started to let my guard down."

"I can guess the rest. Then the incident with the bounty hunters happened after they kidnapped you?"

"I guess so. Whatever happened drove me into a shell of my own making. I don't even remember what happened…even now. Missus Warren told me you brought me back, and were injured while you were fighting with the kidnappers. What happened?"

"You don't remember?"

"No. Tell me."

"What Missus Warren told you pretty much tells it all. I tracked you and the bounty hunters. A couple of them got killed, and another one shot me while he was getting away. You fixed me up enough to get us back. That's about all."

"Did they rape me?"

"No. One tried, and he was the first to die."

There was a silence between the two of them. Andrew didn't know what to say. Was it time to change the subject, or did she have something else to add? Branwen, on the other hand, had a faraway look, as if she was trying to digest what had been said.

She was the first to speak. "Something doesn't seem to add up, Andy."

"What?"

"When you first showed up here, at the Whitaker's, you had been shot in the leg, and they thought you had been shot in some kind of battle."

"And?"

"Well...I've been thinking about that. There was no fighting at the time between us and the British. The fighting on Breed's Hill was over. The only thing happening was Boston was under siege, but it was a quiet siege. We didn't try to storm the city, and they didn't try to break out. How did you get shot?"

"Don't laugh," he said, "but you'd been on my mind for a long time. When I decided to leave Lexington I couldn't quite force myself to go west. It would have been a simple thing to do, to just point Henry west and let him have his head. But I figured I should go to Boston and try to find you."

"You went to Boston! Who shot you, our troops or theirs?"

"Getting into Boston was easy. Nobody on our side tried to stop me. I told the British guards at the neck why I was there, and just waited. Before long, I was standing in front of General Howe and a couple of other generals, telling them my story. Long story short, they locked me up, but they were curious enough to also look for you at the doctor's house. They told me you had left with Doctor Warren."

"How'd you get out?"

Andrew told her how he escaped, and how he had come to be at the Whitaker farm. She bowed her head and placed her hands on her forehead, shaking her head in disbelief.

"Then you got shot—because you were looking for me?"

"Well, at the time, I was just trying to get myself out of Boston."

"I mean, you wouldn't have been shot if you hadn't come looking for me."

"I guess you could say that."

"And my guess is you're finally going to go west. Am I right?"

"I've been thinking about it. I could go west where white men are few, and there are no slaves. Don't know what's there; don't even know how to get there. I might be killed by Indians, or I might live with 'em from time to time, or we might just let each other live as we want in peace. I've thought of clearing land along a river, building a cabin, growing crops, and hunting for whatever I needed."

"I understand there are others doing the same thing, Andy."

"And that, Branwen, is where the big problem lies."

"I'm way ahead of you, Andy. Slavery is just going to go west, too. Is that it?"

"Exactly."

"You have something else in mind?"

"Maybe…I don't know for sure. I haven't put it all together in my mind. What would you do? You're as smart as anyone I've ever known. Should I go back to Lexington and join up with the militia again, and tell 'em I've changed my mind? Should I join the British, because they were the first to offer freedom for slaves, before the Americans offered it? I still can't see a difference."

Andrew was getting worked up now, and his voice became louder. His arms moved as he talked to emphasize what he was saying. He reminded Branwen of the preachers who made the rounds of the plantations and farms, expounding upon why slaves should believe in Jesus, and saying they'd be saved if they obeyed their masters.

Not dropping a beat, he continued, "If the British were, in truth, against slavery, they should have declared their colonies to be slave-free along with imposing all those taxes; couldn't have made the Americans any madder. Then, sure as hell, I would've joined the British, along with every other slave in America. They could still declare it."

He stopped talking. After a pause and a sheepish grin, he said, "Sorry, I didn't mean to sound off that way. Don't recall I've ever done it before."

"My God, Andy, what are you thinking?"

"I'm thinking about two things General Washington said. He said to me, 'A man has to believe in something, and, if necessary, fight for it.' The other thing he said, though not to me, was that the reason slaves weren't wanted in the army was because whites were afraid that if Negroes had guns, there would be Negro uprisings. That was the reason blacks were not allowed in, but that all changed when the Americans needed manpower, and the British were recruiting us with the promise of freedom. Isn't it strange how the two seem to fit together?"

"You're thinking about getting slaves together for an uprising?"

"No! That would be the most stupid thing that could be done. What would be the sense of it? Sure, the slaves would kill a lot of whites, burn down a lot of farms and so on, but in the end, there wouldn't be one of us left alive. And if we succeeded what would we do? A bunch of slaves left to make it on their own without knowing how. Even those whites that sympathize with us would end up turning against us. Killing whites would be as bad or worse than slavery. We need the Friends and their likes."

"So, what's your plan?"

"Don't know yet. But I'm putting things together in my head."

"Go on."

"The way I see it is that on either side, American or English, the people who pull the strings on all us puppets, white and black alike, are those that want to be in control. They pay us slaves nothing and pay white workers next to nothing. Why, I've seen white women and children working all but a few hours a day for little more than a slave makes on his day off working for himself. If you're not born into what I'll call the control class then it's harder than hell to get into it. There are those who do, I know, but for the most part what I say is the way it is."

Branwen never heard Andrew talk this way. Never expressed himself this way. This was an Andrew she had never seen before. "I never knew you to think like this. I never saw this side of you."

"Don't know where it came from 'cept ever since a fellow by the name of Isaac had a sit-down talk with me, I've been thinking about a lot of things. The last few weeks sitting on that porch mending my leg has given me a lot of time to think."

"So?"

"I didn't mention this to you before but, you know who George Washington is?"

"Heard of him from Doctor Warren but not a lot."

"He's the commander of all the American troops. I know him. He even poured me a brandy, a couple of 'em, and we drank 'em together. He wrote a letter that allowed me to get into Boston to look for you."

"Why were you drinking with him?"

"It had to do with my mule, Gage. You see, Gage is a mule that is bigger and stronger than any mule you'll likely ever see. Mister Washington has always wanted to breed mules like Gage. So, he offered me a job at his plantation to do that…after the war of course and as he said, 'If the British don't hang me first.'"

"Would you want that kind of job? Not being a slave but a real job."

"A man does have to make a living and pay his way. So, it would be a good job…eventually. But I really want to try to educate and help free slaves so they can make a living and pay their way on their own.

Here's what I have in mind. First, this George Washington is an important man, and I'm betting that if the Americans win the war, he is going to be an even more important man. Second, he owns a few hundred slaves in Virginia. He's offered me a job there even though I don't want to fight in the war. If I took the job, I would be in a position to teach and influence his slaves while he was tied up with the war. Those slaves might then influence Mr. Washington after the war to do something about slavery."

"Sounds as if you've been doing a lot of thinking about it. Do you believe it could work?"

"I don't know. Maybe I should go west and stay one step ahead of the white man. I thought about it a long time ago, when we were making our way here. But that practicality stuff got in the way, and I ended up in Lexington. Should have gone where I wanted to in the first place, and I wouldn't be walking around with a limp."

"We wouldn't have run across each other again, either. I saved your leg and most likely your life, remember?"

"I know. I'm grateful...I mean, for saving my life as well as...well, us." He looked a little embarrassed, and tried to hide his face by turning his head toward Henry.

"Andy, look at me."

He raised his head to look at Branwen, who was wearing her *listen to me* look.

"You called me smart a while ago. Well, I'm smart enough to know when I'm talking to someone who needs to be dedicated to something. Someone who's smart enough to know what he wants, and how to go about getting it. You want my opinion? Forget about running away out west. You, we, us...we've already run away. Here we are. Now do it."

He saw the serious look on her face dissolve into a devilish grin.

"Andy, as your doctor, I've come to the conclusion that you're prone to being shot, and you shouldn't be allowed to do anything without your personal doctor being with you at all times. It's just too dangerous. Got room for my stuff? I've still got my buckskin dress. I'm ready for..."